Adventures of Max Spitzkopf

Adventures of Max Spitzkopf

The Yiddish Sherlock Holmes

WRITTEN BY JONAS KREPPEL

TRANSLATED BY MIKHL YASHINSKY

Adventures of Max Spitzkopf: The Yiddish Sherlock Holmes
By Jonas Kreppel
Translated by Mikhl Yashinsky

White Goat Press, the Yiddish Book Center's imprint
Yiddish Book Center
Amherst, MA 01002
whitegoatpress.org

Printed in the United States of America at The Puritan Press, Braintree, MA
10 9 8 7 6 5 4 3 2

Paperback ISBN 979-8-9909980-5-6
Ebook ISBN 979-8-9909980-6-3

Library of Congress Control Number: 2025936717

Book design by Michael Grinley
Cover design by Kandy Littrell
Story cover illustrations courtesy of the Jewish Studies collection of Yale University Library

Originally published in Yiddish as *Maks shpitskopf: der kenig fun di detektivs—der viener sherlok holmes* (*Max Spitzkopf: The King of the Detectives—The Viennese Sherlock Holmes*), ca. 1908 (Kraków).

This publication is made possible through the generous support of Esther H. Rose

Table of Contents

Introduction

By Mikhl Yashinsky

I present you with a mystery: What would a great writer—the only Nobel laureate of his besieged but unbounded minority language, the son and grandson of rabbis, a fabulist of phantoms and demons, and a sardonic Jeremiah of his destroyed people—read for pleasure as a child? What could possibly be deep and dark enough to fire the imagination of such a boy?

I speak, of course, of Isaac Bashevis Singer. And what was this writer reading as a child under the covers while his father inveighed against the heretical dangers of modernity and his brother began publishing secular literature in the local newspapers? Why, what else but the detective stories of Max Spitzkopf, the "king of detectives, the Viennese Sherlock Holmes"!

Such were the appellations that accompanied this fictional sleuth's name on the fifteen pulp-fiction pamphlets that cost only twenty Austrian heller for each shabby little shocker of thirty-two pages, published in Kraków around 1908. Young Isaac Singer wolfed down each volumette like it was nothing more than a dumpling—incidentally, the meaning of their author Jonas Kreppel's surname. Here is what the Nobel laureate wrote, in his own memoirs, about these fiction feasts of his childhood:

> In my eyes, these detective stories were high art. They simply enchanted me. A sentence from one of the booklets remains with me to this very day. It was a caption to an illustration that depicted Max Spitzkopf and his assistant Fuchs surprising a bandit, revolvers in hand. And the detective is calling out, "Halt, you scoundrel! The game is up!"

> These naïve words resounded in my ears like heavenly music. I invested them with all of my youthful fantasy.

No Spitzkopf cover exists that adheres perfectly to every detail remembered by Bashevis, a man in his fifties when he set down these memories, but one comes pretty close. Hermann Fuchs, Robin to Spitzkopf's Batman, does not appear on the cover of "The Smugglers," but the master detective is there, bearing his usual firearm and the usual defiant expression on his sharp-angled face as he confronts a gang of miscreants with the words "*Halt! Shurken!*"—"Halt! Scoundrels!"

Pulp can be powerful. A book of fiction need not have the sweep of a thousand-page novel to awe us, and a detective story need not be difficult to figure out in order to surprise us, make us root for the heroes, seethe with hatred for the villains, and wonder if Fuchs will yet again wind up bound in a dungeon somewhere. (Of course he will—and sometimes his hyperintelligent master might, too.) For the mysteries of this supersleuth are not, ultimately, very hard to sleuth out. Often, we do so right along with Spitzkopf, somewhere near the beginning. But how fearlessly he sallies forth into the vortex of danger; how ingeniously he tracks the culprits; how curious his contrivances and costumes; how adorably hapless his assistant; how dastardly the anti-Jewish plots they unravel; how tenderly grateful the victims and their families! It is the colorful settings of wine-and-coffee-soaked Vienna and the faith-immersed shtetl, the lively plotting, the forceful language, the absurdity and slapstick, the vivid and unsubtle characterization, that give these stories their perpetual charm and excitement.

One might not guess that such wildness and derring-do would have emerged from the mind of their stolid creator. In his photograph, the Jewish-Austrian bureaucrat Jonas Kreppel (1874–1940) looks refined and serious, neatly cravatted and mustachioed. But there is a twinkle in his eye and an upward turn to his lips. For all of his serious literary and political accomplishments—and they were many—he also wrote some of the most ludicrous (and ludicrously popular) fiction of his day.

When Kreppel was born on Christmas Day in the shtetl of Drohobych in Austrian Poland, the fourth of seven children, he was called Yoyne by his Hasidic parents, a biblical name meaning "dove." He played on the reference in one of his many pseudonyms—"La Paloma." The Spitzkopf stories were issued anonymously, but it was an open secret that they were Kreppel's handiwork. Perhaps the author left his name off to lend credence to the claim, stated on the back cover of every booklet, that his hero was a real man who "LIVES AND BREATHES" and that "the stories about him are THE ABSOLUTE TRUTH."

This was merely an advertising strategy—there is no evidence that Spitzkopf or his Viennese detective agency, Blitz, actually existed—but it is incontestably true that the crises our hero flew into were nightmarishly prevalent in the reality of European Jewry. The private eye, the back cover goes on to proclaim, "IS A JEW—and he has always taken every opportunity to stand up FOR JEWS." These Jews in trouble are variously accused of treason against the Austrian state (shades of Alfred Dreyfus) or of blood libel, beset with pogroms, abducted and sold into sexual slavery or sent for forced baptism by Christian clergy, or otherwise ensnared in any number of murderous, rapacious, antisemitic plots.

Tales such as these would have seized the hearts of Yiddish readers, already familiar with them through contemporary newspaper reports and the experiences of neighbors and friends. For them, a hero like Spitzkopf not only nabbed the guilty and freed the innocent but did so with irresistible panache and—perhaps most importantly—in their own language. He would have shone as a beacon of comfort and hope, bright as the rays of his omnipresent *elektrishe lampe*. And he was such a wiz, a man whose ultra-sharp deduction skills resided in a "pointy head" (the literal meaning of "Spitzkopf")—that is to say, a decidedly clever mind. The stories of his exploits sold like so many slices of hot strudel. Kreppel became a master at such fare, derided as *shund*—lowbrow trash—in the more rarefied echelons of Yiddish literature but adored by the eagerly reading masses.

Writing Spitzkopf stories was hardly Kreppel's sole endeavor. After marrying Helene Fischer, the daughter of Kraków publisher Josef Fischer, Kreppel put his training as a printer and typesetter to good use when he took over the management of his father-in-law's popular fiction business, the Jüdischer Roman-Verlag (Jewish Novel Publishing House). For both that firm and, a couple decades later, in the 1920s, that of publisher Symcha Freund in the Polish city of Przemyśl, Kreppel penned dozens of the slim-format page-turners that Spitzkopf helped popularize—crime capers, biblical and Hasidic legends, supposedly firsthand accounts of the First World War and of Jews who met Napoleon. Nor was Kreppel's engagement with the personalities and predicaments of his people limited to storybooks. His longest work was in German and amounts to 891 scrupulously researched pages on *Juden und Judentum von Heute* (*Jews and Judaism of Today*), published in Zürich and Vienna in 1925. Even Yoel Teitelbaum, the august founder of the strict Satmar Hasidic sect, had to be impressed by Kreppel's success. Upon encountering the "tall, lanky" man as a youth around the close of the nineteenth century and being regaled by him with one of his homespun yarns, the name Kreppel stuck in the "dumpling" of Teitelbaum's mind, as he put it. Eventually, he started seeing that unforgettable moniker pop up on newsstands everywhere. The man's books, Teitelbaum later wrote, were "being sold and distributed far and wide as though they were Holy Writ. A terrible and terrifying thing."

In 1915, after a successful publishing career in Kraków and Lviv and after serving as a delegate to the famous 1908 "Conference for the Yiddish Language" in Czernowitz, Kreppel moved to Vienna, the royal and imperial capital that had so fired his fancy in the Spitzkopf tales. There he embarked on the second of his grand careers, one fairly unusual for a Yiddish man of letters: serving Austria, of which he was an avowed patriot, as a government press officer, first in the Austrian Foreign Ministry during the waning days of the Habsburg Empire and then, from 1924, in the Federal Chancellery of the Austrian Republic. Setting up shop at his favored Café Arkaden, he gradually gained the approbation of his colleagues and co-religionists. He was a Viennese gentleman at last, one whose suavity and skill matched those of his most famous protagonist. In his adopted city Kreppel edited the German-language journal *Jüdische Korrespondenz*, the organ of the Orthodox Jewish political movement known as the Agudas Yisroel. His twin allegiances, to his people and his patria, are reflected in the title of the only biography dedicated to his life, published in Vienna in 2017: *Jonas Kreppel—Glaubenstreu und Vaterländisch* ("true to his faith and his fatherland").

But when that fatherland turned on him, such fidelity was for naught. As Hitler consolidated power, Kreppel published a pamphlet alerting the German-reading public to the peril of the dictator's expansionist plans and criticizing the appeasement policies that weakly hoped to restrain him. He titled it with his usual flair: *1935—das Shicksalsjahr Europas* (*Europe's Fateful Year*). In May 1938, seven weeks after Austria welcomed Nazi annexation, Kreppel was rounded up along with other political opponents of the new regime and interned first in Dachau, near Munich, then transferred to Buchenwald, outside of Weimar.

His identification card from Buchenwald lists his occupation as a *Staatsbeamter* (civil servant) and his address as Vienna, Seegasse 3, in the ninth district. It is the same area in which the brutally slain Dr. Leon Politzer maintains a couple of handsome residences in the Spitzkopf story "The Forged Will." The author of that story, *jüdischer politischer Häftling* (Jewish political prisoner) #3229, aka Jonas Kreppel, was eventually worked to death in a limestone quarry just outside the concentration camp. He died on July 21, 1940, after nearly two years of forced labor.

Kreppel's writings serve as his testament. As with any Holocaust victim whose life was cut short, the fullness of his existence will remain a mystery: speeches unspoken, books unwritten, deeds left undone. The vast majority of his personal papers were destroyed by the Nazis, and any attempt at biography involves patching together bits and bobs from his own publications, limited reports in the contemporary press, and reminiscences of surviving family members.

How gratifying then that we have the solutions to the mysteries presented in this volume: those of brave Spitzkopf and trusty Fuchs; of the 17-year-old assistant Leon Fein, whose Ganymedean beauty enables him to dress up as a glamorous coquette and serve as a honeypot to trap a pack of scoundrels in "The Child Murderess"; of the coarse and fearsome Frau Mathilde Schoppening, archvillainess of that tale; and of the indomitable young Fraulein Chana Frisch, daughter of Oświęcim, who is "kidnapped for conversion" in the very first tale of the series. Here, each case is neatly cracked. Each ends with justice being served, the detective duly granted his laurels, the admiring public reading of his latest feat in the newspaper and sending him "heartfelt messages of thanks, from every corner, for so passionately championing the cause of the innocent and the persecuted."

The few extant copies of these fifteen "sensation novels" are nearly crumbling but still blessedly conserved in a handful of the world's libraries. Each story is accompanied by a bold cover illustration of the sort Bashevis remembered: in muted monochrome except for a dash of red surrounding the title, and Spitzkopf's portrait, haloed in gold. I have had the *zkhus*, the rare privilege and honor, of rendering them into English in this first complete edition since they were released as twenty-heller pamphlets over a century ago. May their thrilling odes to smart, swift, and beneficent action resound in our ears as they did for the boy Bashevis. And may we endow them with all the spark of our "youthful fantasy"—no matter our age.

Issue 1: Kidnapped for Conversion

ערשטעם העפט. | פרייז 20 העללער.

געראויבט צו דער שמד...

הא, איהר גוינער! איך האב אייך דערטאפט. איך בין דער דעטעקטיוו שפיצקאפף
און ערקלער אייך אלע פיר פערהאפטעט.

Kidnapped for Conversion

CHAPTER ONE

Taken in the Night

A MONSTROUS TERROR reigns in the home of Reb Menashe Frisch, estate owner in the Galician village of Olsztyn, in the eastern reaches of the Austrian Empire. Reb Menashe is pacing madly, rubbing his hands together till one nearly breaks the other. His wife Leah lies about and falls into fainting spells, their tiny children are crying—no, wailing. And the servants are running from one room to the next in the greatest terror.

Because a terrible thing has happened. Reb Menashe's eldest daughter, Chanah, a girl of seventeen, has disappeared in the middle of the night under mysterious circumstances.

Now, Reb Menashe was a rabbi's son. His father had been the rabbi of a small Galician shtetl, and it was expected that Menashe likewise be trained as a rabbi. As a child he had a fine head on his shoulders—very focused and sharp of thought. He would surely have grown up to become a formidable genius. But his health faded from too much sitting and studying, and the doctors ordered that he take rest for a while in a village in the mountains. He would enjoy fresh air there and have some much-needed time away from his studies.

And so his father sent him to a relative, a tenant farmer in the Carpathian Mountains, and the young fellow stayed there a whole summer. The fine air and frequent walks in the forest strengthened his constitution, and he was soon himself again. But he had gained such a love for the free life out in God's creation that to be cooped up in the piddling shtetl, with its narrow alleyways and low little houses, choking air and foul smells, no longer pleased him. Meanwhile he had lost all desire to enter the rabbinate. Soon after he married the only daughter of Olsztyn's most prominent landowner, he took every opportunity to leave town and spent most of his time in the country.

His father-in-law died a couple years after the wedding, and Menashe inherited all of his vast property, including the Olsztyn estate. But he continued to spend most of his time in a village in the country, and when his own father died, and the community selected him to take over his hometown's rabbinate, he did not care to.

While he had rejected the life of a rabbi, he led his household in a strict Jewish fashion. He raised his children traditionally; he was a renowned host and philanthropist. Everyone around knew of Reb Menashe's altruism and great piety.

Chanah, his eldest daughter, was a beauty, and impeccably raised. She was the pride of her parents, and only to see her was to love her. She had received the best education, her father providing her with a private tutor, Isaak Loewenstein, who instructed her in various scholarly disciplines, placing particular emphasis upon Jewish history and literature. For Reb Menashe had a warm Jewish heart, and he wanted his children to grow up good Jews.

It was two days before Purim around the turn of the twentieth century. Reb Menashe and his wife had gone off visiting a neighboring estate owner to see about a potential bridegroom for Chanah. When they came home early the next day, they were greeted by an upheaval in their home: their only daughter had vanished in the night.

Her bedroom window was shattered, and two chairs had been knocked over. Her clothes lay scattered on the floor, and her bedsheets were stained with a massive spot of fresh blood.

None of the household's residents had heard any suspicious sounds in the night. The girl's bedroom was separated from the other rooms by the grand salon and her parents' bedroom. The window opened onto extensive grounds that rolled on a great distance, beyond the village limits.

Not a single object in the house had been stolen. The door to the salon stood open, but even there nothing was missing. It made the whole situation even more inscrutable. The fear and agony of the parents were indescribable. They wept and wailed, wrung their hands, staggered about. The entire household—servants included—looked as if it had been dealt a frightful blow.

The local constable was notified, and he soon came with a gendarme and closely inspected the scene of the horrific crime. But the gendarme could not detect any tracks left by the criminal and left no hope that he would be of any help.

The first to collect himself and to begin to ponder the case with a level head was the tutor, Loewenstein. "This does not," he reflected, "suggest a robbery. Nothing in the house is missing. But the girl also could not have simply run away. What, then, would all the disorder in the room signify, and the bloodstain on the bed? It is equally unlikely that this was an act of revenge, as Chanah, her whole life long, never hurt a soul. On the contrary, whoever had the opportunity to be in her presence loved her—indeed treasured her. Anyhow, she was hardly in contact at all with the wider world. She barely ever traveled or even went out walking without her parents. What we have here, then, is a truly impenetrable mystery. Your village constable and your gendarme will have a tough time puzzling this one out."

The tutor then shared this advice with his employer: "Do as I say, Reb Menashe, if you ever want to recover your daughter. If it is even remotely possible that we shall ever discover what has happened, it is possible only by this path: contact the legendary, top-secret private eye, the King of Detectives, Max Spitzkopf of Vienna.

"Everyone calls him 'the Viennese Sherlock Holmes.' He heads the famous Viennese detective bureau Blitz—'lightning.' The largest bureau of its kind anywhere in the world. He's cracked hundreds of these sorts of cases, which even the police in the big city couldn't begin to figure out. And he does his work with the utmost skill and authority. He's never been dealt a case too difficult for him to crack. He has deputies posted in every major city. He's known everywhere. He's bold as a lion and takes the wildest risks. No, he doesn't shy away from even the most fearsome dangers if it takes conquering them to uncover a clue.

"Reb Menashe, do listen to what I'm telling you and telegraph him immediately. I am certain that if he's free he'll come quickly; otherwise he'll send one of his assistants. They are just as zealous as he is. Only the bureau of Max Spitzkopf can help you!"

Reb Menashe knew the name well. He had often read of Spitzkopf's feats in the paper. And so he needed little convincing after hearing the tutor's speech. He quickly dispatched his valet to the closest city, bearing an express telegram addressed to Max Spitzkopf. It contained a plea that the detective come as soon as he could, as a most dire case had presented itself.

So the bedroom of the vanished girl was sealed up. And the despairing family waited impatiently for the arrival of the master detective.

CHAPTER TWO
Loewenstein: Arrested!

By early afternoon, a judicial commission had shown up to Reb Menashe Frisch's home. It was made up of the local constable and his attending gendarme, the commander of a nearby patrol troop, and the district clerk. The commission once again mulled over and inspected the bedroom and interviewed the Frisch sons and all the servants, asking them whether they had not heard any kind of noise during the night. In the end they even subjected the tutor, Loewenstein, to questioning. Like the others, Loewenstein stated that he had heard no suspicious sound in the night and that the entire matter was a complete mystery to him. But the constable's questions bothered Loewenstein more than they had any of the other interviewees. He grew agitated and showed it in his responses. It led the gendarmerie commander to comment, "Mr. Loewenstein! You are so terrified that it seems to me you do not have a clear conscience. As you were the only adult male in the home last night who had access to the bedroom of Fraulein Frisch, and as the windows of your own room open onto the yard, enabling you to enter it from your room and then creep into that of Fraulein Frisch, I have reason to consider you the primary suspect in this case and hereby pronounce you, in the name of the law, arrested!"

Loewenstein instantly grew extremely upset and wanted to rush at his defamer. But he realized that such fury could only harm him. His earlier agitation had already drawn suspicion, and the best course for him now was to remain as calm as possible. So he bit his tongue and answered with measured cool. "I am innocent, as God is my witness. But I submit to my arrest in the secure hope that the truth soon will out. I regret only one thing: that by my being arrested, this commission is now going down the wrong route, and instead of searching for the actual criminal it will waste time with me. The culprit, in the meantime, will have the opportunity to disappear."

The gendarmerie commander answered him much provoked. It was up to him how he would carry out the investigation, and he had no need of Loewenstein's wisdom. He ordered the tutor to be clapped in irons and confined, for the time being, in the district jail.

Reb Menashe and his wife were sharply affected by what had transpired. They could not begin to believe that Loewenstein would be at all guilty. He had been with them already for two years, and they were well acquainted with his character, his uprightness, his downright noble bearing. Reb Menashe tried to stand up for him and pleaded that he not be arrested.

But it was no use. The gendarmerie commander soon led Loewenstein away, and the constable said quietly to Reb Menashe, addressing him in Polish, "*Panie* Frisch, sir. It is a clear-cut case. This tutor is a young man and obviously fell in love with your daughter. Last night, when you and your wife were out of town, he took the opportunity to penetrate into her bedroom. She, of course, resisted him, and it led to this calamity . . . a struggle and a bloody conclusion. To cover up his tracks, the tutor carried out the dead body and buried it somewhere in the yard or threw it in the lake.

"First things first, we had to shut him away, and now we can search the yard. Then you'll see that we're on the right track."

The gendarme agreed vigorously with everything the constable had said. But since it had begun to grow dark, the commission decided to leave the search until tomorrow, and left.

Reb Menashe and his household remained in the house, their dejection even more complete than before. They had no share in the suspicion of the tutor and were convinced of his innocence. Oh, how could all this be happening?

"Sorrows never come singly!" Reb Menashe sighed bitterly. "Not only have we lost our dear daughter, but now, too, an innocent person has been taken and had his whole life laid to ruin. God alone can help him find a way out!"

CHAPTER THREE
Spitzkopf Makes His Way to Olsztyn

SPITZKOPF CAME UP to Galicia by the afternoon express train. Until they stopped in Oświęcim,[1] he had been occupying a private, first-class compartment with his assistant, Hermann Fuchs. He had brought Fuchs on account of the man's thorough command of the Polish language, which Spitzkopf figured he would have to rely on in this venture.

Before reaching the Oświęcim station, Spitzkopf quickly changed into the garb of a traditional Polish Jew, with a fine beard and long *peyes*. He ended up looking rather like a wealthy Jewish merchant. Fuchs, on the other hand, disguised himself as a simple peasant, wearing an immense fur cap and wide boots.

"We will now be crossing into third class," Spitzkopf told his assistant. "I will find myself some Jewish company and you a compartment where the Christians are sitting. Perhaps we shall hear or learn something about what really happened out there in Olsztyn. We're not too far from the scene of the crime. If a significant event did indeed take place, it would already be well known in the vicinity, and the passengers would be buzzing about it. When we learn what has happened, we will be able to immediately settle upon a plan."

And so Spitzkopf settled into a compartment where several Jews had boarded at Oświęcim. He sat apart and eavesdropped on their conversation. They discussed various matters, first and foremost the condition of Jews in Galicia. Regarding this matter, one of the passengers bitterly lamented that antisemitism in the region was increasing by the day, and furthermore that in the last few years a new trouble had presented itself: the kidnapping and conversion of Jewish girls.

Spitzkopf listened attentively to the sundry stories of these violent kidnappings, which were largely taking place in western Galicia. Most of the girls were eventually handed over to the order of Felician Sisters in Kraków. He had already read about these happenings quite often in the newspapers, and the details of the cases had interested him deeply.

Fuchs, meanwhile, had set himself up in a compartment occupied by a number of Christians whose attire marked them as members of the cultivated classes. He sat in a corner by a window and looked out, smoking from a crude, rustic pipe. His traveling companions were conducting a quiet conversation, so he only half heard a few sentences. But he caught enough to know that they were talking about Jews, because the Polish word for "Jew"—"*Żyd*"—occurred with some frequency, spoken with such an intonation that it was clear they were not paying that population any compliments.

They began chuckling about a prank that had been played on a certain *Żydówka*, a Jewess, and one of this company finally said with pride: "So you see, friends, that when I want something, I get it done. I am stronger than the Devil and sharper than the Jew!"

The group laughed. Our Fuchs took a hard look at their hero. He was a young man about thirty years old, with impishly glittering eyes and a pointy little black beard. He was elegantly dressed and had the air of a schoolteacher or civil servant. Fuchs also realized that he wore a leather glove on his right hand while his left hand was bare. He duly etched this character's appearance into his memory and found that it pleased him none too much.

The remaining journey did not last long. Spitzkopf and his assistant were to get out at the second station after Oświęcim. From there it was a walk of about three kilometers to Olsztyn.

After he alighted, Fuchs noted that his man had also. His friends were calling out to him, "Godspeed for the rest of it!" The man speedily left the depot, and Fuchs followed him for a few paces. A man awaited him outside an elegant carriage, and he stepped into it at once. It was already rather dark out, but Fuchs observed from the light of the streetlamps that the coachman limped a little on one foot and that the top button of his suit coat was coming apart from the frayed fabric below.

The carriage sped away. Fuchs remained standing outside the depot, awaiting his master. It was more than ten minutes before Spitzkopf emerged from the first-class waiting lounge and motioned for the assistant to proceed. Fuchs took large steps until he was out of the vicinity of the depot and well concealed by the darkness beyond. He stood still, waiting for Spitzkopf to catch up with him. Spitzkopf soon did so, also stepping boldly, and Fuchs unraveled his observations to him.

"Meanwhile, I didn't learn anything new," Spitzkopf said. "It appears to me, however, that what you saw and heard, when I combine it with what I heard, will have something to do with our case. Naturally, we must first of all see Herr Frisch in Olsztyn and hear what happened there. He gave us no hints about any of it in his telegram; most likely wants to keep it under wraps. We cannot travel there together, however. I think I should take a carriage. But you ought to go on foot and stop at an inn on the way. I will collect you from there."

Fuchs began walking quickly, and Spitzkopf returned to the depot. But he could not find a single carriage. The few that had been there had already departed. And so he changed course and also set out on foot.

"It could attract attention, a Jew dressed like me walking down such a road at night," he thought to himself. "And I certainly don't want to attract attention. I must come to Herr Frisch quite unobserved. But it is already dark—it would be very hard to spot me. And I do want to be wearing these same clothes when I arrive at Herr Frisch's. Of course, I don't know if he is an Orthodox or progressive Jew. But I would assume that he's Orthodox, considering he signs his name simply as 'Menashe' and not something more refined like 'Emanuel' or 'Max' . . ."

CHAPTER FOUR
In Olsztyn

THE ROAD FROM the train station to Olsztyn is very much a Polish road, ungraveled and unpaved. A soft warm wind was blowing down it, melting the snow. Spitzkopf was up to his ankles in mud as he walked. Three kilometers and three quarters of an hour later, he glimpsed from afar a few glowing windows. It was pitch black outside by then, with an overcast sky and a moon that did not shine.

He had not met anyone on the road, and his assistant Fuchs would have already settled into the inn. Coming into the village, Spitzkopf did not want to ask where Herr Frisch lived, figuring that he would surely recognize the estate house by its appearance alone. And so he wandered nearly the entire village before he arrived at a charming cottage in which all the windows were illuminated. Thinking that perhaps this was part of Frisch's residence, he approached and peeked into a window that was imperfectly covered by its curtain.

Inside he saw the village clergyman sitting with a veiled nun and a young man who matched the description Fuchs had provided of the suspicious fellow he had observed. They were deep in what appeared to be an impassioned discussion. He marked the one young fellow closely and soon continued on his way.

After around two hundred steps he arrived at a large, finely built house with a garden in front and a grand entrance gate. He knew he had arrived at his destination and went in.

The cook—a Jewish woman—was standing in the front room. She quickly ran to Reb Menashe and announced, "Sir, some Jew is here!"

Reb Menashe entered, extended Spitzkopf the cordial greeting "*Sholem-aleykhem*," and led him into an adjoining room. He invited the man to sit down and asked how he could help him.

Spitzkopf did not want anyone in the household to know who he was. And so he answered him, quite convincingly, "I am a distant relative of yours, Reb Menashe, and have an enormous favor to ask of you. But first I must tell you my whole story so that you will understand what I ask is very serious and how you must help me out of my dire circumstances."

"My dear relative!" Reb Menashe broke in. "I do not yet even know who you are or what our relation is. But just this fact—that you are a fellow Jew and are asking a favor of me—that is enough for me to listen to you and if possible fulfill your request. But you must forgive me a hundredfold. I find myself today in a situation that prevents my even hearing you out. I have been struck senseless by a terrible misfortune."

"God be with you, Reb Menashe," Spitzkopf answered, with terror in his voice. "What . . . what is it that has happened, God forbid?"

"Oh, my dear fellow Jew. God has punished me severely. My eldest daughter was taken from me last night. God alone knows if she still lives . . ."

Reb Menashe could not speak any further and broke out in bitter sobs. Spitzkopf let him get properly sobbed out before he gripped his hand in tender sympathy and said, "My dear Reb Menashe! You mustn't lose hope. God's salvation can come in the blink of an eye. Tell me how this happened. Perhaps I will be able to advise you."

The warm intonation with which Spitzkopf spoke these words moved Reb Menashe most agreeably. He found himself able to control his deep agitation and in a few words told his guest what had taken place.

"I have also telegraphed this certain detective bureau in Vienna, as advised by our tutor, Loewenstein. But I have still not received any word from them as to whether the detective would be coming. And even if he does come, the situation has already grown so complicated, even more so by the arrest of our innocent tutor, that I deeply doubt whether this secret agent can bring any light to the darkness. If I could at least get any idea as to the motive behind all this . . . I am, in any case, completely convinced of Loewenstein's innocence."

"I can see, Reb Menashe," said Spitzkopf, "that I must not trouble your head with my own affairs. God must find another way to help me. But I did come to you directly, and now I must ask you to allow me to stay here this night. I am very weary from my journey. Tomorrow morning I will depart and make my way home."

"With pleasure, dear relative," Reb Menashe answered. "It would be the greatest honor. Perhaps I will be able to calm myself somewhat by then, and tomorrow you can finally present your request to me. But now perhaps you will eat something? And afterward, I can point you to our tutor's bedroom. It is empty now, and you can get some good rest there."

"I thank you most sincerely, Reb Menashe. But I won't eat anything—I took my supper at the station, and I would rather lie down at once. I am awfully tired."

"As you wish. Since I cannot help you, I would at least like to be a good host to you. Come, I will show you the room."

Reb Menashe led his guest into the tutor's room, put on a light, and with a friendly good night returned to his own room, sending his valet to make up the guest's bed.

Spitzkopf set himself up in a corner of the room, as if to daven *mayrev*, the evening prayer service. When the valet entered to prepare the bed, Spitzkopf watched him out of the corner of his eye. Perceiving that this was quite an ordinary young man, simple and fairly guileless, he finished his praying and with a sigh said to him, "*Nebekh*, poor soul! God have mercy on him! For such a calamity to befall such a fine Jew as Reb Menashe!"

"*Nebekh, nebekh*," the valet agreed. "Such a calamity. May it not happen again to any Jew! If only that Viennese hotshot would come, the one we telegraphed today. I don't have much truck with the constable and gendarmerie in these parts. They're fooling around. When someone pinches someone else's hen or goose, they turn the whole village upside down. And now a person—and not just any person, but a truly precious child—has been kidnapped, and they don't lift a finger. They went all in on that innocent tutor and clapped him in irons like a common thief. Meanwhile the actual criminal could have disappeared to who knows where."

"And how do you know that they've telegraphed some Viennese hotshot?" Spitzkopf asked him.

"I myself brought the telegram to the post office in the city. I can't read and didn't know what it said. But at the train station I ran into our village schoolmaster, and he asked me what I was doing in the city. I showed him the telegram, and he told me that the boss was contacting some German-speaking gentleman in Vienna, asking him to come search for his daughter. And he said to me, '*Glupi Żyd!*' Stupid Jew. He thinks this fancy-pants from Vienna is going to be able to help him? If our gendarmes couldn't solve the mystery, some little Viennese devil is not going to be able to find out anything.' But I think that if the boss telegraphed him, and Loewenstein agreed with the idea, they must have known what they were doing. But still no word from Vienna . . ."

"*Nebekh*, *nebekh*, poor souls! God have mercy!" Spitzkopf again exclaimed. He began to get undressed, and the valet left the room.

CHAPTER FIVE
On the Track

HERMANN FUCHS had also taken about three quarters of an hour to reach Olsztyn from the train station.

Arriving in the village center, he immediately went to the inn. A few peasants were sitting inside, along with the constable and district clerk. Fuchs sat himself down in a corner by the fireplace and ordered a strong shot of liquor. Emptying it, he lay down his head on the table and pretended to doze. But meanwhile, he had perked up his ears to hear what the company was discussing.

For a rather long while he could not understand the conversation. Finally he caught on that they were predicting something about "*nasz* Menaszke, our little Menashe" soon enjoying some "bitter hamantaschen." And that there would soon be "one fewer

Jewesses in the world." He figured that it all had something to do with what had taken place in the village, but more precise an understanding than that he could not come by.

He sat on pins and needles, waiting for his master to come get him. But the waiting lasted over an hour, and Spitzkopf had still not appeared.

Suddenly a man entered, called the constable and clerk over to one side, and whispered some secret to them. They immediately quit the inn. In the new arrival, Fuchs had recognized the coachman who had been waiting for that certain young fellow at the station. He knew he had to follow them, but quietly.

He walked behind them for about two hundred paces until they reached a charming cottage, its windows brightly illuminated. They entered it and, after two minutes, came back out again, accompanied by two men and a veiled woman. In the darkness he could not see who the two men were. He continued following them from a distance until they reached the church and entered the clergy house.

The elegant carriage he had earlier seen at the station was now parked outside of this house. Light soon shone from the windows. But they were heavily draped, and Fuchs could not make out anything of what was happening behind them.

He stood outside for perhaps fifteen minutes, burning with curiosity. Finally he decided to have a closer look. Having made up his mind, he knocked on the door. A servant answered and asked what he desired.

"I got lost on my way from the train station to the village Zalesie and ended up here," Fuchs answered. "It's very dark, and I'm afraid of walking outside at night. I wished to ask the priest if he would allow me to spend the night."

The servant admitted him into the front room, telling him that the priest was, however, with guests, and that when they left Fuchs could go in to see him. In the meantime, he should wait where he was.

Fuchs remained standing in the front room. He took a flask of vodka out of his lapel and handed it to the servant. "Drink, brother!" he said. "A mighty fine tipple, that is."

The servant did not have to be asked twice. With a "*Na zdrowie*—cheers!" the servant took a hearty gulp from the flask. And the drink had its desired effect on him. The man's head soon became too heavy for his neck, and within a couple of minutes he was lying down on a banquette, snoring.

Fuchs approached the door to the adjoining room. It was dark within, but he made out several voices. Squinting hard through the keyhole, he made out this scene: the priest seated at a large table alongside the constable, the gendarme, the district clerk, the young fellow with whom he had traveled from Oświęcim, and a nun. He could hear their conversation quite clearly.

"Oh, the conditions are just right," the nun said. "It's very dark out. We can travel at midnight and be at our destination by dawn."

"And then let that *Żyd* Spitzkopf come in from Vienna!" the young fellow piped up. "He'll be better off looking for a snowflake in hell!"

"If he's not already here," said the priest. "You don't fool around with his gang. It wouldn't be a bad idea to drop by little Menaszke and see whether or not he has a guest . . ."

"Quite, quite," the constable agreed. "Once our Michałki arrives, we can send him over there. Tomorrow those *Żydzi* celebrate this Purim hullabaloo, the innkeeper told me. Every year Mrs. Menashe gives out these pastries called hamantaschen to the villagers. Michałki will pay her a visit and request his hamantasch a day early. And he can ask their maid, Marynia, whether they might be entertaining a guest."

"And if they are," the nun asked, "what then?"

"If they are, we'll take action!" the gendarme cried out. "I'll go over there myself and have this character introduce himself to us. Ask for his badge, and even if it's the genuine article I'll doubt it and throw him in jail anyway. When it comes time for him to be released, we'll have already finished up our business and can have a few good yuks at his expense."

They all broke out laughing. Meanwhile our Fuchs was standing as if on burning coals. He could not decide what to do. Run to tell his master? Or remain to hear the end of it? He was losing some of his calm. What if Spitzkopf had already gone looking for him at the inn to no avail? At the same time he was feeling a deep urge to produce a magic trick himself this time and at last be the one to figure out the mystery. He could show his master what a capable student he had been. And so he convinced himself to stay put.

But he had become so engrossed, looking into the room and eavesdropping on the conversation, that he had forgotten one very important lesson: a detective must always look and listen in all directions and not become so singly focused as to see and hear only one side of a matter. So he did not at all notice that the coachman Michałki had entered the front room and, seeing the servant snoring, took his lantern and walked toward the adjoining room. At the sight of our Fuchs kneeling at the door, he shouted out, "*Złodziej, złodziej*, thief! Sound the alarm!"

Fuchs was stunned. His eyes went starry from the sudden lantern light, and before he had time to jump up and save himself the company in the next room threw open the door and pounced on him. The constable and gendarme seized him and dragged him into the room they had just left.

"Who are you and what do you want?" they all asked him. Fuchs wished to tell them the same story he had used on the servant. But the one young fellow called out triumphantly, "Aha! Who do we have here but the *Żyd* Spitzkopf! We've captured our little birdie, and now we'll get even with him."

"You're a real bright bulb," the priest taunted Fuchs. "But we're brighter. You've fallen right into our net. Let's see how bright and brave you are now!"

Fuchs could see that he had really stepped in it. Of course, he did have two loaded revolvers on him and could easily get free. But he was afraid he might muck up the whole affair by going that route. He still had not found everything out. He still did not know precisely what had happened or what was still to happen. If he escaped their clutches and fled, this company would alter its plans, knowing that Spitzkopf was underfoot, and his and the detective's work could come to naught.

"Perhaps it's for the best," Fuchs thought to himself, "that this crew takes me for Spitzkopf. Now they won't go searching out my master and will think they don't have to look over their shoulders for anyone. They'll go forward with their plan without a care, and it'll be easier for Spitzkopf to catch them. Of course, I don't know what progress my master's made. But I'm certain he's not sleeping and that he, too, is on the right track. Maybe even farther along it than I."

And so he did not try to resist the assertion that he was Spitzkopf. At first he pretended not to understand, but when they laughed and shouted, "Bravo, Spitzkopf! There's our clever boy!" he finally "confessed" and said, "I am in your hands. Do with me what you will. But I trust that a constable and gendarme who have taken on the duty to uphold the law would not dare to do me harm. My bureau is licensed by the government, and I have the right to investigate these kinds of cases in order to uncover the truth."

The company could not quite sniff out what they ought to do. Of course, they could take this opportunity to strike him dumb forever. But each of them was afraid of giving the word. It's no good when too many people are privy to too much information. They reckoned that the bureau in Vienna was well aware of where Spitzkopf had gone off to. They would know at Menashe's too. They would all come looking and might find something out.

It was most crucial for the whole company to at least get through the night. Once they fulfilled their mission, they would no longer need to fear the detective.

To that end, the priest declared that it was the detective's obligation to demonstrate his credentials to the constable before he could begin carrying out any kind of investigation within his precinct. The detective would also have to find out through the official channels how the matter stood and whether or not the local gendarmerie had picked up any leads on the crime. At this moment, late at night, the constable was not required to answer any such requests for the latest intelligence. The detective had not yet even shown that he was indeed the man he claimed to be. Could be he was just a common thief . . .

"I say," the priest advised, "that we detain this character and confine him overnight in a cell on the grounds. Tomorrow morning the gendarme can hand him over to the constable, and if he can produce the proper papers to prove who he is, we can free him to attend to his business."

They all agreed with his advice. They bound Fuchs's hands and feet, gagged him, and locked him in an isolated chamber in the courtyard of the clergy house.

The conspirators were now certain that they could carry out their plan, with none to bother them.

CHAPTER SIX
In Captivity

MEANWHILE, in a dark, narrow, suffocating little room, with her hands and feet bound, was the kidnapped girl. Soon it would be a full twenty-four hours that she had been lying there, only half conscious. It was a long time before she completely recovered from the shock she had sustained from her assault.

And even then she could only fuzzily recall the events of the night before: how she had been sleeping in her bed, peacefully and happily as always, without a care in the world. It was about midnight when, having just fallen asleep, she heard some sort of noise coming from below her window. She had thought it must be the wind rustling through the thin branches of the trees in the yard. She cocooned herself more tightly in her comforter so that she might continue her rest.

Suddenly she felt two cold hands touching her face. She opened her eyes in sheer terror. But it was pitch black, and she could only make out two dark figures gazing down at her with flaming eyes, like a pair of wild animals. She wanted to scream out, but instantly a cold hand flew to press her mouth shut. With all her might, she bit down on one of its fingers and felt warm blood trickling over her cheeks. In a matter of seconds her head was covered in a fabric so heavy she could barely breathe.

She soon felt herself being wrapped up in a rough blanket, lifted, and carried out of the window. She was carried for over a half hour. But her bearers kept silent, and she had no inkling of what they were going to do with her.

A cold sweat soon covered her entirely. And she gradually lost consciousness.

Then, suddenly, she came to. Opening her eyes, she furtively looked around and found herself lying in a small room, on a plush sofa, dressed in some kind of peasant gown. Her hands and feet were tied up. And beside her stood the village schoolmaster and the priest.

"Where am I, and what do you want from me?" she asked, in great alarm.

"You are among good people who want only what's best for you," the schoolmaster answered her.

"No!" she shouted desperately. "I am not among good people. And they certainly don't want what's best for me. Good people never feel the need to kidnap a person in the middle of the night. And if someone wants to do a person a good turn, they can tell them so in the daytime. They don't need to descend on the person like a thief in the night."

"Calm yourself, dear child," the schoolmaster said to her

softly. "You are agitated. Your nerves have been excited by these unexpected events, and you find yourself unable to peacefully consider your situation. Someday you will thank me for the steps I have taken on your behalf.

"I have loved you for a long time. I love you with every fiber of my being, with every beat of my warm, feeling heart. I couldn't bear to see you blossoming, so perfectly lonely, in the constricting Jewish environment of your family home. No one understood you there. No one there knew how highly to measure your worth.

"So I said to myself: 'It is your duty as a human being to save this noble soul, to ensure that she is allowed to blossom and grow in God's wide world.'

"The steps I have taken are perhaps not proper. But you must forgive me this in the name of my deep, burning love for you.

"Look, I am of aristocratic Polish stock, and you are a Jewess. Your parents were always completely dependent on my parents and served them like the basest slaves. And now see how I, a proud Polish nobleman, am kneeling before you, a Jewish girl, and begging you to utter these few words: that you wish to be mine. You would make me the happiest man in the world."

"Shut up!" she cried. "Shut up, you monster! How dare you let words like 'love' or 'happiness' cross your lips. Perhaps you've learned from your friend the priest that the end justifies the means. But we simple folk don't hold by that. You say you're kneeling and begging on account of love? Is that why I'm lying here, tied up, a little plaything in your hands? One does not beg of someone who's been tied up. You can make them obey you by force! But whether you're begging me or forcing me, it's all the same. I have but one request: to return to my parents. If you truly seek my well-being—bring me home! Think of what a state my dear parents will be in when they return tomorrow and don't find me there . . ."

Such was her ardent plea. She would remember almost every

word she said then and every word they said in response, even though they carried on arguing like this for a very long time—so long that once again she fainted.

How long she lay there unconscious she of course could not know. But this she would remember: that when she came to, she was surrounded by total darkness, still lying bound on the sofa, in the same peasant gown. The air was suffocating, and she breathed with difficulty. As she lay, she tried to recall all that had happened that fearful night to clarify for herself what was going on—where she was and what was wanted of her.

Suddenly the door swung open. The schoolmaster entered, along with the priest and a veiled nun.

"So, dear child," the schoolmaster whispered, with a voice of velvet, "have you changed your mind about what I said to you last night? Do you wish to . . . be mine?"

"No," she answered, dead-set in her resolve. "No, no. All that I ask of you is that you return me to my dear parents. Oh, God! Just imagine the depths of the despair they must be feeling. If God is in your heart, let me go home. I can't take this anymore. I can never love you. Stamp that madness out of your head. If you will let me go home, I will forgive you your barbaric deeds and at least consider you a human being. A human being who committed an error but then made it all right again. But if not, I will despise you for as long as I live."

"Oh, let's have an end of this idiotic chatter!" the nun burst out impatiently. "It's getting late. We have to get going already. And where we're headed, this *Żydówka* will probably start talking a bit differently!"

"Aha, you sweet dear!" the captive bitterly interjected. "So you're bringing me to that spot where you've already forcibly brought so many Jewish girls. You want to enrich your religion with yet another soul. Well, all your effort is for nothing. I would rather give up my life than my holy religion!"

"Come, come," the nun retorted, with a cruel smile. "Cut

out the high and mighty stuff. We'll soon see who's really got the might."

And with that she winked to the schoolmaster, who flung a veil over the captive's face. She inhaled a sharp odor. Her mind blurred. And she fell into a deep sleep. They had chloroformed her.

The nun wrapped her up in a large blanket, the schoolmaster carried her out, and the company boarded the carriage waiting outside the door.

"Michałki!" the schoolmaster shouted to the coachman. "Drive quickly so we arrive before dawn. Such matters as these can only be taken care of in the dark . . ."

CHAPTER SEVEN
Spitzkopf Cracks the Case!

THE VALET who made the bed for Spitzkopf had just barely left the room when the detective bolted the door after him and set about working.

First he removed his Jewish garb and put on a pair of winter shoes, a short jacket, and a felt fedora so that he could move about more easily. Then he commenced on a thorough search of the room. He examined every corner, picked the lock of every drawer with a thin skeleton key, and pored over the writing on every piece of paper, making sure he did not leave a single stone unturned in discovering potential evidence of the tutor's complicity.

He found nothing suspicious nor any sign that the tutor had any kind of untoward relationship with the daughter of his employer.

After searching the room, he attempted to open the window that led onto the grounds. But it was frozen shut, and it was only with great effort that he managed to do it. He could see that it had been weeks since it had last been opened.

"Aha. It appears we are faced with a truly vile crime," Spitzkopf thought to himself. "The commission that suspected the tutor and locked him up did not even take it upon itself to see if the window, through which the man was supposed to have climbed down into the yard, had been opened the day before. It seems someone had a motive to cover the tracks of the true culprit—or to get rid of the tutor.

"Loewenstein appears to have been the only intelligent person in the house who, not being related to the disappeared girl, was not immediately affected by the calamity. He would therefore have been a little calmer, a little more composed, and could have been instrumental in the solving of this perplexing case. The true culprit obviously didn't like the smell of that. And it was Loewenstein who recommended telegraphing me. It would clearly have been in someone's best interest to take the opportunity to dispose of him before I arrived."

Spitzkopf considered all that he had heard and discovered that afternoon, and as he put together the pieces of the confounding puzzle, he pondered: "There have lately been many cases in Galicia of Jewish girls being abducted and penned up in convents to be converted. The specifics of these cases varied. Sometimes the girl let herself be persuaded, or sometimes the girl had fallen in love with a Christian and went willingly to the convent. But in other instances a Christian man had developed a passion for a Jewish girl, and because she wanted nothing to do with him, he requested that she be taken forcibly to a convent, where they had certain methods of 'perfecting' their 'stubborn' victims.

"Such a case is likely presenting itself here. Fraulein Frisch was beautiful and well-educated. A Christian could easily have taken a liking to her, and because he could not get near her, hits upon the absolute grimmest method and steals her away at night. He must have been someone who knew the family. He would have waited for a night when her parents were not at home to carry out the crime.

"After his plan proved successful, he would have learned that the unfortunate father had telegraphed me. My name must not have been unfamiliar to him. He must have known that Reb Menashe had been advised to send for me by the tutor Loewenstein, and so decided to neutralize him.

"The constable and the gendarme were likely convinced by the local clergyman that all of this had to do with a most holy matter and so did everything that was asked of them.

"The Christian who concocted this entire dastardly plan would appear to be that young fellow Fuchs was telling me about, whom I saw in the lit-up cottage together with the priest and the nun. The nun must be from the convent they hoped to force the girl into. In the discussion I overheard they were probably going over their plan, deciding how best to conduct the girl out of the village.

"From all this I can deduce that the girl still lives and is most likely still in the village, and I must now expend all my powers to stop them from getting her into that convent. Once they get them in there, it's hard to get them out."

That is how Spitzkopf saw the matter. And now he had to get to work. Immediately.

The main thing for him was to find out where the girl was at that moment. For that, he would have to undertake a thorough search of her own bedroom and follow the tracks from there.

True, he had promised his assistant that he would be retrieving him from the inn. But he did not want to lose any time now. Every minute was extremely precious.

And he did not want to let Reb Menashe in on his plan just yet. It was possible that the conspirators had a spy in the house, and when the person found out that Spitzkopf was here they would be much more cautious and upset his entire scheme.

Having made up his mind, he immediately climbed down into the front yard from his bedroom window and entered the bedroom of the kidnapped girl on the other side of the house.

It was dark in her room. He turned on his electric torch and began to quietly inspect his surroundings. Everything in the bedroom was as it had been the morning after the girl's disappearance. Two chairs were lying upside down, the girl's clothes were scattered over the floor, the bed was unmade. He closely examined the pillows and quickly found the bloodstain beside them.

"The victim clearly figured," he thought to himself, "that she could not scream, as they probably had covered her mouth, so she would have bit down on her attacker's fingers. Thus the blood."

At that moment, he remembered that the young man with whom Fuchs was traveling had worn a glove on one hand.

"That shark must have been present at the kidnapping! Seems to me I'm on the right track."

Finding no other significant clues, he climbed back out through the window and with the help of his electric torch began to inspect the ground. Near the house he could not usefully identify anything—it had been warm out that day and the snow beside the walls had melted. But about twenty paces ahead, among the trees, the snow was still as it had been. And Spitzkopf noticed footprints in it.

Upon closer inspection, he quickly distinguished two sets of prints: one made by a pair of large, wide feet in rustic boots and another by a pair of small feet in galoshes.

"So two characters must've carried out the kidnapping, working in tandem," the detective deduced. "That young fellow, together with the help of some peasant."

Spitzkopf followed the footprints very slowly until they reached the outer limit of the backyard. There he noticed something else significant. The enclosure had pointed iron posts. The footprints extended just to the enclosure, and on one pointed post he found a clump of rough cloth, of the same material peasants' coats are usually made of. A button was hanging from it.

"Aha!" he cried out, taken aback. "Fuchs told me that he had noticed a torn section on the jacket of the coachman waiting for the young fellow at the station, and that the coachman was limping a little on one foot. When he climbed over this fence, his jacket probably caught, and in his hurry, a piece tore off. He probably also injured his foot in the process.

"It was that young blade and his coachman who did the deed! My work here is nearly finished!"

Beyond the estate grounds, the footprints faded away. On the open fields the snow had turned to slush over the course of the day. Spitzkopf feared crossing them with his electric torch lit lest someone notice the glow from afar. And so he walked slowly through the perfect darkness, straining to see where exactly he was going. Within around two hundred paces he again felt packed snow under his feet. He pressed the button of his electric torch and observed that he was standing in front of a stone wall more than a meter high enclosing a large garden. Beside the wall he again noticed footprints.

"I have arrived at my destination," he sputtered out with glee, and he leaped over the wall in a single bound.

From there the footprints carried on for rather a long distance. He followed them slowly. The weather had improved somewhat; the dark clouds had slid away, and the moon was beginning to shine. He had no more need of his electric torch.

After walking thus for a few hundred paces, the footprints divided. The large, wide feet began heading right, and the smaller tracks of the galoshes continued straight ahead.

Spitzkopf decided to follow the larger footprints. In a few minutes he arrived at a sizable, isolated chamber.

The door was locked. Putting his ear to it, he sensed movement within. He quickly picked open the lock with his skeleton key, turned on his electric torch, and stood there, as if frozen on the spot. His assistant Fuchs was lying on the ground, nearly suffocated, his hands and feet bound and his mouth gagged with a wad of cloth.

Spitzkopf immediately removed the rag from his mouth. The bound man took a deep breath and opened his eyes. Then Spitzkopf quickly slashed the offending ropes with his knife and massaged some snow into his assistant's temples. He soon came to and asked with surprise, "Master! How did you get here?"

But Spitzkopf cut him off. "Now is no time to ask questions or tell stories. Do you know where the kidnapped girl is?"

"Not exactly, no. But I know we are in the priest's courtyard."

"Come," Spitzkopf said, pulling a loaded revolver out of his breast pocket. "Let's find this gang once and for all."

Hotfooting it, they retraced the large tracks back to the point where the smaller ones had diverged. Following the small prints of the galoshes now, they soon arrived at the door of the clergy house. In the meantime, Fuchs readied his own revolver.

The door was lightly closed and stood unlocked. Spitzkopf and Fuchs entered quietly and found themselves in the front room. The servant was still lying there, snoring. Spitzkopf quickly bound the man's hands and feet and covered his mouth with a rag so that he could not move or cry out. They went into the next room, then the one adjoining it. Both were empty. They searched the entire house and found not another soul.

But in a small study with a little window opening onto the grounds, Spitzkopf noticed a sharp odor.

"The scoundrels!" he shouted with fury. "They appear to have carried out their evil purposes. I sense the smell of chloroform. The girl must have lay hidden here the entire day, after which they would have knocked her out and dragged her away.

"But the odor is still fresh. Probably isn't even an hour since they left. Follow me, Fuchs. We must catch them, come what may!"

Fuchs also noticed something. He saw through the window that the carriage was no longer standing outside the door and said as much to his master. "But how can we pursue them," he went on, "when we don't even know what direction they went in? Now, at night, in this mud, we'll hardly be able to follow their tracks."

But Spitzkopf heard nothing. He had made up his mind. He entered the hallway, unbolted the door, and stepped out into the wet outdoors.

"Follow me, Fuchs!" he cried, and began running with everything he had in him. He soon arrived at Reb Menashe's estate, wrenched open the entrance gate, entered the stables, and led out two horses. It all happened quick as lightning.

"Onward toward Kraków, Fuchs!" he called out, and they rode off at a furious gallop.

CHAPTER EIGHT

Freed!

FOR MORE THAN two hours Spitzkopf and Fuchs rode at full gallop. Fuchs fell off his horse several times, but he was never hurt because every time he landed in soft mud. The horses were panting, though. Sweat poured from their bodies and foam ran from their mouths. But Spitzkopf just drove them even harder.

Finally they glimpsed the first houses of Kraków. It was nearing two o'clock in the morning, and the city lay motionless, as if dead. No glow peeked from any window. Only a pair of gas lamps lent any light to the darkness. The sky had once again been covered with black storm clouds, and a cold, driving rain stabbed the riders' cheeks. "I only hope we're not too late," Spitzkopf thought to himself as he pushed his horse to gallop faster.

At last they arrived at the grand Wawel Castle in the center of Kraków. Suddenly Spitzkopf heard the rattling of a carriage nearby. He and Fuchs veered their steeds into a side street and let it pass. With his sharp eye Fuchs recognized the vehicle as the same elegant carriage he had spotted before. He gave a sign to Spitzkopf.

"Look after the horses!" Spitzkopf shouted, leaping off his own with the greatest of speed and sprinting to the gate of the Felician Sisters' convent. He barely had time to whip out his revolver before the infamous carriage approached.

"Halt, you rogues!" Spitzkopf commanded. "One move and I'll shoot!"

Quick as lightning he flung open the carriage door and illuminated the interior with his electric torch. Inside were the priest, that young bearded fellow we know only too well, and the nun, with an unconscious girl, wrapped in a large rough blanket, lying in her lap.

"Ha, you villains!" he bellowed. "I've caught you red-handed. I am the detective Max Spitzkopf, and you are all under arrest."

The passengers were so stunned by Spitzkopf's sudden appearance they could not even open their mouths. The nun swooned, and the priest and his young companion looked as if they had been turned to stone.

The coachman tried to get a good smack at this interloper with his whip. But Spitzkopf got him first, by the leg, and pulled him down from his seat with such force that the man's head struck the ground hard and he lay in the mud, bleeding.

At that moment Fuchs rode up. Spitzkopf immediately dispatched him to the nearest police station, and soon a police commissioner arrived at the scene with a few officers. They commandeered the carriage and brought it into the station. There Spitzkopf presented his credentials and briefly recounted the whole story. The lovely little pack of criminals was so shocked by the proceedings that they denied nothing and admitted everything.

A police medic was quickly summoned to examine the girl and pronounced her to be under the influence of chloroform. He revived her by the proper methods, but she soon retreated into unconsciousness, and it was quite a while before she came to again.

The police commissioner, meanwhile, conducted an exhaustive interrogation of the gang, through which it became clear that Spitzkopf's deductions were correct. The young man was indeed the village schoolmaster, and Fraulein Frisch had pleased him very much. Knowing that his suit was hopeless, he hatched the sinister plan to bring the girl forcibly to the convent and to baptize her there, after which he would be able to do with her as he liked.

He became acquainted with one of Reb Menashe's maids, Marynia, who entertained him quite a few nights on the estate grounds, so the schoolmaster had the opportunity to get a good sense of the place. He then let the priest in on his plan and received his approval. The priest then worked thoroughly on the constable, securing the latter's assistance.

Two days earlier Marynia let her young man know that Reb Menashe and his wife would be traveling to look into a possible engagement for their daughter and planned to spend the night away from home. That would be the optimal time to carry out his plan.

And so that night, enlisting the help of his school's caretaker, the young fellow stole into the estate grounds. The traitorous maid had already unlocked the girl's bedroom window. Toward midnight the company entered the bedroom, quickly bound the sleeping girl's mouth with a rag, then wrapped her in a blanket. The girl resisted and bit down hard on the schoolmaster's hand. But the two men overpowered her, and with the victim in tow crossed the length of the grounds. Upon climbing over the enclosure, the caretaker's coat snagged, and as he was desperate to escape quickly, a piece of it tore off as he fell to the ground and lightly injured his foot.

They carried the girl across the fields up to the priest's courtyard, then through the courtyard and into his house. There they bound her and left her to lie the whole day in a dark study. They gagged her mouth so she could not scream.

That morning, the schoolmaster urgently needed to travel to Oświęcim. At the station he ran into Reb Menashe's valet and read over the telegram. He decided at once to send a friend of his to the priest's, directing him to channel all suspicions onto the tutor Loewenstein and to have him arrested. This friend disguised himself as the commander of a patrol troop in order to make that happen.

Having been telegraphed of these proceedings, a nun from the order of Felician Sisters arrived that same day to give the girl a warm welcome.

If Spitzkopf had delayed and arrived at the gate of the convent but an hour later, all would have been lost.

The police commissioner had the gang detained at once. The ailing girl, meanwhile, was escorted to a hotel. There a very capable doctor sat up with her, never once leaving her side, as her condition was still critical. The shock from her assault, lying tied up for a full twenty-four hours, the chloroform—it had all rather shot her nerves.

Meanwhile Fuchs rode like the wind toward Olsztyn. He arrived early in the morning and brought Reb Menashe the good news. The parents were overcome. They thanked God for his infinite mercy and set off at once for Kraków to see their daughter. The scene of their reunion is difficult to capture in words. Everyone positively wept for joy.

Loewenstein was released that same day, while the constable and the gendarme were arrested. A few weeks later all of the culprits had received their final court hearings and were sentenced to a nice stretch of time in the clink.

Reb Menashe had tears in his eyes when he thanked the great detective at their parting. And he compensated him most lavishly. The girl's naturally healthy constitution allowed her to travel home the same day she was freed. There, Reb Menashe celebrated a very merry Purim indeed, filled with "light and gladness, joy and honor," just as it says in the Megillah.

Spitzkopf, with his assistant Fuchs, traveled home soon after wrapping up the case, returning to Vienna later that day. There, new and highly critical assignments waited for them.

We will tell you all about them in the next issue.

Issue 2: The Counterfeiters

פרייז 20 העללער.   צווייטעס העפט.

באַנקנאָטען־פעלשער.

שפיצקאָפף האָט געהאַלטען אין איין האַנד דאָס ־עמפעל און אין דער־אַנדערער אַ געלאַדענעם רעוואָלווער און האָט אויסגערופען: — איך האָב אייך ביי דער ארבייט דערטאַפּט! דאָ פאַבריצירט איהר די פאַלשע נאָטען! אָבער דאס איז צום לעצטען מאהל. אצינד וועט איהר אייער סוף האָבען.

The Counterfeiters

CHAPTER ONE

Falsely Accused

THERE WAS A grand and sensational trial on at the provincial court of Vienna today. The banker Adolf Lewinsohn stood before the jury under the accusation that he had taken part in the distribution of counterfeit money. And since he was unable to demonstrate from whom he had received the bills in question, the public prosecutor also considered him a suspect in the actual fabrication of the money and consequently increased the charges against the man.

Now the banker Lewinsohn was a well-known personality in Vienna. His father had been a small-time businessman who died young and left his wife with one child—twelve-year-old Adolf—and no money. The mother, who was quite well educated, took to providing for the family, in a most meager way, by giving lessons. When Adolf turned fifteen, he had to give up his studies at the high school and look for a position, as the small livelihood earned by the mother was not sufficient to truly support them both.

Through the intervention of his teacher, who was very fond of his diligent and talented young scholar, the boy received a position as an intern in a small private bank. The position was by no means highly salaried. But the youth soon proved himself very useful, and his boss began increasing his earnings every three months.

After remaining employed there for two years, he was actually earning quite well, such that his mother could afford to stop giving lessons, and both lived very comfortably. He was even able to save up some money.

His reputation as a hard worker soon grew in banking circles throughout the city, and at the age of twenty-four he was installed in a large firm as chief managing clerk and deputy to the director. While occupying that position, his knowledge of the profession grew by leaps and bounds. Furthermore, his pay was so respectable that he was able to store up quite the nest egg, especially because he led a quiet, modest life and was frugal in his habits.

His mother, however, was not so fortunate as to enjoy these days of plenty for long. One day she took ill with a very serious cold, developed pneumonia, and despite all the medical treatments to which she now had access died two weeks after contracting the illness.

Her son mourned for her most grievously. He felt lonely, abandoned. After several months, he decided to marry.

In the same bank where he worked, there was a damsel employed as a clerk. She was a very comely young woman, well-bred and educated. Adolf Lewinsohn developed a close acquaintance with her, and eventually a mutual fondness grew between the two.

She was an orphan. Her father had been very wealthy, and in his life he had set up a trust for her worth twenty thousand kronen, of which she would receive the entirety upon the occasion of her twenty-fourth birthday.

After a short courtship they married. Lewinsohn had saved up a likewise hefty sum, over ten thousand kronen. With the money, he decided to leave his position at the bank and open up his own currency exchange office.

He was proving himself to be quite the able hand. He speculated with success on the stock market and won a small fortune by it. The small *bureau de change* soon evolved into a banking house of the first rank. His wealth, in fact, was popularly estimated to be even greater than it actually was, and he was widely envied for his success.

He lived most happily with his beloved wife. She bore him two fine-looking, healthy children, and his life was one of peaceful contentment.

And then, like a cloud passing over a sunny day, his fortunes darkened. At that time, counterfeit fifty-kronen notes were circulating in Austria. Soon they also popped up in Galicia, in Hungary, and in Bohemia. All the efforts of the police to locate the source of this counterfeit money turned up nothing. The government promised a handsome reward to whomever discovered the identity of the counterfeiters or the propagators of the bills, but no one was able to get their hands on these criminals.

The imitation banknotes, meanwhile, were produced with such exactitude that their inauthenticity could only be determined through close inspection.

A few weeks prior to the trial of the banker Adolf Lewinsohn, a gentleman had shown up at the Vienna police headquarters and reported that he had sold Lewinsohn some securities at a high value and received payment in the form of paper money. Later he discovered among the bills around twenty fake fifty-kronen notes, which he handed over to the police as evidence.

The banker was then called in so that he could explain where he had gotten this money. His information did not assuage the suspicions of the police. He was arrested, and the public prosecutor consequently pressed charges.

We find him now in the courtroom on the day of his trial. The story had caused a splash throughout the city, and the spectators' gallery in the courtroom was full of onlookers from the crème de la crème of Viennese society.

Lewinsohn, sitting in the dock, looked broken down and despondent. His defense attorney, one of the best lawyers in Vienna, tried to buoy his spirits, consoling him with the assurance that the truth must out and that he must not lose hope.

Lewinsohn, however, answered with resigned mien. "What hope? The evidence is against me, and if no one manages to find the actual counterfeiters, I'm lost. If they don't believe my defense, how can I possibly demonstrate my innocence?"

The presiding judge read out the bill of indictment, which laid out the whole story of the ersatz money. It also concerned itself with the character of the defendant. He had been a high-earning officer of a bank when suddenly he decided to give up his position and go independent, though he had no enormous store of capital to draw upon. He had been managing his own business only for a few years but had already become one of the wealthiest private bankers in the city. How could he have possibly amassed such a fortune? Realistically, a person could not build up these riches in so short a time. It was a question that made him the primary suspect in this sordid business of the false banknotes.

Furthermore, the man led a rather secluded existence. He seldom ran in the usual social circles and rarely invited anyone over. Probably it was because he had secrets at home that needed to remain hidden.

His defense was, to put it mildly, weak. One had to assume, circumstances being what they were, that the man was guilty.

When the judge finished reading the bill of indictment, he directed a question to the defendant: "Herr Lewinsohn! Have you understood the charges, and do you consider yourself guilty of them?"

"No, Your Honor," Lewinsohn responded in calm tones. "I have not understood the charges and do not consider myself guilty of them. I have not understood the charges because there are things mentioned in this document that do not in fact pertain to the matter at hand.

"The person who drafted this brief claims that because I managed to build up a considerable sum of money in a short time I must have done it by dishonest means. This is a fallacy! I am the director of a banking firm, and I keep my books very accurately. From my records one can plainly see the extent and the sources of my wealth. Every gain is registered precisely in my ledgers, and if the public prosecutor were to acquaint himself a little more closely with them, he would see at once that my wealth is in point of fact not so very great as is alleged. Furthermore, he would see that what actual wealth I do possess I acquired through favorable speculation on securities, and that success I owe strictly to the expertise in my profession that I have been fortunate enough to gain over the years, something I consider to be beyond reproach.

"Ridiculous, however, is this accusation that because I maintain an unassuming lifestyle, I am worthy of suspicion! Here I address the High Court! It has always been the case that if a person enjoyed an extravagant lifestyle, his habits were taken as a sign that he was reckless or that he did not truly earn his money. Now the public prosecutor proposes quite a novel principle: that he who leads a quiet, modest, domestic life is the one truly to be suspected. Wherein does this logic lie? I have led a quiet and domestic life because I love my wife and my children, and unlike others I have no need to go in search of distractions and frivolous amusements. Neither for this am I deserving of reproach.

"I have chosen to live in the center of the city, in an open, easily accessible home, without clandestine cellars or attics. Indeed, I've nothing to hide there, not a single article to conceal. Anyone who wishes is readily admitted to my home.

"The bill of indictment alleges, furthermore, that on the day in question I provided this man, who appears as the chief witness against me today, with a hefty sum of money in cash, among which were twenty counterfeit fifty-kronen notes.

"Now, first of all, I do not know whether or not these bills that the man has delivered up as evidence even came from me. It is possible, however, considering that half an hour before this man appeared in my office another gentleman bought from me a number of securities for the same high price that I paid the man who followed him. That earlier patron introduced himself as one Count von Fries of St. Pölten, and he paid the entire amount in paper money, among which there were indeed twenty fifty-kronen notes. Because his name was familiar to me, and as the man cut a most genteel figure, I suspected nothing untoward, and I took his money without objection. As for the fifty-kronen notes, I did not recognize them as being counterfeit.

"No sooner had the purported count left my offices than today's witness entered and offered to sell me his securities. I did buy them and furnished him with the same sum I had just received from the other man, which still lay in the box of petty cash on my desk.

"That is the extent of what I know about the source of the money in question. I have nothing else to share. I can only profess, before God and man, my complete innocence."

With those words, the defendant concluded his rebuttal. The speech made a profound impression on the spectators and members of the jury. Then the man who first made the complaint to the police was called as a witness. The presiding judge swore him in, and the man testified thusly: "My name is Anton Schulze. I am a banking agent and live in the suburb of Floridsdorf. Through the years I have managed to save up some money and have acquired a number of stocks and bonds. But most recently I resolved to sell these securities and purchase my own banking house with the money. I brought them to the banker Lewinsohn and received in return their equivalent value in cash. Upon coming home, I counted the money once more, examined it, and found there was something I didn't quite like about the fifty-kronen notes. I recalled that false fifties had been circulating recently, so I inspected these bills more closely until I came to the determination that they were indeed counterfeit. I ran at once to the police and handed over the funny money."

At that point the lawyer for the defense posed several questions to the witness. His answers were cagey, though, and he finally blurted out, with noticeable irritation, "Am I the defendant here and not a witness, that you should be interrogating me so pointedly? I am not duty-bound to respond to all of your foolish questions."

Issuing a rebuke to the witness, the presiding judge told him that in fact he was duty-bound to do precisely that. The judge then made it known, however, that the court had questioned Count von Fries of St. Pölten, and he had declared, with a high degree of confidence, that he did not know Lewinsohn personally and that he had never bought any securities from him.

"We may learn from this," the judge concluded, "that the defendant is not able to, or does not wish to, identify the actual source of the money in question. Perhaps there are some witnesses for the defense or pieces of evidence in his favor that the defendant would like to present?"

"No," Lewinsohn answered.

"With that, then, we conclude the taking of evidence," declared the judge, "and move on to the final phase of the trial."

At that instant, someone rose from the spectators' gallery to hand the defense attorney a note.

"High Court!" the lawyer then cut in. "I have just been informed by a most reliable source that there exists a very significant witness for the defense. However, his testimony cannot be heard today, as he is at the moment not in Vienna. In the name of justice, I ask the court to temporarily halt the proceedings. Tomorrow is Sunday and no court business will be taking place. By Monday, possibly, the witness may have returned to the city."

The officials of the Provincial Court withdrew into the deliberations chamber. After a brief period, they returned with their decision: the trial would indeed be adjourned until Monday.

The crowd in attendance began to disperse. These spectators could be heard expressing both their surprise at the sudden turn of events in the defendant's favor at the eleventh hour and their hope that Lewinsohn's innocence might still be proven. Many of them surrounded his lawyer and asked who this witness could be.

But all he could do was answer, "I have been sworn to silence. I cannot reveal anything. You will just have to be patient until Monday morning, when you shall learn all."

Only one of them was displeased by this sudden development: the witness for the prosecution, Anton Schulze. His eyes burned with indignation, like a wild animal that had swiped its claws at its prey in vain. He left the courtroom with a scowl on his face. He would have given anything to know the identity of the new witness, as well as that of the person who had informed the defense attorney of his existence. He stood and waited at the door of the courthouse, hoping to catch this lawyer on his way out so that he or his associate could walk with him and have the opportunity of finding out who these people were.

The attorney, however, remained in the courthouse for another ten minutes so that he could call Frau Lewinsohn on the telephone and inform her of the change in circumstances. He wished to lend her some strength, telling her that her husband's innocence would, God willing, soon be demonstrated.

Then he exited the building, climbed into a carriage, and made his way to his offices. Anton Schulze realized his vigil had been for naught. He glanced about warily in every direction and then, making sure no one noticed him, he too entered a cab and told the driver to conduct him to the coffeehouse known as the "Wilder Mann"—the Wild Man.

As soon as the carriage drove away, an elegantly dressed young man emerged from the gates of the house next door to the courthouse, hailed a cab, and said softly to the driver, "Follow that cab that just drove off, but make sure they don't notice they're being followed!"

"Very well," the coachman answered.

And so the man climbed in, and the driver spurred his horses on.

CHAPTER TWO

In the Home of Frau Lewinsohn

THAT SAME DAY, Frau Lewinsohn sat in her parlor, her head resting in her hands. Her reddened eyes, pallid complexion, and embittered expression put on full display the suffering and pain that the young woman had endured over the preceding few weeks.

Today she had felt both so weak and agitated that the doctor categorically forbade her from attending the trial, though her heart was compelling her toward it. With dreadful impatience she awaited the news of the trial's outcome, and when her housemaid called her to the telephone, she walked over to it like someone who is about to hear her own death sentence.

The news from the lawyer—that there had been a sudden turn of events—surprised her more than it did solace her. The lawyer spoke very unclearly, and she could not cull from his words whether or not there was any real reason to hope that her husband would be saved or whether all this meant was but a couple of days' reprieve from the inevitable. She asked him, therefore, to pay her a visit and explain everything in person. The lawyer agreed, affirming that he would come later that afternoon.

She waited for him anxiously, thinking to herself all the while, "Oh, God, where can I find the strength to endure these two days of dread? This constant floating between hope and despair—it is the most fearsome assignment for a woman afflicted such as I am. I am afraid, afraid . . . that in these two days I will lose the last crumb of clear thinking I can still lay claim to."

At that moment, the housemaid opened the parlor door and announced in German, "Madam! An elegantly dressed gentleman would like to speak with you!"

"What is his name?" Frau Lewinsohn asked.

"He did not wish to say. But he says that his visit concerns a most important matter and that it's in your own interest to receive him."

Frau Lewinsohn thought it over a moment, then said to the girl, "What have I to lose? Let him in."

In a matter of seconds, a man who was indeed most elegantly dressed stood before her. He bowed in a gallant manner and greeted her with a cordial air.

"Whom might I have the honor of addressing, my good sir?" Frau Lewinsohn asked.

"I could provide you with some arbitrary name, but I won't. Who I am, Madam, is quite beside the point. I wish to take action on behalf of your innocent, wrongly accused husband, and to that purpose I would like you to answer a few of my questions."

"My good sir! I will not permit you to speak in such tones to me," Frau Lewinsohn interrupted. "If I do not know who you are, I can hardly enter into such a discourse with you."

"Madam! Later you shall come to regard me in quite a different light. Your distrust is quite understandable. But you have nothing to fear. I must, for the time being, conceal my name from you . . . but is it possible we are being overheard?"

With that, the man went to the door and bolted it shut.

"Sir! How dare you!" Frau Lewinsohn called out, her voice raised to an excited pitch. "Remove yourself from the premises at once, or I shall cry for help!"

"Shh, shh! Don't be afraid! The fate of your husband is in my hands. Whether you wish to or not, you must listen to me—and answer my questions."

The resolute tone in which the man uttered these words made a profound impression on Frau Lewinsohn. She composed herself somewhat and said, "All right. I shall endeavor to hear you out. Now ask!"

"First I must ask you something of particular delicacy, Frau Lewinsohn," said the man. "Do you have, or does your husband have, any enemies?"

"Everyone has enemies. But we have never done anyone ill.

As far as I know, my husband is well loved and respected by all who know him. Likewise in his business, he is always honest and strictly on the level, such that no one could rightly accuse him of anything untoward. And as for me, I could hardly believe that I have some personal enemy.

"It could be that wicked people, those who would begrudge us our success, may be envious. Maybe a former friend was jealous of me at one time or another for having found such happiness. But there is a considerable distance between envy and enmity!"

"I don't quite mean that," the gentleman said. "You or your husband must have a most formidable enemy for you to have landed in such boiling water. But now for an even more delicate question: Has your husband ever had a relationship with another woman, whether now or before your nuptials?"

The question hurt Frau Lewinsohn to the quick. But she restrained herself and answered curtly, "As for now, surely not. This I could swear to. And as for before our wedding, it would not have been the case either."

She concluded, the agitation rising again in her voice, "What do you want from me, anyhow, with such questions? Why should such things be of concern to you?"

The gentleman did not let her agitation hold him back, however, and he carried on with his questioning. "And you, Frau Lewinsohn, do you have now or did you have before your wedding a relationship with some other man?"

This proved too much for the unfortunate woman. She shook with rage and responded in a raised, trembling voice, "Sir! You have become impertinent. How dare you pose such questions! Do you believe that because I am weak and broken you are permitted to deal with me however you wish? Leave my home at once, or I shall positively shriek for help! Not another word out of you!" With these words she leaped to the door and clutched at the handle.

But the gentleman just kept on sitting quietly in his chair, answering with an icy air, "The agitation you display shows me that I am on the right track. Whether you want to answer me or not is all the same to me now. Naturally it would be more advantageous if you were to give me the particulars that I seek. We would be able to hit our target more quickly. The query that I have just put to you contains in it the key to this entire case. If you wish for your husband to be set free, you must answer this question clearly and with the utmost precision."

Deeply impacted by his words, she moved from the door to the sofa and resumed her former seat, once again holding her face in her hands.

"God, oh God!" she cried, weeping bitter tears. "Why must you torment me so!"

But in time she managed to calm herself and said, "I have never had a relationship with any man besides my dear Adolf, whether before or after I married him. It is true that as a girl, many young bucks made bids for my attention, but I did not enter into a more intimate connection with any of them."

"Fine," answered the gentleman. "And could you tell me whether or not one of these young bucks made a more passionate bid than any of the others?"

"As far I can remember at present, one of the gentlemen, by the name of Anton Sturz, did pursue me for a longer period and even wrote me a number of letters. This was just before my engagement, and as soon as I did become engaged he left me alone."

"What was this man's profession, and what did he look like?"

"He worked as an accountant in a factory that produced printing ink. I couldn't tell you the name of the company, because I had no interest in it. As far as what he looked like, all I remember is that he was a bit cross-eyed in his right eye. Other features I did not take note of. He looked much the same as anyone looks."

"Have you heard any details of him since that time? Perhaps you are still in possession of one of the letters he sent?"

"No! I always burned his letters without reading them. They didn't interest me. I didn't bother myself over him ever again, neither where he is now nor how he is occupying himself."

"I thank you kindly, Frau Lewinsohn, for your information. From my perspective, things are looking up for your husband. I must only insist that you not breathe a word of anyone having visited or making inquiries on these topics. Farewell for now. I leave you with my best wishes."

Again the gentleman made his courteous bow, turned on his heels, and quit the room.

Frau Lewinsohn was left alone. She could do nothing to explain to herself this most singular event. Who was this man, what did he want, and how could his inquiries have been of any use? She asked herself all of these questions but could not come up with a single answer.

In the afternoon the defense lawyer appeared and described to her the mysterious new development that had put a pause to the trial—how someone had suddenly stuck a note in his hand that gave notice of an important witness for the defense that would be able to appear on Monday.

"I figured," the lawyer related, "that the delay, in any case, couldn't hurt. '*Tsayt gevunen*, *ales gevunen*,' as we say—gain time and you gain everything. And so, with that in mind, I asked for the pause in the proceedings. Any further details than that, I simply do not know."

The lawyer's narrative only added to Frau Lewinsohn's astonishment. "Something much to be wondered at is taking place," she uttered. "Maybe yet another wonder awaits us."

She did not tell him of her parley with the unknown gentleman. And after the lawyer left, she remained sitting where she was, lost in her melancholy and uncertain thoughts.

CHAPTER THREE
Sturz or Schulze

ONCE HE LEFT Frau Lewinsohn, the man who had visited her and interrogated her in that most unusual way headed straight for the police headquarters, where he entered into a conference with the chief.

"Good day, Mr. Spitzkopf," the police chief greeted him. "You must have some news for me. What's happened?"

"I happened to have some free time today," the famous private detective answered—for yes, that finely dressed gentleman who had paid a visit to Frau Lewinsohn was none other than he! "And to fill it, I decided to attend the court hearing of the banker Lewinsohn. I had read about the case in the papers and taken an interest in it."

"Well, what did you see and hear there?" the chief asked.

"Not so much, as it happens," the detective answered. "But as far as I could tell from the proceedings, the banker is innocent, and I came to consider it my duty as a human being to investigate the matter and consequently protect the innocent man from injustice. And it seems I am on the right track."

"Not a doubt in my mind that you are, my private colleague!" said the police chief. "When Master Spitzkopf takes on a case, it's bound to get cracked. I take every opportunity to tell my officers that the government really ought to seize your private license so that you would have to join the force. Your continual success damages our own reputation. The public gets to thinking that the police aren't worth a hill of beans—and that if something big is brewing, it's Spitzkopf who's gotta be called!"

"And yet," Spitzkopf responded, "I always need the help of the police when I carry out an investigation. That's precisely what has brought me here today.

"But before I reveal anything else, I need to demand that this remain confidential, my having taken an interest in the Lewinsohn case. My method is always to take the most important steps before anyone knows I'm on the case. That's what I did today. At the trial, I surreptitiously had a note handed to the defense, informing the lawyer that I have an important witness lying in wait and that he must convince the court to delay the proceedings until Monday. The man did not know the note came from me. I hope that by Monday I will have been able to discover all that there is to be discovered, and to do that, Chief, you will have to give me the information I'm seeking."

"Fine!" he answered. "I'll do whatever can be done. So what do you need?"

"All the intelligence you have on a certain Anton Sturz, who, some eight years ago, worked as an accountant in a local factory of printing ink. I want to know what became of him and where he is now."

The chief had his inspector Springer called in and related to him Spitzkopf's wishes. Springer left and soon returned with the following information: "Eight years ago, Sturz was an accountant at the ink factory Grün & Co. He led a most lavish, profligate lifestyle, and at the end of his time there he stole quite a handsome sum from his employer. He was arrested and sentenced to eight months in prison. After serving his time, he left Vienna, and what became of him after that is unknown to the police."

"I thank you sincerely for these details," the detective said. "If you would now please let me know the date he was sentenced and the date the convict was freed, I would be most obliged."

The police inspector provided him with the dates. Spitzkopf recorded them in his notebook and left. He then got into a carriage and made his way homeward. While sitting in the carriage, he pondered everything that had taken place up to that point and said to himself: "It seems that Frau Lewinsohn did not tell me the whole truth. Sturz was sentenced barely three months after her wedding. The newspapers surely reported on the case at length. It is impossible that Frau Lewinsohn could have been so uninterested in the matter that she was completely unaware of what happened to the man.

"Admittedly, I do not know what reasons she could have had to keep secrets from me. Perhaps she forgot about her prior agitation and did not realize how any dissembling would make me suspicious. Now I am curious, though, what news my assistant Fuchs might be sitting on. I told him to follow today's witness for the prosecution, Anton Schulze.

"I have a hunch that Anton Sturz and Anton Schulze are one and the same man. In any case, both of them are cross-eyed on the right. I'll just go and ask for the file on Anton Schulze at the police station in Floridsdorf and see if my suspicion bears out.

"And as it happens, here I am back at home. Soon I shall enjoy hearing that news."

The carriage had drawn up to his house. Spitzkopf exited in one swift motion and dashed into his office.

CHAPTER FOUR
In Dire Straits

HERMANN FUCHS, assistant to the renowned detective Spitzkopf, was the young man who had pursued Anton Schulze after the witness left the courthouse. He had attended the trial that day with his employer. When the proceedings finished, Spitzkopf gave him a sign to follow Schulze and find out where he was headed and what his business was.

Fuchs had been tracking him for about a quarter of an hour when the man started looking around nervously, seemingly aware that someone was following him.

"It's no good," Fuchs thought to himself. "The man's noticed that I'm on his trail. It's time I play a little trick on this flyaway chickadee."

He told the driver to stop and got out. The other carriage,

meanwhile, had sped away. Fuchs disappeared into a side street, from which he emerged onto another street. There he called another cab and told the driver to take him to the Wilder Mann coffeehouse.

Upon entering, Fuchs sat himself down in a corner and made as if he were deeply engrossed in a newspaper. What he was actually doing was scrutinizing all of the patrons, but he could not find Anton Schulze among them. He walked through all of the café's rooms—including the one with the billiard table and the spot where people sat and played cards—and still no Schulze.

"Aha," Fuchs thought to himself. "The birdie made out that I was hot on his flight path, and so he headed somewhere else. I'm loitering around here for nothing, and my master will have a right good laugh at my expense that the lout outsmarted me.

"And yet—I did hit upon a bit of good luck! It's clear now that Anton Schulze is treading carefully and has reason to hide . . ."

While he sat pondering, a special-delivery man entered and handed a letter to a gentleman sitting nearby. Fuchs observed the man closely and noticed that he read through the note quite quickly, was surprised at its contents, put on his things, and left the premises immediately.

"I want to follow him," Fuchs thought. "There's something about this character that rubs me the wrong way."

And once the thought popped into his head, it was as good as done. He called over the waiter in charge of settling up, paid him for the coffee he had drunk, and asked him, "Among your regulars, would there chance to be a man by the name of Anton Schulze?"

"No!" the waiter answered at once. "The name is not familiar to me. Are you perhaps a friend of this gentleman?"

"If you don't know him, you also don't need to know whether or not I'm his friend," Fuchs retorted, throwing the waiter a sharp look.

"I do apologize," said the waiter. "I meant nothing by it."

But Fuchs had noticed that the waiter was taken aback by his inquiries, and he left the coffeehouse lost in these thoughts: "It's a pity I didn't notice every possible detail of the patrons and personnel here. Because there's something about the waiter I don't like either! I'll have to find my way to this coffeehouse again before long."

Upon exiting into the street, Fuchs spotted the man who had left before him standing a few buildings away, hiding behind an open door as if looking out for someone's arrival. As soon as he noticed Fuchs, though, he quickly retreated into the building and slammed the door shut.

Fuchs went over to give the place a good once-over. It was an old three-story affair with a broad arched door at the entrance. Having inspected it from all sides, he made a spur-of-the-moment decision to enter.

"It's true I don't quite know what I mean to do by entering," he thought. "But I feel I should have a look at the place from the inside."

Having stepped through the door, he made his way into a pitch-black corridor. There he took the opportunity of throwing on a new ensemble. He drew out a lightweight hat of glazed cloth from his pocket and stashed the felt hat he had been wearing. Then he pasted on a dark moustache and a goatee that came to a fine point and set a golden pince-nez before his eyes. He looked entirely different from before. And naturally he did not forget to lock and load his revolver . . .

Then he lit a match, preparing to begin his inspection of the corridor. Suddenly a door creaked open and out came a filthy, raggedly clad man and asked him a question with a leery air: "Who is it you're wanting to see, my good man?"

"I am a doctor," Fuchs answered. "I've been summoned to this house to tend to someone who is ailing. I've forgotten his name, though, so I thought I'd check the doors to see if I could find a name placard on one that might help me remember."

As soon as he got out this little speech, a door just opposite the stairway was flung open and a voice called out from within, "Please come in, Doctor. The patient lives right over here."

Fuchs knew it was a trick. And precisely for that reason, he entered.

Without overthinking the matter, our Fuchs strolled right into a dark room, its curtains shut. He could barely make out the person who was leading him along, but go along he did, quite peacefully.

They walked through several small rooms. Then the man opened another door and announced, "If you please, Herr Doktor. The patient is through here."

Before Fuchs had the chance to look around, the man gave him a forceful shove from behind. Suddenly Fuchs felt himself flying down a number of narrow, stone steps, his head being knocked about something awful in the descent.

"Enjoy the view from down there, you dirty spy!" he heard someone baying from above in wild tones. "Maybe next time you should try being less curious—and not go looking for trouble."

Fuchs lay there for a long while, semiconscious. Warm blood trickled from his head, all his limbs hurt, and he thought he was surely done for.

He did not know how long he had been on the ground when he slowly began coming to. He did remember, though, how he had gotten there, and thought to himself: "Well, at least I can be sure I'm on the right track. Seems it wasn't to that goon's taste how I was following him, and he thought he could do away with me for good. We'll just see about that. I've been in such straits before, and in the end I always got what I was after. First, let's just see where exactly I am."

And so he switched on his electric torch, blessedly still intact, and gave his prison a once-over.

It was a dungeon-like room, damp and cold, without a single door or window to be seen.

Fuchs was stunned.

"What could it all mean?" he thought. "I tumbled down here from somewhere up there. So where's the opening leading to the floor above, and where are the steps? It must be that after I fell, that man shut some trapdoor into which I'd fallen. Now it falls upon me to find that door."

While assessing himself and his surroundings, he found that he was bleeding from a number of wounds to the head and that the skin on his right hand had sustained abrasions in several places. But none of the injuries were very dire, and they caused Fuchs almost no pain.

He duly wiped the blood off his face using his pocket handkerchief and bound the wounds on his head with the same. Then he got right to work. Using a small hammer that he happened to have on him, he gave every wall that surrounded him a resounding bang, seeing whether he could detect any opening. It was no use, though. Nowhere did he find anything that might even suggest the presence of a door.

"The trapdoor must be somewhere up above," Fuchs determined. "How could I possibly get up there, though? The ceiling has to be rather high up, and there's no way I could clamber up there. The walls are smooth and damp, and climbing them would be a herculean task."

He sat back down and considered his sorry lot but could not hit upon a way out of it. He finally resolved to wait. Perhaps some bright idea would come to him—or, more likely, help from outside.

CHAPTER FIVE
In the Lair of the Counterfeiters

EN ROUTE in his carriage from the courthouse to the Café Wilder Mann, where his co-conspirator Franz Grobschmied was waiting for him, Anton Schulze's eyes darted about constantly. He was afraid he was being followed. He did not like the story of the defense witness who would be testifying Monday. He feared his secret would soon out.

He then noticed a droshky was tailing him, and he began to eye the vehicle with a certain uneasiness. As he watched the droshky stopped, and Hermann Fuchs got out and fled into a side street. Schulze was now afraid even to enter the café. He got out of the carriage near a bridge over the Danube, and by way of a *Dienstmann*, one of Vienna's class of errand men, he dispatched a note to his partner telling him to visit him immediately at home—for he was being followed.

Franz Grobschmied, in the meantime, was sitting in the café waiting for him. This particular café was a rendezvous point for a certain crowd of people who were always elegantly attired and gave the impression that they were people of distinction, whereas, in point of fact, they made a living off of fraud, filching, forgery, and the like. They were regulars at this café, and nearly all of them knew each other. Even the waiters were well acquainted with most of their secrets, and their silence was bought with handsome tips.

After Hermann Fuchs appeared in the coffeehouse and began his close inspection down to the last corner of the place, the unexpected guest quickly became an object of suspicion. None of the gangsters bothered him, however, not wanting to draw attention in case he was searching for one of them.

As soon as Grobschmied received the message from Schulze informing him that he was being followed, Grobschmied ascertained that it must be the very same man who had infiltrated the café as a spy. And so he immediately quit the premises, deciding to wait in the doorway of his home until the stranger exited the coffeehouse so he could observe where he was headed next.

Meanwhile, Schulze was peering out the window of the house, stealing furtive glances under the curtain, and when Fuchs left the café, he gave a sign to Grobschmied indicating this was the man who was pursuing him. Grobschmied immediately retreated into the shadows, believing he had evaded detection.

When Schulze found to his surprise that Fuchs was entering the home, however, the two decided to incapacitate him. They lured him through with their various tricks and flung him down into the cellar. Then they sat down to discuss what their next steps would be. Three others who lived in the same house and belonged to the same gang were also parties to the discussion.

"You're to blame for all of it!" Grobschmied thundered at Schulze. "We've been doing our work for months now in perfect peace and quiet. We've got our regular customers, and we all had enough dough to kick back a bit and enjoy ourselves. It wouldna been long before we saved up a nice bundle and coulda lived it up like God Himself enjoying a leisurely ride on the Ferris wheel at the Wurstelprater. But then our Schulze up and gets the notion he wants to reignite an old flame and get his sweet revenge on some knob who nabbed a girl that got away. So he goes and shows him what's what and meanwhile puts our own faces to the frying pan!"

"Look who's talking now!" Schulze cut in, roaring back at him. "When I first laid out the plan to you and told you to dress up as some Count von Fries and slide some of the funny money Lewinsohn's way, I didn't hear you crying none. And why's that? Because I promised you a cut of the cash I'd eventually be winning off my old gal in the process."

"What's all this claptrap good for?" the other gangsters cried out. "We're practical lads and just wanna do a bit of business. We don't give a damn about some old love story. If you all can't quit it with that nonsense, we're out. We get the smallest cut anyway."

"And who asked you, my sweet boys?" Schulze asked with a wicked smile. "If you don't got the eagers, we don't need ya! You all forget that I'm the captain of this whole operation. I got the ink plates and I know what colors get printed on which bills, because my old boss, that filthy dog Grün, who had me sent up the river, used to supply them to the government mint. It was me what masterminded our whole enterprise. You all just lend a hand with the dirty work. Got any more complaints against me?

"You think I'm scared you'll rat me out? Not a chance. Because if you do, it's the chokey for all of us. I'm not scared o' that spy either. We've dealt with him already. He's lying in our cellar with a coupla broken arms and legs. Tonight, when we go to check up on our handiwork, I'mma stick a gas hose through a hole in the cellar wall and crank it up so he'll be suffocated. You can bet we'll soon have washed our hands clean of him and whatever miserable company he keeps."

"You're right," said Grobschmied. "But I'd tone down the highfalutin attitude if I were you. It ain't gonna be so easy to find another crony who's got his own house to install secret dungeons in, complete with trapdoors and hanging flights of stairs and other such fixtures that you need to run a little factory operation like ours.

"You need us just as much as we need you. And I'm not so crazy for the coupla thousand kronen we've got coming our way if it means a coupla years in the clink. It'd be better to lay off the manufacturing for a few months. Then when things quiet down and folks've forgotten all about this whole scandal, we'll get back to work."

"Agreed!" the other three conspirators called out. "Our cut of the cash really ain't too hot anyhow. In the meantime, we can do some better business elsewhere."

"For my part, I say fine!" Schulze responded. "I'm not gonna force anyone who's too scared to press forward. But as you know, we're in the middle of fabricating a hundred blue banknotes. They're almost done—all they need is one last run through the printing press. It's a job of no more than two or three hours. So I think we should finish it tonight and divvy up the bills. Then we'll take our little rest from it all. But I'm positive you lot will be the ones asking me to get the fabrication up and running again before I ask you!"

"Let it be so," said Grobschmied. "But so's to be safe: just

Schulze and I will finish up the printing work tonight. You three will stand just outside the door, in the courtyard, and on the steps, keeping watch to see that no one comes to raid us."

"Good, good, it's a plan," the three lackeys agreed. "When do we get to work?"

"Midnight," Schulze answered.

The gang babbled on a little further, then the co-conspirators retreated to their rooms in the house. Schulze remained behind with Grobschmied. Although during these deliberations he had pricked up his courage, wanting to show what a tough sort he was, his heart was in fact pounding in his chest. He was afraid to go outside—afraid even to be seen on the streets of Vienna.

CHAPTER SIX

Another Innocent Arrested

WHEN SPITZKOPF returned from the police headquarters to his home, he expected he would find his assistant Fuchs waiting there, or at least a message from him about the man he had been following. But Fuchs was nowhere to be found, nor any message he had sent. It was already late afternoon, and Spitzkopf was growing a little impatient.

In the meantime he telephoned the Floridsdorf police to request all the details from the file on Anton Schulze. But he was not satisfied with what little information they had. The police could only relate that he had come from a small town in the Czech region of Moravia, had been living for two years in the Viennese suburb of Floridsdorf, and was a machinist. The police were not at all acquainted with the particulars of his person—the matter remained to be investigated.

"The way I see it, I'll simply have to go to Floridsdorf myself to get down to the nitty-gritty," Spitzkopf reflected. "I want to wait a bit longer before I do, though. Maybe Fuchs will come back or send along a bit of news."

So Spitzkopf remained in his office for a good while, but there was still no sign of Fuchs.

"Well, I'd better get going then," Spitzkopf said to himself, promptly changing his attire. He donned an old, tattered jacket, patched-up shoes, and a wrinkled hat so that he looked altogether like a poor laborer. Then he strapped on, as always, two loaded revolvers, a ring of lockpicks and skeleton keys, an electric torch, and a few other necessities and set forth to Floridsdorf.

He had gone down only a few streets when he saw a pack of people all running off in one direction. He rushed after them and observed a police watchman leading an aged Jewish junk dealer by the arm. Scurrying behind in their wake was a whole gang of urchins, porters, wagon drivers, and other such types, all shouting, "Counterfeiter! Counterfeiter! Jew! Jew!"

Spitzkopf asked them what was going on. They told him that the Jewish junkman had bought something in a shop and paid with a fifty-kronen note. The shopkeeper recognized the bill as a fake and had his clerks detain the man until he was able to call a watchman to drag him in to the police station.

Spitzkopf followed the group there, where he presented his credentials to the police inspector and asked permission to be in attendance when the arrestee was interrogated. The inspector agreed and brought in the man for questioning.

The junkman laid out his account of things. That morning he had bought an old suit jacket from some fellow with whom he was not previously acquainted. After paying him, the man asked whether or not he could get change from the dealer for a fifty-kronen note. The dealer provided it, seeing as he had a good number of smaller bills on him and, moreover, the fellow was dressed very finely and so he had no suspicions against him.

"What is this fellow's name, and where does he live?" asked the police inspector.

"I couldn't say for certain," answered the junkman. "I had

been wandering around with my pack of goods through a number of streets and was in a great many houses. I didn't take stock of what street or house it was where I bought the suit jacket. But if I retrace the path I took this morning, perhaps I'd be able to recognize the street and the house."

"Your excuses don't quite add up for me," said the inspector. "Maybe what you want is for the watchman to follow you around a few hours just until it gets dark, and then in some shadowy house or back alley you'll hightail it. We're very familiar with such maneuvers! I don't think so. You'll sleep tonight in our holding cell. Maybe you'll remember who you got the fifty from. If not, I'll let you traverse the streets under the strict supervision of a patrol, and maybe you'll find the spot you're looking for.

"Guard! Conduct this man to the holding cell."

The guard was just about to do so when Spitzkopf piped up. "Please, just one moment, Herr Kommissar. If you'd permit me to ask the arrestee one question."

"*Bitte sehr*," answered the inspector. "By all means, ask away."

"Please just tell me, good sir," said Spitzkopf, "do you still have the jacket you bought off this fellow?"

"Yes!" the junkman answered. "It's in my pack of goods."

"Show it to us," Spitzkopf requested.

The junkman unraveled his bundle and searched among various articles until he found a black jacket, which he handed over to Spitzkopf.

The detective turned the jacket over and over, examining it from every angle and turning out all the pockets. Finally he discovered a monogram stitched into the lining, the letters "F. G."

"Something of a clue," Spitzkopf remarked to the inspector, jotting down the letters in his notebook. "It seems to me this man is actually innocent. Now I don't have the right to ask you to free him, but I hope I shall soon manage to demonstrate his innocence to you."

Then Spitzkopf turned to the junkman and said, "If you don't remember the name of the street where you bought this jacket, you'll at least remember in what part of town the streets are that you went wandering down today. Maybe you remember some landmark that was nearby, say a hotel, a coffeehouse, a bridge, a train station, anything like that?"

"Yes, I can remember that much. Not long before I had passed a coffeehouse with a big red sign advertising the 'Wilder Mann.' More than that I can't recall, I'm afraid, as I haven't been in Vienna long, and that was my first time setting foot in that part of town."

"That information will suffice," said Spitzkopf.

The guard then led the junkman away, and Spitzkopf left the precinct.

CHAPTER SEVEN
In Floridsdorf

AFTER LEAVING the building, Spitzkopf hopped on the tram and journeyed off to Floridsdorf. He had gotten Anton Schulze's exact address from his telephone call with the police earlier, and upon arriving at the man's street he soon found the house number.

It was already quite dark, and a paltry few gas lamps just barely lit the narrow, crowded lane. Not a soul could be seen. The low-slung houses with their tiny windows made the environs look more like some obscure rural district than an industrial suburb of Vienna.

Spitzkopf had a good look at house #15. It was a single-story building with six windows in the front, none of them illuminated. The door was closed. He opened it cautiously and entered a dark, cramped corridor that led out into a small yard on the other side of the house.

Upon inspecting the yard, Spitzkopf found that none of the windows on that side of the house were lit from within either. "It seems no one is at home in the whole building," he thought to himself. "So I can have a good search of Schulze's rooms. I just have to find out which door is his."

He returned to the corridor, illuminated it with his electric torch, and noticed on one door a placard bearing the name "Anton Schulze." He tried turning the knob, but the door was locked. After opening it with his skeleton key and entering, he locked the door behind him by the same device.

"Good thing the windows here face the courtyard," he thought. "I can use my electric torch without worrying that someone passing on the street will notice anything. But I'll draw the curtains closed anyhow."

After doing so, he began his close inspection of the apartment. It consisted of three small rooms, simply but attractively furnished. One could tell that the individual who lived here was a man of means.

Spitzkopf looked through every corner of all three rooms, sliding open every cupboard and every drawer by the aid of his special keys. But he found nothing that might raise any suspicion. He was growing a touch disappointed until finally he spotted, lying upon a sideboard, an old photo album. He picked it up, leafed through it, and peered closely at a number of the photographs within. Then he cried out in amazement. "Ah! What have we here? The lady in this picture very much resembles Frau Lewinsohn. This is how she must have looked as a girl some eight or ten years ago. Turns out my hunch was right on the money. Anton Schulze is indeed the same man as the Anton Sturz who once courted the present-day Frau Lewinsohn. And it seems I figured correctly that the only reason the man has gone after Lewinsohn is to get his revenge on him for winning the lady's heart."

Spitzkopf slipped the photograph into his pocket and recommenced his search of the premises.

"Seeing as I've already made such a weighty discovery, I've got to keep on going," he resolved. "Maybe I'll find something of equal importance."

He searched and searched and then at last, in the pocket of an overcoat, came upon a business card bearing the inscription "Franz Grobschmied—Landlord—Vienna."

"Franz Grobschmied! Franz Grobschmied!" Spitzkopf erupted, seizing his notebook from his pocket. "Aha! On the suit jacket that the junkman bought today, two letters were embroidered: F. G. That could very well be Franz Grobschmied. If Schulze and Grobschmied are friends—and both of them have something to do with counterfeit money—then perhaps they themselves are the counterfeiters. The plot thickens.

"Now I just have to find out where this Grobschmied resides. That will be easy enough. I should be able to find his location in one of those address books that can be found in any coffeehouse in Vienna. And then I'll send these hoodlums packing.

"I needn't search here any longer. What I've found already will suffice for the moment. And in any case, I shouldn't tarry. Someone could show up and send *me* packing first!"

With those words, Spitzkopf switched off his electric torch and, taking care to walk quietly, exited the apartment.

But as soon as he opened the door leading into the rest of the house he was met by an old woman carrying a kerosene lamp. Seeing a strange man coming out of Schulze's rooms, she raised an alarm: "Help! Help! A thief!"

Spitzkopf's first instinct was to run out as fast as he could. But on thinking the matter over for a moment, he realized his would-be captors might follow him, and he might not be able to hail a carriage so quickly. And what good could such a hullabaloo as that do, being chased through the streets thus by all the denizens of Floridsdorf? Maybe better to declare himself a thief right there on the spot. Then when Schulze comes home and finds someone has been rummaging through his rooms, he would pin it on having been burglarized. More convenient to be classified as a common crook, Spitzkopf figured, and allow himself to be clapped in irons than to have the real criminals thinking a detective was on their trail. He would of course, in the end, be able to identify himself accurately to the police and would immediately be set free.

And so, playing the part, Spitzkopf laid the startlement on thick and made as if he wished to flee, while the woman's hue and cry attracted a number of neighbors to the scene, who seized Spitzkopf at once. One of them then went off to alert a watchman.

Indeed, Spitzkopf's external appearance, looking as he did at that moment like some sort of vagrant, was highly suspicious. So when the watchman arrived, he did not delay in grabbing the alleged thief by the collar and hauling him to the nearest precinct. And Spitzkopf calmly let himself be thuswise hauled. As soon as he was before the police he made his true identity known to the commanding officer. Having done so, he snuck out of the precinct through the other side of the building so the voracious gawkers on the street would be none the wiser.

CHAPTER EIGHT
The Counterfeiters Are Cuffed

AFTER EMERGING from the Floridsdorf precinct, he lingered on the street for a moment plotting his next steps.

"I ought to go home first," he thought, "to see whether Fuchs has returned with some news. But if Schulze comes home and gets to thinking it was a detective, not a burglar, in his room—because nothing of value was taken—he would alert his accomplice, and then my plan would come to nothing.

"Considering that possibility, it would be more expedient for me to drop in at one of the hideaways I maintain throughout Vienna. There I can change clothing and set out to search Franz Grobschmied's residence. Maybe there I'll find the key piece of evidence."

Embarking upon this new course, Spitzkopf boarded the

tram back to the center of Vienna and alighted near his hideaway in the district of Brigittenau, with its significant Jewish population. Once inside he took off his tattered jacket and threw over his usual suit such habiliments as made him look altogether like a junkman. He then slung a small pack over his shoulder and marched out into the street.

His first destination was the Wilder Mann coffeehouse. The junkman said he had bought the suit jacket not far from that establishment, so Grobschmied must live somewhere nearby too. Spitzkopf intended to thumb through the coffeehouse's address book and have a look at the house. Then he would know what to do next.

The Wilder Mann was rather far from this particular hideaway. The tram ride there took over half an hour, and when he arrived it was past ten at night.

There were only a few people still lingering in the coffeehouse at that hour. Spitzkopf sat himself down at a little table off to one side and asked for a glass of beer and the Vienna address book. While he waited, he took the opportunity to have a good long look at the other patrons. A new guest had entered, attracting the attention of the server. Spitzkopf felt the guest's eyes on him, but not wanting to reveal that he had noticed anything, he pretended to be engrossed in the address book.

There he quickly found the name he was looking for. Grobschmied in fact lived no more than a few houses away. He downed his beer, paid, and left the establishment.

As he left, however, he took one last look around him and noticed the waiter winking to yet another patron, signaling to him to keep an eye on Spitzkopf.

"That other customer must be a member of the gang too!" Spitzkopf thought. "I think I'll soon be ensnaring the whole lot of them at once. I've got to be careful."

He walked away briskly just as a tram was passing through. He sprang onboard with great alacrity, leading the conductor to shout that it was forbidden to get on as the tram was moving and he would be taking down his name so he could be fined. Spitzkopf pretended not to hear him until the tram turned onto another street, at which point he jumped back out, leaving the conductor standing there like a fool.

"Now to pay Herr Grobschmied a little visit," he said to himself, directing his steps to the house where the man lived. As soon as he arrived, he saw the café waiter emerging from the house.

"Aha!" thought Spitzkopf. "Seems the birdie flew over here to give word that something fishy was going on. Good thing he didn't see me just now. It's rather a risky thing to enter gang members' homes. But enter I shall. It'll be worth it as long as they haven't yet had a chance to do away with any damning evidence."

And so, with confident steps, he walked up to the massive arched door and rang the bell. The building's caretaker opened, gave him a sharp look, and asked through gritted teeth, "What do you want here, Jew? Fine hour to be going traipsing about selling your dirty wares!"

"I am in urgent need of seeing Herr Grobschmied," Spitzkopf answered evenly. And before the caretaker had a moment to consider the situation, he had already made his way inside. By the light of the caretaker's lantern he immediately noticed a door placard bearing the name of Franz Grobschmied, and he rang.

The door soon opened. Anton Schulze poked his head out and asked, "Who is it?"

Spitzkopf recognized him at first glance. He was stunned but did not let it affect the calm tone of his reply. "Is Herr Grobschmied at home? I have some business with him."

"Yes, he's here. Do come in," answered Schulze, his eyes blazing like a tiger's.

But Spitzkopf was not afraid. He stuck his hand down one of the pockets where he had stowed away a loaded revolver and strode into the room with his head held high.

There he found Grobschmied sitting at a table along with a

couple of rounders, all of them playing cards.

"What is your wish?" Grobschmied asked him.

"I am the junker you sold the suit jacket to earlier today," Spitzkopf answered. "The one who changed a fifty for you. I paid with that same fifty at a store later on, and they wouldn't accept it because it was phony. I've come here so you could give me my money back. I'm a poor man and can't afford such a loss."

As he spoke Spitzkopf was examining the men, registering their minutest movements. Schulze received his closest scrutiny.

Then, quite out of nowhere, he received a dramatic wallop to the back of his head with some unknown object, and he fell to the floor half conscious.

One of the three underlings from the gang had done it. He had been hiding in the front room and had come up behind Spitzkopf, cracking his pate with a hammer.

"Now down to the cellar with this lump!" Schulze commanded. "He'll find his little friend there, and we'll soon put an end to their meddling with one blow."

The men hoisted him up by his arms and legs, lugged him through a few rooms, and heaved him down into the cellar where Fuchs had now been lying for a good number of hours.

"That's the second spy taken care of!" Schulze sniggered. "But now things are getting serious. We have to finish printing the last bills tonight and then tidy up. I'll bring the plates and the ink back home with me. Then if they come searching tomorrow, it'll be a wild goose chase."

"Yes. But first we have to pipe gas into the cellar," said Grobschmied. "Snuff out this pair of sleuths. It was the devil what must have made me hand over that fake fifty to the junkman today, and it's gotten me into a real mess. He could come and testify against me as a witness. Why, the man was an undercover rat! And now I've gotta exterminate him."

"All in good time," Schulze answered. "We'll make quick work of it, never you fear. Come, Grobschmied, into our workshop. Meanwhile, our three friends will keep guard so that no one sneaks up on us unawares."

Hermann Fuchs had been lying in the cellar for what seemed an eternity. He had recovered from his injuries, and they barely hurt anymore, but he was in a state of despair. He thought and thought and could think up no plan to get him out of the vile dungeon.

All he could do was hope that his master had also gotten onto the right track that day and would soon be coming to rescue him, as had happened more than once before. But one hour followed another, and the air in the cellar seemed to grow more damp and stagnant, his breathing more labored, his thirst and hunger more acute. He feared that if he had to wait much longer, he would be suffocated or die for want of water.

He was sitting, moreover, in total darkness. He did not want to use his electric torch lest the overuse should make it lose power.

Suddenly he heard footsteps overhead, felt a momentary change in the air, and was thwacked by some heavy object falling directly onto him. It all lasted just a few seconds—not long enough for him even to notice that a door had been opened up above—and just as quickly the door slammed shut again.

He switched on his torch, illuminating the room, and rose, standing on the spot as if he had been turned to stone—it was a human body, apparently near death, lying there at his feet.

He shone the light right into the figure's face, and to his growing horror recognized it as none other than that of his master.

"*Ach, mayster*! What happened?" he gulped out in a voice choked with anguish.

Spitzkopf opened his eyes. The plummet down the steps had made him come to. He recognized his assistant at once and said weakly, "Thank God, thank God I've found you here. These scoundrels could have their way with us as long as we were each alone. But against both of us together? They're bound to fail."

"But Master! Your head is bleeding!" Fuchs cried, afraid half to death.

"Oh, it's not all that bad. I've survived much worse. The wound is only skin deep—I'm confident my skull is still in one piece. I know because my pain is only slight. Now take off my junkman's jacket and open up my pack. There you'll find everything we need: wound dressings, a rope ladder, and other articles of that sort. I've come forearmed against all eventualities."

Fuchs tore open the pack, snatched out the dressing materials, and bound Spitzkopf's head. Using the jacket he rubbed away Spitzkopf's blood, then cleaned himself off by the same method.

Spitzkopf took out a bottle of cognac. Both took a swallow and refreshed themselves.

"Now I'm going to take a minute to rest," Spitzkopf announced, "and then we'll get to work planning out our next steps."

The detective laid the old jacket on the ground and stretched himself out on it. As soon as he did so he smelled a sharp odor. He jumped up and said, "The scoundrels are trying to gas us. They're piping in gas through a hole in the wall. But they're in for a surprise. I've brought along a match with me. We'll ignite the gas and find the cellar entrance lickety-split. They'll just save us the trouble of having to use our lamps."

He then set about his stated plan, lighting a match and walking with it beside every wall of the cellar until the gas ignited. A massive flame formed and, all at once, the entire room was brightly illuminated.

"Presto! We've got the gang to thank for shedding a little light on the situation. Now we'll find the entrance in no time . . . but hush! I hear a noise."

He inclined his ear to the wall and detected, only just, the faint whirring of a machine on the other side of the wall.

"There's where the counterfeiting operation must be!" Spitzkopf said. "Now I hear it clear as day, the sound of their press printing away. We've got to get out of here at once so we can catch these menaces in flagrante delicto."

He undertook a close inspection of the room and said, "The secret opening to the cellar must be somewhere high up. I think I detected it as I fell. Get up on my shoulders, Fuchs, and try pressing on the ceiling."

And so Fuchs hoisted himself up onto his master's shoulders and right away found what felt like the outline of a trapdoor. Using a skeleton key, he opened the lock that held it fast and quietly pushed the door open.

He clambered onto the flight of stairs that ascended therefrom, and Spitzkopf tossed the rope ladder up to him. Fuchs pulled his master up to join him. They returned the trapdoor to its closed position and climbed the stairs together until they entered a dark chamber. They illuminated it with Spitzkopf's electric torch and saw that the chamber had two doors, one to the right and another to the left.

Moving very quietly, Spitzkopf opened the door on the left. It led to yet another flight of stairs that descended to yet another door. From there he again heard the printing press going at full tilt.

"Their workshop is down here. I'll go in and surprise these grifters in the middle of their work. Meanwhile, Fuchs, you go and open the door on the right; that probably leads to their residences. Climb out into the street through the first window you see and alert the police."

Fuchs made a quick getaway. It was pitch black on the other side of the door on the right, but he managed to open a window and hop right out. He moved too swiftly even to notice a man racing after him shouting, "Stop, thief!"

Fuchs sprinted until he found a street watchman and called to him, "I am the undercover detective Max Spitzkopf! Alert the police—we have found the counterfeiters!"

The watchman blew his whistle and a cluster of his colleagues gathered from all sides. Fuchs led them all to Grobschmied's house, where a frightfully dramatic scene was currently playing out.

After Fuchs left, Spitzkopf had, without making the slightest noise, pushed open the door leading from the cellar and flashed his electric torch. The light fell upon Grobschmied and Schulze standing beside a small hand-operated press. By the light of a kerosene lamp, they were printing one banknote after another.

The two scoundrels were nearly blinded by the sudden light and found themselves unable to move a muscle. Spitzkopf, gripping his torch in one hand and a loaded revolver in the other, boomed, "I've caught you red-handed! There you are printing the funny money! But you're doing it for the last time. You've met your end, right here and now!"

Schulze pulled himself together a bit, preparing to make a run at Spitzkopf. The detective noted it and said in ice-cold tones, "You'd better stand off, you scallywag, if you don't want me to shoot you like a dog."

At that moment he heard heavy footfalls from above. Certain that it must be Fuchs and the police, he moved away from the door so as to give them space.

But it was not they. The three underlings had shown up, one of them having noticed Fuchs leaving by the window and immediately recognizing him. At first he had thought to detain him, crying out, "Stop, you thief!" But then, realizing he would not be able to catch up with him and that the police would soon be following in his wake, he instead notified his two cronies, and the three of them made their way down to the cellar so as to warn Schulze and Grobschmied and to do all that was necessary to prevent the workshop from being discovered.

Upon entering the room, they spotted Spitzkopf and made to tackle him from behind.

But the detective caught sight of them just as quickly and fired a shot. One of the accomplices was hit in the right leg and, issuing a piquant curse, fell to the ground. Meanwhile Grobschmied seized a heavy screwdriver that had been lying beside the press and hurled it at Spitzkopf. His aim was poor, though, and it managed to hit one of the other accomplices in the head. Spitzkopf then fired again, wounding Grobschmied.

No further action was needed on his part. As soon as the melee broke out, the officers dashed in, and there was nothing the gang could do other than get marched right off to police headquarters.

There the police doctor treated the wounds of the injured, and the police chief was telephoned to be informed of all that had occurred. He made his way over to the station at once and congratulated Spitzkopf on his tremendous success.

"You've done well, Master Spitzkopf. To have uncovered everything in such a short time. Truly a tour de force!"

The chief then took it upon himself to interrogate the men who had been arrested. They confessed to everything. Anton Schulze was indeed the same person as Anton Sturz—he had taken on another name so that no one in Vienna would recognize him.

He had been engaged in the fabrication of the fake banknotes for several months together with Grobschmied and their three accomplices. They found a market for them in the Café Wilder Mann, where buyers would rendezvous with them. The waiter was their liaison and took a cut of the revenue.

Schulze bore a deep resentment against Lewinsohn in his heart because he felt the banker had stolen away his beloved. He meant to destroy the man because of it. But the plot would lead directly to his being discovered.

That very night the police chief notified the court of the new developments, and before dawn Lewinsohn was freed. The Jewish junk dealer, too.

All of Vienna would soon be reading about it in the Sunday morning papers—the latest, most magnificent feat of the master detective Max Spitzkopf. He was praised throughout the entire city, his name vaunted to the high heavens. Lewinsohn, meanwhile, rewarded him handsomely for his efforts. And from every corner the detective received heartfelt messages of thanks for so passionately championing the cause of the innocent and the persecuted.

Issue 3: The Blood Libel

דריטעס העפט. פרייז 20 העללער.

עלילת־דם (דאס בלוט בלבול.)

די וואַנד פאַלט אָב און עס בעוויזט זיך דער טויטע קערפער פון דעם פערשוואונדענעם קינד.. — אָט דאָ איז דאָס פערשוואונדענע קינד, פרוי האלטשיצקא! — זאָגט שפּיצקאָפּף קאלטבלוטיג, זיצענדיג ביום פיאנאָ — וועגען וועלכען איהר האָט די יועלט איינגעריסען או, אונשולדיגע מענשען אונגליקליך געמאכט

The Blood Libel

CHAPTER ONE

A Pogrom

It was eight days before Passover. After a long, hard winter, temperatures were starting to rise a little. For a few days a soft southern breeze had been blowing, and the snow had begun to melt. A deep layer of thick mud now coated the streets.

The Jews of the small Galician shtetl of Dorokhov[2] were hard at work preparing a suitable welcome for the springtime holiday, their dearly beloved annual guest. The severe frosts that had dominated the landscape up until the first of the month of Nisan, shortly before Passover, had delayed their preparations and made them gloomy for a while. But now they turned with full hearts to their work.

In all the houses of the shtetl, families were whitewashing the walls, sweeping, scrubbing. The wives ran to and fro with their heads wrapped in kerchiefs, tidying each room, even the cellars and attics. And laid out in front of every home for later cleaning and refurbishment you could find broken tables and chairs, cots and cupboards, straw that had been found rotten in the sacks that cushioned each bed, and linens to be laundered.

Meanwhile the matzo bakers were working day and night. On every corner one met porters' apprentices with heavy baskets of the unleavened bread on their shoulders. In cheder, the religious elementary schools, the teachers had already stopped their instruction, and the mud-spattered schoolchildren ran free and wild in the streets. A Passover's eve in the true Jewish style.

Today the tumult was at an even higher pitch. It was Thursday evening. Friday would mark the beginning of *Shabes-hagodl*, the Great Sabbath, which immediately precedes Passover. On those two days, preparations for the festival were not allowed. Instead one had to bake challahs one last time before the holiday. For that purpose, the usual kneading troughs were brought out again, those used for non-Passover food, food containing leavening. And one still had to put up cholent, the Shabbos stew, in the usual, nonholiday vessels, those that would be forbidden for use on Passover. Only after *Shabes-hagodl* could one complete the final cleaning—scalding the pots to rid them of any leavening and banishing every last crumb from the house—all in honor of the sacred holiday.

It was a dark and dreary day, black storm clouds covering the sky, the air damp and heavy. The melted snow dripped from the roofs and windows, and the deep, viscous mud on the streets crept all the way up to one's ankles. With sundown approaching Jews were racing to pray *mincha* and *mayrev*, the afternoon and evening services, before the day drew to a close. Soon a perfect quiet would spread over the shtetl. The sort of quiet one finds in a graveyard . . .

Most of the Jewish shops in Dorokhov were located around the *Ringplatz*, as the main square is called in Galician towns. Suddenly a mad rush was seen in that place and a cacophony was heard, a terrible clamoring, the sounds of utter riot. The shops were quickly bolted shut. Jews were tearing away in every direction, horror etched in their faces, shooting glances this way and that, glances wild and unbelieving. Women screamed and children wailed. Total chaos had taken over.

For from the other side of the town, where the Christian population lived, the bells of the church could be heard pealing loudly as a mob of peasants and laborers armed with crowbars, clubs, and axes set out for the *Ringplatz*. They walked with threatening steps. They emanated terror and sent forth waves of fear.

A pack of elderly Gentile women ran behind them, shrieking curses. "Get the Jews! Kill them! They are taking our children and slaughtering them for their Passover matzos!"

Soon this savage gang reached the first row of Jewish houses and the attack began. Heavy stones flew through Jewish window-panes. The front line of the assault force—the men—began to smash open the doors of Jewish stores. Meanwhile the few gendarmes stood opposite the attackers with raised bayonets, shouting, "In the name of the law, return to your homes or we'll shoot!"

The pogromists stood still for a moment. The gendarmes' command had startled them somewhat. But the pause was very brief.

The rear of the mob—the old women—was already pressing the front of the line forward, screaming, "You should be ashamed of yourselves, Christians! You're afraid of three lousy gendarmes? And you gendarmes! You should be doubly ashamed! Taking the side of these *Żydy*, these damned kikes, and threatening to shoot at *us*, honorable Christian souls all!"

And so the gang took courage and resisted the uniformed men. The gendarmes wavered, not knowing what to do. They were just three against a wild and fanatical mob, a hundred or so people burning with rage.

A steady hail of rocks began to fall on the gendarmes—the mob's way of telling them to get lost.

"Once more we demand that you stand down!" a gendarme called out. "Do not force us to shed blood today."

"*Hura, na Żydów i żandarmów!* Have at 'em, the *Żydy* and their buddies the gendarmes, too!" the mob cried as it tightened around the uniformed men.

The situation was growing more perilous by the moment. Darkness had almost completely descended. In a quarter of an hour it would be pitch black. And at that point the mob would be able to do whatever it wished . . .

Suddenly the district governor arrived with a few of his officers and called out at the top of his voice. “Subjects of the realm! Listen to me! Return quietly to your homes, and I give you my good Christian word that I will do everything within my power to find the culprits of this crime you speak of and punish them. Don’t force me to call in the military. It would be a terrible shame for Christian blood to be spilled.”

The governor was revered by the people in his district, and his words began to have their desired effect. Some of the so-called subjects went along with his orders. But for most of them, “returning quietly home” was the last thing on their minds. The rear pressed ahead, pushing and shoving. The three gendarmes and the police officers were powerless against these masses.

The clatter of broken glass was heard again, and the splitting and crashing of doors being wrenched from their sockets. The governor and his officers were quickly enveloped in the swarm of people and could barely move an inch. It was only with great effort that the governor was able to extricate himself and run to the telegraph office. There he sent an order for military reinforcements to be brought in from the nearest city.

The governor had barely exited the office when he noticed a red glow illuminating the entire town. The *Ringplatz* was burning. The deranged crowd had set the nearby Jewish homes on fire.

The fire expanded slowly at first, as the roofs were so wet. But soon the wind carried the flames far and wide, and the entire *Ringplatz* became an inferno.

As the homes were burning, the mob did not sit idly by. The fanatical peasants took the opportunity to continue smashing windows and doors of Jewish homes, those not yet engulfed in flame. They then forced their way into them and looted as much as they could carry. That which they could not take they destroyed and rendered useless. Feathers from comforters and pillows flew everywhere and mingled in the air with the sparks the wind heralded from roof to roof and from house to house.

The small-town fire department was making an attempt with its solitary hand-powered pump, but it was no use. The firefighters barely knew where to begin. Meanwhile the plunderers could not be stopped.

The Jews who lived around the *Ringplatz* escaped through their yard fences into the backstreets and then hid in cellars and attics or in the little tradesmen's shuls and study houses. They waited, petrified with fear that the fire would reach them where they hid or that the feverish mob, once it finished its work in the *Ringplatz*, would then proceed onward to the backstreets . . .

The wailing, the shrieks and shouting, were impossible to describe. These Jews looked just how their coreligionists of Jerusalem must have when their Holy Temple was burned to the ground and the Romans slaughtered Jewish children openly in the streets.

Suddenly a wild howling was heard, coming now from the Christian quarter. The winds had driven the sparks of the conflagration there, too, and some of the houses began to burn.

The pillagers noticed it and immediately began making their way back. All of them returned to save their hovels and meager possessions. Little by little the *Ringplatz* emptied out, as the firefighters also returned to the Christian quarter to do what they could to save it. The Jewish homes of the *Ringplatz* were left to burn undisturbed. Some of the roofs had already fallen in, and in other homes only the chimneys were left standing, sticking out like gravestones. The state of the place was enough to make one shudder.

Meanwhile the Jews hiding in the backstreets were completely unaware that the rabble had vacated the town square. They remained shut away in the cellars and the attics, in the tradesmen's shuls and study houses, afraid even to move a finger.

At about midnight it finally began to rain, and hard. The

downpour gradually extinguished the fire that had raged over the houses, but their interiors continued to burn. Dozens of houses continued to burn in the Christian quarter too, so their inhabitants were kept busy, and they did not return to their "work" in the Jewish streets.

At about two o'clock on Friday morning, the military detachment arrived to find the shtetl looking like an embattled and ruined fortress. These soldiers no longer had any property left to secure and no persons to defend. Meanwhile the rain continued to come down like whole bathtubs were being emptied out. The district governor billeted the soldiers for the night in the town school and police station, where they waited in readiness for the coming day . . .

CHAPTER TWO
A Blood Libel

THE FIRE BURNED through the night. Around morning the rain subsided, and the dawning day illuminated a shocking and horrible picture.

The Jews began to rouse themselves from their hiding places. Seeing soldiers marching in the streets, they gained resolve and went to inspect the ruins of their homes.

Almost the entire *Ringplatz* was in ashes. In the Jewish homes, all of the windows had been smashed, the doors torn off their hinges. All of the residences and shops had been ransacked. For the Jews of Dorokhov, the radiant eve of *Shabes-hagodl* had become instead a dark *Tishebov*, the ancient day of mourning.

The most dreadful aspect was knowing nothing about why this calamity had befallen them.

Up until then they had lived peacefully and contentedly alongside their Christian neighbors. The district governor was an upstanding servant of the state and had never bothered them.

The mayor, to be sure, was a Jew-hater, and the priest would, of course, incite against the despised *Żydy* from time to time—but both of them still loved Jewish money, and it could be counted on that their threatening hand would be stopped whenever a handsome present was stuffed into it.

But now, out of thin air, this fearful attack, this shocking pogrom—why, what for?

In the largest of the shuls, the chairs of the official Jewish community gathered—along with the rabbi and the most prominent heads of households—to discuss what was to be done. First they decided to send a deputation to the district governor. The delegates would express the Jews' appreciation for the governor calling in the military and hopefully find out what complaint the town's Christians suddenly had against them. The pogrom could not have happened without some instigating factor. But before they appointed the men to serve in this deputation, two gendarmes entered.

They asked the assembled men, "Is the rabbi here, and the kosher slaughterer, and the community president?"

"Yes," the Jews answered, with some fear in their voices. "Why do you ask?"

"We have received orders," said one of the gendarmes, "to arrest them and take them away."

"But why?" the Jews asked, shaking. "What crime have they committed? Why this new trouble, on top of everything else?"

"We cannot tell you that," the gendarme answered. "We were told what to do, and now we must do it."

He and his fellow seized the rabbi, the kosher slaughterer, and the community president, cuffed them, and dragged them away. The other Jews were left standing there, looking for all the world as if they themselves had just been murdered.

Only after a long while were they able to speak again, and a few of the prominent heads of households declared themselves ready to march to the district governor immediately and question him as to what was going on.

"The governor is a kind man. He stuck up for us yesterday, telegraphing for the military so that they'd come to offer protection. We can count on him to give us a clear notion about why the Gentiles have turned against us."

And so these Jews set off for the governor's residence. On the streets and on the *Ringplatz* some soldiers were strolling about. But aside from them, there was not a living soul to be seen. And as soon as the Jewish delegates entered the Christian quarter, a sudden dread took over them . . .

Ominous figures appeared in that neighborhood's windows, with clenched fists and hateful expressions. On the streets, these citizens had clearly been afraid of the soldiers. Not so once they were behind their own windows and bolted doors. From there the men could scream out shocking threats to the Jews, which the women complemented with the most vulgar curses.

With hearts pounding, the Jews arrived at the home of the district governor. In front of it a large crowd of people had gathered, all of them shouting, swearing, and arguing. They noticed the Jews and leapt upon them like so many hungry wolves who have encountered a man coming into their neck of the woods.

It was only with great effort that the soldiers who had also assembled there managed to protect the Jews and conduct them through a back gate into the governor's courtyard. From there they entered the kitchen and proceeded into the living quarters. But a maid had seen them and ran out to the crowd with a terrible scream: "Help! Save me! The *Żydy* want to slaughter me too for their Passover!"

The Jews, meanwhile, stood in the governor's front room, waiting for someone to come out to announce them. But no one appeared. And from the other room, they could hear a number of distinct voices. "I refuse to keep quiet about this!" a woman's voice raged. "They have barbarously murdered my precious child, my only child, and spilled her blood so they can bake their matzos with it. I will not keep quiet. I will tear apart heaven and earth before I do! All these kikes ought to be exterminated for their crimes."

"Calm yourself, *pani* Kulczycka!" the district governor could be heard telling her. "I've already given you my word that I will do everything in my power to find your child, and if something terrible truly has happened, the guilty parties will of course be punished accordingly.

"If you want my investigation to be successful, please do not disturb the process. Your shouting and arguing will only make it harder for me to carry out my search."

"What kind of *investigation*, what kind of *search*?" the woman's voice erupted again. "What is it you're searching for? I have witnesses who can testify that the kikes slaughtered my baby girl. Let them burn, these murderers, these . . . subhumans!"

"And what kind of eyewitness testimony do you have?" the governor asked. "I have accommodated you and have had the Jews' rabbi and kosher slaughterer and president arrested. You can see that I've done everything you've asked for. So leave me alone now, and do not disrupt the proceedings of the law!"

"What kind of testimony do I have?" the woman's voice continued to blare. "The police guard saw everything with his own two eyes, and he'll tell it all to you!"

"That's right, Your Honor!" the guardsman piped up. "The day before yesterday, around midnight, when I was walking to my post in the Jewish quarter, I saw a wagon pulling up in front of the synagogue. A few Jews lifted out some kinda big sack. And these awful sounds were coming from it. Sounded like a kid screaming.

"They carried the sack into the synagogue. I followed them. I stopped behind a closed door and peeped through the keyhole. Saw them pulling a three- or four-year-old girl outta the sack. The little lamb was screaming so hard it could stop your heart, and flailing its little arms and legs. But they held it down and hauled it over to a big table. Then one of them took out this huge knife . . .

"After that I didn't see nothing else, because some Jews came out and I had to get away. But in that group of Jews who brought in the child I could make out the rabbi, the kosher slaughterer, and the president of their community."

"Why did you not call out and try to save the child?" the district governor asked him. "And why would you not tell us this immediately and are only coming out today with this wild story?"

"I was scared something awful," the guardsman answered, "and was afraid of hollering. And afterward, once I'd run away, I thought to myself, 'Maybe it was only a Jewish kid anyway.' And if it was, why should I care what they were doing to it!

"It was only yesterday evening when I heard that *pani* Kulczycka's daughter had disappeared, and the priest said it must have been the Jews what done it, because they need it for their Passover, Christian children's blood. Right away I remembered what I saw and went running to Mrs. Kulczycka to tell her that I knew what happened to her baby."

"Answer me this: Is all that you've told us true?" the governor questioned him.

"I swear to God and all the saints! Every word of it," the guardsman answered, crossing himself.

"So you see, Your Honor?" the woman's voice again broke forth. "You know now, sir, what these kikes did. I cannot keep quiet about it! I will have my child back, or all the kikes will be killed!"

"Please calm yourself, *pani* Kulczycka!" the governor begged. "I will once again give you my word that I will do everything I can to punish the criminals. But now I must ask you to leave me be so I can deliver the proper orders."

But the woman carried on shouting, and it was only with great effort on the governor's part that he was able to prevail upon her to leave the premises.

Meanwhile the Jewish deputation was standing just outside, completely stupefied. Now the men knew what all this was about: the old dreaded blood libel, which had already claimed so many Jewish victims, had returned to oppress them again. They knew what was coming.

They had no need now to ask any questions of the district governor, but they did need to ask for his protection. After he finally called them in, though, their fear stopped them from uttering a single word. They just lifted up their hands in a gesture of supplication.

"I know that the whole story's a lie," the governor said. "I will assign my gendarmes to investigate the whereabouts of the child. When they find it, the truth will out.

"For the moment I am unable to do anything for you. But the military is here to offer its protection. Return home and be careful to avoid meeting any of your Gentile neighbors."

With broken spirits, the representatives of the Jewish community exited through the back door of the governor's home. A few soldiers accompanied them until they reached the Jewish quarter.

As they passed through the Christian streets, throngs of their neighbors ranted and raved, threatened and agitated, and only restrained themselves from wholly renewing yesterday's pogrom because the Jews' military escort struck fear in their hearts.

By the time the Jewish delegates at last returned to their own neighborhoods, their faces were drawn and their hearts sunken. Their brothers and sisters were left nearly paralyzed by the news: that the ancient blood libel was now sweeping anew over their own shtetl, the ancient lie that the Jews make use of Christian blood to bake matzos for the Passover holiday.

They were sure, of course, that the entire story was manufactured out of whole cloth, that the child of Mrs. Kulczycka, the priest's sister, was probably still living and most likely had been hidden somewhere in order to incite the murderous rabble against the Jews. They also figured that the whole story originated with the priest, who would have convinced his sister to take it up and then worked up his flock into a fever over it, setting the parishioners upon their Jewish neighbors.

Their only possible salvation was this: to find out where the child of that fine lady Kulczycka was hidden. But when and how could they ever do that?

The district governor had already set in motion his own investigation, but cowing to Christian pressure, he had ordered the gendarmes to begin their search in the Jewish quarter. Of course, they would find nothing there, and in the meantime no one was searching in the Christian neighborhood, the only place actually worth being searched.

The whole of the Jewish community was in despair. And none of them knew how the matter could be helped.

CHAPTER THREE
Spitzkopf Is Summoned

News of the pogrom in Dorokhov spread quickly through the region. And the looming peril of further pogroms in the surrounding shtetlach spread with it. Those towns, too, were not lacking in antisemites who would eagerly use the proud example of Dorokhov to incite their Christian populations against the Jews and get some trouble of their own started.

In one of these shtetlach lived a well-educated Jewish merchant, the type who always reads the newspaper. Having learned of these terrifying events, he thought instantly of the famous Viennese detective MAX SPITZKOPF. The man knew that in such knotty situations as this, only Spitzkopf could help. Only he would be able to figure out what had happened to the Christian child and thereby bring disgrace upon this renewed persecution against the Jews.

The merchant did not wait to ponder the matter long and dashed off a telegram to Spitzkopf, in which he informed him briefly of the situation and begged that he come at once.

But the detective had already read about the shocking pogrom in the papers. That such misery could befall so many innocent people upset him deeply, and though he had certain important cases to complete in Vienna, he transferred them over to one of his subordinates and set off for Dorokhov himself, taking with him only the most dynamic of all his assistants, FUCHS.

It was Saturday night around eight o'clock, and at the home of Dorokhov's priest a secret meeting was underway.

The priest chaired it, assisted by his sister, Mrs. Kulczycka, the widow of Dorokhov's district secretary. She sat weeping, her face covered with a black veil.

"Dear Christian citizens!" the priest said. "I have invited you here so that we may come to a resolution on what we must do. You are all aware of the terrible crime that took place in our locality. These accursed, fanatical Jews, who live among us and eat of our bread, this year selected our community as the place where they would carry out their most barbaric custom. They cruelly slaughtered a tender Christian child, the precious daughter of my own sister. We must not let this pass without taking swift action.

"The district governor acceded to our demands and had the kikes' community leaders arrested. Since yesterday their rabbi, livestock slaughterer, and community president have been pent up in the police station's jail and tomorrow will be handed over to the county judiciary.

"But do you think we ought to be convinced that they will receive their deserved punishments?

"To think so would be an error. Jews all over the world will pipe up in their defense. Millions and millions will be raised on their behalf to stuff the judge's pockets, and their lawyers will work their most deceitful wiles in order to free the defendants.

"It has always been thus. Any time our fellow Christians have caught Jew criminals, their cousins have always managed to jump them out of the brig through bribes and lies, tricks and tall tales.

"But we cannot let it happen again. Not only because on this occasion my own family has been affected. Not only because this time my sister's child was the chosen victim of the Jews' savagery and inhumanity. But rather because my Christian heart and my Christian faith command me to not rest until the guilty are punished to the full extent of what they deserve.

"The eyes of all Christendom are trained on us at this moment. We must show our fellows that when such a thing takes place in one of our communities, no amount of Jewish gold can help, nor any number of bribes or lawyers or filthy tricks.

"The blood of that innocent and pure Christian child cries out to us: 'Avenge me upon the Jews!' Let us heed her call!"

The priest spoke with fire in his eyes. He pounded his fists on the table with such force that the windows shook in their frames.

"Christians! Brothers!" Mrs. Kulczycka rang out, with a sob in her voice. "Avenge the blood of my blameless child, the blood of my little lamb. Do not rest! Do not be silent! Not one Jew in Dorokhov should be suffered to live!

"And do not believe the governor! He has been bribed by the Jews. He let those few kikes be arrested to stop us doing anything to them ourselves. He'll free them later, you can be sure of that. So we must execute our own justice! We cannot allow the Jews to free themselves through their swindling.

"Tomorrow they will be led out from here to the county seat. They'll be protected from us there in the city. Their own kind will take up on their behalf, and we'll be left to sit and watch in silence. But we must not let that happen. We must deal out justice here before they're brought away!"

"Quite right!" affirmed her brother, the holy man. "Even tonight we must take our revenge on them. I am of the opinion that when total darkness falls, we should infiltrate the police station, drag out those kikes, and do unto them as they did unto an innocent Christian child. Their blood must spill, as they spilt Christian blood."

"I agree!" said the teacher, Mr. Krispin. "I have read extensively about these kinds of stories, and I know that the Jews have in every case managed to free themselves as soon as they were allowed to unravel their wild speculations in court.

"But if we deal out their sentences ourselves, all Christendom will thank us. Let's make sure that no one disturbs us while we're working, though. We've been keeping quiet these past two days, and the governor has no inkling that we're bent on starting something up against the Jews again. Around midnight, let us each make our way to the police station separately and meet up there. I'm acquainted with the warden. I'll pay him a visit earlier. Get him good and drunk. The man loves a tipple.

"Then, when we're all met, we'll bust open the doors and haul out the kikes. Each one of them will have to get stuffed in a big sack and carried away. This all has to happen very quickly, before the police or the military hears anything. Meanwhile, some of us should tear through the Jewish quarter like bats out of hell so that the military will head there to defend it.

"While they're distracted, we'll bring the Jews over to my cellar. And there . . . we can do with them whatever we like."

"Good. Is the plan clear to all of you?" the priest asked.

"Oh, yes!" cried all of the assembled, as with one voice. "We'll get our revenge on the Jews! Let their children's children be warned never to provoke us again."

"Thereby will you, my own dear children, fulfill a most sacred duty," said the priest, as his eyes turned to the ceiling. "I give you all my blessing."

"And I, a poor widow and a most unhappy mother," his sister

cut in, "thank you for carrying out your Christian duty in avenging the blood of my child!"

"Down with the kikes!" the assembled cheered. "Not a one of 'em will survive! Let's finally get rid of these bloodsuckers!"

"Good, I thereby close this meeting," the priest said. "Let each of you return quietly home. Keep our plan a secret. And at midnight, let us carry out our work."

The assembled went their separate ways. Only the priest and his sister remained.

"We've gotten this far," the priest said, "but we don't know yet how it will end. So let's be careful and wipe away the last traces of our earlier deeds . . ."

"There'll be time for that!" his sister answered. "No one will find the child. I hid it so cleverly that not a hundred Heebs' heads put together could guess where it is."

"I still think we'd be well-advised to clean up after ourselves, so to speak . . ."

"No! There is time yet! First we have to snuff out those *Żydy* who are suspected of slaughtering the child so that they can't deny it in court. After that we can abandon the child somewhere in the Jewish quarter and leave the police to confirm its death."

"Very well, let it be so," the priest answered. "Until now, all has gone precisely according to plan. Let us hope it continues to."

CHAPTER FOUR
Their Plan Is Disrupted

SPITZKOPF AND HIS assistant, Fuchs, meanwhile, had been in Dorokhov for hours. Having learned all the crucial details about the incident that had taken place, they decided en route that they should disguise themselves as peasants and integrate themselves among the shtetl's Christian population. First they would learn whether a new pogrom was being planned, and meanwhile they might also find out what had happened to the disappeared child.

Many workers and peasants from the surrounding villages had also shown up in town the day the detective arrived. Their clergymen had used the recent chaos to instigate their own flocks against the Jews, and a mob of farm laborers had headed to the town to help their brothers or simply to get in on the looting of Jewish homes.

Because of all the new faces, the appearance of two more strangers wandering around was not noticed. After Spitzkopf and Fuchs had gotten a handle on who was who in the town, particularly whose child was missing and who the chief rabble-rousers were in the latest pogrom, they fixed their plan and divided up the necessary work: Spitzkopf would follow the tracks of the missing child, while Fuchs would continue mixing in with the citizens of the town and the village peasants in order to find out what business they were bent on carrying out.

Fuchs soon managed to hear about the gathering being planned at the priest's residence and made sure he was in attendance. There he learned what action was being organized for midnight.

"Your plan will never succeed!" he thought to himself. "I'll be keeping a close eye on you all and will put an end to your dirty work. You won't be touching a hair on the heads of the arrested Jews, not on my watch!"

When the meeting split up, Fuchs was intent on being the last to leave the clergy house. Even after all but the priest and his sister had gone, he still did not leave, instead choosing to stand a while behind the door of the room where the two were speaking to eavesdrop on their conversation.

Though he heard only broken bits of it, and did not perfectly understand even those, he had a fairly solid idea of their subject. It certainly wasn't kosher—*that* he was sure of.

"It seems to me," he thought, "that the priest and his sister know quite well where the child is and what happened to her. It would also seem they have a certain interest in the child disappearing.

"Now I must go posthaste to tell my master everything I've seen and heard here. It may prove very useful to him."

Fuchs had already arranged to meet with him around ten o'clock that night in an alehouse not far from the church. So there he went, ordered a beer, and sat waiting for the detective's arrival.

But ten o'clock passed, then eleven, and there was still no sign of him. Meanwhile the tavern was emptying out. Only a few of the townsmen were lingering, and they too were preparing to leave. Fuchs could not remain much longer—even just sitting about that long could attract undue attention. He had no choice but to pay his tab and leave.

Outside a cold wind was blowing, and with it a rain so frigid and sharp it pricked one's cheeks. Fuchs wrapped himself in his fur-lined coat, pulled his fur cap down over his forehead, and placed himself under the roof of a house that stood beside the police station.

He stood there for nearly an hour, his hands in his pockets, but with his ears perked to hear the slightest rustling nearby. The bell in the clock tower, which rose up from the church, struck twelve. Fuchs pulled out a small package from his pocket and held it ready in his hand.

A few shadowy figures began to appear. They moved silently and positioned themselves around the police station.

In the room where the police officers had their desks, it was dark and quiet. Because of the poor weather, even the police guard who would normally be found posted outside the station had sought refuge within and fallen asleep there.

No soldiers were to be found either. After two uneventful days, the district governor had been misled into thinking that things had truly quieted down and that most of the soldiers who had been patrolling the streets through the night were no longer needed.

Meanwhile the crowd around the police station was growing. About twenty people now stood there. Others continued onward, making their way toward the Jewish quarter.

The town clock read twelve thirty. A number of small groups had formed around the police station. Not a word was exchanged between them; they only gestured with their hands toward the station's jail, waiting for a light to appear there. That would be a sign that the warden was well in his cups and they could get to work.

Fuchs flung the small package he was holding onto a mound of stones that lay in the middle of the street. A stunning crack like cannon fire followed. Sparks jumped through the air. The stones flew in every direction. The windows of the police station and of the nearby houses were instantly shattered. It seemed as if a violent earthquake were taking place.

The police officers and the inhabitants of the nearby homes woke with a start and stumbled half-dressed into the streets. Soldiers appeared, too. The entire shtetl stirred.

But the explosion had harmed no one. The little package of dynamite that Fuchs had thrown was of a weak variety—his only object was to disrupt the priest's plan. And he had achieved it.

The mob broke up as though a fire had erupted. No one knew whence the explosion had come. The peasants crossed themselves. The priest ordered the bells of the church to be rung. They were all convinced some Jewish magic had been enacted or that it was the work of demonic spirits.

Seeing that the deed was done, and done well, Fuchs retreated to a nearby lane and watched the scene unfold with much contentment. The heroic rabble, which had moments before been desperate to murder three innocent people, were now fleeing, they thought, to save their own lives, bewildered and afraid.

"That'll put a kink in your plan, you savage beasts!" he called out to them in muted tones. "May the same be true for your renewal of the old blood libel myth and the rest of your wicked endeavors!"

As he stood there and spoke to himself, he suddenly felt a pair of hands placed heavily on his shoulders. He turned around with great trepidation, which was shortly eased by the sight of his master.

"Bravo, Fuchs!" Spitzkopf murmured to him. "You've acted with the utmost skill. I see that I can trust you thoroughly in this case. Come with me to my lodgings, and we'll go over what we must do next. For I believe that I too am on the right track."

They both withdrew and vanished into the darkness of the rain-soaked night.

CHAPTER FIVE
The Detective's First Moves

SPITZKOPF HAD begun his time in the shtetl by making his rounds dressed as a peasant until he had learned all the particulars of the dreadful case and had become confident in his knowledge of the surroundings.

Afterward he returned to his lodgings to change his clothes. His new getup was that of an elegant young professional—he held a leather case in one hand, filled with papers, and went out thus to visit with the Christian residents of the shtetl.

Every time he knocked on a door, he introduced himself as the agent of a fire insurance company and convinced the people within to insure their homes and furnishings. Naturally, the conflagration that had broken out days before was a great help to his cause.

"So you can plainly see," he said to the town dwellers, "what obvious worth an insurance policy has! Every one of you, I do not doubt, has experienced great damages, and even those few whose homes did not catch fire surely spent the whole night petrified with fear that they would.

"And remember, you had to give up your laudable work against the Jews when the fire spread into the Christian streets . . .

"Now, if you were to have been insured, the fire risk would have been as child's play. Whosever house burnt would have ended up receiving a pretty penny with which to build a lovely new one. Whosever furniture was consumed in the flames would have received money with which to buy replacements, brand new!"

Spitzkopf carried on this way and was able to exchange a few words with every Christian householder and every peasant in town, meanwhile getting a decent once-over of every home and stick of furniture, keeping an eye open at all times for anything that might appear suspicious.

The Christians, meanwhile, were delighted to entertain the elegant and friendly agent and listen to his pitch. By getting in their good graces, Spitzkopf was furthermore able to eke out a good many details concerning the events of the last few days and to hear what these people thought of it all.

Most of them took as gospel everything the priest had told them. A few of them did not even make a secret of the fact that as soon as the military eventually evacuated from the town, the citizens were planning on making a fresh start of the anti-Jewish pogroms. And for that reason they were glad to get the chance to insure their homes so that they would have no reason to fear the fire jumping over into their side of town when the rioting recommenced.

Only from a precious few of the Christian citizens—those who made a living off of their business dealings with the Jews—did Spitzkopf hear bitter criticisms of the priest's incitements.

"Your holy man in black is trying to dust off some old wives' tales," said a Christian baker. "The Jews have been my loyal customers for over twenty years, seen them nearly every day on the street. Been to a lot of their homes, too. Never saw a bit of wrongdoing from any of 'em.

"I don't buy one word of this story. But what am I suppose ta do? I gotta keep silent. If I try to argue, you can bet the priest will immediately say I'm the Jews' slave cause I live off o' their commerce."

Spitzkopf could see that he was dealing with a clever and open-hearted fellow—the sort you could get to talk. So he did just that and asked him a question. "But what are you saying? The child of the priest's sister has disappeared, and the police guard swore that he saw with his own two eyes what the Jews did with it in their synagogue. Surely it must be true."

The baker broke out in belly-bobbing laughter. "I'mma let you in on a secret, baby boy. Your Mrs. Kulczycka ain't the priest's sister. She's some relative, a cousin or who knows what. She also doesn't have any kids. The kid that disappeared wasn't hers; it was her brother's. He died three years ago, and Kulczycka took in his baby."

The story hit Spitzkopf like a ton of bricks.

"Well, this is all quite new to me," he thought to himself. "If it's true, the whole story looks a little different. This baker talks too much for his own good. I must get one other item out of him."

"Seems to me you're an utter blasphemer," Spitzkopf said to the man. "You don't believe in the priest and his sister. Here you are telling tales out of school. But what would you say to the guard who saw it all? He's a common yokel, seems the kind of fellow you can see right through."

"Sure, the guard is a yokel," the baker answered, "and a big lush too. For the money to buy a shot of whiskey he'd sell you his ma and pa. Heck, he'd make a solemn oath against the whole church and everyone in it, too, for a nice dram.

"The governor knows that and doesn't believe a thing the fella says. But he doesn't want to start any trouble between himself and the community, and he's trying to play nice so the whole thing quiets down."

Spitzkopf bade the baker farewell and departed. "Seems to me I've hit upon the right path," he reasoned. "An important discovery is within my sights."

He continued paying visits to the Christian citizens until late in the night, hoping he would uncover something else of significance. But everywhere he went, he heard the same hoary old stories. Around midnight Spitzkopf retired to his lodgings.

He entered the inn at the very moment that Fuchs produced his explosion. And then immediately set off to fetch him back.

CHAPTER SIX

Fuchs Is Arrested!

SPITZKOPF'S ROOM was in Dorokhov's tiny guesthouse, the only one in town. The innkeeper was a Jew, and it took a lot of trouble on the detective's part to convince the man to give him a room.

The Jews of Dorokhov were, after all, in a state of terrible fear, afraid even of their own shadows. And since Spitzkopf was dressed as a Christian peasant, he made the Jewish hosteler tremble.

Only after extended supplications and the most solemn assurances that he had not come to loot the inn but rather had purposes to attend to in town did the man let him into a small room.

This was the room in which Spitzkopf and his assistant Fuchs were now sitting. Fuchs first recounted to his master all that he had seen and heard in the home of the priest.

Spitzkopf sat and listened in a posture of contemplation, giving every word his closest attention. When Fuchs finished, the detective said: "Well, it's certainly a pretty kettle of fish. I myself have recently discovered this: that first of all, the disappeared child is not the daughter of Mrs. Kulczycka but rather her niece, her brother's daughter. The brother died three years ago and entrusted the child to her because his own wife had died but a few months earlier.

"Secondly, Kulczycka is not the priest's sister but rather some cousin or another. She only poses as his sister so that the curious companionship between the two of them will not attract attention."

"*Nu*," Fuchs interrupted him, "are you thinking that maybe the two of them have—"

"I am thinking many things," Spitzkopf stopped him, "and have not yet come to any definite conclusion.

"But this much I do know: that we must, most importantly, find out in what condition the child is, whether she is dead or still living. But our search is hindered considerably by the agitation of the locals.

"I don't wish to present myself to the district governor and tell him everything we know. Sure, the fellow seems upstanding enough for a government official. But we won't be able to hammer a bit of our suspicions about the priest or his supposed sister into his head. He wouldn't let us help in the investigation anyway.

"We must, therefore, act alone. I would have wished to search the residences of the priest and his 'sister' today. But I had to seize upon the opportunity to take some other important steps.

"Tomorrow is Sunday. Priest and sister will surely be at church in the morning. I'll pay their houses a visit then and see if I can't find some tracks.

"In the meantime there's nothing we can do. Let's rest and return to our work early tomorrow morning."

And so they both lay themselves down in bed. Spitzkopf was tired to the bone, and it took him mere seconds to fall asleep. But Fuchs was too excited by the events of the past hour and could not do the same. He decided he would instead go out and see what was going on in the Christian quarter, whether the townsmen there remained shaken over the unanticipated explosion.

He slowly slid from the room, not wishing to wake his master. He moved soundlessly through the Jewish streets so that no one would notice him. After a few moments he encountered marching soldiers on patrol, but he remained near to the houses lining the street, hoping the men would not spot him in the shadows.

Finally he arrived at the grounds of the church and the clergy house. An anterior room of the priest's home was illuminated. Very gingerly, Fuchs opened the gate and went to listen at the front door.

Through the keyhole he discerned two figures: the church sexton and the police guard who had served as a witness before the governor. They were whispering, but Fuchs was able to make out nearly every word.

"You're a simpleton," said the sexton, "to be afraid of such things! Do you really believe that God is looking out for these damned Jews, who crucified our Savior?"

"But you were there too, by the police station," the guardsman answered him. "You saw yourself how that pile of rocks suddenly started spitting out these flaming sparks. There was thunder and lightning in them, I tell ya. You're telling me that's a perfectly natural thing to happen?"

"No, that's not what I'm telling you!" the sexton interrupted him. "I can't explain it myself. Of course the Jews are actual demons, and their best friend is the devil. I only think you need not be any more afraid than the rest of us are."

"Oh, do I ever gotta be afraid! I'm the only bloody witness in this whole thing. It was because of my testimony that those kikes were arrested, and it's gonna be my testimony that sentences 'em to hang! So I got just cause to be more afraid than any of yehs!"

"No! If Kulczycka and our priest aren't afraid, you needn't be either. You don't know the whole truth. You don't know where the little one is . . ."

"She's not alive, is she?" the guard asked, shocked.

"That I don't know," the sexton responded. "I only know that she's in Kulczycka's house. And even considering that, they don't fear what might happen. But you're positively shaking in your boots."

"Ah, what do I know!" the guard sputtered out finally. "I'm so riled up I can barely tell what's the matter with me.

"After that display in the street, which was not like anything I've seen before on God's good earth, I wanted to run to the governor and tell him the truth. I don't want to sell my soul over for eternity just for a coupla gold coins. Those kikes never did me any wrong anyway. I make a living off of looking after them . . .

"Who knows? Maybe I'll feel better if I go see the priest tomorrow morning. Could be he can put my mind at ease."

"Now you're talking," the sexton agreed. "Don't lose heart. All will come right; you'll see."

Fuchs noticed the guard rising and preparing to go, so he withdrew quickly from the gate and started walking back to his lodgings. He walked quickly, eager to tell his master the news. He was so eager that he was not as careful as usual and neglected to open the gate of the guesthouse very quietly.

The hosteler was not asleep, and hearing the opening of the gate he leaped out of the house and spotted Fuchs in his peasant's costume. The man began to raise a clamor, and Fuchs tried to make a run for it. But within seconds several soldiers arrived on the scene and declared him under arrest.

Fuchs thought better of identifying himself to the soldiers, not wishing to let it be known that Spitzkopf was on the premises. And so, as they dragged him to the jail, he kept perfectly quiet.

CHAPTER SEVEN

The Will

JUST AS SOON as Fuchs was arrested, the hosteler rapped at Spitzkopf's door and told him his presence at the guesthouse was no longer welcome.

"I made an exception for you," he said, "because you gave me the impression of being an upstanding fellow. But when I see some peasant heading to your room in the middle of the night, I can only assume that you are one of that crowd—those folks who want to start up the pogrom against us Jews again. You are clearly in cahoots with them, and I no longer want you staying here with me.

"I had your buddy arrested. I could have the same done to you, but I wouldn't want to give you the pleasure of saying that the Jews are two-timers and that I deliberately accepted you as a guest so that I could do you dirty. So I'm asking you nicely, with the most honest intentions: clear out at once!"

Spitzkopf instantly understood what had happened: that his assistant had gone out while he was sleeping and that on his return, the hosteler had become suspicious of his activity and had him arrested. Without delay he paid for the night's stay but said to the hosteler, "I am leaving you, as you demand—even though I have no idea as to what you're going on about. I know no one in this town. I also don't know who might have wanted to come in to my room tonight, or even whether or not this person was planning to do so.

"But I'll leave because I have already taken care of my business in town and was going to depart today anyway."

With those words, he quit the guesthouse. "There's that classic Fuchsian luck again," he thought. "Always getting himself into some scrape. But it won't trouble him a jot. My man's worked a fine little trick tonight. The Christians in town were left terrified by his little explosion and will soon be singing an entirely different tune. I must make use of their vulnerability and see if I can glean some worthy bit of intelligence."

Outside, the light of a new day was already settling in. Spitzkopf made his way out of the Jewish quarter and infiltrated the Christian streets. Coming to the clergy house, he spotted the priest leaving.

The man was clearly disturbed by the night's events. The sudden explosion had shaken him. He could not understand what had happened and had been unable to get a wink of sleep. At the first sign of dawn he had left for his church.

"It's all working out beautifully," Spitzkopf thought to himself. "I can easily pay a little visit to his house now."

The coast was clear—no one else was on the streets at this hour. Spitzkopf waited only a couple minutes after the priest's departure before he climbed over the gate and entered the yard. He managed to open a back door with a skeleton key and made his way inside.

The windows were still shuttered. With his trusty electric torch in hand, he crept through each room, closely observing each minute detail.

In the priest's office, he found a massive writing desk. Using a thin lockpick, he opened all of its drawers and inspected the papers lying within them. There were various letters, documents, and the like, none of them of much interest to the detective.

But then he happened upon a rather small, hidden compartment in the desk. Opening it, he found within a little packet of papers on which the following appeared, in large letters: THE LAST WILL AND TESTAMENT OF ADAM GRABOWSKI.

"Ah, now here seems a worthy discovery!" Spitzkopf exclaimed, stowing the packet away under his arm. "This just might have the answer inside."

He quickly restored all of the drawers to their closed and locked positions, left the house, and locked the door back up so that no one would notice someone had been within and potentially touched anything.

Meanwhile the morning had advanced outside. It was turning out to be a rather dreary day, overcast with dark clouds, with a thick fog choking the streets. Spitzkopf walked carefully through the priest's grounds until he happened upon an expansive garden. He hopped the fence and carried on a little distance until he was deep within the garden—until he was certain that no one could see him.

Then he took the packet in both hands, opened it, and began to read.

The more he read, the more excited he became. When he finished, his hands were trembling. "Aha, so that's the way the cookie crumbles!" he cried out. "In these pages is revealed the full treachery of Mrs. Kulczycka.

"I can barely believe that a person's evil could go so far. I've never seen anything before quite so wicked as this. I must have another look through the will in case my eyes deceive me."

He removed the papers again and examined each page, from every angle.

"The date is correct," he remarked to himself. "The baker told me that Mrs. Kulczycka's brother died three years ago. The will has also been legitimately composed and signed by a notary. There can be no doubt that it's the genuine article. Now I can't help but look it over again."

And so he read:

> I, Adam Grabowski, being ill for a number of years, and knowing that my days are numbered, and not wishing to suffer much longer, hereby give over the entirety of my estate, consisting of several properties, houses, and gardens, as well as 50,000 in Austro-Hungarian kronen, cash, which is held in the savings bank of Lemberg, to my only child Marynia, currently one year of age.
>
> My beloved daughter should be entrusted to my sister Henryka, the widowed Mrs. Kulczycka, that she may raise and educate the child.
>
> Until the child reaches the age of 24, my sister should be allowed to enjoy the interest accrued on the money held in the bank, as well as all income that is raised from the rental of my properties, houses, and gardens.
>
> In the event that my child should die before that time, my sister will receive the entirety of this inheritance.
>
> She must, however, prove to the courts that she

> reared the child faithfully, as though the child were her own daughter, and that she bore no guilt in the child's early departure from this world. If, however, she cannot prove this, or if it appears that she mistreated the child, she loses her right to my estate, which should instead be portioned out to charitable societies in the city of my birth, according to the best judgment of that city's mayor.

Spitzkopf hid the will away in his pocket and thought to himself, "It's clear to me now, the whole sordid story. Kulczycka's late brother had no great trust in his sister. He doubtless knew her well and suspected that she would be set upon receiving the entirety of the inheritance. In order to do so she would ill-use the child so that the girl would not live to receive it herself. It was for that reason that he saw fit to include that sharp stipulation in the will.

"His worst nightmare seems to have come true. Kulczycka clearly ill-used the child. She was perhaps sick, and Kulczycka did not see fit to call a doctor. And so the girl died.

"But she would have feared that the court wouldn't find her worthy of receiving the inheritance on that account, so she hit upon another bright idea: to let the word get out that the child had vanished. And since it was just before Passover, clearly it was the case that the Jews must have slaughtered her.

"The priest helped her spread the slander. They got the police guard good and drunk and had him parrot back the testimony they provided him.

"Now it would be the general consensus that others had dealt the child a violent death. And Kulczycka would get her hands on the inheritance. That must be the plan.

"And through it, hundreds of innocent Jews will suffer in vain. An entire people will be villainized, its name dragged through the mud. Guiltless men and women will be arrested and by false testimony condemned. And that treacherous crew won't be bothered a bit by any of it.

"But their schemes will not come to pass! Not if I can make one final discovery. The child is no longer living, that's clear. But the body must be hidden somewhere. Probably in Kulczycka's very house, or on her grounds.

"I have to search the place. And then, I sincerely hope, the final truth will out."

CHAPTER EIGHT
The Guilty Are Arrested

THE CHRISTIAN POPULATION of Dorokhov rose with the dawn that Sunday. The happenings of the night before had left them in no condition to sleep. The church filled up far earlier than usual, and the priest used the opportunity to spit out a fresh new sermon of incitement against the Jews.

"They are not merely murderers," he bellowed, "but sorcerers too! We must not rest until we wipe them out entirely.

"Do not fear the military! I will lead you with the cross in hand, and we will see if those Christian soldiers would dare fire upon me."

The incitement worked. The mob was radicalized, made bold and wild, and rushed out of the church intent upon storming the Jewish streets. And as promised, the priest marched at their head, bearing an immense crucifix in his hand. At the *Ringplatz*, a row of soldiers stood opposite them. The priest held high his crucifix and said, "Would you stand up for the Christ killers and meanwhile shoot upon the holy cross?"

The soldiers remained standing, now indecisive. They awaited an order from their commander. But he wanted to first consult with the district governor on what the proper course of action ought to be. He did not want to shed any blood, though he also feared a new pogrom breaking out.

The savage mob on one side, the soldiers on the other. Both awaited a sign that might tell them to rush against their opponents. It was a stand-off thick with tension—and full of danger.

Fuchs, meanwhile, had already spent several hours in the police lockup. As soon as he noticed through the tiny window of his cell that a new day had begun, he banged ferociously on the door and called out to the warden. "I have something very important to tell the district governor! Please lead me to him immediately!"

The warden was still reeling somewhat from the liquor that the teacher, Mr. Krispin, had plied him with the night before. At first he refused to hear anything that the prisoner was about. "Wha', to the gubbernor hisself?" he grumbled. "You'be gotsa be platient. Firss why's dontcha tell me what'sit you were looksing for in the Jewzish streets las' night."

Fuchs could see he would not be able to get anything from this fellow through clever persuasion. He did have a loaded revolver on his person and could free himself by force. But he also did not want to start any kind of ruckus. And so he hit upon another idea and stuffed a handsome banknote into the warden's hand.

Spying a bit of cash, the warden became a different person entirely. He called over to a police officer and ordered the man to conduct the arrestee directly to the district governor.

The governor, meanwhile, was still lying in bed but had been well informed of everything that had taken place the night before. Still, it was all a complete riddle to him. He could not wrap his head around a single detail.

And now in comes Fuchs, led directly to his bedside. Fuchs asked that the officer accompanying him remove himself because he had to reveal sensitive and significant new information to the governor. When the two of them were alone, Fuchs finally revealed whose assistant he was.

"The famous detective Max Spitzkopf is here in Dorokhov!" the governor burst out, thoroughly astounded. "It's many times now I've heard of his wondrous deeds. I'm quite sure he'll succeed in cracking this case wide open. But why did the two of you not come directly to me? Surely I could have been of some help in your investigation."

"Our system has always been to undertake everything ourselves," answered Fuchs, "before anyone knows that we're on the scene. We're already on the right track, and it's quite possible that at this very moment, as we're talking here, my master has already found out everything there is to know.

"I wouldn't have come to you now either. But as I've sensed the threat of another pogrom, I couldn't be silent, and so thought it best to tell you all that I know so that you might do all you can now to protect the innocent Jews of this town."

And so Fuchs unraveled to the governor all that he had seen, heard, and done up until that point.

"Bravo!" the governor congratulated him. "I see you're the kind of bang-up fellows who can get the job done. It's no nonsense with you!"

At that moment a messenger sprang into the bedroom and announced that another pogrom was beginning. The governor ran out with a fury, just barely throwing on his coat and hat.

Seeing the fevered mob of townspeople in the streets, standing ready to storm the Jewish quarter, he called out to them at the top of his voice. "Citizens! Do not be misled! The mystery has been solved—I know now what has happened! You will soon see who the truly guilty parties are!"

Upon hearing the steely words of the district governor, the commander of the military detachment strengthened his own resolve. He commanded his troops: "If anyone tries to resist you with force, shoot!"

Now the mob simply stood there, deeply confused. The priest, who stood at its head, let down his hands, which had been holding high the crucifix. He looked about blankly. He could not fathom what to do.

Suddenly Spitzkopf appeared, leading a shackled Mrs. Kulczycka. Beside them walked her maid, carrying the dead body of the disappeared girl.

"Regard the murderess of her own brother's daughter!" Spitzkopf roared. "And here, her 'missing' child! See for yourselves: she was not slaughtered with a knife. She was suffocated! Do not let yourselves be deceived any longer, citizens! The guilty parties are your own priest and the woman Kulczycka!"

The priest stood still as a statue. For the first time he was entirely without speech.

And his crowd of followers slowly drew back. All looked with amazement at the handcuffed Kulczycka, who stood before them with her head bowed, ashamed to show her face.

Spitzkopf approached the priest and cuffed him too. "Here stands your second culprit!" he announced. "Lead them both to the jail."

The district governor gave a nod to the assembled police, and the priest and Kulczycka were brought away. The Christian rabble dispersed, all of them booking it back to their homes, staggered by this latest reversal.

CHAPTER NINE
The Whole Truth

After Spitzkopf had read through the will, he had taken a circuitous route away from the priest's grounds, leaving the garden for the open fields beyond it, then returning to the shtetl. After asking around as to its location, he made his way to the home of Mrs. Kulczycka.

Upon entering, he did not find her within but did find her maid. He presented himself once again as an insurance agent and told her he would wait until her mistress returned, as he was leaving town later that day and still had some business to attend to with her.

The girl let him wait inside, and he figured he might as well strike up a conversation, hoping to question her about Kulczycka and the woman's way of life. The maid was a young, ordinary village girl, frank and perfectly artless—it was easy for him to get her talking.

"I'm not certain I shall be able to close my insurance deal with Mrs. Kulczycka," Spitzkopf said to her. "She is obviously in great distress over her disappeared child and I expect won't have the patience to think about such things."

"Ha, to be sure, distressed," said the maid. "You know, she never especially loved the child. She used to hit her all the time, torment her something awful, so bad it would near give me heartache just to see."

"But now she's moving heaven and earth to find her," Spitzkopf drove her on.

"Yes, but that's only for show, for people she doesn't barely know," the girl remarked. "Behind closed doors she's perfectly at ease. Having a gay old time getting dressed up and decoratin' herself, just as always. You'd barely notice a change in her.

"I'm sure she'll buy your insurance; no need to worry in that respect. Last week's fire gave us all a good fright, and everyone's now keen on securing themselves against damages like that."

"In that case," said Spitzkopf, "perhaps you will permit me to look through all the rooms so that I can make an estimate on the value of your mistress's home and possessions, and when she gets back I won't have to delay her long."

"That'll be fine," said the girl. "Have a look around."

She opened a door and admitted him into the dining room. He made a note of the furnishings and pretended to record it all in his register, meanwhile actually having a good look at every corner of the home and keeping his eyes open for anything suspicious.

The girl walked him from one room to another until they came to a handsomely appointed parlor.

"Hmm, is there not a very sharp smell in this room?" observed Spitzkopf.

"The mistress poured carbolic acid in here yesterday," the girl said. "Couldn't tell you why, but she did say that the room was damp and the acid would help it dry up."

Yes, Spitzkopf could certainly smell that something was off. "Something is in here," he thought to himself. "I'll have to inspect everything very closely." And so, slowly and intently, he examined every piece of furniture from every possible angle.

A piano stood in the corner. Spitzkopf remained beside it for rather longer than the other pieces of furniture. His finely developed sense of smell told him the suspicious odor was coming from here. He knelt beside the bottom panel of the piano and then suddenly sprang up, astounded. "I've found it," he murmured. "Now I have to send the girl away and make absolutely sure that I am not in the wrong."

At that moment the kitchen door could be heard opening. "Someone's coming," said the girl, running out of the room.

Now with none to observe him, Spitzkopf pried away one small board of the piano's bottom panel and realized that, yes, he'd found what he was looking for. He replaced the board and sat at the piano as if he were about to play it.

Meanwhile Mrs. Kulczycka had entered the kitchen. She had been off visiting a friend and was now planning to go for a walk with her. But the maid told her that an insurance agent was waiting for her in the parlor. Kulczycka charged off to the room to see him.

Spitzkopf introduced himself to her and expressed what business he had with her.

"Yes, I would like to insure my furniture with you," she spat out, "but at the moment I have no time, and no patience either.

Perhaps you could come back tomorrow."

"I am truly sorry," Spitzkopf answered, "but I am leaving town today. This won't take long. I've already taken the liberty of describing in my register everything I've seen here; you need only tell me at what price you would like to insure your things, and the matter will be done with."

He sat back down beside the piano, as if preparing to take out the relevant contracts. But he could see just how impatient Kulczycka was. She clearly wanted to get rid of him as soon as possible.

"No, no," she argued. "At present, I simply do not have time. My friend is waiting for me; I am just about to leave to meet her. If you'd like to finish this business, I'm afraid you will have to wait until tomorrow."

"In that case, we are quite finished," said Spitzkopf, making as if to go but meanwhile giving a kick to the bottom panel of the piano. It fell open.

Inside was the corpse of the missing child.

"Here is the child who 'disappeared,' Mrs. Kulczycka," Spitzkopf icily intoned, sitting back down at the piano. "The child about whom you lied to half the world, ruining the lives of innocent people."

Kulczycka was petrified. She had not predicted anything like this happening and could not speak a word. But Spitzkopf did not delay. He slung a pair of handcuffs out of his pocket and snapped them around her wrists. "I am the detective Spitzkopf, from Vienna," he now introduced himself accurately, with a little bow. "I came here to find the missing child, and my efforts have paid off. I have not only found the child. I've found her murderess too.

"Come, sweet lady. Let us now show your incited, inflamed neighbors who it was that actually killed the child in question."

He called in the maid, showed her the body, and said to her, "Take the child and come with us. We'll go into the center of town and demonstrate what our dear Mrs. Kulczycka is capable of."

The maid was dumbfounded and would not dare touch the corpse. But when she saw her mistress bound in irons, she became afraid lest Spitzkopf should suspect her of having been an accomplice to the murder. And she followed his orders.

Kulczycka, meanwhile, had not lost a whit of her consuming shock. Incapable of resistance, she let herself be conducted out of the house by Spitzkopf. She followed him through the streets of the shtetl. And when they reached the mob, Spitzkopf presented her to it as the child killer.

At that moment Kulczycka lost all her strength. After issuing a bitter, savage cry, she fell to the ground unconscious.

The district governor had the priest and the police guardsman arrested. When Kulczycka came to a few minutes later, he ordered that she also be brought to the town jail.

The governor appeared in the jail himself to attend to the case, and the interrogations of the arrestees were carried out in his presence.

They confessed to everything. They knew that their denial would not help them. No, Kulczycka had not liked the child. Yes, she used to beat her constantly.

Last Wednesday, the child was sobbing because the maid had gone out of the house. Kulczycka grew furious with her, and for several minutes held the child's mouth closed. When she finally let go, she realized the girl had suffocated.

In terror, she locked the body away in the parlor and ran off to the priest, seeking his counsel. He hit upon the ingenious idea of hiding the dead child and spreading the news that the Jews had kidnapped her. With the gift of a couple gold coins, they had the guardsman pronouncing himself ready to testify that he himself had witnessed the Jews slaughtering the child.

Kulczycka then returned home and hid the body inside the piano. No one would find it there—she thought.

The blame was successfully flung onto the Jews. Kulczycka hoped that the guardsman's testimony would be enough to convict a few leaders of their community, and she would be able to get her hands on her late brother's entire inheritance. She would give half to the priest if all went according to plan.

All did not go according to plan. Once again, Spitzkopf had worked up one of his masterpieces.

As soon as the interrogations were complete, the confined Jews were freed, and the news of all that had taken place quickly spread through the Jewish quarter. The hosteler begged Spitzkopf's forgiveness for having wrongfully suspected him. And all the Jewish residents of Dorokhov came out to thank the detective personally for his work.

The same day, the district governor had the priest, Kulczycka, and the police guard driven to the county seat and confined in its prison. There, things were brought to a close: Kulczycka received a sentence of ten years hard time; the priest and the police guard, two apiece.

The military presence remained in Dorokhov for two days, until the tempers in town were thoroughly settled. After that the soldiers marched away.

And the Jews celebrated a very joyous Passover—just as God instructed them long ago, when the Israelites were freed from Egypt.

The news of Spitzkopf's little miracle was disseminated throughout the country. As he and his assistant Fuchs rode the train back to Vienna, Jewish delegations awaited them at every station. They brought lavish gifts and expressed their gratitude to the detective for his wondrous deed, for freeing the Jews from the blood libel, for this liberation renewed.

Issue 4: A Mysterious Murder

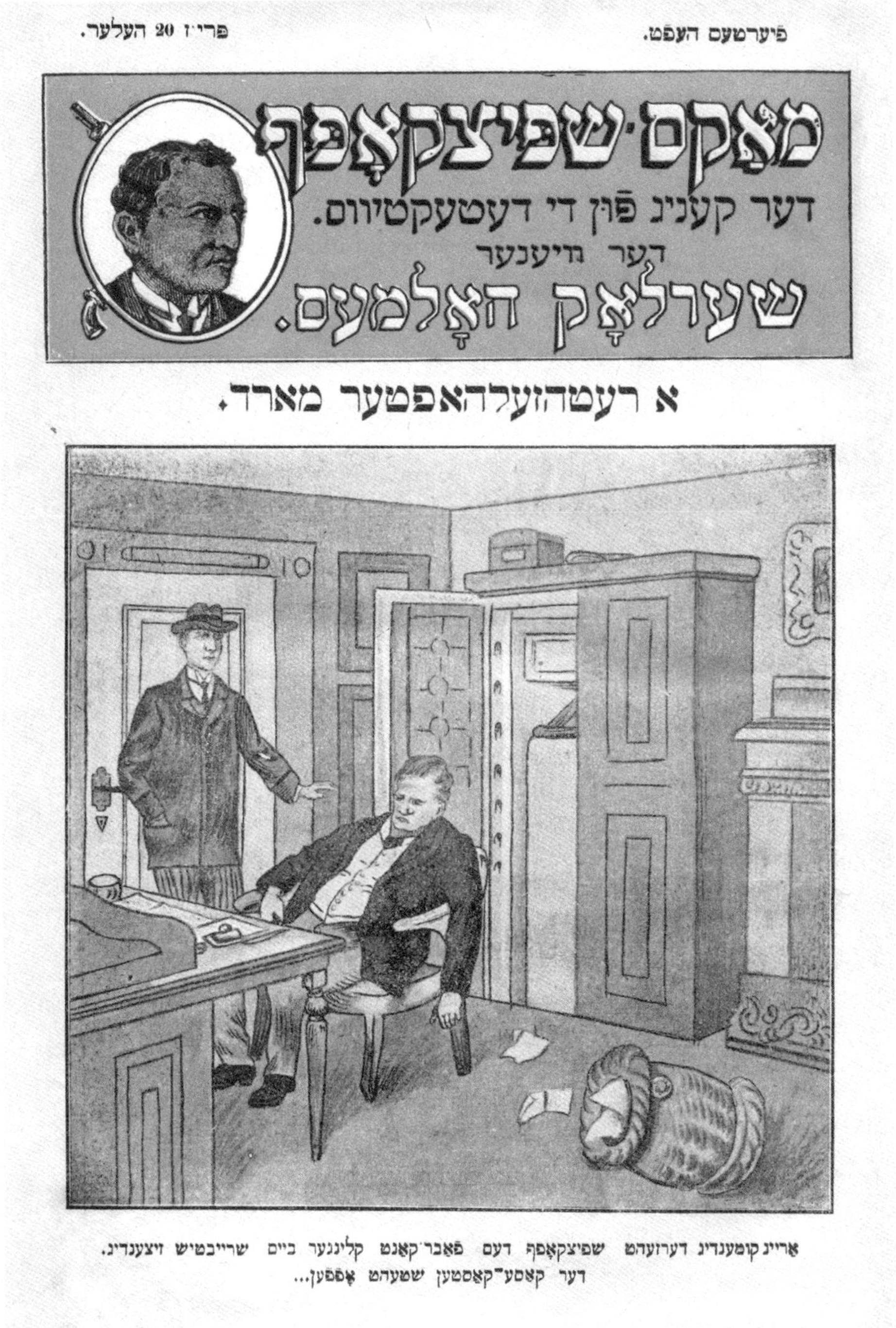

פּיערטעס העפֿט.
פרייז 20 העלער.
מאַקס · שפּיצקאָפּף
דער קעניג פֿון די דעטעקטיווס.
דער אידישער
שערלאָק האָלמעס.
א רעטהזעלהאפטער מארד.
אריינקומענדיג דערזעהט שפּיצקאָפּף דעם פֿאַבריקאַנט קלינגער ביים שרייבטיש זיצענדיג.
דער קאַסע־קאַסטען שטעהט אָפֿפֿען...

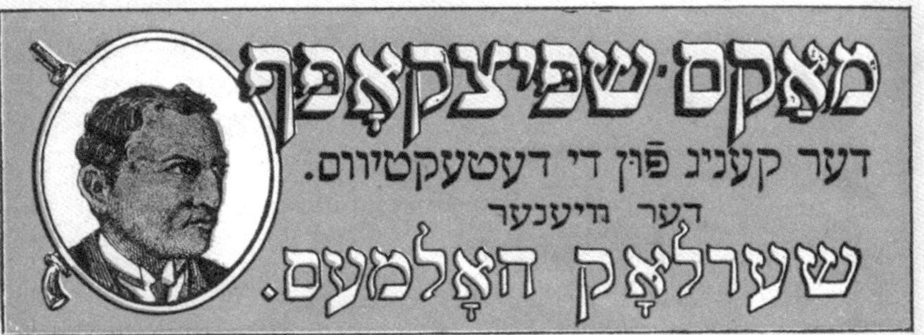

A Mysterious Murder

CHAPTER ONE

A Mysterious Murder

THE RENOWNED DETECTIVE Max Spitzkopf is sitting in his elegant office, engrossed in his newspaper. It is a lovely warm day, around nine in the morning.

Spitzkopf does not have much to do today. There are but a few less-than-important cases on his docket, which he has handed over to his assistants to finish taking care of. Now all he would like is at least one whole day to get some decent rest.

And so the detective has stretched out on his sofa and is browsing his paper.

That is, he had been until someone suddenly rang the doorbell and his manservant entered to hand him a calling card.

"Dr. Gottfried, Provincial Court Judge," Spitzkopf read on the card. "Oh, this must be rather an important case if this celebrated criminal justice jurist is paying me a visit." With those words, Spitzkopf turned to his manservant and said, "Let the gentleman come in at once."

"Good morning, Sir Provincial Court Judge!" Spitzkopf greeted his guest. "To what do I owe the honor?"

"That which leads me to you, famous man," answered Dr. Gottfried, "is a most unusual matter. I do not even know, as a judge, if I should be doing such a thing. But my conscience will not let me rest.

"Today I presided over an important trial by jury, for a case of murder. The defendant swears by all that's holy that he is innocent. But there are very strong grounds of suspicion against him, and it appears to me that he will certainly be found guilty.

"I am convinced, however, that he is innocent. And it breaks my heart when I realize that I shall have to read a death sentence for a person who, I am quite sure, is not the culprit.

"Therefore, I would like to ask you, when you have time, to attend the hearing. Perhaps you can help the man somehow. I won't relate all the details of the case to you. It would be better for you to hear the whole indictment and the exact charges, as well as the testimonies of the witnesses. That way you will have a clear picture of the whole case."

"Most gladly," Spitzkopf answered. "I would like to attend the trial. You know me, and therefore you know that when it comes to helping an innocent person, my presence can be counted on.

"In fact, I have time today, so I'll appear at the court right away. When does the hearing begin?"

"In fifteen minutes," the judge answered. "I must dash so that no one is waiting for me. But first I must thank you for your readiness to grant my request. I trust, with some certainty, that if I am not mistaken and the man is indeed innocent, you will succeed in saving him and in discovering the actual culprit, as it has been your fortune to have solved so many mysterious cases before!"

With these words the judge bade his farewell to Spitzkopf and left.

Spitzkopf scribbled a note for his assistants and left it on his desk, instructing that the first of them to show up at his home office that day should depart at once for the provincial court.

He then changed his clothing, throwing on a gray wig, an old-fashioned ladies' hat, a dress of similar vintage, and a broad jacket, setting a pair of blue-tinted glasses over his eyes. He looked like a poor old woman, supporting herself with a rough-hewn cane. In this attire, he quit his office and went off to the provincial court.

The courthouse was not far from his office, and he made it there in good time, just as the trial was getting underway for the day.

The public gallery was full of curious spectators. No one could have noticed that the old woman, taking great pains to prod her way in to find a seat in the first row so that she could hear and see everything with perfect clarity, was the famous detective.

The presiding judge, meanwhile, constantly glanced over at the spectators' gallery, his eyes searching to see if the detective had arrived. He did not want Spitzkopf to miss a moment.

But naturally he did not recognize him and did have to begin reading out the charges. The indictment was quite brief and related the following: The accused, Wilhelm Grünfeld, had for several months been a correspondence clerk for the manufacturer Leopold Königsberg. Königsberg's silk factory was outside of Vienna, and in the central district he maintained only his city office, occupied by himself and a single employee—Grünfeld.

Königsberg was an older man, around sixty years of age. He visited the plant rarely, and his son led its operations. At his city office, the factory would send him the most important letters and merchandise orders of the day, and he would take care of them and issue the necessary instructions back to the factory.

There was always a good deal of mail to handle, enough to keep Grünfeld working into the evening. The office was also home to a large vault that was intermittently used to store vast sums of money and securities.

On the tenth of March at about eight in the morning, Grünfeld, quaking with fear, appeared before the police with the message that, upon coming into the office that day, he had found his boss dead, slumped over at his desk.

A team of police officers was dispatched at once to the office. There they found Königsberg sitting in his desk chair, his hands lying at his sides, a stab wound in his chest.

The police doctor asserted that the wound was produced by a fine-pointed dagger and that the death occurred quickly, with quite minimal blood loss. The murder had taken place some twelve or thirteen hours earlier.

The vault stood wide open—and had been thoroughly emptied.

The team of officers at once began questioning Grünfeld, and his testimony was so unclear—and his ability to answer their questions so weak—that they immediately suspected him as the assailant and arrested him. He had not succeeded in demonstrating his innocence and was now to be tried for the murder and robbery of his employer.

After the judge had finished reading out the indictment, he addressed the defendant. "Well, Leon Grünfeld! Do you consider yourself guilty?"

"No," the defendant answered, in resolute tones. "As I already explained at the inquest, the following is precisely what took place.

"On the ninth of March, there was a great deal of mail to attend to. I was scribbling away until seven in the evening and still had not finished. My boss then said to me, 'Go home now; it's late already. For the less important letters, I'll sketch out some short replies, and you'll come in a little earlier than usual tomorrow and answer them in full.'

"Such a situation had presented itself several times before, so I thought nothing of it. I took my leave of my employer and headed down the stairs of the building. On the last step I encountered a sort of veiled lady, and before I exited the premises I seemed to hear the lady opening the door to our office and entering. It did not worry me, and I continued on my way.

"The next morning, at around eight, I entered our office again. I always had a key on me so that I wouldn't have to wait for my boss to get in. He often arrived after me and sometimes left before I did.

"On this occasion, as soon as I inserted the key, I noticed that the lock did not turn—the door opened on its own. My initial idea was that my boss had locked up imperfectly or had simply forgotten to. But coming into the main room, I saw the curtains closed and him sitting at his desk. At first I thought that he was sleeping. I called out in a loud voice, 'Good morning!' so as to wake him. It was surprising to me that he would be at the office so early.

"But he didn't answer me, so I approached him. Then, to my horror, I saw that he was dead. Terribly afraid, I ran off at once to the police and relayed to them what had happened. In those brief moments in the office I had not even noticed that the vault was open and had been emptied, such was the extent of my shock and horror.

"That's all I can say. As God is my witness, I am innocent in this terrible murder."

The public prosecutor posed a question. "How late was it when you left the office?" he asked.

"After seven in the evening," Grünfeld answered. "It was dark outside."

"And when did you arrive to the office the next morning?"

"Around seven-thirty."

"As the police doctor certified after eight o'clock a.m., the victim had been dead for around twelve or thirteen hours. The murder must therefore have been carried out at that spot the night before, at around seven. That is exactly when you left. It should therefore come as no surprise to you that you are under suspicion for this crime.

"Your coming to the office the next day at seven-thirty is also suspicious. No one goes to their office at that hour, and you yourself say that the boss would routinely come later, so you had enough time to take care of the rest of the correspondence without arriving quite so early.

"The story of the veiled woman who apparently went to visit your boss after you left work strikes me as not entirely plausible. Even if it turns out to be true, that such a woman had gone up the stairs at that time, it would be impossible for you to know with such certainty that she had indeed visited your employer. It just seems so to you, but it is equally possible that she went somewhere else in the building.

"You see, then, defendant, that from whichever angle one considers the case, you come out consistently as the likeliest suspect. The most sensible thing for you to do now would be to confess and thereby hope to achieve a more lenient sentence."

"I have nothing to confess," answered the defendant. "It all happened just as I described."

The public prosecutor proceeded to pepper him with various other questions, trying to tease a confession out of him. But he answered everything calmly, with the utmost composure, just as an innocent man might, one who hoped against all hope that the truth would out.

Then various witness testimonies were heard.

Among those who resided in apartments in the same building, not a one had seen a lady going up or down the steps. Meanwhile, the police investigators had not found any suspicious evidence that might lead them to such a person. The case was quite clear-cut: the suspicion fell squarely on Grünfeld.

The trial went on in this manner until around noon, at which time the presiding judge called for a recess of two hours.

When the proceedings recommenced that afternoon, the prosecutor began by giving a speech in which he called for the defendant to be found guilty and punished.

"We consider this case to be eminently straightforward," he said. "Grünfeld was sitting with his employer in the office. He knew that there was a great sum of money being kept in the vault at that time. He murdered his employer, locked up the office, and went home.

"The next day, quite early, he ran to the police, twisted his face up so as to look shaken, and announced that he had found his boss murdered.

"The police doctor maintains that the man died over twelve hours earlier—that is to say, on the ninth of March at about seven o'clock in the evening—just when Grünfeld left the office. It is therefore quite clear, as clear as day, that only he could be our killer.

"We cannot take the story about the veiled lady seriously. When someone wants to cover up their wicked deeds, he always concocts some kind of veiled lady. I need only remind you of the trial of Captain Alfred Dreyfus, in which a veiled lady played a similarly significant role. However, we must not let ourselves be deceived by cockamamie stories."

The defense attorney then took pains to refute the claims made by the prosecutor. "For the public prosecutor, the case is quite clear. He wishes the defendant to be convicted, and he cannot be bothered to think otherwise.

"But for us ordinary people, the case is not half so clear. When any kind of crime takes place, first we must ask ourselves if the suspect is indeed capable of having carried it out; second, for what purpose he would have carried it out; and third, whether or not there is any kind of direct evidence connecting the crime to the suspect.

"Not a single one of these factors is present in our case. No one could logically contend that this individual is capable of carrying out such a nefarious deed. And if he had stolen the money—then where is it? He could not have hidden it in a single night so effectively that an investigation couldn't uncover some trace of it. And where is the weapon with which he is supposed to have committed the murder? Where is any kind of concrete evidence?

"The public prosecutor is calling for the defendant to demonstrate his innocence. But it seems to me that it is, before anything else, the responsibility of the prosecutor to demonstrate his guilt. That has not occurred. The case is very mysterious, and I am certain that the gentlemen of the jury will therefore move to acquit the defendant. They must consider carefully that we are dealing with a murder here. If they convict this man, it will cost him his life. In such a case one must tread very carefully."

Then the prosecutor spoke again, and the defense attorney answered him. The presiding judge then had the last word, and the mixed panel of judges and laymen retired to the deliberations chamber.

Their deliberations lasted for approximately half an hour. The panelists could not come to a consensus so easily. But in the end, they moved to find the defendant guilty while at the same time expressing their wish that the kaiser allow him to live.

All throughout the defendant sat perfectly calm and collected. The thought could hardly enter his mind that he would be convicted. Only when the judiciary panel returned from its chamber and made their judgment known did he let out a cry of despair and fainted to the ground.

He was duly brought to an adjoining room while the judge, with a trembling voice, announced that the court would be sentencing the convicted man to death but with the recommendation that the kaiser take mercy on him and commute the sentence.

Throughout the day's hearing Spitzkopf remained in his seat. He listened closely to every word and observed all present—the defendant, the witnesses, his fellow spectators—with intense focus.

Even during the midday recess he did not budge from his spot, even when the bailiff was about to lock up the courtroom. But as the other spectators had already removed themselves, he asked the old lady to follow suit. So Spitzkopf left but did not go far, sitting on a bench just outside the door. The bailiff had barely opened up the doors again at the end of the recess when the old lady came right back in and resumed her former spot, remaining there until the end of the day's proceedings.

Spitzkopf had become entirely convinced that Grünfeld was innocent. But every trace that might lead to the actual culprit eluded him. And none of his assistants ever appeared. "Apparently they have not finished their other work yet," Spitzkopf thought to himself.

At the end of the trial, when Grünfeld fell unconscious, a great agitation spread among all of the spectators. At that moment Spitzkopf felt someone brushing up against his shoulder. He turned around quickly and recognized his assistant Fuchs, dressed as an old man, as he shoved some kind of note Spitzkopf's way.

After briefly scanning it, he remained sitting at his place as before, but directed his gaze at the right side of the public gallery, fixing his attention on an elegant young man. The man was sitting there with a distinctly composed posture and a widening smile on his lips. As all the spectators went into a tumult at the end of the trial, expressing their sympathy with the unfortunate defendant, it appeared that the matter was of no great concern to him—that on the contrary, he was enjoying it deeply.

Spitzkopf did not lift his gaze from him for a moment. He noted his physical appearance with exactitude, and after the proceedings ended and the spectators left the courtroom, Spitzkopf shoved his way in among them so that he could get to Fuchs and whisper in his ear, "Don't let that man out of your sight. And drop some proverbial breadcrumbs for me along the way so I can retrace your route later. That scallywag is one dangerous character!"

CHAPTER TWO
The *Plattenbrüder*

The man whom Fuchs was told to follow left the courthouse. At the entrance he met another man and off both went together, strolling slowly. Fuchs followed about twenty paces behind them on the opposing sidewalk. Every ten steps, he let a chunk of chalk fall to the ground and crushed it with his foot so that white tracks were left on the pavement, allowing Spitzkopf to eventually follow the route Fuchs had taken.

After an hour this route had stretched quite far. The mystery men had now arrived at one of Vienna's outer districts, where they finally disappeared into what seemed to be a small, low-slung coffee shack. Fuchs made close observations of the building from every angle. The place left him with a wary feeling.

"It doesn't seem prudent for me to enter in the clothes I've got on," he thought to himself. "This appears to be an establishment of the lowest sort, and appearing inside in my very decent habiliments would arouse suspicion. But I don't want to lose any time. While I'm changing clothes, that fellow might just disappear from the place, and it would be a terrible shame for him to put me off the scent."

And so, making a snap decision, he entered the drinkery. Thick smoke from stinking cigars filled the suffocating air, and a powerful odor of schnapps and beer all but walloped Fuchs in the face. With some effort he managed to come to his senses and start taking stock of the main room. There were about twenty little café tables, nearly all of which were occupied. And those who occupied them left a most unsavory impression—wildly contorted, drunken faces, characters who had fallen quite low in the world. Only a few of them looked a little more refined. But even they belonged to that former crowd, the whole lot sitting together in close company, jawing away.

Finally Fuchs spotted an empty table standing off to one side.

He made his way to it and procured a mug of beer. Then his eyes began searching out the character he had been following, but he could not locate him or the man who had accompanied him. So Fuchs gulped down his beer, paid his tab, and made to leave. At the exit, however, he was waylaid by a rather inebriated creature, who hollered out to him, "Leaving so soon, my very good sir? What, don'tcha likes it here with us?"

Fuchs did not deign to make a reply and carried on his way, but the man grabbed him by the jacket and pulled him right back. "Hey, buddy!" he growled. "Seems you ain't one of our kind! But we won't take any jokes here. Ganged together, hanged together, that's what we say. What, y'ain't never seen a *Plattenbruder*, a Tabletop Brother?"

Fuchs now realized he was among a truly decent lot—decently despicable, that is. The *Plattenbrüder* were the vilest gang in all of Vienna. Their name came from their tactic of unscrewing the *Platten*, the round tabletops in the city's cafés, then instigating a quarrel with one of the guests or a waiter and using the heavy marble disks as weapons, swinging them wide and fearfully injuring their opponents.

The *Plattenbrüder* were a deeply dreaded group in the city. Even the police preferred not to deal with them, ever since one of their officers had gotten involved in a melee with the brothers and had been dealt several mighty blows from the marble slabs that he would not soon forget.

Because of that incident, the police decided that only rarely would they mix it up with the Tabletop Brothers, and when an officer found himself in the vicinity of one of their signature brawls, he would go hide until it was over and done with.

Fuchs had buzzed right into the nest of this very swarm, and he could not figure out what to do next. He did have his loaded revolver in his pocket and could therefore defend himself quite ably—but if he were to use it, the gang would take him to be a spy, and he would no longer be able to effectively shadow the man he was looking for. And so he resolved to simply cheese it as quick as he could so as to get the meddling gang member off his back.

"Let me go my way, my good fellow," said Fuchs. "I am an old man, and I was ever so weary, so I stepped in here to rest a bit. And now I'll be carrying on. What could you want from the likes of me?"

At that moment, a back door opened and in came two characters, whom Fuchs at once recognized as the two people he had been following from the courthouse. But now they were dressed quite differently. Instead of the natty attire they had worn earlier, they were now dressed in old, ragged suits and torn shoes, and their hair was disheveled. One of them had pasted on an unkempt red beard, and the other, who had been sporting a black goatee, was now clean-shaven. An ordinary person would surely not have recognized the two men from before. But Fuchs, with his trained eye, knew them at once.

When they entered, the younger of the two, the one whom Fuchs had seen in the courtroom, shouted out: "Well, brothers! Here's a nice fish you've caught! That man has been following me since I left the courthouse. He'll reach his target yet. Yes, he'll soon learn who I am—and what I am!"

All of that he bellowed so that the whole room could hear him. The *Plattenbrüder* arose from their chairs, wanting to make a rush for Fuchs. Fuchs, meanwhile, saw he had little to lose. These men were already on to him. And so, thinking quickly, he whipped out his revolver and started firing.

The first two bullets hit their marks. Two Tabletop Brothers crumpled with wild screams on their lips. But Fuchs could fire no more. From behind he received such a terrible blow to the head that he fell to the ground senseless.

Like feral animals, the whole gang pounced on him, getting to work with clubs and chairs such that Fuchs started bleeding from a number of fresh wounds. Then they bound his hands and feet, gagged his mouth with a rag, and dragged him out into the yard.

There in the yard stood an old shed surrounded by half-ruined crates and old bits of iron. Entering it, the *Plattenbrüder* moved aside a big heavy crate, revealing an interior door. They flung Fuchs through it and down into a cellar.

Then they shut the door, pulled the crate into its former spot, and returned into the tavern to pour a few out for their terrific victory over the spy.

CHAPTER THREE
A Treasure Is Found on the Trail

SPITZKOPF, MEANWHILE, had left the courthouse and gone directly home. Entering his office, he found a few of his assistants, who briefed him on their activities that day. Spitzkopf listened closely to their reports and pronounced himself satisfied—they had done their work with care and alacrity.

"You are all excellent young people," he praised them. "And I see that one can depend on you. When I die, you will be able to lead my agency."

"Oh, there our chief goes talking about dying! There's time yet for that!" they cried in one voice. "You have, it's true, achieved a great deal and performed wonderfully daring feats in your time. But you're still young and healthy—and will probably end up surviving more than one of us!"

"Sure, healthy and strong—that I am," Spitzkopf responded. "But a detective must always count on the greatest dangers lurking along his path, and he can never know what's coming just around the bend. Take, for example, our friend Fuchs! How many times has he been in mortal danger? How many times has he looked the Angel of Death straight in the eye?

"And he is, it so happens, a very healthy and dexterous young man! But somehow he always extricates himself by dint of his own powers, or at least manages to hold himself together until help comes from some other party, whether me or one of you. In fact just today I set him upon a most dangerous task. I'm actually rather afraid he'll end up with a cracked skull by the end of it. There's no kidding around when it comes to the *Plattenbrüder*. But I ordered him to mark out his path on his way to them, so if he doesn't return soon I'll be able to go looking for him."

"Chief!" the assistants pleaded. "Maybe send us after him instead? We could take care of a job like that too maybe."

"No!" Spitzkopf answered. "We're not talking here only about a dangerous undertaking. Indeed, if we were, I would be able to use you, as you are all strong, courageous young men, and you know how to conduct yourselves in such situations. But here we also happen to be dealing with the discovery of a tremendous secret.

"The scoundrels whom I will now be pursuing are extremely crafty. Until now they have carried out their crimes so deftly that no one has been able to catch them. The character whom Fuchs pointed out to me today—I have been pursuing him for longer than just this morning. Since I've been on his trail, he has found fresh new knaveries to commit, and still he eludes me.

"I won't flatter myself by saying that everything is bound to go my way. But this is an important case, and I want to handle the investigation on my own. If I were to hand some of it over to you and it didn't turn out right, I'd just end up taking myself to task—that maybe things would have turned out differently if I'd gone myself.

"Therefore, go about your business, all of you. I won't need your personal attention any further today. I shall wait a little longer in case Fuchs comes back with some news for me. But if he doesn't return by the time it starts to get dark, I'll set out on the trail."

So the assistants left Spitzkopf on his own. He waited for another half an hour. It was starting to get dark outside. Then he put on the raiments of a common laborer and left the building.

With swift steps he made his way to the provincial courthouse. He scanned the sidewalk closely from all sides until he noticed the first white spot Fuchs had left for him there. Then he started quietly sauntering down the sidewalk, every couple of minutes looking down at the pavement to make sure he was still following the markings. He walked in this manner for a good while, until the sky had grown quite dark and the gas lamps were burning.

The path had now led into the outer districts of the city. Spitzkopf started to think, "Who knows in what kind of hole Fuchs may be lying now . . ."

Suddenly he realized that the white spots on the sidewalk had crossed over to the other side of the street. He remained standing where he was and assessed the building across from him.

"Ah, I know that coffee shack quite well," he thought to himself. "I've been there more than once. It must be there that Fuchs went into—so it's no surprise now that he never came out again.

"This is where the most dangerous of the *Plattenbrüder* hold their regular covert coffee klatch. This is where the most corrupt capers and crimes are conceived and carried out. I shan't need to go in. These gangsters are so cozy with each other that any unfamiliar face would draw their attention, and they'd immediately start to doubt that I'm one of theirs. And anyway, now's not the time to go searching for our suspect.

"First I've got to free my Fuchs. He must be tied up somewhere in this yard—and I know this yard well. I'll wait until it gets darker. Then I'll enter and find my Fuchs. Everything else will sort itself out."

He spent half an hour loitering until the sky was pitch black.

Then, through a dark side street, he neared the building. On that street stood an old, fallen-in house, its yard bordering the yard of the gang's coffeehouse. No face dared show itself in these decrepit surroundings. Spitzkopf seized the opportunity of creeping into the neighboring yard and jumping the fence that separated it from the gangsters' den.

Here too there was no one to be seen. Even the coffeehouse's windows facing the yard were not lit. Spitzkopf quickly oriented himself to his surroundings and, seeing the old shed, went in. The door was only closed, not locked. He shut it behind himself so that he could use his electric torch without being discerned. After illuminating the chamber and inspecting it closely, he could see that, not long before, people's feet had trod the area surrounding a massive, heavy crate. In the thick layer of dust one could plainly make out footsteps.

"There must be something here," thought the detective, and with a hearty effort he shoved away the crate.

"I've found it!" he said, spotting the door, which he opened with a skeleton key. He shone his lantern into the next room.

There he saw a long flight of narrow, crumbling steps. He descended carefully, and as he continued downward, downward, he heard a deep groaning, a human voice . . .

Perceiving that Fuchs must be down there, he now positively flew down the steps. Finally he came to a cold, dark cellar and saw Fuchs lying on the ground, bound hand and foot, bloodied and covered with dirt.

Spitzkopf quickly sliced off the offending ropes and freed him. Then he wiped off the blood that seeped down all over his body and wrapped his head wounds with a kerchief.

Fuchs had indeed suffered awfully from the blows he had received, but his robust health had protected him this time from too grievous a harm. After he had lain there for quite a long time, he eventually came to and remembered all that had happened to him. And he knew that his master would soon be in hot pursuit—

he had, after all, left behind the chalk marks. Now that Spitzkopf had come and put him to rights a bit, he began to rebound so nicely that he was able to shlep himself up the steps and quit the site of his captivity.

Spitzkopf, meanwhile, stayed behind in the cellar for a few minutes, once again surveying the surroundings. He sighted yet another door, opening into another compartment of the cellar. He managed to enter it, again using his skeleton key, and found in this second space what could only be described as a treasure chamber.

Alongside the walls were large boxes filled with merchandise of different kinds, as if in a shop. In the corner was a giant safe.

"This is where the gang keeps all its loot," he thought. "This is where it all must be. Just you wait, scoundrels. I'll soon have you all shelved away, too."

He closed the vault door and went up the steps, pushing the crate back into place so that no one would suspect anything was amiss. Fuchs was waiting for him outside. With Spitzkopf's help, Fuchs was able to climb over the fence and drag himself over to the neighboring side street. There they hailed a carriage and made their way back to Spitzkopf's lodgings. Once they got there, Fuchs climbed into bed and a doctor was summoned who examined his wounds and confirmed that they were nothing too severe. He applied some provisional dressings, and Fuchs soon sank into a deep sleep.

Spitzkopf, however, got right back to work.

CHAPTER FOUR
Another Mysterious Murder

Spitzkopf left his office again, although he had not yet determined what his next steps would be. He was well acquainted with the man whom Fuchs had drawn his attention to in the courtroom. He had long been aware that this was one dangerous bird, but it had not yet been his happy lot to catch him with his own two hands. And now—the man's behavior at the trial that day, his monstrous laughter at the moment when the innocent defendant was sentenced to death—aroused the suspicion in Spitzkopf that he must know the particulars as to who committed the mysterious murder in question. And perhaps that he himself had played a part in it.

The way Fuchs had been waylaid on his reconnaissance mission that day strengthened the premonition in Spitzkopf that this crowd must be absolutely quivering with fear lest someone discover its secrets. And once he had liberated Fuchs and found the secret treasure chamber, there was not a trace of doubt left in him that this was a pack of hustlers with which they had crossed paths—hustlers so prolific that they needed an entire storehouse in which to stash the spoils of their thievery.

A plan began to take shape in the detective's mind. It involved waiting for the thieves at night, then surprising them in the cellar when they went to tuck away their takings. But he quickly cast that plan aside.

"First things first. I want to find out who killed that manufacturer. And anyhow, if I go to sneak up on these villains in the cellar, I'll not have gained any tangible evidence that they were involved in the murder. If I know anything about this lot, it's that it'll be tough going to pin anything on them without some concrete evidence.

"It follows that the only plausible course of action is to spy on them tonight from afar. Maybe I'll hit upon some trace of their dirty work. I'll go and camp out a few houses away from their coffee shack and watch for whatever's doing there."

And so he set off walking in that direction. The path led him along the Franz-Josefs-Kai, the street running along the western bank of the Danube near the center of Vienna. While there, he saw a large assembly of people standing in front of one of the buildings. He hotfooted it over and learned that a murder had just been committed therein. Spitzkopf made himself known to the police officers present so that he could be let through. He soon found himself in the office of yet another manufacturer, a man named Klinger.

Entering, Spitzkopf saw Klinger sitting at his desk. His vault was wide open. The manufacturer, meanwhile, was sitting peacefully, just as if he were sleeping. But upon bending close toward him, Spitzkopf could see that the man was dead. The vault, meanwhile, had been emptied. The wastebasket had been overturned, and several pieces of paper lay scattered on the floor.

Spitzkopf inspected the corpse closely and deduced that he had been killed in the very same way as Königsberg. A hole had been stabbed through his chest by a fine-tipped blade, so fine that it was hard to discern the opening it had made in his vest, an aperture no wider than the eye of a needle. There did not even appear to be any bloodstains. The blade of the dagger must have been poisoned; the death would have occurred instantly.

After completing his inspection of the body, Spitzkopf directed his attention to the room—the doors and windows—but could find no indication of breaking and entering. The footprints in the room were of ordinary size.

Meanwhile the team of police officers had entered. Spitzkopf apprised them of his findings, and the police doctor pronounced his judgment that the murder had taken place some two hours earlier.

Soon the manufacturer's office personnel were summoned. They related that the man would often spend the evening alone there, remaining until around ten o'clock, as he was in the habit of handling some of the accounting as well as dispatching the most important letters. Today was one of those days. When the staff had left around six o'clock that evening he had stayed behind, telling them he had much to do.

The building's landlord and the neighbors were called too. None of them, however, had heard or seen anything suspicious.

But a little girl no older than ten, the landlord's daughter, recounted that at around nine o'clock that night she had caught sight of a veiled woman ascending the stairs. But the child was terribly frightened by the strange lady and skedaddled into her family's apartment as soon as she laid eyes on the woman.

The police officers set to cordoning off the office suite and sealing it. In the morning a new team of officials would be dispatched there to continue the investigation.

"So what do you say, Herr Spitzkopf?" the police commissioner asked. "Seems to be quite the puzzler, eh?"

"Puzzling, certainly. But I'm afraid I don't have fairly anything to say in these first moments. I've not yet had the chance to think it all over."

But it was not so, really, for Spitzkopf. For him the case was not at all puzzling. He was already hot on the trail.

"Another mysterious murder!" he thought to himself. "And another veiled lady . . ."

Even the manner of death was the same as with the other manufacturer.

"If I am not mistaken, the same murderer that took Königsberg's life took Klinger's, too. And these gangsters must have spread their branches quite wide. They know exactly when these rich fellows might be sitting alone in their offices. One of them would have come disguised as a lady, on some social pretext, and once the boss had engaged in a sort of chat with 'her,' she would have used the first advantageous moment to stick her blade into the poor unsuspecting fool. Then she would have gotten the key to the vault from off of his person, emptied it, and quickly made her getaway.

"In Königsberg's case, no one had asked after the manufacturer the whole night. He remained there for hours on end, and not until morning did the unfortunate Grünfeld come upon his dead body.

"But on this occasion, around eleven at night, Klinger's

household started wondering as to his whereabouts, asking why he was not home yet. The family sent someone to check on him. And so the sad occurrence was discovered much sooner.

"And that's all we know about that. Now on to the next. Tonight. Tonight has to be the night I go and sneak up on these scoundrels—and finally send them packing. If I wait till morning, the newspapers will have gotten wind of the new murder case, and it may be too late to catch the criminals unawares.

"I'll proceed to them presently, that pernicious pack of plunderers."

CHAPTER FIVE
A New Hiding Place

AFTER FUCHS had fallen into the clutches of the *Plattenbrüder* in their covert café, after he was bound and tossed down into the cellar, the brothers threw a rollicking party, swilling down alcohol as if it were on the personal tab of God Himself.

"We did it!" roared the one whom Fuchs had followed out of the courthouse. "We damn well did it! The story about the veiled lady everyone took for some tall tale concocted by the defendant. And so he got the judgment that was coming to him! No one suspects us in the slightest. We can carry on with our work! I've got a whole list of these fat cats who are in the habit of staying late at their offices. Why, tonight's as good a night as any for catching another of 'em in my trap!"

"Fine, fine!" cheered another member of the gang. "But then who's that tweety bird who went fluttering after you all this way? It seems someone does suspect you . . ."

"Right you are," the first man responded. "But he was stalking me for a different reason. Two years ago I broke into the jeweler Jamber's, down in the center of town on Kärntner Strasse, and pinched a heap of merchandise. I was working at that time as an independent operator, no partners, which is why you lot don't know about it.

"Once I'd finished my work, suddenly Jamber scuttles onto the scene. He lived on the premises, and to this day I don't know what demon inspired him to wake up before dawn and see what was doing in his shop.

"To make a long story short, he caught me off guard and seized me by the collar. But I gave him such a wallop straight to the chest that he hit the deck instantly, at which point I cheesed it immediately.

"Now this Jamber is probably the same old coot who recognized me today and followed me here. He'll soon lose his taste for that kind of funny stuff, though. If our fists today weren't enough to knock out his appetite for it, then tonight I'll serve him the full meal.

"The man isn't getting out of here alive. Of that we've gotta make damned sure. Because if anyone finds out where we meet, soon a whole flock of birdies like him are gonna be swooping in to pay us a visit." The gangsters went on drinking until it was very dark, then each of them went off to their work, at different sites around town. The two whom Fuchs had followed remained at the hideaway.

"I'll let you in on a secret," said the man whom Fuchs had pointed out in the courtroom. "There's something about that guy what followed us today that I don't like. I told our friends a story about the jeweler called Jamber so they'd cool their jets on him. But the God's honest truth is that the fella has me spooked. I think he may be a spy.

"I won't let it get in the way of my work tonight, though. I don't want to miss my moment. But when it's over and done with, I mean to put in the request that we clear out our treasure room, and not even wait till tomorrow.

"We've got to abandon our shack for a while too and find some other safehouse. This one ain't so safe anymore.

"I'll soon be off on my way. You go off to the treasure room and make sure everything's in order there so that we're ready to transport the loot later. Make sure you're back by around ten tonight. And if anyone from the gang shows up, don't let him leave. Once I'm back we're getting right to work."

True to his word, right around ten our man returned weighed down with sacks full of cash. His plan had worked. Through his handiwork, the factory owner Rudolf Klinger was now dead and cold and his vault emptied.

A good number of gang members had already gathered at the hideaway. They hailed their leader with a "Hurrah!" and thought they would get down to drinking right away.

"First we get a good gulp down, then we have a look to see what you've brought, and each man will claim his share," they shouted.

"No, brothers," answered the man who had hauled back the laden bags. "Today we're going to switch up our usual schedule a bit. We're going down to our treasure chamber first—to empty it. I've already arranged for another safe spot to stash our booty. See, I'm a touch afraid that someone's on our trail."

That made the gang *very* afraid.

"What? Who?" they all cried out. "Ya gotta tell us more."

"I cannot and will not tell you anything else. Not now," he answered sharply. "There isn't any time to lose. Now c'mon!"

The men obeyed. One by one they emptied out through the back door and into the yard. One by one they squeezed into the old shed and waited till all were assembled there. The heavy crate was then shoved aside and they opened the door. One by one they descended into the cellar. Once they were all in, they opened the doors of their bull's-eye lanterns, turning them on.

"The little tweety bird's winged it outta here!" one of them exclaimed, a deathly fear in his voice. "Someone's on to us!"

"You're right! It's true!" the others agreed. "How could he have gotten out?"

They searched the cellar on all sides, but the prisoner had not left behind a trace.

The door that led into the adjoining cellar room was shut just as it had been earlier. Indeed, how *could* the man have gotten out?

"Like I said, boys, we've gotta clear outta here," said their leader, a quaver in his voice. "And really step on it, too.

"It'd be a shame to leave all our treasure here—all together it's worth a king's ransom. But we're more than twenty of us together. If everyone takes a good bit of it we can be done by midnight. I'm sure no one'll surprise us here before then. As for after midnight, though . . . I have a feeling we're being pursued by a particularly proficient private detective and that it will probably be around midnight when he plans to stage his ambush."

And so the gang got to work. The most precious merchandise was immediately packed away into parcels, and each man took a parcel onto his shoulders and vanished into the dark. They stored the packages away into the attic of their coffeehouse, making the speedy clearing of the cellar a priority. The cash they divided amongst themselves. For the time being, the leader kept on his own person the fresh money he had raked in that night.

The less-valuable articles they brought up and hid in the old crates that lay about the shed. "Let the bloodhounds find this old junk," they said.

It took barely an hour to clear the cellar. The door to the treasure chamber was locked up again. And down the stairs to the cellar the gangsters threw splintered planks of wood, rags, rocks, and other such refuse, giving off the appearance that no human soul had been down there for years. They then restored the large crate to its former place in front of the door to the cellar and locked up the shed.

Only a part of the gang was engaged in this work of concealing the evidence. The others were up in the attic, dividing the parcels of treasure into even smaller parcels. Then, jumping the fence into the adjoining yard, they went off to the storehouse they had chosen to succeed their former one.

It was not far. They used to hold their meetings there several years earlier. It was a small cellar into which they gained entry through an old, crumbling well. They used to open the cover of the well and then, employing a rope ladder, lower themselves into the shaft. Several meters down there was a door that opened onto the small cellar that had formerly served as their hideaway.

As accessing it was so difficult, however, and as they could only enter it on very dark nights so as not to attract attention, they had eventually found it necessary to seek out more suitable headquarters.

"Today, however, as this threat looms over us, we've got to scurry back to our old hole," they reasoned as they transported all of their most prized possessions to the well.

Once they had finished their work, they sat down for a moment of rest. The clock had already struck midnight. The ruffians broke out their bottles and started imbibing, thinking to themselves, "All the way down here, three meters underground, no private eye will be able to find us, no matter how proficient!"

CHAPTER SIX

Nabbed!

Spitzkopf, meanwhile, had left the office of the slain manufacturer Klinger and headed straight to the chief of police, where he requested that several skilled undercover officers be dispatched for his use in executing an important arrest. They immediately fulfilled his request, and he and the officers went off at once to clap this gang in irons.

He imagined he would very shortly be bearding the *Plattenbrüder* in their own den, to which they would have repaired to divvy up their recent spoils. Then he would go fetch the officers, ambushing the criminals and arresting the whole motley crew. He imagined it going so smoothly that he had not even found it necessary to go in disguise, as he often did, but rather set out on the mission in his everyday apparel.

It was already past midnight when he arrived at his destination. All the lights were turned out in the coffee shack, though a waiter sat next to a sideboard dozing. Spitzkopf went into the yard by his now-familiar route, the police right on his tail. He opened the door of the shed and saw the large crate in its usual spot.

"Probably one of the gang remained outside while the others went down and blocked the door after them," the detective thought to himself as he pushed aside the obstacle.

He then opened the door and shone his light down the flight of stairs. Upon them he noticed a whole heap of rubble—moldering bricks and rotted wooden boards all lying in a great jumble.

He could not quite fathom it. Something had to have happened here in the interim. Descending into the cellar, he opened the door into the treasure chamber. It was empty. Every box and every shelf: empty. The safe: empty, and wide open.

"The vultures have flown the coop," he muttered to himself. "They saw that Fuchs wasn't here anymore and understood they must have been found out. I've galloped somewhat in the wrong direction this time, it would seem.

"But their race is run—of that I'm sure. I'll find their tracks soon enough."

He returned to the shed and told the officers what had happened.

"Two of you go into their coffee shack and wait there. Maybe something novel will turn up. The others should station themselves at different niches along the street and keep a close eye out.

"As for me, I'm going to follow their tracks. They've managed to clear out their merchandise in a very short amount of time, but they can't have gotten far with it."

With that he left the shed and started to look for footprints, illuminating the yard with his electric torch. But it was tough going. The gang members had crossed several times between the shed, the coffee shack, the shed, and back again, such that it was difficult to discern whither their steps ultimately led. He rotated around the yard for over a half hour and still could not come to any conclusion.

Finally he decided to jump the fence to see where the footprints would lead on the other side. But the second yard was overgrown with tall grass, and on such a dark night he could not make out a single footfall. And he did not want to use his electric torch there, reticent of giving himself away lest the gang should be somewhere nearby.

"They've really done me dirty this time," he thought to himself. "It's one clever gang, I'll give them that.

"I've got to put a pause on my investigation for now, as long as it's still night. In two hours the new day will start to dawn, and I'll be able to follow their tracks more easily."

And so, in rather low spirits, Spitzkopf exited the yard and went back out into the street. In the coffee shack all was the same as before. Two police officers were sitting in a corner, drinking beer. The waiter was still snoozing next to the sideboard. Meanwhile, the officers who were stationed on the street had not yet seen anything to arouse their suspicion.

All their work that night, it turned out, was in vain.

For about a quarter of an hour Spitzkopf wandered the streets and alleyways in the vicinity. His eagle eye scanned in every direction, and his keen ear pricked up at the minutest rustle. But he discovered nothing worth discovering.

"Might as well make my way home," he decided. "And when I continue my search here in the morning, I must remember to change my attire so no one recognizes me."

At that moment the detective heard, from some distance away, a sort of whistling. "That's one of my own team of assistants," he called out in astonishment, answering the signal with a corresponding whistle.

Not a minute had passed before his third in command, Julius Haupt, was standing in front of him.

"What is it you're looking for here, Chief?" asked the young man, a note of surprise in his voice. "Have you maybe come to help me?"

"I had no idea you were in the area," Spitzkopf answered. "Neither do I know what you're doing here. But I'm glad our paths have crossed. Something most unusual has just happened to me, and it's a very good thing that I have one of my own people here now. But first tell me what led you to this neglected corner of town."

"I was here doing some fieldwork," answered Haupt, "for the case you had sent me out to investigate. At around ten tonight, I observed a suspicious-looking character with a parcel under his arm sprinting down the street.

"This fellow, well, he raised my eyebrows somewhat. I followed him. But then suddenly he disappeared from my sight. And since then I've been stalking around here, convinced he would at some point have to come back out of wherever it was he vanished to. I'm certain he entered one of these houses."

Spitzkopf took a moment to ponder this new intelligence. "Something about this second house on the left rubs me the wrong way," he said. "Let's try to go in."

He opened the door with his skeleton key and walked down a corridor until he came to a large courtyard. Carefully he pointed his electric torch at their surroundings, then eked out with a stunned sort of joy, "Ha, you lot of fowl! I gave you my word I'd get you in my cage one day! And now I've reached your roost!

"Quickly, Haupt, go run off to the third street on the right from here. There you'll find a number of undercover officers patrolling. Order them, in my name, to come here at once. Meanwhile, I'll remain where I am and start making the necessary arrangements . . ."

Once Spitzkopf had shone a light on the courtyard he noticed the decaying well, beside which were fresh footprints. To his trained eye, it was enough. He knew it must be the gang's new hiding place.

He had sent away his assistant to call up the police officers, so now, quite alone, he approached the well and removed its cover. Several meters down he noticed a faint light as from a door that had been cracked open. Without wasting too much time in thought, he wound a rope around the top of the well and shimmied down.

Once he had descended to the spot he had noticed, he grasped the doorknob and pressed his ear to the door. He heard a number of different voices, ranting and raving, snickering and scolding and squabbling. Not a doubt was in his mind—he was in the right place.

Moving quickly, he clambered back up again, grabbed his two revolvers, and waited for the policemen.

Some minutes later they turned up. Then Spitzkopf fired a shot down the well. The bullet pierced the door. And the gangsters inside were pierced with fear. No one was hit, but the warning was keenly sensed by them all. They had just gotten to the point of dividing up the loot that they had seized that day. They were just starting to feel so very sure of themselves—and then, at that very moment, for someone to shoot at them?

One of their number cautiously poked his head out of the door. And Spitzkopf called down to him: "Hello down there, *Plattenbrüder*! Why don't you all come on up here?"

"Who are you?" the man shouted back up.

"A good friend to the lot of you. Come on out and we'll get nice and brotherly, *Plattenbrüder*!"

Soon several more heads emerged. Spitzkopf then flashed his torch down the well, and one of the heads recognized him. "Ah, you bloodhound!" he bellowed upward. "Yer that one, the one what's been stalking us! But just you wait. Soon it'll be our paws digging into *you*!"

With those words he flung up a sharply honed dagger, which managed to hit Spitzkopf and tear open a wound in his left hand. That hand now let go of his revolver, which went plummeting down the well shaft. Spitzkopf drew back to tend to his injury. The wound was not deep. He bandaged it quickly with a handkerchief and returned to the mouth of the well.

The door to the cellar was now closed. The gang had retreated. Again Spitzkopf let himself down the shaft. Again he pressed his ear tight against the door. But now he heard not even the slightest murmuring. It was as if all life within had expired in the blink of an eye.

"Who knows," he pondered. "Maybe these birdies have another way out of their nest through which they'll manage to fly away once again."

Making up his mind in moments, he pushed open the door and crawled through, at the same time calling out an order for the officers to also shimmy down the well shaft and follow him into the cellar.

Not a speck of light pierced the gloom of this subterranean chamber. Spitzkopf waited for a few officers to descend, then illuminated the darkness with his bull's-eye lantern. This special device was designed to flood any space with bright light but leave the bearer of the lamp in total shadow.

As soon as he turned it on, Spitzkopf could make out his targets: the gangsters were hiding under various boxes and crates. He issued a quiet command to the officers: "Be ready to fire."

And to the others present, he thundered, "Surrender now, *Plattenbrüder*. Or I'll have you shot like dogs."

They did not move.

"Once again I am insisting of you. Surrender."

Not a muscle.

"For the third and final time, I demand. Surrender yourselves. One . . . two . . ."

"Don't shoot! We surrender!" a few of the gang cried, worming out from under the boxes.

Spitzkopf bound them hand and foot and set them aside in a corner. Soon all of the gangsters had crawled out and likewise allowed themselves to be restrained.

"Is anyone still hiding?" Spitzkopf called out.

"No," they answered. "You've got us now. All of us."

Spitzkopf scrutinized each one's face. The man he had seen in the courtroom was not among them.

"Aha, *Plattenbrüder*. You can't fool me. One of you is still missing."

At that very moment a gunshot rang out, and Spitzkopf's ear was grazed by a bullet.

"Well, *Plattenbrüder*!" Spitzkopf jeered. "It seems you can steal much better than you can shoot. You've missed your mark and given yourself away in one shot."

And with that Spitzkopf fired off his own revolver in the direction whence the other's had come.

A wild scream resounded through the cellar. Spitzkopf, it seemed, had better aim.

From under a crate the policemen dragged out a bloodied body. It was the nasty character we have been following. Spitzkopf had got him in the leg, and soon he too was lying on the floor bound with ropes.

Spitzkopf set about transporting all these gang members up to ground level. First he climbed back up along with two of the police officers. Then they let down a thick rope into the well shaft, reaching the cellar. The officers below tied each of the criminals to the rope, and those above hauled them up. The *Plattenbrüder* ground their teeth with rage at being shlepped up in such a manner, more like a bunch of rocks than like living human beings.

By the time the work was finished, hours of daylight had already passed. People whose work required them to be up early dotted the streets with their morning traffic. And the transport of the criminals over these same streets was causing a stir. Everywhere people were opening their windows and gawking with considerable pleasure at the sight of the most dreaded gang in all Vienna being towed off to the police station.

"Finally, finally they've managed," they all said, "to arrest the *Plattenbrüder*. They'll be raising a ruckus no longer. No longer threatening to overturn our entire city."

Once they arrived at the police headquarters, the first order of business with the *Plattenbrüder* was to register into the police log all of their various robberies, which they duly confessed to.

Only the man who had been suspected of the two recent murders did not wish, by any means, to admit to those crimes: killing the manufacturers Königsberg and Klinger. Even after the station personnel found among the stolen items, wrapped up in a parcel, the costume of a lady with a voluminous veil, he denied everything. That package, he explained, was simply part of a bunch of loot he had stolen.

Spitzkopf almost began to despair at the man's hardheadedness. His chief task had been to uncover the murderer of the two factory owners. Now here the culprit was protesting his innocence, and no tangible evidence had yet turned up.

The detective decided to repair back to the cellar under the well. Maybe there was still something there waiting to be found. Again he carefully inspected the environs, but to no avail. While searching, though, a thought occurred to him. He should go back and search the previous treasure chamber too. It could be that there, at last, he would hit upon what he was looking for.

And so, just as soon as the thought struck him, he made his way to the storehouse in the yard of the coffee shack and started combing through every pebble, every rag, every scrap of paper.

And this time, fortune favored him.

Among the papers he found an old calling card belonging to Königsberg, on which someone had also jotted down the addresses of other major manufacturers—first among them Klinger's.

When Spitzkopf showed the criminal this card, he turned pale. He could plainly see that denial would no longer be any use.

So he confessed to everything. He even explained how he hit upon the plan and precisely how he carried out the murders. Meanwhile, it was clear from the card found by Spitzkopf that the man had his eye on still other manufacturers and people of great wealth. But now, thanks to the detective, the dangerous man had been rendered harmless.

As soon as possible the police apprised the provincial court of the new development in the case. The innocent Grünfeld was immediately released. The gang, meanwhile, was thrown into jail. Before long, decisions were handed down, and each associate was sentenced to several years' hard time.

The murderer of the manufacturers was sentenced to death and hanged.

To the last, he refused to give his name. It seems he must have been a very serious criminal, with still other murders weighing on his conscience.

Meanwhile, the detective's golden success in the case polished his name to an even brighter burnish than it bore before. All Vienna thanked him for solving the MYSTERIOUS MURDERS and for liberating the city from the predations of the *Plattenbrüder*.

Issue 5: The Smugglers

פינפטעם העפט. פריין 20 העללער.

דער שמוגגלער.

אין דעם מאמענט בעוויזט זיך שפיצקאפף אויף דער לייטער, מיט'ן רעוואלווער אין דער האנד, רופענדיג:

האלט! שורקען — דער מאן האט אייך נישט פערראטהען — איהר אליין האט אייך פערראטהען.

The Smugglers

CHAPTER ONE

A Nighttime Visit

IT WAS eleven at night.

The famous detective Max Spitzkopf was lying in bed, resting his bones after a day of hard work. He had been tasked with a most difficult assignment on what was a very hot summer day. He had spent it running and riding around the city, pursuing the tracks of a most appalling criminal.

He had not been successful this time.

The case had originally been assigned to a different detective, but that individual had conducted the investigation so clumsily that not only had he wiped away some of the most significant clues, seriously endangering the process, but he had also managed to make it plain to the criminals that they were being pursued, making them quite careful of themselves.

"We have a disaster on our hands with some of these younger detectives," said Spitzkopf to one of his assistants, who sat beside him as he lay in bed. "Truly a disaster. Just as soon as a new case drops into their hands, half the city already knows about it, and the culprits can make their moves unnoticeable. And once it's clear that these kid sleuths aren't worth half a heller, it all falls into my own lap.

"But what am I supposed to do about it? It's not so simple to sweeten a sauce that others have scorched. I've spent the whole day in hot pursuit, but whatever track I set out on it becomes quite clear that my predecessors have already mucked it up.

"Meanwhile these rascals get terrifically cautious and make themselves damn near uncatchable. I can do nothing but let the case rest for a couple of days so they can return to their work and crawl out of their hidey-holes—and right into my hands."

At that moment the doorbell rang.

"Rather a late guest, eh?" Spitzkopf said, quite surprised. "Go see who's there."

His assistant opened the door to the detective's rooms and in tumbled a well-dressed man in middle age. He was terribly agitated and pale, his eyes bright red from too much crying.

"Is Herr Spitzkopf at home, and might one see him now?" he asked in trembling tones.

The assistant first wanted to question the man as to his precise wishes. But Spitzkopf had heard the stranger's quavering voice from the next room and immediately felt that his was a most urgent matter. He leaped out of bed, threw on a dressing gown, and opened his door. "Do come in, my dear man!" he called to the stranger. "How can I help you?"

The man duly entered the bedroom, sat himself down on an armchair, and said, "Please do help me, you most renowned gentleman! I have been met with a terrible calamity."

"I always do what I can," Spitzkopf replied. "And whenever I have found I could be of use to someone, I have never refused them my assistance. But first you must calm yourself down somewhat and tell me everything in as much detail as you can manage. Only then will I be able to tell if I can truly help you or not."

The man sighed deeply and said, "I must admit that I am finding it very hard to be calm. These recent events—they have driven me half insane. But I shall try with all my energies to compose myself—so that I can tell you everything.

"My name is Heinrich Rosenbaum. I own a factory in Warsaw, a vast operation with vast profits. I have two children, a boy and a girl. My son is sixteen and my daughter seventeen. They are dearer to me than anything in the world. Ever since my wife died some years ago, I live only for their sake and would surrender up my factory and my fortunes just to make them happy.

"For a long time now they have been driving me fairly mad saying how badly they want to travel abroad. Now, the political situation for us in the Russian Empire must be well known to you, pogroms and revolution and the like. We live in constant trepidation, and not one of us goes a day without fearing for his own life.

"Still, it was difficult to think of acceding to their wish. At first I didn't even want to hear it. But I soon saw for myself that remaining where we were would grow more and more uncomfortable for us. We all decided that we would emigrate together.

"But they were desperate to leave the country as soon as they could. I would meanwhile remain for a certain length of time in order to put my business concerns in order, maybe even sell the factory. Then I would be able to leave the country too and settle with them abroad.

"And so ten days ago my beloved children left. I accompanied them until we were just a few miles from the border.[3] We decided that as soon as they found themselves on the other side they would send a telegram.

"But one day passed, then two, then three and four—and I heard not a word from my sweet dears.

"So I traveled to the border, asked everywhere, investigated, but I couldn't discover a trace of them. I figured they must have been detained at the border. I asked the border guards, sent word to the Okhrana, you know, the tsar's secret police, along with as much money as those fellows could ever want. But to this day I've heard nothing.

"In desperation I turned to a private eye in Warsaw. He traveled to the border, spent a couple of days there, and came back with nothing.

"Yesterday an acquaintance told me about you; said you were a master, a legend. I set off at once on the high-speed rail for Vienna directly to you. You'll forgive me for disturbing you in the middle of the night. But my nerves, my absolute terror—they won't let me rest."

"You haven't disturbed me in the slightest," Spitzkopf reassured him. "You couldn't possibly. I've long grown accustomed to such 'disturbances.' What does disturb me is that another detective has already had his paws on the case. I can bet you the man has already erased any relevant tracks, and the culprits have gotten careful."

"What do you mean, 'culprits'?" cried the man in anguish. "Who said anything about a crime?"

"Calm yourself, Herr Rosenbaum. I myself at the moment have no idea as to what happened. I only meant that it's possible that what you've told me suggests a crime has been committed. But first you must answer a few questions for me. Did your children have passports?"

"No!" Rosenbaum answered. "I am not a native of Warsaw, so we had to wait quite a while until I could get passports for them. But they were keen to rush things and decided to smuggle themselves over the border. How did you guess that?"

"I realized," Spitzkopf answered, "when you expressed your fear that they might have been detained at the border that they must not have had the proper documents. Now, where exactly along the border were they trying to cross?"

"Not far from Kraków," Rosenbaum answered. "I don't know the spot precisely. The smuggler had said that he would have to look around to find the best place to lead the children through."

"Had you known this smuggler from before?" Spitzkopf asked.

"No. I went with my children only so far as a small shtetl not far from the border. I looked into a smuggler there, and they sent a certain man to us."

"Can you give me a description of the man?"

"I regret that I cannot," said Rosenbaum. "It was at night, and we made our arrangements in a small shed outside the inn where we were staying."

"What was the name of the inn?"

"The Hotel Grigoriy. I do have the address; the owner gave it to me."

"Did the smuggler know who you were?"

"No. I only told him I would reward him handsomely once he got my children safely over the border."

"Did your children have much money on them?"

"Just a few hundred rubles."

"Would you happen to have a letter with your children's handwriting on it?"

"Not on me. But I have many back home. I used to travel often on business and demanded that the children write me every day. I have always kept those letters."

"That's good," Spitzkopf remarked. "Go to your hotel and get some rest. Tomorrow morning at eight we're headed to the border. You can go directly to the train station. I'll meet you there."

"Do I have reason to hope?" Rosenbaum asked.

"I can't say," Spitzkopf answered. "But it seems to me that you will indeed see your children again."

Rosenbaum bade him farewell and left. Spitzkopf put himself back to bed.

CHAPTER TWO
A Forged Letter

THE NEXT DAY at seven in the morning, Herr Rosenbaum again came knocking at Spitzkopf's door.

Spitzkopf had been awake a long time and was at that moment busy packing his necessaries for the impending journey.

The appearance of the factory owner surprised him.

"I'm afraid, Herr Rosenbaum, you've unnecessarily troubled yourself by coming here so early," said Spitzkopf. "Didn't I tell you that you should wait for me at the station?"

"Yes," said Rosenbaum. "But I've come to tell you that our journeying together has become unnecessary.

"When I arrived at my hotel last night I found a letter waiting for me, sent by the express mail from home. Enclosed was another letter, this one from my children, telling me they had safely crossed the border and are now traveling toward Switzerland. The entire issue has been resolved. I'll admit, they've written very little. But they'll surely be writing more soon.

"I beg your forgiveness for having put you to work to prepare for this journey, all for nothing."

"It's no bother," Spitzkopf said. "A detective is always prepared. I've not had to do much at all. I'm pleased to hear that your children have been found and that you can travel home now in a peaceful state of mind.

"I must, however, ask you to show me your children's letter."

Rosenbaum looked at the detective in astonishment.

"The case is solved! What good would it do you to see the letter?" Rosenbaum asked.

"And what harm would it do *you*?" Spitzkopf responded. "There are no secrets in it, surely. I am curious to see your children's handwriting."

"Fine. If you really want to see it," said Rosenbaum, "I'll show it to you."

He removed a letter from his briefcase and handed it to the detective. Spitzkopf examined the envelope from every direction.

This was not sent from any city postal office but rather thrown into a train car traveling on the Warsaw-Vienna line, Spitzkopf observed.

He then opened the envelope and spread out the letter before him. It read:

> Dear Father!
> We are writing to tell you that we have safely crossed the border and are progressing toward Switzerland. If we stop somewhere on the way, we will write you with all of the details.
>
> Your dear children,
> Anna and Leon

"The letter has no date nor any notice of where it was written," thought Spitzkopf to himself. "Rather strange."

"Tell me this, Herr Rosenbaum," he said. "Do you recognize the handwriting as your children's?"

"Oh, of a certainty! No doubt at all in my mind. But what are you asking me such a thing for? What are you hinting at? In any case, I must be off right away. The train leaves in three quarters of an hour. I don't want to be late."

And with those words he attempted to remove the letter from Spitzkopf's grip.

"But it seems to me, Herr Rosenbaum," Spitzkopf said very softly, "that you've made a mistake. Your children did not write this letter."

"What are you saying?" the man screamed with terror in his voice. "How could you possibly know that?"

"From the signatures," Spitzkopf answered. "I don't know your children's handwriting, so I couldn't say whether the body of the letter is genuine or not. But the signatures are certainly not. Too formal and stilted, by far.

"The fact that the letter is undated, and the place of writing unspecified, and there's not even a stamp on the envelope telling us its point of origin and it having instead been thrown into a train car—it's all suspect. What it tells me is that your children are likely in great danger."

"Great God!" cried Rosenbaum in despair. "What are you saying? Have mercy. Please, tell me what you're thinking."

"I am thinking many things," Spitzkopf told him. "I cannot tell you clearly how matters stand now. One thing I do know: your children are still living. And we have a hope of saving them. We must not tarry for one minute, however. We must depart at once. But we must also be careful. It is imperative that we not travel side by side. And by no means should you reveal to anyone en route that you saw me or that I am accompanying you on the journey.

"Set off for the station immediately and purchase a ticket to the border. I will leave separately. I also intend to so alter my appearance that you won't be able to recognize me. En route I will make it known to you where we should de-board. And what we are going to do after that."

Rosenbaum stood there motionless. How he had rejoiced upon discovering that all of his fears had amounted to nothing, that his children had safely crossed. And now all of a sudden—those same terrible fears came rushing back, just as before.

Somehow he found himself being dragged down the stairs, as if not by his own two feet, and his body making its way to the hotel, where he quickly paid his bill and ordered that his things be brought to the train station.

He presently set off for the same destination in a hired carriage.

CHAPTER THREE

Followed En Route

Heinrich Rosenbaum arrived at the platform for the northbound train just minutes before it was scheduled to depart. He quickly purchased a first-class ticket and climbed aboard.

He did not see Spitzkopf, nor had he really any time to look for him. The train began moving and Rosenbaum seated himself in a corner, lost in his own thoughts.

The train made few stops. And where it did stop, it did so for barely two minutes. At the first large station it came to, in the Czech town of Prerov, it remained for ten minutes. Most of the passengers got out to walk around a little.

Rosenbaum did too and paced about the platform. Eventually he made his way back to the train, entered the buffet car, and ordered a glass of beer.

"Don't drink so fast, *mein Herr*," he heard a strange voice say. "You're perspiring and could catch a cold."

Rosenbaum glanced around. There appeared beside him a distinguished-looking man, finely attired. It was he who had called out to him. Rosenbaum bowed his head politely and answered: "I thank you most kindly, *mein Herr*. But I am well used to these things, and a bit of lager isn't likely to do me any harm."

Most of the travelers were now approaching the refreshment counter to order lunch, but not Rosenbaum. He had only agita now, not appetite. Proceeding to his own railcar, he absentmindedly took a seat by the window and gazed out.

"And you're not eating a thing," said the same voice again. Rosenbaum looked around and saw that the same man who had spoken to him in the buffet car was now sitting directly in front of him.

"Oh, I suppose not," said Rosenbaum. "I don't care to eat when it's so hot out."

"Probably you don't have far to travel, and you're waiting to eat until you arrive at home?" the man questioned him further.

"Au contraire," Rosenbaum answered. "I'm going all the way to Warsaw."

"Aha, so you're a Warsovian," said the man. "Then it would appear we are neighbors. I am Ludwig Bittner, from Łódź."

"Very pleased to meet you," said Rosenbaum, introducing himself.

"Ah, your name is familiar to me," said the man. "I worked

for several years as a manager in a factory in your sector of the industry. We were in contact with your own company not infrequently."

And so the man began a conversation with Rosenbaum, first about political and social matters in Russian-controlled Poland. Eventually they came to discussing their families. Rosenbaum told him of the misfortune that had recently come upon his, how his children had vanished and how all his efforts to find traces of them had turned up nothing.

"And was it this that brought you to Vienna?" the man asked him.

Rosenbaum was on the point of blurting out yes, as he felt like unburdening his heart to the man, but he soon remembered what Spitzkopf had advised him: that he should by no means tell anyone why he had traveled to Vienna, or that the great detective was now traveling with him. And so he decided not to answer the last question truthfully.

"No! I am on a business trip . . . I wish to sell my factory and settle abroad . . . so I wanted to get to know the situation in Austria, thinking that maybe I'd stay there."

At that moment the conductor entered and checked their tickets. Their conversation was interrupted. Rosenbaum felt a woman sitting beside him now pushing a note into his hand.

He left the car and stepped out onto the platform. There he unfolded the note and read: "Be careful. Stop speaking to that stranger."

Rosenbaum was stunned. He had no idea who the woman might be. He remained a moment outside, then returned to his seat beside the window. But he struck up a conversation with other passengers so that the man would no longer bother him.

CHAPTER FOUR
Buyer and Cellar

In a deep and dark cellar, lying with their hands and feet bound, are the two Rosenbaum children.

A masked man stands beside them, a long whip in his hand. His eyes are flashing with delirious rage, his teeth gnashing.

"You made up yer minds yet to write that letter I want?"

"No!" the captives cried. "We won't do it. We won't have our dear father pay any exorbitant ransom. How can we be sure that we'll be freed even if you receive the money? You could just ask for even more money and go on holding us prisoner.

"If you really want to receive the highest possible sum from our father, you will take us over the border. He would surely give it to you then. Whereas if you continue down the path you're treading now, you can be assured of not receiving a kopeck. But we give you our word of honor that if you let us go free, you will receive fifty thousand rubles before three days have passed. We swear to you that no person on earth then will know what you did to us."

"Ha!" the masked man guffawed. "I should setcha free, eh? What, so ya can set the cops on my tail? You really think I'm such an imbecile? For that alone you deserve one or two healthy smacks."

And he brought the whip down on them mercilessly. The brother and sister let out piercing cries.

"Oh, just go on screamin', ya damned stubborn asses," he bellowed, spitting with scorn. "No one's gonna hear ya from down here. Ya don't know yer ten meters underground? There's only one way yer gettin' outta here, and that's if ya write the letter I want."

"No!" they repeated. "Do what you will. We'll never write your letter. Your threats don't scare us in the slightest. Beat us as much as you like. We know you won't make good on your threat to kill us. We're no use to you dead."

"Good!" he replied. "I'll letcha live! And I'll burn out yer eyes in the meantime. Slice off yer hands and feet. Rip out yer tongues. There's the prize yer pigheadedness will getcha."

And again he lashed them monstrously across their faces, then across their arms and legs.

And again they cried, heartrending cries. But not a living soul heard them.

This same scene played out over and over for ten days straight.

When Rosenbaum had arrived with his children at Niedzwiedz, a Polish village on the Russian side of the border, and inquired about a smuggler who could lead his children over the border, he was very ill met. He had stopped over at a diminutive inn whose owner happened to belong to a band of smugglers. Whenever these men found that a fat cat had landed in their paws and sought their help, they would instantly begin to scheme, ensuring that when he eventually crossed the border, he did so with his pockets well emptied.

On the other hand, if they sniffed out that the individual was wealthy or belonged to a wealthy family but happened to be traveling without cash, they would lead the person into a dark chamber and confine them there so long, and deal out such savage beatings, that the person would be compelled to write home or to their relatives telling them to deposit a certain sum, as much as the criminals asked for, in such and such a location.

They would threaten their captive with death if their family dared to inform the police with the intention of apprehending the gang member who came to collect the ransom.

Such was the basic scheme of their criminal handiwork, which they carried on for years, always successfully. It was into this gang's net that Rosenbaum had fallen.

He promised that if his children were brought safely over the border he would lavishly compensate the smugglers, so they understood that it was quite a pretty little fish they had caught.

They also questioned the children and found out from them too that their father was a man of serious net worth.

And so, in the dead of night, just when the border crossing was to have taken place, they instead led Rosenbaum's children into the cellar and ordered them to write a letter to their father telling him to send along a hundred thousand rubles to grant them their freedom.

It is easy to understand, then, the terrible fear and agony of the youngsters. They fainted, wept, wailed, and begged for mercy, begged to just be freed, and swore that if they were, swore by all that is holy, that as soon as they were released the gang would receive a hefty reward.

The thugs would hear nothing of it. They daily afflicted the children with the most horrific tortures and beat them nearly to death, all in order to persuade them to write the desired letter.

But these children were tough as nails. It was not that the sum was of any great concern. They knew very well that their father would be only too eager to pay it. What they feared was that as soon as the gang received it the criminals would immediately kill them so they could never reveal what had happened.

And thus their torments grinded on for ten excruciating days.

The criminals had never before been met with such stubbornness, so eventually they hit upon a different scheme. Among the captives' luggage the men had found a few notebooks containing the children's handwriting. They handed over the notebooks to an associate of theirs, a man frightfully skilled in forgery. It was he who fabricated the letter that Rosenbaum later presented to Spitzkopf in Vienna.

If Rosenbaum had received the letter within two or three days he would have had no cause to be suspicious of it, and the gang would then have been able to fabricate a second letter intimating that the children had fallen into the hands of bandits and would need to be ransomed.

Such was their plan. But they got to it too late. Having not heard from his children for ten days, Rosenbaum had grown increasingly panicked and left no stone unturned in pursuit of their whereabouts. When the forged letter had arrived to his home in Warsaw, Rosenbaum was out conducting his search, so it was forwarded on to him.

Meanwhile, the gang had learned that Rosenbaum was out looking for his children, seeking out every possible means to find them, and they decided to have him watched in order to make sure he would not discover their tracks.

A man followed Rosenbaum to Vienna, staying close on his heels, and observed him heading to visit Max Spitzkopf. By no means could the gang allow Spitzkopf to be hired on to the case. His legendary name was well known to these men. They were aware that there would be no kidding around once Spitzkopf got involved.

So the lookout was surprised to find that Rosenbaum was returning on the train alone, sans Spitzkopf. He struck up a conversation with the manufacturer in order to find out if the detective had taken the case on and, if so, when he would be arriving at the border.

But Spitzkopf *was*, of course, on the train, just not as himself but rather as a woman. And such a nicely put together one too that no person would be able to recognize that the fine lady was in fact a gentleman in disguise.

The detective sat himself near Rosenbaum and monitored him closely the whole trip, making sure he would not utter a word to anyone regarding Spitzkopf and thereby blow his cover. When he observed the manufacturer on the very point of doing so, he slipped him the aforementioned note—and so managed to stop him before it was too late.

CHAPTER FIVE
Off the Rails

THE EXPRESS TRAIN in which Spitzkopf and Heinrich Rosenbaum were traveling arrived around one in the afternoon at the station of the Polish town known as Oświęcim, or, in German, Auschwitz.[4]

For the remainder of the journey Rosenbaum had not spoken a word to the strange man who had engaged him earlier.

He guessed that the woman sitting so close beside him must be Spitzkopf and secretly wondered at the detective's skill in so masterfully passing himself off as a woman.

"I see now," Rosenbaum thought to himself, "that I can really count on this fellow. If he knows how to disguise himself so convincingly, and could recognize at once that the strange man was not to be trusted, that he must be one of the thugs who have their hands on my children, he'll certainly be able to sniff out the kidnappers' tracks."

Spitzkopf, meanwhile, did not let his eye wander from the stranger for one instant during the entirety of the trip—but so inconspicuously that the man never guessed that he was being watched.

From the first minute that Rosenbaum had told him what he knew, Spitzkopf could imagine all that had taken place. And when Rosenbaum brought over the letter, which Spitzkopf had immediately recognized as a forgery, his suspicions were confirmed, and likewise his hope that he might eventually track down the culprits.

He was also sure that one of the gang members must be following Rosenbaum and therefore disguised himself so that none could recognize him.

Indeed, up until arriving at the station at Prerov, the strange man had not an inkling as to who his womanly neighbor might be. Only when Rosenbaum was handed the note and exited the train did the man start to become suspicious that Spitzkopf must be nearby but in disguise.

And so he lumbered through all the train cars, giving each and every passenger a good once-over—but didn't recognize the detective in any one of them.

"Cunning as a fox, that Spitzkopf," he thought. "Did himself up so nicely that the devil himself wouldn't know who he was. But the devil take me if the great detective doesn't soon find out that our gang ain't to be played with."

The express train stopped at Auschwitz for a few minutes, and the man climbed out and went into the station. But then Spitzkopf, observing him from the window of the railcar, saw him turn about and start walking back toward the train. Something seemed fishy. He would have to watch the man closely. But he could no longer see him.

"He must have entered a car where an associate of his is sitting," the detective guessed.

The train began moving again. Spitzkopf started to pace down the aisle with the intention of entering different carriages once the train arrived at the next station and finding where the man now sat. Naturally, he had no idea that the man had realized Spitzkopf must be on the train.

The train had only been chugging for a few minutes when an awful boom resounded through all the cars. Spitzkopf's had been dealt a monstrous wallop while the other cars had piled atop it. A shocking accident had taken place.

The locomotive at the front, the postal car, and the first two passenger cars had remained whole. But all of the other cars, which had been in back of the battered car, were damaged beyond repair.

All things considered, however, the result of the disaster could have been worse. No one was killed, though several passengers were badly wounded. Others had sustained more minor injuries. Among the badly injured was Rosenbaum. Spitzkopf had received only a grazing blow.

A rescue train was soon dispatched and came bearing doctors, wound-dressing materials, and other first aid supplies.

The severely injured were brought to a hospital car, and after the doctors completed provisional wound dressings, the car was to be transported back to the station in Auschwitz.

The wounds of the more lightly injured were also attended to. Some of these passengers desired to be brought back to Auschwitz, while others who urgently needed to continue onward decided that they would do so as soon as the train's undamaged cars could be assembled and prepared for travel.

Spitzkopf had been only lightly maimed on his left hand. A doctor wrapped it, and the detective began to wander around the scene of the accident with the air of an unaffected spectator.

A police commission had also arrived with the rescue train, there to investigate what had caused the crash. The officers closely inspected the rails, the wheels, and the track but found no sign of damage that could have caused such a catastrophe.

Spitzkopf stood near them, still posturing as a curious bystander. He too searched over everything with his trained and sharp eye. Then he jumped back in surprise.

"What kind of dirty work has been done here?" his mind stormed. "Just look at that, under the running board—someone's placed dynamite so the whole car would be blasted to smithereens! I can plainly see the scorch marks left on the shattered board!

"Luckily it seems someone washed off the running board before the train departed. The dynamite was dampened and didn't go off with its full force.

"I have no doubt the man who placed it is the one who has been following us all the way from Vienna. He must have recognized me and, upon realizing that he couldn't easily rid himself of me, latched on to the most horrible means of doing so. Hundreds of lives could be ruined, fine, as long as he and his fellow thugs remain free from my meddling.

"Never have I seen such villainy! I must hunt down that gang and turn the whole lot in to the criminal courts. But if I have this one scoundrel arrested now, the rest of them will know it, get extra cautious, and make sure they can't be found.

"Besides, I have no direct proof implicating the man. Nothing can be hung on my bare conjectures, and nothing would happen to him. So I'll have to hold my tongue. But I won't let the little birdie out of my sights. My injury couldn't be more trivial. I can certainly continue onward. Meanwhile, Rosenbaum's badly hurt. He'll have to stay in the hospital for the time being. I don't need to look after him. I can keep going."

It was about two hours before the tracks were cleared again. A new train was put together, and it soon set off in the direction of the Russian border.

Meanwhile, Spitzkopf proved unable to stay hot on the trail of his suspect. He could not find the man again.

"The bird's flown," he sighed. "Maybe he fled the scene and escaped to the Prussian border, or maybe he hid somewhere while I was busy investigating the accident. In any case, I mustn't lose a second. I'll head straight over the Russian border and carry on. My first stop will be Niedzwiedz. I should be able to find some breadcrumbs to follow from there."

CHAPTER SIX
Danger Amid Darkness

AROUND EVENING the train clattered into Niedzwiedz. When it arrived at the border, Spitzkopf took the opportunity to quickly change, stuffing the women's clothing into his valise. He asked around after the Hotel Grigoriy, but no one at the train station could give him any information about such a place.

"There's only one guesthouse here in Niedzwiedz," he was told, "and the proprietor's name isn't Grigoriy. He's called Jan Ostrowski, and his inn is called Ostrowski's."

Spitzkopf took his valise in hand and walked into town. Darkness had already fallen when he turned into a small lane and was confronted by a man walking toward him. The man asked, "Would sir happen to be looking for a hotel to spend the night?"

"Why, yes," answered Spitzkopf.

"Come with me then," said the man, and Spitzkopf followed him. At the end of the lane stood a large, low building with a wide gate at the entrance. The man led Spitzkopf through it, opened the door, and told him to enter. "This is the spot," he said. "Now gimme something for bringing you to it."

Spitzkopf handed him a few kopecks and the man disappeared.

Meanwhile the proprietor had entered from the next room. He was a short, round fellow with disheveled hair and a face red from too much drink.

"Good evening, sir!" he said with a cordial smile, which somehow made his face look even uglier than before. "Does sir desire his own room or just a bed in the large dormitory?"

"My own room," Spitzkopf answered. "And I would like to be able to lie down at once. I am very tired."

"Very good! Come with me."

He opened a small, low door and led Spitzkopf up a few narrow steps into a kind of attic, surrounded by more doors, each with a number hung on it. The proprietor opened door number 4 and motioned for Spitzkopf to enter.

It was a small and crowded room with a tiny window looking out onto the yard. The proprietor lit a tallow candle, made up the little cot, and said, "Well, here you are. You can get right to sleep."

With those words, he left. Spitzkopf noticed him suppressing a chortle as he made his way out.

As soon as he had gone, Spitzkopf quietly locked the door behind the man, snuffed out the candle, and sat down on the cot. His keen ear told him that the man had not yet descended the steps but rather remained standing just outside the door. Spitzkopf remained sitting quietly for a few minutes.

Meanwhile the innkeeper was listening too. As he didn't hear even the slightest rustling, he reasoned that his guest had indeed lain down immediately and so proceeded to galumph down the stairs.

At that point Spitzkopf rose from the bed, walked to the window, and surveyed the yard. As it was a fairly large expanse, he could not discern the enclosing fence through the darkness. A few sheds stood at one end and at the other was a sizable heap, most likely of garbage or stones. He could not quite make it out. He stood watch at the window for a number of hours, not letting his eye wander for a moment.

At around eleven he spotted a shadow hurrying across the yard. It was soon followed by a second shadow, a third, then several others. They vanished into one end of the yard, the end Spitzkopf's eye could not reach. But he was afraid to illumine the darkness with his electric torch lest anyone should notice his vigil. So he squinted up his eyes and peered out as best he could, but it was no use.

He stood there, undecided. Suddenly he heard someone climbing the steps outside his door. He readied his revolver for shooting, seized his bull's-eye lantern, and stationed himself in a corner of the room, squeezing himself in beside the cot so that he had cover on all sides.

Then he heard someone start to push a key into the lock. He dashed over and inserted his own key from inside such that the other key could not enter so easily from without. The man in the hall, meanwhile, fumbled a while with the lock until eventually Spitzkopf's key fell out and the intruder's key went in.

The door opened. Spitzkopf could see two figures entering in the darkness. One of them crept quietly, catlike, to the bed and, his eyes flashing, searched out the sleeping man. When he realized the bed was empty he rose up irresolutely, waving over the other man to join him and help decide on a course of action.

Spitzkopf knew that the critical moment had come. He had not a second to lose. He did not want to shoot and risk waking up the whole house. So he maneuvered quietly to the bed and dealt the first man such a resounding blow on the head with the butt of his revolver that he immediately dropped unconscious to the floor.

The other man approached. Spitzkopf struck him too, and let him have it good. The man slumped at once onto his fellow.

It all happened in a matter of seconds. He then pulled his iron shackles from his pockets and chained the two men together so tightly they could not move an inch. Then he stopped up their mouths with cloth and stowed them under the bed.

All was quiet again. Spitzkopf crept to the door and pressed his ear to it, listening for anyone standing outside. He did not hear a sound. These people must have not expected resistance and so had not considered it necessary to provide themselves with any backup.

Spitzkopf remained standing a few minutes, considering what to do next. Then he flung open the window and climbed down the wall into the yard.

It was pitch dark now, and no one would be able to see him. He quietly darted around the whole of the yard, trying to find any tracks left by the shadowy figures he had seen crossing earlier. But he could see nothing in the darkness. About a hundred paces away from the inn he came to a high fence.

"Either the gang has some secret hiding place here in the yard," he thought to himself, "or they climbed over the fence. But I can find nothing here at this time of night, and it's dangerous to keep looking. The gang could surround me at any moment, and I wouldn't be able to defend myself. Climbing the fence is the only way out. At least on the other side I won't be subject to a surprise attack coming at me from every direction."

And so he bounded over the enclosure. And found himself in an open field.

CHAPTER SEVEN

The Smugglers' Gang

THE GANG KEPT itself busy with a number of pursuits, though its main beat was smuggling. But the smugglers didn't just hustle their customers over the border—they stole everything they had on them too, shaking them down until they had not a single kopeck left in their pockets. They also smuggled merchandise across the border, often keeping it for themselves.

And where did they hide all of their misbegotten loot? They had their own special cellar, dug deep into the ground, that they could enter through a covert hole in the middle of the forest outside Niedzwiedz.

From time to time they also perpetrated fairly ambitious robberies in that shtetl and its environs, stashing away in the cellar the takings from those missions too.

The top dollars, though, came from kidnapping and confining the rich people that needed smuggling. When those kinds of fat fish wriggled into their net, they could get an impressive payday out of squeezing them or their family for all they were worth.

The guesthouse sometimes known as the Hotel Grigoriy served as their headquarters. The proprietor was himself a member of the gang, and he lent it the place to use as the nest for whatever unsuspecting quarry one of the associates managed to drag in from off the street.

It was now midnight. The gang was holding a secret meeting in their cellar hideout. These villains' spies had informed them that the manufacturer Rosenbaum, whose children were currently in their clutches, was turning the world upside down to retrieve his son and daughter. So they had him watched by one of their number. When the gang learned that Rosenbaum was headed to Vienna, the spy had gone along too.

In the city he had seen Rosenbaum stopping over at the residence of the famous Spitzkopf, whose name was well known to everyone in the gang. The spy knew that with him involved, it would have to be a fight to the death.

On the train journey to Poland, the spy had tried to tease a few pieces of information out of Rosenbaum: whether or not Spitzkopf was accompanying him and when and where he planned to get off. But the attempt was unsuccessful. The spy realized Spitzkopf must be on the train after all and must have warned Rosenbaum not to spill the beans.

He had to hinder the detective from hitting upon the right track. So he strapped dynamite to the bottom of a train car while he himself skipped off to one of the front cars, which he knew the explosion would not impact.

After his little masterpiece went off (and how!), he took the next train over the border to Prussia, passed through the towns of Myslowice and Sosnowiec—which contained the famous tripoint between the three great empires, Russian, German, and Austrian—and arrived in Niedzwiedz.

Once he made his way back to his associates, he told them everything that had happened. He did not know whether Spitzkopf was wounded or not; he had not been able to recognize him. He had seen, though, that Rosenbaum had been hurt very badly and so figured that Spitzkopf had not made it out so hot either. After all, nearly all the passengers in the detective's car were injured from the blast.

In any case, it seemed to him that his handiwork had been successful, and the gang would have nothing to fear, as he now told them there in the underground lair. Rosenbaum would take quite a while to recover in the hospital, and while he rested they would all perhaps have the time required to finally wangle that letter out of his measly kids. And Rosenbaum would, a million times over, rather pay out than put his children in harm's way.

Such was the spy's report, and all the gang was satisfied with it. Well, perhaps not all. One of them soon piped up, "You didn't do right to cheese it and leave Spitzkopf alone. He and his buddies are a dangerous crew. Whether he's hurt bad or only grazed, we can't get rid of him so easy as that. Who knows? That bloodhound could be on our trail this very moment.

"You really mucked it up, that's what I think. We'll have to get going, and quick, and force those bull-headed little brats to write us that damn letter. Couldn't we try any tactics with them that might be a bit, well, sharper?"

"I've already been givin' 'em the whip for several days now!" the man assigned to torture the children answered. "But it's no use. Threatened 'em with a lot worse too. But there's no scarin' 'em.

"They tell me they're convinced that even if we get the money there's no chance we'd let 'em go alive on account of we'd be afraid that they'd betray us. That's why they're so bloody stubborn about it."

"We don't have all this time to lose!" another cried out. "If we keep waiting and waiting that Spitzkopf will up and surprise us. Lemme tell you something: If the whip won't work, then we've gotta give 'em a flash o' the ole branding iron."

"And let me tell *you* something," said the torturer. "These two are such mulish little brats that there's no threat evil enough to change their minds. If we give 'em anything worse than we've been givin' 'em already, it will only be worse for us. Say we end up stamping out the little scamps out of frustration. We'll have lost our one bargaining chip.

"Anyhow, we're not murderers. We just want a bit of cash. Sure, we ain't afraid of a few drops of blood. But only when it can get us the gelt."

"There's nothing else to do," remarked yet another member, "but try out the new method we used on that university student Grinberg not long ago. We write, plain and simple, to Rosenbaum, telling him that we've gotten ahold of his kids and we've got clear evidence that they've allied themselves with the anti-government revolutionaries. If he doesn't want us turning them over to the Okhrana, the tsar's secret police, in whose hands death would await them willy-nilly, he must send us the exact sum that we demand.

"When we wrote that very letter about the Grinberg kid, we got ten thousand rubles out of it. This time we'll get a hundred thousand."

"Bravo!" his fellows cheered. "It's the best way out. The simplest too. Let's do it."

"But first let me talk to 'em one more time," said the torture master. "Maybe they'll write the letter after all. A letter from them could wrap this up a lot speedier than the Okhrana business.

"Grinberg was politically suspicious to begin with, not as kosher as these two. His family was ready to do what we said immediately if it meant protecting him from the Okhrana.

"But we're talkin' about two young kids now, and that factory owner Rosenbaum is rich as Midas, with all the power and pull that comes along with it. Could be he's not as afraid of the Okhrana as ya think. And anyway, as we've heard, he's already asked the Okhrana whether they'd arrested his kids. It doesn't really seem he's so scared of 'em after all."

"As you say, then!" the others agreed. "Let's pay the boy and girl a visit together and see if we can't knock some sense into the little bastards.

"But if it doesn't work, we'll have to try the Grinberg trick."

CHAPTER EIGHT

Betrayed

THE GANG'S BOSS took a massive key out of his pocket and opened a solid, heavy door that stood in a corner of the cellar. From there, around twenty steps led down to another cellar room below.

Down the associates trudged and found the Rosenbaum children there, sleeping on sacks filled with rotted hay. The poor souls were so exhausted, so thoroughly depleted, that the soundness of their sleep prevented their being awoken by the heavy tread of the gang members descending the stairs.

A few of the gang forced the children awake by shining lanterns in their faces. They opened their eyes and searched the room with growing panic. The sudden appearance of so many strangers startled them and filled them with fear.

But before anyone in the gang was able to get out a single word, they all heard the swift patter of two feet descending the stairs. The door opened. In ran a man with a wild appearance and disheveled hair. He exploded in a shout: "Come quickly to the Grigoriy! Something's gone wrong there."

The gang members asked no questions and bounded back up the stairs. The young Rosenbaums remained in the dark below, unable to contain their dread and despair, unaware of anything that had happened—just as they were unaware of the fact that they were not going to suffer for much longer and that help was on the way.

The gangsters, meanwhile, huffed and puffed all the way to the Hotel Grigoriy. The man who had brought them the news led them directly to the room where Spitzkopf had been staying.

There they saw the innkeeper, Grigoriy, and his lackey Ivan lying bound together with long chains wrapped so tightly that they were cutting into the men's flesh, turning it black and blue from the pressure. The chains were not tied together but rather secured with a padlock, so it was impossible to undo them. The gangsters were forced to saw at the chains with a file.

Once that was accomplished, the two manacle-mates began to breathe freely again. With great effort they rose to their feet, and Grigoriy gave his report of all that had taken place. "Earlier this evening," he explained, "my agent, Maksim, brought me a guest who needed lodgings for the night. He didn't look as if he needed to cross the border, so I didn't see the need to tell you about him.

"He did look like he had a fair bit of coin on him, though. So I thought I'd have a go at lightening his load.

"At around midnight, we sneak into his room, Ivan and I do, and just as soon as I get to the bed I see our honored guest isn't in it. So I wave to Ivan, telling him to come over, but before he does I get such a blow over the head that I start to see stars and fall into a complete daze.

"Meanwhile Ivan comes to the bed and is treated to the same welcome, right over the noggin. How long we lay there unconscious neither of us knows. But Maksim was waiting for us below, and seeing that it had been quite a few minutes, he comes up to see what was taking so long.

"It was dark in the room and he couldn't see anyone. So he lit his lantern and looked around till he found us under the bed, chained together and barely alive.

"Then he dragged us out, splashed water on our faces, and managed to rouse us. But he couldn't undo the chains, and he saw that they were cutting into our skin something awful. That spooked him, so he ran to call all of you to the scene."

The gang listened to Grigoriy's story in amazement. It was all a complete riddle to them. But the gang's boss, that masked man whom we espied earlier in the cellar with the Rosenbaums, trying to whip them into line, interjected. "Grigoriy! You've acted like a complete imbecile. You tried to do a bit of business entirely without us. And now you've gone and blown our cover.

"The story, as you've told it to us, makes it plain that this fellow, who sought lodgings with you, was no ordinary traveler but rather a spy. On a mission.

"It's clear that he anticipated an ambush from you and stood ready for it, ready to neutralize whomever came to attack him. And he had those chains ready for you. Those are the type used exclusively by undercover policemen . . . or private detectives.

"We can also assume that your guest did not leave through the door but rather the window. He must have understood that others were standing watch below, so he would have chosen to climb down the outer wall, right down into the yard. At which point he would have then shinnied over the fence to reach the open field.

"You've really got us in the royal jelly this time, Grigoriy. That bloodhound will know now that the kennel he thought he could catch a coupla winks in tonight wasn't exactly doggie heaven. The police could turn up here any minute and send us packing.

"We can't stay. We have to go back to our cellar and keep talking things over there. But we have to cross very carefully, one at a time, so no one notices us. Could be they're already having the hotel watched."

The gang listened to his words with extreme trepidation. To utter even a word in response was unthinkable. One by one the associates left the building, climbed over the fence, and entered the field and forest beyond. There, groups of two or three of their fellows were waiting, on every side, watching for any interloper who dared approach.

CHAPTER NINE

Busted

SOON THE WHOLE was gang was assembled in the hideaway.

Their lanterns lit, the men sat down to discuss a plan of action. The cellar was silent as death. The gang was waiting for its boss to begin speaking. Grigoriy sat like a defendant in a courtroom. He knew that a very dark sentencing awaited him.

Suddenly the silence was broken by an unfamiliar noise. It seemed to the gang that it came from the second cellar room below, where the young Rosenbaums were being held.

The boss sprang up and bounded to the cell door. He jammed in the key and jiggled it, but it would not budge.

When he tried to bust through with a push, however, the door easily gave way. It seemed that it had not been locked after all. The men thought that perhaps in their rush to leave earlier they had forgotten to lock it.

Now the boss and two of his men went down the stairs. They returned in a matter of moments, shock and fear etched in their faces. The lower cellar was empty. And not a trace could be seen of the two hostages.

The associates looked as if they had been turned to stone. During the very brief period in which they had been at the inn, something untoward had clearly taken place.

A wild clamor arose among them. “We’ve been betrayed! We have to run!”

“Yes!” the boss called out. “We have to get away. Don your masks, all of you, and let’s dash in every direction so no one can track us.

“But first things first—we have to take our revenge on the traitor who brought this whole disaster on our heads. Our Grigoriy has let us all down. He tried to keep something from us and ended up betraying us.”

“Death to the traitor!” all the men cried. The boss, who had meanwhile slid his mask over his face, seized Grigoriy by the hand and dragged him into the middle of the cellar.

Grigoriy trembled like a fish out of water. He knew that this gang would not grant him a long trial. And then . . .

Spitzkopf arrived, bolting down the cellar steps. With his revolver in hand he barked out, “Halt, scoundrels! That man did not betray you. You betrayed yourselves."

The men's heads whirled around. They were terrified. They wanted to fling themselves upon the detective, but he stopped them dead in their tracks with these words: "Hands up! Whoever makes a move gets shot."

None of them dared. They put their paws in the air and waited. Then Spitzkopf whistled, and a whole troop of gendarmes and police officers spilled into the cellar. The criminals were cuffed, then hauled out of the cellar and off to jail.

Spitzkopf, however, booked it to the police station, where the two young Rosenbaums were being kept.

Earlier, after Spitzkopf had quit the inn, crossed the yard, and entered the open fields beyond, he had spotted from afar a man scurrying across the landscape.

It was Maksim, the innkeeper's agent, running to tell the gang what had happened to Grigoriy. Spitzkopf followed him from a comfortable distance until they reached the forest, where the detective saw Maksim climbing into a concealed pit dug in the ground. He hid himself behind a broad-trunked tree and watched to see what would transpire.

Soon there appeared the whole gang, crawling out of the same hole and running in the direction from which Maksim and Spitzkopf had come: back to the hotel.

Spitzkopf suspected that this must be the gang he was hunting. But he did not think about it for long. The men had only gotten about a hundred paces away when Spitzkopf sprang to the pit and let himself down into the cellar. Lighting the interior with his electric torch, he saw the second door, which he opened with his skeleton key. He descended.

There he found what he was ultimately searching for. The young Rosenbaums were lying bound, wounded and bloody. He did not delay. He did not answer their stunned questions. He simply tossed them over his shoulders, sped up out of the cellar, and ran with all his energy into the shtetl.

Finding the night watchman, he asked him as to the whereabouts of the police. Upon entering the station, he identified himself and asked for a few of their number to assist him in apprehending the criminals.

He left the Rosenbaums back at the station, where a doctor tended to them. Both were running a very high fever. The doctor explained that they would need to recuperate in bed for several days before they were entirely themselves again.

Spitzkopf and the police officers dashed into the forest, meanwhile, snuck up on the gang, and arrested them all.

Later that same day, the manufacturer Rosenbaum was informed by telegram that his children had been saved, and although his injuries from the train bombing were quite severe, he left the next day for Niedzwiedz.

Naturally, he compensated Spitzkopf with a prodigious reward and thanked him heartily for his most dedicated—and successful—labors.

THE SMUGGLERS received a fitting sentence. Most of them were given ten to fifteen years in Siberia and were sent east without delay.

Spitzkopf, meanwhile, headed west, and the day after his reunion with the manufacturer he took the train back to his hometown of Vienna. No dynamite lay in wait for him this time.

Issue 6: The Forged Will

זעכסטעס העפט. פרייז 20 העלער.

דאָס געפעלשטע טעסטאַמענט.

זעהט אירר, געעהרטע ריכטער! — זאָגט פוקס — עס איז אמת, אז מין טעסטאַמענט איז פאַלש... אָבער דאָס טעסטאַמענט, וואָס מען האָט געפונען אין דער קאַסע ביי דר. פאָליצער, איז אויך פאַלש!

The Forged Will

CHAPTER ONE

Murder Most Gruesome

THE RENOWNED DETECTIVE Max Spitzkopf has come home after a long journey abroad, where he cracked a most critical case. He is exhausted. He kicks off his shoes and lays himself down for a good long snooze.

But as soon as he falls asleep, he is awoken by the telephone's cacophonous ringing.

He jumps out of bed, runs to the confounded machine, and shouts into it, "Hello! Max Spitzkopf speaking! Who's there?"

"A criminal most vile!" answered a voice in great distress. "Who has committed a vile crime! Come quickly, Herr Spitzkopf, and save us!"

"Where are you, and who is speaking?" Spitzkopf inquired.

"*Oy gevalt!* Don't ask so many questions! Just come, right away!" the voice rang out in a bloodcurdling scream. "He is killing us!"

"But for the sake of heaven!" Spitzkopf cried out in return, his own voice growing in desperation. "At least tell me where you are! Or your telephone number! I don't know where to go!"

"*Gevalt!* Help! Anybody! Save us!" These were the last words he heard emitting from the telephone.

The detective stood there as though his feet were stuck in red-hot coals. Something horrific was clearly underway, and he could do nothing to help.

Through the telephone's speaker he heard more wild, clamorous cries. He was able to distinguish both a woman's voice and the wails of a child. And then—a bang, like a gunshot. A heartrending scream followed it.

But then the screams grew fainter and fainter until all Spitzkopf could make out was a soft, sorrowful moan. And then . . . utter silence.

Spitzkopf felt for a moment like he had lost his senses. He had never been in such a situation before. But soon he dialed a number and was quickly connected with the central telephone exchange.

"This is the central office. Who's speaking?" asked the woman operating the switchboard.

"This is the detective agency of Spitzkopf. Please be so good as to tell me what number rang me just a few minutes ago."

After a few seconds the operator responded. "You were connected to number 1730."

"Very good, *danke sehr*." Having thanked her, Spitzkopf took out his address book and began to flick through its pages.

He soon found the name beside #1730: "Leon Politzer, Doctor of Medicine. Döblinger Strasse 169."

He threw his clothes back on and flew down the stairs of his apartment building.

It was already past midnight, and dreadful outside. The heavens were veiled with black storm clouds, and tubfuls of rain were coming down. Spitzkopf ran in the downpour for some thirty steps until he came upon a hansom cab. He launched himself in, thundering, "Döblinger Strasse 169! But take it at a gallop!"

The journey took about half an hour, enough time for Spitzkopf to be able to calm down and regain his usual composure. He leaped out of the hansom and paid the coachman. After the man drove away, Spitzkopf took a moment to examine the exterior of No. 169.

It was a small villa with a flower garden out front and a large backyard. The front gate was locked. It seemed perfectly quiet inside. All the curtains were drawn closed over the windows, through which no trace of light could be perceived.

Spitzkopf circled the perimeter, closely considering the environs and the surrounding homes. Then he jumped a fence and made his way up to the front door. It was locked, but he quickly sorted that out with the aid of his trusty skeleton key and entered.

Now in the front hall, he switched on his electric torch and soon found another door, which he duly entered.

He strode through a number of elegantly appointed rooms, but there was not a soul to be seen nor any sign of recent suspicious activity.

But when he stepped into a large bedroom, he encountered a most horrific sight.

In one bed, an older man was lying with his throat sliced open. He was bathed in his own blood . . .

The sheets on the other large bed, along with those upon a little child's bed, were tossed about in every direction. The door to the adjoining room stood open.

In that room, an even more terrible picture met Spitzkopf's eyes.

Lying prone on the floor beside the telephone was an older woman, her breast pierced with bullets and her throat likewise cut . . . Beside her, a river of blood.

In a corner, next to a desk, was the body of a child. A girl no more than ten years old, her throat slashed. Blood pooled around her on every side.

In the middle of the room, a maid, wearing only her nightgown, her head smashed in and her throat slashed.

Spitzkopf was a man who was accustomed to seeing homicide scenes. He had seen more than his share of murder victims. But so much blood all at once, so many people slain in one spot . . . it was too much even for his iron nerves. He was seized by a forceful wave of nausea. Nearly fainting, he folded in upon himself, landing in a chair.

He sat thus for nearly ten minutes before he came to a little. "A most hideous crime has been carried out here," he said to himself. "And I heard it happening through the telephone . . . and could do nothing.

"It must be a terribly knotty case, though. The lady called me for help instead of the police. For me, it's a sign that I have to keep looking around here for clues. I won't rest until I solve the case of this quadruple murder."

And so he hoisted himself up and began a thorough inspection of the house.

Nothing appeared to have been stolen. All of the cupboards and drawers were very much locked. All the windows were shut too, and because the front door was locked, it was a mystery to him as to how the murderer had entered and exited.

Later, however, he noticed that one window in a small study was only closed but not locked. That window opened onto the backyard. It was that window through which the murderer must have exited the home, and perhaps entered it too—that is, if he had not been simply invited into the home earlier.

The detective could not find anywhere the knife and revolver with which the murders were committed—nor any other traces of the criminal's deeds.

Considering the downpour that had been coming down ceaselessly all night, it was impossible to detect any footprints in the wet grass of the backyard, which would have helped to determine where the murderer had fled to.

This yard stretched out quite far until it hit another street. It was bordered on the other sides by adjacent yards, while the villa itself stood apart, at some distance from the surrounding homes. The screams of its slain inhabitants would therefore not have been heard by their neighbors.

Yes, Spitzkopf was confronted by a most obscure mystery indeed. But one thing was clear to him: the dreadful deed was carried out by a single criminal, acting alone.

"That much is apparent from the woman having had time to run to the telephone to ring me," the detective thought to himself, "and to spend a few minutes standing there until she too was slain. That must have taken place whilst the murderer was taking care of the other individuals."

The fact that even the ten-year-old child was not spared, moreover, indicated to Spitzkopf that the murderer and the family were acquainted with each other such that the girl could have divulged the killer's identity. Or perhaps he had some other motive for not leaving a single survivor from this family.

"The case is confounding," Spitzkopf considered. "But I've a feeling that it will be this very web of these most unusual particulars that shall make it easier to uncover the tracks of the culprit.

"But first things first: I will notify the police."

So resolved, he went to the telephone and asked to be connected to police headquarters, to which he summarized all that had occurred.

Within a quarter hour a police commission had arrived at the scene, and the officers took careful notes on what they found there. These men were also much affected by the horrific sights in the bedroom and Dr. Politzer's office. But they too were unable to find any clues, besides the few bloodstains that the inspector Springer noticed beside the window through which the murderer must have escaped. Having shown them to Spitzkopf, the detective responded: "Yes, I saw them earlier. I've not a doubt the murderer fled through this window. And the drops of blood demonstrate to me that he didn't clean himself off here in the home but rather somewhere outside.

"Unfortunately it was coming down so hard tonight that the rain would have wiped away all traces of the blood outside along with any footprints. And in any case, we'd have to wait until daybreak to see them. Maybe we'll uncover some other significant clues then."

"And what is your take on the case?" the police inspector asked.

"I've not arrived at any clear judgments yet," Spitzkopf answered. "One thing's for certain though: eventually, we're going to get our man."

"How?" asked the inspector.

"It's clear as day," Spitzkopf said. "The culprit, as far as I can see, did not steal anything. Every door in the place is sealed shut. Even the dead man's golden clock, along with his wallet, are still here intact on his nightstand.

"And so I think the raider will be coming back for his loot. And that's when we'll nab him."

The inspector looked at Spitzkopf with eyes as big as saucers.

"You speak as if . . ." said the officer, "as if you've already got it all figured out."

"Well, I don't," Spitzkopf answered evenly. "But I think it's by this route that I eventually will. Naturally, we have first to learn more particulars of this family's background, the extent of its wealth, and its present condition . . . or rather, its former condition.

"A judicial commission will have to conduct a thorough inspection of all the papers of the deceased. We need to know who Dr. Politzer's inheritor is—who might have had a reason to not even allow the small child to remain living."

"I marvel at the brilliance of that Spitzkopfian mind," the police inspector remarked. "I'm convinced you've already found the key to unlocking this mystery."

"I haven't even convinced myself," Spitzkopf responded. "I have often had the experience of my sturdiest conjectures crumbling under their weight.

"But this time, it's true—I feel that I am hypothesizing on rather more solid ground. For instance, it seems to me that the culprit did not break in tonight on the spur of the moment but rather was invited in a good deal earlier, before the downpour began. We can determine this by the absence of any wet footprints in the home.

"So the criminal must have been well acquainted with the family and this home. And I dare say he'll be coming to get acquainted with it further before long."

Outside, meanwhile, the sky was beginning to lighten. The rain had stopped. Together with the team of officers, Spitzkopf made his way into the backyard to seek out footprints.

But their efforts were for naught. The tall grasses were washed so thoroughly by the deluge that not even a trace of a footprint could be found among them.

While tramping back to the villa, Spitzkopf noticed a crumpled-up bit of paper in the garden, not far from the open window.

The rain had not managed to wash the paper clean of a few scattered flecks of blood.

"This may lead me to my target," Spitzkopf thought, secreting the wet paper away into his pocket.

CHAPTER TWO
The Will

THAT DAY the judicial commission arrived at the home of the murdered Dr. Politzer to take stock of all that had taken place. Accompanying them was a notary public who had agreed to take charge of the family's possessions until it became clear who their intended inheritors were. The notary opened up every cabinet and drawer in the house, logged everything he found, then locked them all up again.

After this process was completed, the family safe was opened with the help of the keys that were found in the murdered doctor's pocket. In it were found a number of stocks and bonds, thousands of kronen in cash, and several checkbooks in which deposits of some very significant sums of money had been recorded. In a small, separate compartment of the safe was a sealed envelope bearing the inscription "My Will."

The notary broke the seal on the document and unfolded it. It consisted of one large sheet of paper with Dr. Politzer's own handwriting upon it. Reading it out loud enough for all present to be able to hear, the notary revealed its contents:

> I, Politzer, Doctor of Medicine, domiciled in Vienna, at Döblinger Strasse 169, being 65 years of age, and in weakened health, do record here in detail what is to be done with all of my worldly property in the event of my death . . .

There followed a comprehensive accounting of all the man's property: the villa where he resided along with two houses in Vienna's ninth district, bank savings amounting to 128,000 kronen, stocks and bonds worth 90,000 kronen, and so forth.

The notary went on reading:

> A third of the monetary value of all the aforementioned assets I hereby will to various charitable concerns which I shall name at the end of this document. The rest shall go to my wife in the event that she should survive me.
>
> In the event that my wife dies before me, however, my granddaughter, the daughter of my dear son, shall receive these two thirds of my wealth.
>
> But if, however, it should please the Almighty God for my granddaughter too to be called to Him before me, the share shall fall to my cousin Franz Rotter.
>
> I do not know, however, where this cousin is currently located, as when we became embroiled in a feud

some three years ago he cut off all contact with me.

Therefore, if he is ultimately to be the inheritor, the ENTIRETY of my wealth should be safeguarded temporarily by the courts, with announcements printed in the newspapers calling upon my cousin to present himself.

The interest that accrues on the money before such time as my cousin presents himself, meanwhile, shall be entrusted to the president of Vienna's Jewish community, who should divide said money up and donate it to the poor on my, my wife's, and my granddaughter's *yortsaytn*, the anniversaries of our deaths.

Dr. Leon Politzer

Vienna, the 10th of December, 19—

"This will was composed three years ago," said the notary. "And it has turned out to be the case that neither the wife nor the granddaughter of the murdered man are still living. The inheritance falls, therefore, to the cousin, Franz Rotter, who must be sought out by notices printed in the newspapers."

The entire time that the notary had been reading out the will, Spitzkopf had been standing off to one side. The first thing that drew his attention was the sealing wax on the envelope. He immediately noticed, with his eagle eye, that the wax was quite fresh . . .

When the notary finally got to reading out the date of the will, and remarked that it had been written three years earlier, there was not a doubt in Spitzkopf's mind that the will was fake.

He asked the notary to hand him the document. Then, with his magnifying glass in one hand, he read it over, going through it carefully, word by word.

It became even clearer to him. The document was not authentic but rather forged with a deft hand.

The signature, however, was different, each minute dash, each dot, precisely where it was supposed to be.

"Could the rest of the will truly be fake and just the signature authentic?" he asked himself. "It would be quite the extraordinary surprise."

He examined the signature once again even more closely—then he sprang up as if he had been bitten by a snake.

"Ah, you tricky little bird!" he inwardly exclaimed. "You sure know how to fly nimble! But it won't do you a bit of good. We'll soon show you that your very nimbleness will be your undoing.

"For the meantime, I've got to keep mum. Even the police commission mustn't know what I know because then my little birdie might find out he's under suspicion, and he'd fly.

"Let the call be put out in the newspapers first. And let this Rotter raptor come and present himself, beak first. Then I'll light such a fire under his feathers as will have him remembering the name Spitzkopf forever!"

And so the detective returned the will to the notary, commenting that everything in it seemed to be the genuine article, leaving no cause for suspicion. But he made one request: for the notary to allow him to take a few of the murdered man's letters containing his signature, as he would need them for his investigations. The notary duly entrusted him with said letters.

The bodies of the murdered family were conducted to the hospital, where autopsies were performed on them.

The villa, meanwhile, was sealed off as a crime scene, and the notary took away all of the paper money, stocks and bonds, and deposit slips so that the wishes expressed by the doctor in his last will and testament could be fulfilled.

In Vienna's newspapers, a notice was published to the effect that one Franz Rotter was being sought, cousin to the medical doctor Leon Politzer, so that he might claim the inheritance of the slain.

CHAPTER THREE
Rotter Comes Calling

A NUMBER OF days had passed since the horrific murders. The people of Vienna had forgotten all about it already, and even the newspapers had stopped printing stories about it.

Spitzkopf, after all, had asked the police to refrain from keeping the public informed about their investigations into the identity of the killer, and they had abided by his request.

A few weeks passed. Then the courts received a telegram from London in which the cousin of the late Dr. Politzer, Franz Rotter, declared that he had lately learned of the horrific murder of his relative and that he was on his way to Vienna to claim the inheritance.

Spitzkopf was immediately notified that the man had been in touch. He had asked the court to tell him as soon as Rotter turned up under the pretext that he wished to converse with the man for the purpose of obtaining from him further intelligence on his murdered family's circumstances. The detective threw such a veil over his true intentions that even the court did not know what his plans were.

He did eventually have to inform the police of them, though, as he did not wish for the officers to continue carrying out their investigations. If they did, the murderer could get spooked at the idea of showing himself in Vienna, endangering their chances of nabbing him.

On the day the detective received notice from the court that Rotter had telegrammed, Spitzkopf immediately sent for his assistant Fuchs and said to him: "From now on, your name is no longer Fuchs. It's Markus Politzer, cousin to the lately murdered Dr. Leon Politzer. You're to present yourself before the court and produce the paper will that I have for you here.

"According to the will, you are to be the sole inheritor of the doctor's entire wealth, should Frau Politzer and their daughter no longer be living.

"The will was written a year and a half ago and was then entrusted to you.

"You are a resident of Switzerland and have lately gotten wind from the newspapers about what took place. And so you have come to claim your promised inheritance.

"You are to stay at a hotel until the matter gets resolved. And naturally you'll have to alter your appearance such that not a soul in all Vienna will be able to recognize you."

"You can count on me, Master," Fuchs answered. "I'll arrange it all just as you've prescribed, down to the letter."

"Good," said Spitzkopf. "Now run along and present yourself to the court."

And so Fuchs ran along and did just as his boss had commanded.

Two days later Franz Rotter appeared at the court, produced his own documents, and demanded that the inheritance be paid out to him.

The judge answered him that another claimant had presented himself, bearing a second will, written a year and a half later than the one naming Rotter. Both wills were written by the same hand, and both bore an authentic signature. Therefore, because this newly discovered will was written later than the first, Rotter's was rendered invalid, and the court would of course be recognizing the new claimant as the inheritor.

Franz Rotter's shock was so tremendous that he could barely hold himself together. He sprang up from his chair as if he had been pricked by something sharp and bellowed, "Your Honor! This second will is fake. It's been forged. The proof lies in the fact that my cousin did not destroy the first will after he supposedly drafted this one to replace it, but rather left the original sequestered away in his safe.

"It must also raise a red flag that this character had the will just lying in his bag while mine was safely stored away and sealed."

"You may be right," said the judge. "But I cannot help you. Both wills bear the signature of the deceased, and as long as you are unable to demonstrate beyond the shadow of a doubt that the second will is not genuine, we must assume that your rival carries the day, for his was written later.

"This is, naturally, my private opinion. You must present your suit formally before the court if you wish to pursue your claim, and a trial will then decide between the two of you."

Franz Rotter could see that getting what he wanted would be no picnic. He told the judge that he would be putting the matter in his lawyer's hands and promptly left the courtroom.

But as soon as he had entered the corridor just outside, he balled his fists and gnashed his teeth, seething with anger as he hissed to himself, "I know not who this knave may be who's presented himself here as an inheritor and who's got ahold of this so-called will. Maybe it's the real McCoy, who can say. But if it is, all of my good work has been in vain.

"But heaven help me if I don't find a way to fling this challenger off my back. Yes, I'll have washed my hands of him before long . . ."

CHAPTER FOUR
A Neighbor for Fuchs

FUCHS, MEANWHILE, ensconced himself in the Grand Hotel, where he had taken two elegant rooms. Of course, he would only ever be in the suite to sleep. During the day he would take care of the tasks required of him by Spitzkopf. But he would never show his face at Spitzkopf's offices, as the detective had temporarily banned him from entering.

Two days after Fuchs checked in there, our Herr Franz Rotter took a room in the same hotel—incidentally, the room just across from his own. Fuchs, of course, immediately realized who his new neighbor was, even though Rotter had checked in under a pseudonym.

The same day he alerted Spitzkopf about the new development. The detective warned him to be quite careful at night. The criminal, who had murdered four people so as to get his paws on some money, would surely have no qualms about doing away with a person who was to be his sole competitor for the inheritance.

The first couple of days, all was quiet. Fuchs would be sure to lock himself in quite thoroughly at night and kept a loaded revolver on his nightstand. Upon hearing the slightest noise, he would pop up and grab hold of the weapon.

But he need not have been so afraid just then. The man never did turn up at his door.

A few days later, Rotter did happen to sit down at the same table as Fuchs in the hotel's dining room and attempted to reel him into a conversation. But Fuchs routinely deflected the attempt.

Once, though, just as Fuchs was sitting down to dinner, Rotter approached him, introduced himself, and before Fuchs could get up Rotter had already occupied the chair next to him and spoke. "Excuse me, my good fellow! I know who you are and that we shall soon enter the fray of a trial over the inheritance of my cousin, Dr. Politzer . . ."

"Yes, and?" Fuchs responded. "So let us have a trial, and let the best man inherit."

"But I must be that man," Rotter answered sharply. "And I refuse to participate in this trial because I don't know what the outcome will be . . . an outcome upon which my entire existence—my life—depends."

"That's your affair," Fuchs answered in calm tones. "If you feel you must receive the inheritance, you must be sure to try to win the case. Of course, for my own part, I shall also be endeavoring to win. I also want to receive the inheritance. It belongs to me, for the late Dr. Politzer was my first cousin."

"That so? You actually consider yourself his cousin?" Rotter laughed. "I know all the particulars of the deceased quite well, and I am sure that besides me, the man left no next of kin."

"Then things would seem to be in your favor. Prove that at the trial, and you're sure to win."

"I refuse to litigate the matter," Rotter countered, growing quite impatient now. "I cannot wait as long as such a trial will take. I demand that you give up your claim."

Fuchs answered coolly. "That . . . I will not be doing."

"What if I give you a portion of the inheritance?" Rotter asked.

"Certainly not. I refuse to surrender a penny of what is due to me. For I am certain that I shall triumph in court."

"You are extremely stubborn," Rotter fumed. "One can simply not reason with you in good faith. But I shall warn you that it would be in your interest to retreat from this trial in an amicable fashion. If you don't . . . it could be bad for you."

"Ha!" Fuchs laughed, quite loud enough for other guests to hear him. "You're threatening me. You want to force my retreat by way of violence. But you're mistaken if you think it'll work. I'm no sucker. I won't allow myself to be intimidated."

Rotter could see that further talk would not get him anywhere. He left the table in a rage, gnashing his teeth after his usual fashion and saying to himself, "Just wait, you dirty dog. I'll soon figure out a solution as far as you're concerned."

Fuchs, meanwhile, remained at his table in the dining room for over an hour, reading his newspaper. Rotter had decamped to a different table, also seemingly engrossed in the paper. At around eleven Fuchs left for his suite, and Rotter remained below.

The hotel's corridors were still brightly illuminated, though most of the guests were already asleep. When Fuchs entered his corridor, however, he was greeted by total darkness. It surprised him. He thought of lighting a match in order to locate his room number. But at that moment his head was dealt such a resounding blow from behind that he keeled over unconscious.

He soon came to, however, as the wig he was wearing to render him unrecognizable also had the unexpected virtue of protecting his skull. The impact was not quite as dramatic as it could have been.

Fuchs took a moment to look about him. But he saw no one; it was still pitch black in the hallway. He could tell that the blow had come from Rotter's side. In order to figure out whether Rotter himself had dealt it or some crony of his, he pretended as if absolutely nothing had occurred and went back down to the dining room, though his head still smarted something awful.

Upon entering, he saw Rotter sitting at his table as before, still engrossed in the newspaper. Fuchs asked a waiter whether or not the man had happened to leave the dining room recently and come back again.

"No," the waiter answered. "He's been there the whole time, as if nailed to the spot, absorbed in his paper."

But when Rotter noticed Fuchs had entered and looked as merry and serene as ever, he turned a pair of eyes on him wide as the hotel's dinner plates. It was as if he were looking at a corpse that had been revived.

"Aha, a bit startled I'm still alive, then, are we?" Fuchs thought to himself. "If this isn't an irrefutable sign that you're well aware who assaulted me . . . so it seems you're not alone after all. You've got accomplices. Very well, then. We'll get them too."

Fuchs ordered a glass of tea, swallowed it down, and leafed through another newspaper. Then he went up to his rooms—a bit more carefully this time than before, as might be expected—locked the door tight, and crawled into bed. But he could not sleep a wink. Not so much out of fear that someone would come to attack him again as out of utter shock that he had been so attacked.

His thoughts turned over in his brain. "It must be one crafty pack of brigands they've got. Seems to me now that this Rotter isn't Dr. Politzer's cousin at all but just some hardened, violent criminal. He needs to be kept from harming anyone else."

Rotter, meanwhile, stayed down in the dining room another half hour, then ascended to his room to sleep. But not a wink could he get either. Instead he spent the whole night hatching another scheme for neutralizing his rival. He was also confounded by his colleague's inability to complete the task they had discussed.

He did not know whether Fuchs might have already been in his room by the time the accomplice turned up or whether perhaps someone else had entered the corridor just as he did, rendering the surprise attack impossible. Of course, he would be finding out on the morrow exactly what had occurred. In any case, a new plan must now be worked up. The rival had to be destroyed, that much was sure.

And so Rotter thought. And thought. Until his mind hit upon a plan.

"That's it!" he yipped, rubbing his hands together in utter glee. "It's a surefire way to get rid of this dog once and for all. And the best thing: no one will guess that it's me what's done it.

"Of course, my hands might get singed some in the process. But if you can't stand the heat . . ."

Once he had finished working out all the details, daylight had already begun to stream through the hotel windows.

CHAPTER FIVE
The Conflagration

It was two days later. Two in the morning. And Fuchs had been lying in bed for two hours.

Again—not sleeping.

That evening, upon exiting his room, he had heard a suspicious sort of noise coming from his neighbor's room.

He did not want to make any trouble over it because Spitzkopf had told him not to trouble the sly bird over trivialities, lest the criminal should begin to suspect that his neighbor was aware of his crimes. And besides, all of Spitzkopf's dealings in the case had the ultimate goal of proving that the man was the murderer of Dr. Politzer and his family. If he were to be arrested on a different charge, it would become trickier to prove that more serious offense.

And so Fuchs lay in bed. It seemed he would just have to wait and see what new bit of knavery the man would be getting up to that day.

But then a sharp odor wafted to his nostrils, like something was burning. He sprang out of bed, threw his clothes on, and flung open the window. It was the last possible moment for it, for just then his whole room was engulfed in flames.

He heard wild screams from every direction, and cries for help: "Fire! Fire! Rescue us!"

Fuchs could see that the entire hotel was burning. There was no time to delay. He evacuated through the window. Gripping tightly to the ledges on his climb down, he descended slowly until his feet touched the solid ground of the street.

Just then the fire brigade arrived and began to fight the flames. It took about an hour for the inferno to be put out, at which point the damage could at last be assessed.

Fuchs was not hurt a bit. Other guests were indeed injured, but only mildly. The suite Fuchs had been occupying was reduced to ash. The room facing it on the other side of the hallway, meanwhile, was intact. Franz Rotter suffered a few minor injuries to his hands, but his room was hardly damaged at all.

The conflagration, of course, attracted a massive crowd of onlookers. Among them was Spitzkopf, whose first aim was to make sure his Fuchs was not hurt. Upon catching sight of him on the street, he became, of course, ecstatic. Then he made his way to the hotel's dining room, where the injured were receiving treatment from a cluster of doctors.

Spitzkopf's attention was directed toward Franz Rotter. He had a good look as a doctor was in the process of tending to him. His burns were few in number and slight, concentrated on the left hand. Spitzkopf could see that they were not caused by the great conflagration in the hotel but rather by something like a candle.

Ignoring the scene for a moment, he took to observing the condition of the whole group of injured guests until the doctor finished his work with Rotter and turned away to treat others.

Spitzkopf then gestured to the doctor, indicating that he wished to meet with him outside for a moment. Once they had both emerged, Spitzkopf approached him and introduced himself, saying, "I beg of you, Herr Doktor, to give me a written report detailing that young man's injuries. The one you've just finished wrapping up. It seems to me that they were not serious burns sustained during the blaze itself. I have my suspicions that this man in fact started the fire."

"Very well," said the doctor. "I shall examine him again later and give you my written testimony."

After half an hour, once the doctor had finished tending to all the patients that required his attention, he returned to Rotter, telling him that the dressings he had applied before were only temporary, and he needed to reinforce them.

Rotter told him it would not be necessary. He was not in any kind of pain, and his own doctor would be able to make any modifications to the bandaging.

Spitzkopf, standing off to the side, heard all. He had no doubt that the burns Rotter sustained had been self-inflicted so others would think he had also been injured in the blaze and not, heaven forfend, that he was the one who started it.

"This chickie's got something more than a bird's brain," Spitzkopf thought. "But we'll soon see who rules the roost."

He then went up to the second floor to examine the areas most affected by the fire. With his trained eye, he quickly recognized, at the threshold of the suite Fuchs had been occupying, signs indicating that the surface had been doused with some highly flammable liquid. The suite's walls and floor had turned to pure charcoal, while the walls of nearby rooms only showed the signs of having been exposed to smoke.

"*Nu, nu*," Spitzkopf considered. "The first hearing of the inheritance trial is in a few days. We shall have to guard our Fuchs very closely, allowing nothing to happen to him. Already twice now he has been in grave danger of falling entirely into the hands of his nefarious adversaries. As the day comes closer and closer, Rotter's exertions to eliminate him will only grow more dramatic.

"I shall have to install another of my people nearby to keep an eye on Fuchs and protect him. He must remain safe at all costs."

CHAPTER SIX

Rotter and His Cronies

AFTER THE CONFLAGRATION in the Grand Hotel, all of the guests had to find new lodgings. Fuchs ended up at the Hotel National. And as chance would have it . . . our Rotter took a room there later that same day, off the same hallway as Fuchs.

Fuchs immediately telephoned Spitzkopf to notify him, and the detective then dispatched his second assistant, Julius Haupt, to book a room at the National. It was right next to Rotter's, separated from it by only a thin wall.

Haupt was disguised as an old man, complete with a gray beard and gold-rimmed spectacles. He gave his name at the front desk as Professor Georg Huldmann, from Bonn. He walked hunched over, supported by a cane with a silver handle. He carried off the part so well that no one could have perceived he was but a young man, barely twenty years old.

Spitzkopf tasked him with keeping an eye on Rotter and making sure that neither he nor his friends tried any funny business with Fuchs.

The court hearing over the inheritance money was to take place in two days. Spitzkopf warned Haupt to be especially vigilant during this period. He was not to let Rotter out of his sight.

It was now ten at night. Haupt was sitting in his room. He had turned all his lights out so that his neighbor would figure he had already gone to sleep. But he was of course wide awake, leaning against the door between his room and Rotter's. All was perfectly quiet in the hotel, and Haupt could hear the slightest rustling that came from his neighbor's room.

Suddenly he heard the hall door onto Rotter's room opening and someone tip-toeing in, trying not to make a sound. Then another slunk in, followed shortly by a third. Rotter greeted them in a hush, and they all took their seats. Overhearing this, Haupt hurried into the hall and telephoned Spitzkopf to tell him that Rotter had convened a meeting.

The detective dashed out of his office, dressed as an elderly woman, and assumed a post outside the hotel, ready to observe the gang as it left the premises. When Haupt returned to his room, he could hear the men still holding their hushed conference. He pressed his ear to the door—and could now discern every single word that they spoke.

"So. The day after tomorrow, at court, you'll have to show your hand," a rough voice rumbled. "You'll have to prove that the will naming you as inheritor is the genuine article."

"I'm not worried about that," said Rotter. "It seems to me the court will have to recognize mine as authentic, because it was found in the dead man's safe, while my rival produced his out of thin air. You see now, boys, that I was correct when I insisted that the will should bear a recent date and not one from three years ago.

"If only you had listened to me, my rival wouldn't have a case, as his would have appeared to have been written earlier than mine. There wouldn't even have been a question.

"But you all always think you're so clever. And now you've put me in a bind."

"Well, can't you just get rid of the birdie?" the rough-voiced conspirator could be heard asking. "Clip his wings, so to speak? You're always a dab hand at that kind of dirty work."

"The devil knows why, but twice now I've tried to cut him down, and nothing doing!" Rotter answered. "He must be some kind of devil himself, not a human being!"

"Third time's a charm," said another.

"Blast it all!" Rotter fumed. "All of you with your confounded bits of advice! And never a bit of actual help.

"When I asked you to treat him to such a nice blow to the head as would hammer out all of his appetite for an inheritance, it seems instead you, I don't know, blew his nose with your pocket handkerchief!

"The bloke showed up in the dining hall not more than fifteen minutes later, for all the world fresh as a daisy, healthy as a damned ox! With me there in the corner shaking like a bloody leaf."

"Go ahead, take your swipes at me," the other man said. "But you forget that it's thanks to me that you're even going by the name Rotter."

"To be sure!" answered Rotter, much provoked. "Your mother must be so proud of you! My own feats have been twenty times as bold, and you won't catch me bragging.

"Sure, you strangled that raggedy Rotter in your basement, and buried him, and transferred over his papers to me. And what have I done? Torn into an entire family, slaughtering the lot of 'em like a brood of chickens. I wasn't a bit afraid, either, when mother hen Politzer rang up some Spitzberg or Spitzmann or other and called for help.

"I had such ice in my veins that after the whole family was lying there dead, swimming in blood, I was able to pull out of the geezer's pocket the key to his safe, slip the forged will in, lock it back up, and put the key back where I found it. All executed so masterfully that no one would suspect a thing."

"A bit of derring-do here, a bit of derring-do there!" pronounced the rough voice. "You're all a buncha downright heroes when no one's there to bother you! I wanna know what'll happen, though, if you lose the trial. What'll we get out of it then, huh?"

"The same as I get!" Rotter answered.

"A real genius we've got on our hands, eh?" the others tittered. "This whole business with the will was your scheme. We wanted to get it done much more simply. There was a nice fortune right there in the safe, ripe for the taking. We would have all gotten enough just from that.

"You were greedy, though, and wanted the houses, too. You wanted to be a homeowner in Vienna, a bigshot, maybe even serve on the municipal council under Dr. Karl Lueger![5]

"And so, if you win and get your hands on the inheritance, then good, we'll all get our share. But if not—you're obliged to give us what we're due anyway."

"Give you what you're due, huh?" Rotter chortled. "Oh, that's rich! With the greatest pleasure, my good sirs! And where is it I'm going to be getting that which I'll be giving?"

"That's your affair!" his cronies answered. "But if we don't get our share—it'll be your head."

Rotter could not help but laugh out loud. "A lot of good that'll do ya! Now, friends, we've gotten on the wrong track again. Nothing's going to come of this endless arguing. And these empty threats will lead us nowhere.

"My advice is for us to have a conference tomorrow with the entire gang. At our headquarters. Then we'll figure out how to bury this birdie—before he even gets a chance to perch up at the trial."

"So let it be written," said the rough voice. "I know you're just angling for more time. But allow me to warn you that we're done playing games. We won't be giving up our share."

The conspirators crept out of the room. Only Rotter remained.

Meanwhile Spitzkopf, en travesti, was pacing around the streets outside. As the men left the hotel, he had a good look at them and recognized them as serious criminals who had ended up in prison on more than one occasion, and for extended periods of time too, all thanks to his efforts.

"Seems the 'heir' has been working with this gang," thought Spitzkopf. "I've not a doubt in my mind that he's one of their number—and that the name Rotter is not actually his own.

"I won't be needing to follow these men. I know quite well where their hideaway is located. If the need presents itself, I'll be able to find them there.

"But first I'll listen to what Haupt has to tell me. Maybe he's got some news."

And so he wended his quiet way upstairs. Not wanting to knock at Haupt's door lest Rotter should hear, he opened it with his skeleton key and entered.

At that point Haupt had been lying in bed, though not sleeping. When he heard someone fussing with the door, he jumped to his feet and grabbed his revolver. But upon seeing the old woman come in, he knew it must be one of his own team. With a wave, he told her to sit down.

"You're being careful, my boy," whispered Spitzkopf. "That's good. Now tell me what's happened."

Haupt told him all that he had overheard.

After listening to his account, Spitzkopf responded, "I know this gang. When I saw them I immediately deduced that Rotter is a common criminal, one of their own. And is going under an assumed name.

"But now, of course, his grand plan has blown up in his face.

We know everything. And in two days, the whole measly band will be right where we want it."

CHAPTER SEVEN

The Trial

FINALLY, THE DAY they had all been waiting for arrived.

It was the morning of the trial to adjudicate between the two competing wills. The courtroom was crammed with spectators. The case fascinated everyone, not just because all wished to know which of the wills was authentic. They also wished to learn the dark secret that lay behind the mass murder of Dr. Politzer and his household, committed three months earlier. The public was, of course, deeply disappointed in the failure of the police to uncover who was behind this horrific crime.

"It's a travesty," the populace could often be heard saying. "Such a gruesome murder to have taken place here in Vienna, right in the heart of town, and even though the police were notified a half hour after, they could find nary a clue as to who did it. Then they let the whole matter rest, didn't bother themselves with it. Our lives aren't safe here in Vienna!"

Of course, they did not know that the total silence of the police was purposeful, the intent being that the killer should identify himself and thereby fall into a trap . . .

Such was Spitzkopf's plan. And it worked. At court today he was prepared to reveal all the particulars he had learned in his covert investigation.

See, the night before, Spitzkopf had disguised himself as a drunken beggar and stumbled into the tavern where Rotter and his associates had gathered.

On this occasion Rotter was not dressed quite as elegantly as was his wont. He was wearing a threadbare jacket, and his hair was in disarray. He did not want to stick out among the band of criminals with his usually smart attire.

And now it was very plain to see—the man had the uncompromising face of a true-blue criminal.

Spitzkopf sat off to the side, a bottle of vodka in front of him. He was hunched over the small table. And he snored.

Nearby, Rotter and his cronies confabulated. Spitzkopf was able to learn all the particulars of their plan by listening in closely. "It's a tight little outfit they've got," he thought. "But tomorrow I'll show they're not quite the masterminds they think they are."

It was quite late, after midnight, when Spitzkopf finally staggered out of the tavern. He looked so besotted with drink, so bedraggled, that even the experienced gang of criminals had not the slightest suspicion that he was a detective in disguise.

At nine o'clock, the presiding judge called the court to order.

Rotter was accompanied by his lawyer. Fuchs was alone.

The judge read out the statements of both parties, made a few remarks, then called up Rotter to present his claims.

Rotter explained that he was the only cousin the late Dr. Politzer had. They were indeed, he said, first cousins, Politzer's mother having been his own mother's sister. In his youth, Rotter spent much time with Dr. Politzer, who was very fond of him. The doctor wanted him to study medicine, but the youth was not much interested in scholastic endeavors and preferred the life of a businessman. Politzer grew angry at him for the decision, and Rotter left for America.

He spent three years there, then departed for London, where he also lived for a good deal of time. He did not write to his cousin throughout these long years, as they had left each other on bitter terms.

When he had first left Vienna, Politzer's son was still living, and so Rotter had not the slightest premonition that he would eventually be situated to inherit the doctor's wealth. It is easy to imagine, then, the utter horror and astonishment that he felt when, a few weeks earlier, he happened to come across the court's notice in the newspaper. There he learned of the shocking murder of his cousin together with the man's entire family, and that he, Rotter, had become the solitary heir.

"My pain, it is tremendous," Rotter concluded. "The loss of such a beloved cousin. I see now that he still loved me too, and I regret most deeply that I had broken off all communication with him.

"After arriving in Vienna and making myself known to the court, I of course heard the news that a second will had been presented, one that some unknown cousin had been toting around in his pocket . . .

"But as far as I know, I am Dr. Politzer's one and only cousin.

"I must therefore humbly ask of my opponent in this trial to demonstrate for us to what extent he was in fact related to Dr. Politzer. I have sufficiently proven myself before the court and have left no doubt that I am indeed the same Rotter that my late cousin named as his heir.

"Secondly, the will that so named me was actually found in my cousin's own safe, while my opponent's was simply on his own person. And furthermore, yes, his will was apparently drafted later than mine. But if his is authentic, then my cousin surely would have destroyed the first will, seeing as it had been replaced by a new one. I therefore believe that only the will that names me is authentic, and that I am consequently the sole heir of Dr. Politzer's estate.

"And it follows that my opponent's will has obviously been forged."

He spoke clearly and firmly, shooting his rival a triumphant look as if to say, "Well, what do you have to say about that?"

The judge made sure all that Rotter said had been taken down in the court records, then turned to Fuchs, asking: "And how do you answer your opponent's claims, Herr Politzer?"

"Don't you see, Your Honor?" cried Fuchs. "It's true that my will is forged . . . but so is the one that was found in Dr. Politzer's safe!"

The speech left the judge and spectators astounded.

Rotter sprang to his feet as if a serpent had just sunk its teeth into him. He turned pale as death. His eyes blazed like those of a wild animal.

"You are obliged, Herr Politzer," said the judge, "to explain to this court more clearly what it is that you mean. You admit your will is counterfeit. We may take your word for it. But this of your opponent's will being the same? That you must prove to us."

At that moment Spitzkopf thrust his way forward to the front of the courtroom, facing the bench, and declared in resounding tones: "Your Honor! I hereby present myself to you as an important witness. My name is Max Spitzkopf, Viennese private eye, and I am in a position to unravel this entire matter for you.

"But first, I must demand that several guards be immediately ordered to surround and keep a close eye on this Franz Rotter, as he is a most serious felon and the confirmed killer of the Politzer family."

Rotter lunged at Spitzkopf. A knife flashed in his hand. He was trying to plunge its long blade into the detective.

But then something flashed in Spitzkopf's hand, too: a loaded revolver. "Don't you dare move a muscle, you murderer," said Spitzkopf in a state of perfect calm. "Or I'll shoot you down like the dog you are."

Rotter stood stock still. He let the knife fall to the floor. As soon as it did, he was encircled by a clutch of policemen, who seized him and fettered him in shackles. Gnashing his teeth and cursing up a veritable storm, Rotter now took a seat, howling at Spitzkopf: "Just you wait, you bloodhound! I'll soon get even with you!"

"Yes, yes," said Spitzkopf. "Perhaps after your death. Your little friends have already been locked up in private cells. They'll not be able to get you out of any binds anymore—being bound themselves."

Upon hearing this Rotter said no more. He had lost all courage now—and all hope. He was finished. But Spitzkopf was not. He gave an exhaustive account to the court of all he had witnessed and discovered.

First was the scene late at night when he was called on the telephone, how the voice begged him to come rescue them, then how he arrived at the villa and what he saw there.

"At first, it seemed to me," Spitzkopf recounted, "that the puzzle lay in such a grisly crime having been committed and nothing having been stolen. Some kind of intricate scheme must have been at play.

"When the team of officers came, opened the safe, and found the will there, I immediately perceived that the wax with which it had been sealed was freshly adhered. When it was read out, and we found that it bore a date of three years prior, I became absolutely certain that the will had been forged.

"Upon inspecting it closer with my magnifying glass, I found that Dr. Politzer's handwriting had been quite ably imitated. The signature too appeared at first glance like one Politzer had written out with his own hand. But upon closer examination using the glass, I noticed some faint lines that made it clear it had been applied with a facsimile stamp. The whole will, in fact, had been written out quite recently but using a kind of chemical ink made to appear old.

"Later, in the garden, I found a bit of paper that the murderer had used to wipe the blood off of his hands. When I cleaned off the blood, I saw that it was a receipt from a stamp factory in Berlin, made out three weeks before.

"I immediately dispatched one of my assistants to Berlin so he could visit the factory. A few days later he brought me a second stamp cast from the exact same mold as that which had been used on the will.

"I then had a talented penman write out a second will, and another of my assistants, the man participating in the trial today, presented himself as a rival heir, bearing that new will in hand.

"There was not a doubt in my mind that the murderer had himself slipped the will into Dr. Politzer's safe and that he would be waiting a couple of weeks to present himself to the court so as not to arouse any suspicion with his hastiness.

"My conjecture proved correct. The man sent his letter from a far-off city, as I thought he might, namely London. Naturally, he had never visited the place before."

Spitzkopf went on to relate, in thorough detail, how the man had made several attempts to eliminate Fuchs, how he had set fire to the Grand Hotel, and what Haupt had overheard in the gang's conference at the second hotel, as well as all that he had himself heard when listening in on them at the bar the night before, just hours before the trial.

From Spitzkopf's account, it was clear that the man who had presented himself as Franz Rotter was in fact just a common criminal, one who had been imprisoned several times before.

The gang had murdered the actual Franz Rotter three months prior, after he, by a most unlucky coincidence, had fallen into their clutches. They soon learned that there was a chance he could be the heir to Politzer's fortune, though he had fallen out with the doctor some time before. And so the gang formed a plan to do away with him, have one of the members assume his identity, annihilate the entire family, then deposit in the safe a newly fabricated will naming Rotter as heir.

So that no one might think any sort of swindle was on, they decided, for good measure, to put in the will a clause providing for part of the money to go to charitable concerns.

"And just like that," Spitzkopf concluded, "this forged will shall be their undoing. May the court now deal with them as the law dictates."

You might easily imagine the amazement in which this speech left the judges and the assembled spectators.

In the days following, from every corner of the city, Spitzkopf was hailed with words of congratulation for the astonishing way he had cracked the case. The Viennese newspapers covered the story in lengthy articles rich with detail. The name of SPITZKOPF was now more famous than ever before.

The band of crooks, meanwhile, confessed to everything. And the ersatz Rotter was sentenced to death, along with his accomplice who had killed the actual Rotter. The others in the gang received sentences of up to twenty years strict confinement in prison.

The state took possession of the Politzer family's assets, as there were, after all, no living heirs. It made sure, however, to award a hefty prize to Spitzkopf, as well as a medal. To such stunning feats as his, such rewards were a fitting testament—and not at all a fake one.

Issue 7: The Spy

זיעבענטעס העפט. פרייז 20 העלער.

דֶער שְׁפִּיאָן.

ווען פוּכס קומט אין מיטען פון דער בריק, פאקט איהם פלוצים איםיצער ביים האַלז און וויל איהם מיט ג׳וואַלט איבער די פארענטשים אין וואַסער אריין שמירצען.

פוּכס ווערט זיך מיט אלע כחות. ער האָט זיין געגנער ארומגענומען מיט ביידע הענד און קריצט צווישען די צעהן: — ווען איך זאָל אַראָבפאַלען, פאַלסט אויך דו מיט.

The Spy

CHAPTER ONE

Military Secrets Betrayed

IN ALL THE Viennese newspapers on the tenth of August, 19—, one could read the following telegram:

> Innsbruck. The offices of the Franzensfeste Fortress, which stands at the border with Italy,[6] were recently broken into. In these offices were kept the most confidential military documents. Among the papers stolen were the Austrian military's plans for mobilization in case of war with Italy. The stolen documents are of extreme significance. If the particulars of their theft are not discovered soon, and war breaks out, it could spell disaster for Austria.
>
> An atmosphere of great crisis prevails at Franzensfeste. Upon discovery of the theft, the fortification command immediately initiated a thorough investigation.
>
> The lieutenant Leon Silbermann was quickly suspected of having perpetrated the burglary and has been jailed.
>
> Leon Silbermann serves in an artillery regiment that was recently transferred from Przemyśl[7] to Franzensfeste. Silbermann is deeply disliked by his brothers-in-arms, and when the regiment was stationed at Przemyśl he was

> already suspected of being in contact with Russian spies. He had eventually been able to extricate himself from the charges, though, as the matter could not be proven.
>
> There is clear evidence for the present charges, however: Silbermann was found to be in possession of letters written in Italian, as well as a floor plan of the Franzensfeste Fortress. Witnesses have also testified to having seen him outside of the town boundaries in the company of two foreigners—Italians—engaged in a drawn-out conversation. Who knows what other significant documents the traitor may have delivered up into Italy's hands.

The antisemitic press got all stewed up over the case, made a real *tzimmes* out of it. One of them published an article with the headline AN AUSTRIAN DREYFUS.[8]

In the article, the antisemitic broadsheet fulminated against all the world's Jews, declaring, "This is what occurs when we let a Jew become lieutenant and put him in a position to learn crucial state secrets."

"Well, what do you say?" the famed detective Max Spitzkopf asked his assistant, Hermann Fuchs, after the two had finished reading about the case in the morning papers.

"What is there to say?" Fuchs asked. "What—are you feeling the urge to get involved?"

"Of course I am!" Spitzkopf answered. "You know I take an interest in every case of great import. And I don't wait until they call me, either. This time the case is even more important to me because it concerns a Jew, and the antisemites are having a field day with it. And what's more—it seems to me that this Silbermann is entirely innocent."

"You couldn't possibly know that already!" Fuchs interrupted. "The newspaper accounts are so unclear that we don't even have a clear picture yet of what has taken place, let alone what sorts of evidence they've got on the lieutenant."

"Still," Spitzkopf asserted, "I would put my money on Silbermann being innocent. And what's more—I hope to prove his innocence myself."

"If you're so sure," Fuchs said, "then I think we'd better make our way to Franzensfeste at once and get to work."

"Took the words right out of my mouth," said Spitzkopf. "It just so happens we have a bit of free time right now. We'll leave this very night. But not to Franzensfeste. To Innsbruck. We'll be able to plan our next steps and make our way onward from there.

"Pack everything we need for the trip. And then we'll soon be off." Fuchs stayed back at the office to pack while Spitzkopf went off, he said, to carry out a few minor errands that needed attending to before they departed.

In truth, however, he made his way directly to the Vienna offices of the Ministry of War. He introduced himself and declared his intention to take the Silbermann case into his own hands. In order to make the investigation easier, he put in a request for all the known particulars of the case to be relayed to him. The ministry official he asked, however, told him that he could not be furnished with such information, as it was still top secret. He did, however, provide him with a letter addressed to the command of the Franzensfeste Fortress, asking for the detective to be given permission to investigate the case on the premises.

It was evening already when Spitzkopf returned home. Fuchs had gotten everything ready, just as Spitzkopf had asked, and both of them set off for Innsbruck on the evening express train.

CHAPTER TWO
The Franzensfeste Fortress

Franzensfeste boasts one of the mightiest fortifications on Austria's border with Italy. It is situated on the Eisack River, and a bridge 180 meters long rises 80 meters over the water to meet it. It is very solidly built. Its embrasures—the openings through which guns and cannons may be fired—are ingeniously arranged. The fort stands in proud command of the so-called Brenner Pass and the entrance to the vast, verdant Puster Valley.

The Brenner Pass and the Puster Valley contain the primary routes by which Italy could potentially invade the Austrian province of Tyrol. They form the only opening amid the immense Brenner mountain range in the Alps, which forms a natural fortification between Austria and Italy.

The Franzensfeste Fort, then, is of immeasurable significance to Austria's security, and its secrets have always been guarded most closely.

Ground was broken on the fort in the year 1833, when revolutionary activity was beginning to heat up in Italy. Austria had to be on guard lest it be surprised by a unification-minded Italian populace.

Since the year 1882, however, when Germany, Austria-Hungary, and Italy entered into a triple alliance and a treaty of peace—and Austria no longer feared an invasion from its southern neighbor—the fortress had lost some of its importance, and fewer military men were stationed in the environs.

But in the last ten years Italy had begun itching for war again. Its hottest hotheads got back to shouting about the urgent need for every bit of land where Italian countrymen resided to be reunited with the motherland. At the same time they feared the military prowess of England and France, which were in possession of whole swaths of territory and entire islands that were host to Italian populations. So Italy has lately considered it most expedient to try its hand at Austria first, thinking the country not as imposing an opponent.

The Italians' intentions are well known in Austria. It has been considered a matter of course here that Italy was just waiting for the moment to attack. The Austrian army, however, is not willing to let itself be dealt such a nasty surprise from its tempestuous neighbors. And therefore in recent years the Austrian military presence in Tyrol around the Italian border has been continually strengthened. Entire regiments were even brought over from Galicia, in the eastern stretches of the Austro-Hungarian empire—including from the fort of Przemyśl—so that a well-manned and able army could stand ready in Tyrol in case of war.

The Franzensfeste Fortress, as the gate that the Italians would have to batter down if they wished to fall upon Austria, was of prime importance.

Thus one can easily imagine the shock and horror felt in Austrian military circles when they learned that extremely valuable plans had been stolen from the fort. Their horror intensified when the primary suspect turned out to be a lieutenant serving at the very site.

"If we can't trust our own men," these military folk expressed, "then things are certainly dire. And we don't even know whether or not, aside from Lieutenant Silbermann, other officers or soldiers took part in this treasonous activity. It is very hard to protect oneself from one's enemies if those enemies are coming from within the house."

It was decided, therefore, to carry out as intensive an investigation as possible into the actions of the traitor. His punishment would be likewise severe so that "All the people shall hear, and fear," as Deuteronomy describes the death sentence for wrongdoers—lest anyone dare to imitate the deeds of this dastardly fellow.

The investigation had been going on for several days without any clear results. The chief witness against Silbermann was a man serving in his own regiment, one Corporal Ivan Czechowicz. He was telling all manner of stories. One had Silbermann ostensibly engaged in dealings with certain suspicious Italians and meeting them for an extended rendezvous in the forest outside the fort. Another told of how the lieutenant would spend his free time studying the fort from every possible angle and sketching out its floor plan on bits of paper.

None of these stories resulted, of course, in the military court that was carrying out the investigation collecting any demonstrable evidence against Silbermann. Still, the letters in Italian and the floor plan that were found on him were duly sent to headquarters in Innsbruck so that they could be read carefully and translated to figure out exactly what they contained.

Silbermann himself swore on all that is sacred that he was innocent of all charges. He had not had any communication with foreigners, he did not even understand Italian, and the letters as well as the floor plan must have been planted on him. Corporal Czechowicz, meanwhile, had been his enemy for a long time, ever since Silbermann had given the man a punishment for neglecting his duties at the fort back in Przemyśl.

In the course of its investigation, the military tribunal sent a dispatch asking that the Galician base furnish it with a report on Silbermann's activities there, as Czechowicz claimed that even then the lieutenant had been consorting with someone suspected of being a Russian spy.

At that time, back in Przemyśl, the fortress command had ordered for Lieutenant Silbermann to be observed by two officers of the secret police over an extended period. They tracked all of his movements but found nothing suspicious, and the investigation had been suspended. The report sent by the fort at Przemyśl to the one at Franzensfeste, then, provided the commanders there with little new information.

Ultimately, any of the soldiers and officers at Przemyśl could have been communicating with the Russians. Silbermann had first been identified as a suspect by way of a letter, its anonymity making it highly likely that it had been written by an enemy of his. But still, the investigation at Przemyśl had carried on with some urgency, the community there eager to determine the guilty party, until it was eventually suspended for good due to a total lack of any significant evidence. But it meant Silbermann's name was never entirely wiped clean. A shadow of suspicion still hung over him.

And now a break-in had taken place at Franzensfeste shortly after his transfer there, and a witness, Corporal Czechowicz, had come forward to testify that he had seen Silbermann engaging in all manner of funny business.

It had to be believed, then, that this Silbermann was indeed quite the flighty little finch, capable of the worst kind of treason—and such a bird had to be hunted.

Furthermore, he was a Jew. And you can believe anything about a Jew.

But the investigation at Franzensfeste had not managed to turn up a thing. Mittewald,[9] the hamlet where the fort lay, and the city of Brixen,[10] where the top government official of the region was stationed, were stuffed to the gills with secret police. Every local resident was questioned, every hotel and guesthouse searched. Every corner of the territory, indeed, was rifled and rummaged through. Maybe someone had seen something suspicious, heard something untoward.

But still—nothing. And still—the investigation went on.

Meanwhile, Silbermann was behind bars in a military detention facility, watched closely day and night.

CHAPTER THREE

The Italian

SPITZKOPF AND FUCHS were now in Innsbruck, having arrived the morning after their departure from Vienna.

"Until now we've been able to behave however we wanted," Spitzkopf said to Fuchs before they alighted from the train. "But from this point forward we'll have to be quite careful.

"I'm off to the Hotel Habsburg, where I'll check in under the name Rudolf Spring, a merchant from Prague. You take a room at the Hotel Viktoria, directly across from the train station, and introduce yourself as Franz Schwedt, a traveling salesman from Salzburg. For the moment I'm not giving you anything much to do. When there are any new developments, I will let you know.

"But as you'll have some free time, and as you'll be staying right across from the station, whenever a train arrives, perhaps pop over to the platform to have a look at the passengers stepping off. It couldn't hurt, in any case."

As soon as their own train stopped, Spitzkopf exited in a flash, before Fuchs even had a moment to get his bearings. Fuchs did not delay either. He called over a porter and asked him to bring his trunk to the Hotel Viktoria. When he made his way there shortly after, he asked for a room with a view of the train station. Then he made himself comfortable beside the window, where he watched his fellow passengers slowly pouring out of the station's broad exit gates.

Spitzkopf, meanwhile, went from the station immediately to the Hotel Habsburg, which was not far. After acquiring a room and entering it, he locked the door and sat down to smoke a cigar and meditate over what he might do next. Contrary to his usual tendency to hatch a plan of attack as soon as he took on a case, this time he was quite planless. Until now he had not fully considered how he might approach the matter.

When he had first read of what had taken place in the newspapers—and when he learned that the suspicion had fallen upon a Jewish lieutenant and that antisemites were stirring the pot most vigorously—he was seized by the overwhelming feeling that he must intervene in the matter. He must find the actual perpetrator and come to the rescue of the innocent.

When he went to the Ministry of War, however, to learn further details of the case, he was received most rudely and told in no uncertain terms that the matter must be kept confidential, even from the likes of himself. In the eyes of the official dealing with him, he had read most explicitly, "You can go to hell! That traitor was a Jew—now of course his fellow Jews want him freed!"

Spitzkopf realized he would get nothing from the official channels. His first idea—making inquiries about the case at the military headquarters in Innsbruck—would not, alas, lead him to his goal. Still, he decided to go there first. He knew that precious few tourists visit the hamlet of Mittewald and the small town of Brixen during these dog days of summer. The appearance of an unknown individual in those parts would surely attract attention, thereby making his investigation far more difficult.

And so he sat in his room in Innsbruck for a good long while, lost in thought over what his next steps would be. Stray ideas and strategies floated across his brain, but not one of them pleased him. Impatient, he vaulted himself out of his chair and tripped down the stairs to the dining room to have a bit of breakfast. As he was descending he encountered the hotel porter ascending and carrying a small trunk which appeared to Spitzkopf to be much heavier than its proportions would have made it seem. Accompanying the porter was a tall, muscle-bound man with sparkling eyes and a black beard that culminated in a sharp point.

There was something about the man that Spitzkopf did not like. He remained below, trying to listen for where the porter was conducting him. Thanks to his keen ears, he could make out that they had stopped at the second floor and entered the corridor on the left.

"Seems the new guest is to be my neighbor!" he thought to himself. "I shall enjoy getting to know him a bit better."

He entered the dining room and ordered a coffee and a slice of buttered bread. The waiter brought these to him along with that day's newspapers.

Just then the new guest entered the dining room and put in his own breakfast order. Coincidentally, he sat not far from Spitzkopf, in just such a spot as would make it possible for Spitzkopf to train his gaze on him without being noticed.

The man sat there quite quietly, drinking his coffee and

taking some pulls on a fine cigar as he leafed through an Italian newspaper. He appeared to be quite contented, like one who has just pulled off a nice bit of business.

Spitzkopf scrutinized him from every angle, taking careful stock of his physical appearance. Then he paid for his breakfast and returned to his room.

While passing through the corridor, he noticed the room numbered 26, directly across from his own. It was open. The chambermaid was inside, briskly putting the room to rights. He extended her a polite greeting and casually asked, as if just by the by: "And who might be my new neighbor?"

"A gentleman from Italy!" the maid answered. "Signor Luigi Verdi, from Florence."

"Ah! A grand sort of neighbor!" Spitzkopf commented, before retreating to his own room.

He did not remain there long but rather changed out of his traveling clothes and set off at once for the Hotel Viktoria, where he asked after Fuchs.

Fuchs was taking his breakfast in his room. The train journey had made him somewhat weary, and he had asked for the food to be brought up to him.

"Seen anything unusual?" Spitzkopf asked him right upon entering.

"How should I know?" Fuchs responded. "But there was a tall, strapping sort of fellow who came by the train that arrived after ours. He had a pointy black beard and eyes that glittered. Something about the way he looked was unsettling."

"Ah, so that character caught your eye, too?" Spitzkopf asked, rather astonished. "Seems we share a pair of eagle eyes! What was it about him, specifically, that rubbed you the wrong way?"

"The triumphant look on his face!" Fuchs answered. "Peering at the world around him with a smile, like he'd just grabbed God Himself by the ankles. And his eyes flashing so madly that it seemed to me the knave must have just got done bumping off a millionaire and robbing him for all he was worth."

"Good, good!" Spitzkopf broke in. "We'll have to follow his movements. I'll leave that to you. Track him like you're his shadow. But be careful."

"Course I will," said Fuchs. "After all, we've got nothing concrete that needs doing right now for the case that brought us here, as far as I can tell. So I can keep an eye on that strange bird. Maybe it'll lead to a juicy morsel of roast pigeon falling right into our mouths."

"Come now, Fuchsl, oh, sweet, innocent little Fuchs!" Spitzkopf teased. "What makes you so sure this fellow has nothing to do with the case that brought us here?"

Fuchs gaped at him, his eyes as big as saucers.

"What are you saying, Master?" he asked. "You think we've stumbled upon a significant track for our case? Whatever would make you think that?"

"There's something about the trunk he traveled here with that I don't like," Spitzkopf answered calmly. "It seems to be too heavy for its size. There must be some awfully weighty gold coins in there, or maybe it's crammed full of important documents. As it happens, I was able to snatch a glance into his room and didn't see it there. He must have locked it away into the cupboard and probably keeps the key on his person."

"And now you want me to bring the trunk to you, I'm guessing?"

"Hold your horses! Remember—we're not a pair of common pickpockets and cat burglars. When we take something, we make no secret about it.

"Sure, Fuchs, sometimes you like to show off what a dab hand you are, pulling off a little feat of derring-do. You won't be doing it this time, though. I don't want to recover only the important documents this man may have. I don't want only to deliver him up to the state penitentiary. I also want to find out who sent him and who assisted him.

"That we can only do by being extremely careful. We simply cannot rush things. For now, your single and solitary task is to watch the man—see where he goes, whom he meets with. Other than that, let him be. But if you sense him planning to leave Innsbruck, you must let me know immediately.

"You will generally be able to find me in my hotel. And if not, you'll be able to follow my path out of the hotel. I'll mark my route with spots of chalk on the sidewalk according to our usual method: every few steps I'll let a bit of chalk fall onto the pavement and squash it with my foot. You should have no problem tracking me."

With that, Spitzkopf quit the room and returned to his own hotel.

And Fuchs got right to work.

CHAPTER FOUR
Making Strides

AFTER BREAKFAST, Signor Luigi Verdi did not sit in his room for long before changing clothes and heading out.

Meanwhile, on the street just in front of the hotel, an elegantly dressed young woman was promenading about, her face covered in a wide veil. No one would have recognized that it was actually our very own Fuchs in disguise.

Verdi passed her, strolling along and whistling a merry tune. Keeping to the other side of the street, the girl followed him, strolling just as nonchalantly but not letting him out of her sight. He walked down several streets until he arrived at the busy Innsbruck boulevard known as Maria-Theresien-Strasse. There he entered the building that housed the Italian consulate.

"Well, well," Fuchs thought to himself. "So you're going to see the consul from Italy. Seems my master was on the right track when he deduced that this bird has his talons in the espionage affair."

Fuchs waited on the street in front of the consulate for over an hour before his man appeared again. When he finally emerged, he was deep in discussion with another fellow Fuchs did not recognize. The two of them entered a breakfast bar.

Fuchs could not decide whether or not he should follow them in. But the two men were so engrossed in their conversation that there appeared to be no danger in it. They seemed not the least bit wary of being tracked. And so Fuchs made up his mind and entered.

The establishment consisted of one spacious room with a number of windows facing the street. The two men were sitting in a corner at a little table. They had ordered a couple glasses of liquor with some snacks.

The undercover Fraulein sat a few steps away. She ordered a coffee.

Even though he spoke Italian, Fuchs could only catch a few isolated words here and there of the men's conversation, as they were speaking in such low tones. Eventually Signor Verdi stood up and walked through a back door to the courtyard just outside.

As soon as he was outside the second man winked at Fuchs. To his astonishment, Fuchs now recognized his face. It was his master, Spitzkopf! He also recognized what the wink meant: "I won't be needing you anymore right now. You can run along."

For a moment he could do nothing but admire his master's skill in disguise, so clever that even he, his trusted second, had not recognized him. Then he paid for his coffee and left the establishment. When he was at the threshold, he turned around in time to spot the Italian returning and sitting back down across from Spitzkopf.

The two of them remained chatting for a good while longer before Spitzkopf ultimately left the bar. Verdi remained behind, leafing through a newspaper. Once Spitzkopf was out of earshot, the Italian exploded with laughter and muttered quietly to himself, "The man wants a slice of the whole pizza pie! But first things first—let him help me get what I need. Then I'll figure out what to do with him."

He sat there for a spell, then paid and left. Whistling a sunny sort of air, he sauntered along till he got to the Hotel Habsburg. On the steps, he bumped into our Spitzkopf, dressed in his usual manner. Naturally, it did not occur to the Italian for a second that he had been sitting with this man no more than half an hour earlier, discussing a plan of some importance with him.

Verdi then went up to his room while Spitzkopf made his way to see Fuchs at the Hotel Viktoria. He found Fuchs standing at his window and gazing down at the train station. Let any train arrive or depart and Fuchs would be there, just as the detective ordered, scrutinizing every one of the passengers coming or going in case he should notice anything suspicious.

Spitzkopf wanted to tell him what he had been up to today at the Italian consulate and what he had discussed with Verdi. But at that very moment they both caught sight of the Italian hurrying off to the depot, holding in his hand a small paper-wrapped parcel.

"Don't delay, Fuchs," Spitzkopf commanded. "Run after him. We must know where he's headed."

Fuchs shot out of the room like an arrow leaving a crossbow. Verdi was within his line of vision before he had even reached the waiting room.

In the first-class section of the room, Verdi exchanged greetings with another man, then handed over the parcel to him and said, "Careful with it! This is some real precious merchandise. Make sure it falls into the right hands, then come right back. There'll soon be more where that came from."

Fuchs heard every word. "I must follow that man," he thought to himself, "and prevent this special delivery from taking place. Of course, my master won't know where I disappeared to. But I'll send him a telegram on the way to let him know where I'm headed."

Verdi bade farewell to his fellow and left. The second man then shoved his way up to the ticket window, Fuchs right on his heels. Overhearing the man purchase a ticket for Brixen, Fuchs did the same and made sure to board the very train car he did and sit in a place that would allow him to watch the man closely.

The journey lasted several hours, with the train stopping at various stations on the way. At one of them, Fuchs telegraphed Spitzkopf to inform him of his destination.

It was already fairly late at night when the train arrived in Brixen. At the station, a porter from the Hotel Kaiserhof was awaiting the travelers with a carriage. Fuchs saw his man making his way to it and so made sure to hop on too, and at the hotel they happened to receive rooms right next to each other. A jolly pair of neighbors.

Just after Fuchs had run off from the hotel to the train station to follow Verdi, Spitzkopf had hurried back to his own hotel.

With his skeleton key he opened up Verdi's room and locked the door behind him. He soon had the cupboard opened too and spied the little traveling trunk inside, the one that had appeared to be so heavy before. But now it was half empty. There were only a few letters inside, along with a couple of cards and old newspapers. Spitzkopf absconded with some of them and locked the room door after him.

Just in time, too, for he had barely entered his own room when he heard Verdi's footsteps ascending the staircase, accompanied by the merry tune he was whistling. In the safety of his room, Spitzkopf began to look over the couple of letters he had taken. From their contents he was able to determine that Verdi was in contact with various people who would have been apprised of military secrets at the Franzensfeste Fort.

Whether they were indeed Austrian military personnel or civilians he could not tell from the letters. What he could tell was that whoever betrayed these secrets to individuals abroad must indeed be operating behind the Franzensfeste ramparts—and that he must work to have the traitor found out and arrested as quickly as possible.

The next train to Franzensfeste was leaving that evening. He would still have time to make his preparations. And so he packed all the necessities for the adventure ahead, then decided he would amble down to the dining room to take a cup of coffee.

On the steps down he encountered the hotel's letter carrier, who handed him the telegram from Fuchs.

"So!" Spitzkopf thought. "Fuchs is in the area of Franzensfeste already. We'll be able to work together. But first I've got to speak to the Italian again. I have to tell him that I've been called away on urgent business so that he doesn't begin to worry that I've deceived him."

He went back to his room, changed into what he had been wearing that morning, and positively flew down the stairs so that he would not coincidentally run into Verdi en route. Then he made his way to the Italian consulate, had the man called up on the telephone, and conveyed to him that they needed to speak, and pronto. Verdi told Spitzkopf he would be there prontissimo and arrived ten minutes later.

"So what's new, *mio amico*?" he asked Spitzkopf.

"Nothing, for now!" the detective answered. "But I happen to have received a most urgent telegram and must be leaving tonight to spend two days at Bregenz."

"That's too bad!" the Italian answered. "And here I was about to invite you to come with me tonight to Franzensfeste.

"See, after returning from the consulate this morning, I happened to receive a letter from my informant saying that it would be an opportune time to go down there and find out . . . everything."

"What a pity," said Spitzkopf. "But I must truly be leaving right away. You'll be able to manage without me in the meantime. And afterward I'll make my way to Franzensfeste to deliver to you the documents I promised."

"If it's impossible," Verdi answered, "we'll just have to do without you. Make sure you arrive in no later than two days though. Time won't stand still for us. We must strike while the iron's hot."

"Righto!" said Spitzkopf. "I'll be there in two days, you can be sure of that. Just tell me where I shall find you there."

"I'll be staying just nearby, in Brixen, at the Hotel Kaiserhof," said Verdi. "And if I happen not to be there I'll be in Mittewald, at the Gasthaus 'Wilder Bär'—the Wild Bear."

"Very well!" Spitzkopf answered. "I'll find you one way or another!"

They made their goodbyes, then Spitzkopf sprinted home quite as fast as he could so that he could change his clothing yet again before Verdi returned to the hotel.

"Well, here's a pretty pot of *pesce*," the detective thought to himself. "Either this man's a very sly schemer indeed or a total dunderhead. He's not being the least bit careful, conducting himself as freely as if the whole enterprise weren't so dangerous after all.

"He immediately accepted my offer to assist him in his espionage, without thinking for a moment of making inquiries as to who I am, whether or not I may be, oh, I don't know . . . a detective in disguise.

"A very pretty kettle of fish indeed. All I can hope is that the key to this mystery is bubbling away somewhere inside . . ."

CHAPTER FIVE
On the Bridge

It was a pitch black night.

Fuchs was sitting in the Hotel Kaiserhof in his dark room, his ear inclined to the wall that separated his quarters from those of the unknown individual he had been following. He could hear a whispered conversation emanating from the other side, and his trained ear was able to pick out three distinct voices.

What they were saying, though, he could not make out. He could not even tell what language it was, but it seemed to him something in the Slavic family. Finally he heard something in German: "*Fertig! Vorwärts!* Finished—onward!"

Then the interlocutors rose. Fuchs heard a shuffling of chairs and the locking of a cupboard. Their room door opened, and he could make out soft footsteps in the hallway.

Fuchs dashed to his window and spotted three dark figures exiting the hotel and moving quickly along the street that led to Franzensfeste. He waited for some ten minutes, then rushed off to catch up with them.

For over half an hour Fuchs was positively flying down the street. But there was no sign of the men. Eventually he figured he must have lost his way and that his effort had been for naught. But then—from a distance—he saw three darksome shadows hovering. He knew he had finally found them.

Now he moved along much more slowly and was sure to keep about two hundred paces away from the men lest they should notice him. He followed them at this speed for over an hour until they arrived at the bridge leading to the Franzensfeste Fort.

The clock struck midnight. Not a single beam of light from a single star could be seen through the ashen clouds that covered the heavens. The men in front traveled over the long, high bridge slowly, carefully—indeed so quietly that even Fuchs, with his sharp hearing, could not make out their footfalls. Groping the handrails, he felt his way along the bridge as he walked behind them.

When he arrived at the midpoint of the bridge, someone seized him by the throat and forced his whole body to the rail, trying to pitch him into the water. Fuchs struggled with all of his strength. He grabbed his opponent with both hands and muttered through gritted teeth, "If I'm going to fall, then you're coming with."

It was no use crying for help. He knew that the only other people in the immediate vicinity were the men he had been following, and when it came to Fuchs, they were not likely to be the goodest of good Samaritans.

In fact, he was certain the man grappling with him was one of their same criminal enterprise. He must have been standing watch to ensure the others were not being followed.

Their silent, scorn-soaked struggle lasted for several minutes. Fuchs could feel his energy dwindling. His opponent must have had the strength of Hercules—the way he wrapped himself around Fuchs made him feel he was being bound with iron chains, and he could feel his breath being choked out of him. Finally the man pinned Fuchs into a position of defeat, rammed up against the guardrail with his head hanging perilously over edge.

Just a bit more force and Fuchs would go plummeting from the eighty-meter bridge down into the deep, roiling waters below.

Fuchs defended himself from this fate with mad desperation. He bit the man, sinking his teeth deep into the meat of him, and wriggled with all his limbs to try to free himself.

He had almost lost all hope. He could feel himself getting dizzy and felt a stream of warm blood trickling from his mouth. Soon . . . soon . . . his last ounce of strength would leave him.

But suddenly he felt the man's grip relaxing. And before he even had time to see what had happened, the light of an electric torch flashed in his face. Behind it—his master. Spitzkopf.

Lying at his feet was his attacker—a tall, strong boor of a man, his face wildly contorted. He was flat on the ground with his limbs spread wide, unconscious.

Spitzkopf had dealt the man such a thwack over the head with the handle of his revolver that he had gone out like a light.

As for his own light, Spitzkopf quickly shut off his electric torch so that the beam would not alert anyone to the presence of unexpected visitors on the bridge.

Fuchs, meanwhile, was gasping for air. He huffed and puffed

as he wiped the cold sweat from his forehead.

Spitzkopf let him recover for a moment as he got to work dealing with his attacker. He bound the brute's hands and feet and tied him to one of the bridge's support beams. He wanted to be sure the man could not move, even after he came to.

Then he carried Fuchs down off the bridge to the side from which they had entered. "Come away from here," he said to him as he toted him away. "It's dangerous. I'll tell you everything when we've reached the open field."

As soon as they had, Fuchs spread out on the grass. The deathly struggle had left him fatigued, like every muscle had been drained of its vigor. Spitzkopf sat down at his side, intending to brief him on all that had taken place.

But before he could get a word out, a piercing whistle was heard from the other side of the bridge, three tones in a row.

"That signal's for me," Spitzkopf said. "They're calling. I have to run over there at once."

With those words he bolted up and tore off once more to the bridge. Fuchs remained where he was, stunned. He had no inkling of what to do next. But soon he made up his mind and ran, with the last of his strength, in the same direction whither he had seen Spitzkopf vanishing into the darkness.

CHAPTER SIX
Spitzkopf's Plan

WHEN SPITZKOPF was still in Vienna, paying his call at the Ministry of War to inquire into the particulars of the Franzensfeste case, he had realized that he would not be getting much information out of the military brass. And it would be near impossible to identify the actual traitor if he were not allowed access to all the intelligence that had been collected nor permitted to enter the place where the crimes had been perpetrated.

The military was very cautious—and not at all trusting—when it came to such matters. It was even worse this time, as the officials already suspected Lieutenant Silbermann and were confident that the military inquest would discover everything in due time.

But after traveling to Innsbruck and noticing the peculiar Italian there, whom he had soon suspected of being involved in the case, Spitzkopf hit upon an ingenious idea of his own.

He strolled over to the Italian consulate in Innsbruck disguised as a former officer in the Austrian military who, because of a petty offense, had been punished with undue severity and pushed out of the service. This character claimed to know plenty of military secrets, especially from the Franzensfeste Fort, where he had served for a substantial length of time. He was prepared, if the price were right, to betray these secrets to the Italians and also to infiltrate the fort so as to steal further plans that could be of utmost strategic importance to them.

The consul answered saying that he was not capable of, and uninterested in, getting his hands dirty with such deeds himself, but that it just so happened that at that very time a likely collaborator for the project was in Innsbruck. This was a trusted man of confidence to the Italian war ministry, one who was already engaged in such work. If Spitzkopf wanted, he could easily be introduced to the man.

Naturally Spitzkopf agreed to it. The consul then telephoned the man, inviting him round. When he arrived Spitzkopf unfurled his full plan of action to the two of them, and they assented to every bit of it. They also settled upon quite a hefty reward for Spitzkopf—but in order to receive it, he had to supply them with all the juicy secrets of which he had boasted. In addition to that, he had to assist in the planned break-in at Franzensfeste to collect the further documents they expected were stored there.

Verdi went along with all of it. And he did not think for a moment of looking into this curious new gentleman's background. The detective had played his role well, and the Italian was left with not a drop of suspicion. And so, naturally, the man proceeded to regale Spitzkopf with all the details of his schemes, the documents he had already managed to have stolen from Franzensfeste, and those remaining in the fort on which he still had designs.

For Spitzkopf, it was of prime importance to figure out who within the fort had managed to procure the documents for him. But he was sure not to ask everything at one go, lest the Italian grow suspicious.

Later, though, when Spitzkopf noticed him carrying a parcel to the train station, he began to fear that the man had duped him—that he already had a new scheme underway and meant to make a fool of Spitzkopf. And so he resolved to travel to Franzensfeste immediately. He wanted to be on site in case anything took place. When Verdi told him at the consulate that he was also bound there that day, Spitzkopf rejoiced. He could pin down the birdie there in the midst of his knavery, when he least suspected it.

Of course, he made sure to put on such attire as would render the Italian entirely powerless to recognize him: he disguised himself as an elderly man, hobbling along with the aid of a crutch, a black-rimmed monocle fixed over one eye. He sat in the same train car as Verdi, in the compartment just next to his and observed that the man was traveling alone. No accomplices had joined him—at least not yet.

CHAPTER SEVEN
In the Fortress

THEY ARRIVED AT Franzensfeste late that night.

Spitzkopf alighted a minute later than the Italian and spied him positively galloping off from the train station and making his way directly to the bridge. The detective immediately cast aside his monocle and crutch, smeared the age makeup off of his face, and bounded off toward the offices of the fortress command.

The commandant was already asleep. Spitzkopf woke him up and identified himself, telling him that he was ready to go and have the traitors arrested.

At first, a look of distrust twisted up the man's features. Somehow he could not quite wrap his head around whatever extraordinary thing the detective seemed to be telling him. But Spitzkopf's resolve impressed him very much, so the commandant granted his request for a number of soldiers to be dispatched who would answer to him alone and who would be kept unaware of exactly what mission this was to which they had been assigned.

Spitzkopf positioned them in a dark corner of the fortification, ordering them to keep watch and not to move from the spot no matter what they saw. But as soon as they noticed anyone slipping in through a window, they were to whistle loudly three times.

They were not to do anything else. They were not needed for anything else.

The soldiers posted themselves in such a way that they had a view of the entire fortification, but no one had a view of them.

Meanwhile, Spitzkopf went back to the bridge to try to find out where the Italian had gotten to. But he had spent half an hour with the commandant, and so he bolted down the bridge at a lightning-fast clip until he came to the spot where he found his Fuchs grappling with the unknown accomplice.

After freeing him and bringing him to the open field, he intended to receive from his assistant an account of all that had happened to him. But then he heard the whistle blowing. He had to return to the fort.

He ran back over the bridge as fast as his feet could carry him. Arriving at the fort's archives, he hid under a desk and waited, watching . . . he was ready.

He lay there for several minutes until he heard a sort of knocking on the wall. Then a small window opened and two faces appeared. He remained curled up under the desk, stock still, waiting for the two men to clamber into the room.

Once they did, one of them took a ring of keys out of his bag and attempted to open a large drawer full of papers. But at that very moment Spitzkopf climbed out from under the table and shone his electric torch right in the two men's faces. In his other hand he grasped his revolver. "Move a muscle and I'll shoot," he roared.

The intruders stood petrified. They wanted to charge at Spitzkopf, but the revolver glinted in their eyes in such a way as to render them immobile. They did not dare.

They remained thus, in a silent standoff, for several moments. Both of Spitzkopf's hands were occupied—in one he held his torch and in the other his revolver. He could not do anything with them unless he set one of these items down. He feared setting aside the revolver lest one of the men should attack him, and likewise the torch as it would leave the room completely dark, and who knows what might happen then.

But then the door opened—and in sprang Fuchs.

"Bravo, Fuchs!" Spitzkopf cheered. "You've been very clever. Now be so good as to treat these two men to some nice handcuffs."

Fuchs did not tarry for a moment. He extracted the iron handcuffs from Spitzkopf's pocket and immediately shackled the men's wrists. They gritted their teeth out of sheer rage, but were too afraid to move.

Once Fuchs had finished his handiwork, Spitzkopf felt safe putting down his revolver and torch, saying to his assistant, "You remain here. Keep watch over this pair of characters. And make sure no other hotshot comes in here ready to cause some trouble. I'm going off to search for their cronies."

He hotfooted it out of the room and made a circuit of the fortress, peering into every corner—but saw no one suspicious. Meanwhile the sun had begun to come up. He figured the other conspirators must now have taken great care to hide themselves.

Not overthinking matters, he ran back over the bridge, back to the beam to which he had tied the man who had attacked Fuchs.

But now—there was no sign of him. "My plan to nab the whole gang . . . it's leaked . . ." he thought to himself. "They must have seen the man tied up here and guessed that they were being pursued. But they can't hide forever. Ready or not, here I come."

He sped back to the fortress and called back the band of soldiers the commandant had left at his disposal.

"Come with me!" he ordered. "I'm going to run ahead. You keep fifty paces behind. And make sure not to lose sight of me."

CHAPTER EIGHT
Come Out, Come Out, Wherever You Are

SPITZKOPF REMEMBERED the Italian telling him that in Mittewald he would be staying at the Wild Bear guesthouse.

"That's where the gang's hideout must be," he figured. "And that's where I'll find them."

He walked for three quarters of an hour, on winged feet, until he could just discern the first houses of Mittewald. It was already quite bright out. Upon turning onto the first street of the town, Spitzkopf saw the great sign from afar: *Gasthaus zum Wilden Bar.*

He waited for the soldiers to catch up with him and gave them an order: "Post yourselves up around the perimeter of the building. Let no one out!"

Then he banged on the door of the guesthouse with his fist. After a few seconds the proprietor, in a dressing gown and nightcap, poked his head through a window and asked, "Who's there?

And what do you want?"

Spitzkopf could tell at once he was not quite as sleepy as he was acting. "Open up at once! I have something most urgent to tell you!" he called up fervently. Meanwhile he thought to himself, "Seems I've come to the right place. It appears that man is one of their confederates."

The forceful tone of Spitzkopf's cry had made its intended impression on the innkeeper. The door soon creaked open.

Spitzkopf entered. The man asked him what his desire might be.

"I need the gentlemen who checked in here some forty-five minutes ago," Spitzkopf answered evenly.

The innkeeper stared at him. His eyes widened. "What gentlemen are you talking about? Not a soul has stopped here for the night." But Spitzkopf could tell by the man's stunned reaction that he was simply keeping up the act.

"Listen to me, my good fellow!" Spitzkopf demanded. "I'm not here to play games. I know quite well who is staying here. And you can be sure that I'll find them too. Now play your part nicely, and things'll go just fine. If not they could get quite nasty. Because if you don't stick to my script, I'll know that you yourself are one of the star villains of this ragtag troupe."

"But what do you want from me?" the innkeeper asked, aquiver with fear. "I don't understand you. I don't know what you're on about. I'm an honest, upstanding citizen. I'll go and complain to the mayor you're disturbing my nighttime rest, I will!"

Spitzkopf could not help bursting into laughter. "You, an honest upstanding citizen? One who refuses to say where a bunch of dangerous criminals are whom you happen to be hiding in your very honest, upstanding establishment? But I'll get you talking before long. See this bit of iron? Know what that is?" Spitzkopf held out a revolver. It shone in the light of the streetlamps.

"Heavens!" the man cried out in desperation. "Help me! Rescue me! He's going to shoot me dead!"

But Spitzkopf stood his ground, turning the revolver over and over so it sparkled right in the man's eyes. "Go on and scream!" he said, totally unbothered. "So your friends rush to your aid! Right into my waiting arms."

The man stood there in abject horror. He realized how he had given himself away. His hue and cry had drawn the crooks up from the basement where they had been hiding. It had not in the least occurred to them that they, ultimately, were the intended targets of this clamor. They had fallen into quite the trap.

A door hidden in the floor opened and up popped the head of our infamous Italian. Spitzkopf made sure his revolver flashed in the man's eye and called out: "Remain where you are, Signor Verdi! I'm coming right down, and I've got the Franzensfeste plans for you."

"Mamma mia, it's you! A damned spy!" Verdi snarled back, through gritted teeth. He recognized in Spitzkopf's face the man who promised to be of assistance in his reconnaissance mission at the fort. "So this is how you mean to help me! Well, here's your reward!"

And with that, he launched a dagger at Spitzkopf—and missed.

"Well, that's not what I call polite," Spitzkopf laughed. "Is that usually how you receive your guests? You told me yourself I could find you in Mittewald at this guesthouse, the Wild Bear."

"Yes . . . I've betrayed myself!" the Italian cried out, his tone wild and desperate. Then, seizing another dagger, he stabbed himself in the heart. "But you won't be capturing me alive."

A fountain of blood gushed from his breast. The dagger had penetrated his heart deeply. He screamed out again, in blackest despair, and his body dropped like a stone down the stairs that led up to the trapdoor.

Spitzkopf went to the opening to peer through it. Three others remained below. He could not make out their faces in the darkness.

"Come up at once and surrender yourselves willingly if you

wish to live," he called to them.

But not one of them moved.

Meanwhile the innkeeper took the opportunity while Spitzkopf was diverted with the goings-on below and escaped through the window.

But the soldiers stood outside, and they immediately detained him.

Spitzkopf had a free hand now. He did not have to trouble himself over the innkeeper potentially attacking him from behind. And so he knelt down over the trap door, shone his electric torch into the hideout below, pointed his revolver, and bellowed out an order: "Come up one by one or I'll shoot."

The men below remained silent. He fired off his gun, aiming at a vacant corner.

They realized he was not kidding around—and called back in unison, "Don't shoot! We surrender."

"Good," Spitzkopf answered. "Now come up one by one, with your hands up."

They did as they were told.

He clapped them all in handcuffs and entrusted them to the custody of the soldiers, who had in the meantime brought in the likewise restrained innkeeper.

In the yard of the guesthouse stood a spacious wagon. Spitzkopf had two horses led out of the stall and hitched up to it. Then the flock of shackled birdies were pent up in the wagon like so many geese bound for market. With the help of the soldiers, Spitzkopf hauled up Verdi's corpse and laid him out beside his confederates. Then he returned to the Franzensfeste Fort.

It was high noon there. The fortress commandant had fully arisen from his slumber now and was running to and fro in the courtyard, stunned. He had not yet been told all that had taken place.

Fuchs was sitting in the archives, meanwhile, keeping an eye on the handcuffed intruders. He was wary of giving the commandant any information until Spitzkopf returned.

When he did reappear, the detective gave a full report to the commandant, in the presence of all of his officers. The captives were brought in for interrogation. One of them turned out to be none other than Corporal Ivan Czechowicz, he who had first pinned the blame for the theft of the documents on Lieutenant Leon Silbermann.

Czechowicz could not be induced, however, to reveal further information on who exactly his contact Verdi was or how he was first introduced to him. None of the papers found on the Italian's body, nor in his room at the guesthouse, provided any clues as to his background. These papers did include, however, all of the documents that had been stolen from the fort several days before.

The letters that Spitzkopf had taken from his hotel room in Innsbruck managed to fill in more of his story. The man hailed from Rome and was an agent of the Italian Ministry of War. The other captured accomplices were his countrymen, all of them deeply involved in the espionage scheme. The innkeeper of the Wild Bear was likewise partner to the whole enterprise.

Verdi was later buried in Mittewald. The arrestees were delivered to prison, and in time the courts dealt them severe sentences.

Silbermann, the Jewish lieutenant, was freed from his military detention at once. Soon after, as a means of making amends, he was promoted to first lieutenant.

On the same day that they apprehended the criminals, Spitzkopf and Fuchs returned to Vienna—and to a most generous monetary award, bestowed upon the brave detective by Austria's Ministry of War.

Issue 8: The Flesh Peddler

אכטעס העפט. פרייז 20 העלער.

דער מערכען הענדלער.

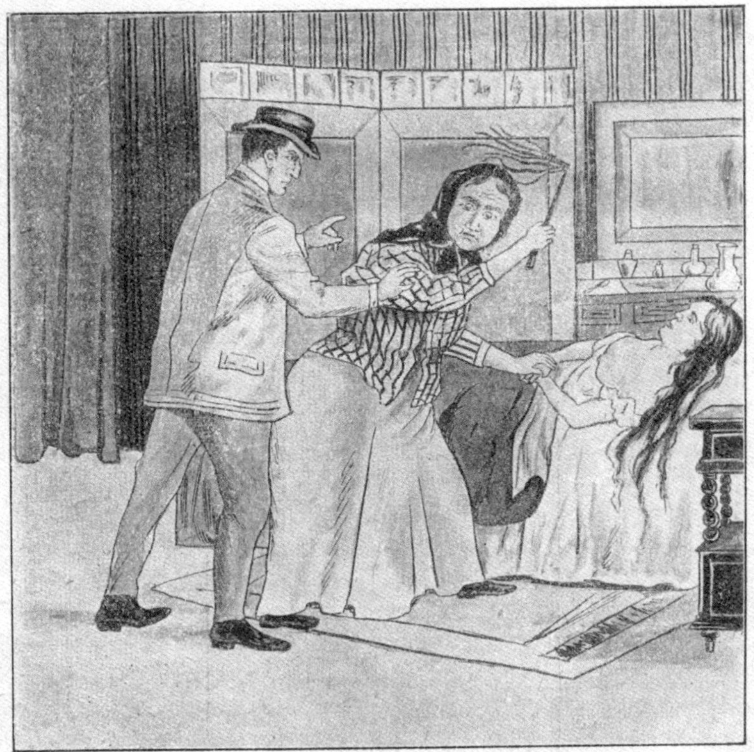

אין בעט ליגט א יונג מיידעל האלב נאקעט, מיט אראבגעלאזטע לאנגע האר. נעבען איהר שטעהט די „מוהמע”, מיט איין האנד האלט זיא איהר צו די צוזאמענגעבונדענע הענד, אין דער אנדערער האלט זי הויך אויפגעהויבען א גרויסען קאנטשוק מיט א גראבען בונד ריעמענס. — דאס מיידעל שרייט יעמערליך.. די „מוהמע” האט גאר נישט געמערקט, אז אימיצער איז אריינגעקומען און שפיצקאפף לויפט שנעל צו און האפט זי אן ביי דער האנד.

The Flesh Peddler

CHAPTER ONE
Wedded Bliss

It is a most joyous day in the home of Mr. Leybush Suchestow. Reb Leybush's eldest daughter is to be married. And not only that but Rivke, or, as she prefers to be called, Regina, is marrying just the sort of man she has dreamt of: a secular, modern sort of Jewish fellow, and a rich one to boot! A second Midas, a man with money to burn.

Reb Leybush is no slouch, either: a respectable householder, a learned fellow, and with a pedigree of some distinction. His father was a rabbi in a Galician shtetl, where his eldest brother happens to preside as rabbi still today. Leybush himself was supposed to have become a rabbi too. But finding a position proved difficult, and having married into a wealthy family and receiving a dowry of several thousand Rhenish florins,[11] he went into business instead and remained a merchant for the rest of his career.

For a good while he was considered a wealthy and important man. He was manager of the *khevre-kedishe*—the burial society—and trustee of the Jewish community in his municipality as well as the trustee over its funds. Money set aside to serve as dowries for poor brides and aid for orphans and widows was deposited in the coffers he guarded. He had earned a name among his fellow Jews as the most trusted person in the region.

But after a number of years the wheel of fortune started spinning in the opposite direction. He was starting to bleed cash in his various dealings, but as he was an honest man, he insisted on paying back his investors down to the last cent, such that he was left hardly any capital with which to run his business.

Still he slaved away for several years, making sure to at least earn enough to lead a respectable lifestyle and raise his children in a respectable fashion.

And he had quite the brood. Besides the eldest, sweet Rivkele, he had three other grown daughters. When fortune was still smiling on him he had seen to it that their manners were cultivated and their minds keenly educated, such that now they put on lofty airs, and it was difficult for Reb Leybush to provide for them in the fashion they expected.

Once the girls had grown up and matches began to be proposed for them, disaster was imminent. He could not give them much at all in the way of a dowry. And as they say: *Ven a tate git nisht di meyes, hot er oykh nit keyn deyes*—if Papa can't pay the piper, he can't call the tune. No matter what groom was suggested to Rivkele, she did not care for him, shrugging off the match as if she were to the manor born.

Of course, she had been very finely brought up, and she was lovely to look at. If she had lived in some large city it would not have been hard to locate a man eager to marry her and worthy of her charms, ready to take her just the way she was, without needing much in the way of compensation. But in Milanowo, the small Polish shtetl where she lived, and which indeed she had never left, such volunteers were nowhere to be found.

Reb Leybush's qualifications for the man were primarily characteristics that he himself bore: he should be a Jew, of good parentage, and a Torah scholar. But as he had little gelt to throw around, he could not quite net anyone who fit the profile.

Rivkele, however . . . she simply laughed at every candidate her father brought before her. Romantic novels had been her daily bread. She dreamt of a groom like the ones that populated their pages: the very ideal of a modern gentleman.

Father and daughter often squabbled—sometimes outright

battled—over the matter. And Reb Leybush's heart grieved for his eldest girl, seeing her growing older and older and her younger sisters not getting any younger, and he, poor soul, lacking the means to support them all according to their expectations. He rued the day he first hired a private tutor for his daughter and arranged for her to be educated in the modern fashion.

"If only she were raised up to be a nice Jewish girl like her friends," he used to sigh, "she wouldn't have her nose so high up in the air as she does now. She wouldn't dream of a castle in the clouds knowing she could only reach the treetops." But now she was *gebildet*—cultivated, much to his chagrin—and she wanted a dandy. And such dandies demanded dollars.

"And I, sad to say it, am a pauper now!" he would lament to himself. "What am I going to do?"

Rivkele—or Regina—rued the day also. The day she was born, that is. She cursed her lot at having been raised out in the sticks, in some godforsaken shtetl in the middle of nowhere and with such a zealot for a father. "If only I'd been born to other parents, to civilized people, in a big city, my life would have been quite different. My parents would know to treasure me. And the young people would simply fawn over me. I would have but to wave my hand and ten bridegrooms would be groveling at my feet."

But what was done was done—and it spelled doom. Reb Leybush was intransigent in his traditional religious beliefs, and a pauper besides. As for Fraulein Regina, no denizen of the shtetl could quite understand her. These days, not a single happy moment passed in the Suchestow household. But then, altogether out of the blue, a modern gentleman appeared in Milanowo[12]—one who looked like he had sprung right out of Regina's books. His face was beardless, but he sported a long moustache. A golden pince-nez perched atop his nose. His collar stood straight up, and his shoes absolutely sparkled. He looked like nothing less than an aristocrat.

And that was not all. On his fingers he wore gold rings studded with diamonds. A golden tiepin, likewise with a diamond at its center, shone at his throat. It was all testament to his being a confirmed man of wealth, a real magnifico.

He had checked in at the only guesthouse in the shtetl, a tiny place, and told the front desk that he was the owner of a petroleum refinery in Romania. He explained that he had come because he heard that there were oil deposits in the region waiting to be tapped.

The appearance of the strange gentleman in Milanowo, meanwhile, proved to be a major event on the shtetl calendar. When he went out promenading on the street, the entire populace gathered to gaze at him. In the small synagogue, not to mention in the bathhouse—if you'll excuse me for mentioning them in the same breath—he was the topic of every conversation, and everyone relished in guessing at just how much he was probably worth.

Reb Yankel, who ran the almshouse, took him for a man of no less than fifty thousand.

"You're a know-nothing!" Leyb-Ber the tailor informed him. "Just the things he's got on him, the watch and all that, are worth that much! He must have at least a hundred thousand."

"Oh, so we have a couple of experts here," Yekheskl the cobbler teased them. "You ninnies ever even *seen* an oil refinery? Just one tiny barrel of the stuff is worth more than a hundred thousand! I'd give anything to own what he owns, that being over a quarter of a million! Heck, I'd gladly share it with the two of you!"

"You ever heard of such a thing in all your life?" exclaimed Shloyme the *mekler*, the man whose trade it was to buy and sell anything he could get his hands on in the shtetl but who owned almost nothing himself. "He's got it in his head to buy up all the fields around the shtetl, from here to deep in the mountains. Ya know what that smells like to me? To me it smells like half a million! I'm telling you, the gent's a millionaire, plain and simple!"

"It would be a bit of luck for the shtetl if he really did buy the oil fields," added Ruvn the bathhouse attendant. "He'd end up settling here, and we'd gain a rich man, a real bigshot. We could all make a good living off such a guy!"

"Ya know the one thing I'm curious about, though?" Khone-Leyb the town matchmaker piped up. "Whether this character's a bachelor. If he is, making a match for such a person wouldn't be a bad bit o' business, not by half!"

"So whaddya waitin' for?" the *mekler* encouraged. "Go ahead and ask him! I've been to see him a few times already, and you better believe I managed to carry off a few sweet deals in the process! Why, he's not liable to smack ya!"

"I'm sure he's right," the matchmaker thought to himself. "Sure as I am that I'm a Jew."

So that very day Khone-Leyb sought out the millionaire and asked him outright, there on his threshold, whether or not he was a bachelor, and if so, whether he might be amenable to a match being made for him.

Before answering, the gentleman made sure to welcome him in most graciously and treat him to a Cuban cigar. Then he responded to the question: "I did come here to make a business match, you know," the man answered. "Not a marriage match. But I have seen quite a number of comely maidens in this town, and to tell you the truth I like them better than the girls we have back home in Romania. There's something about them that's more delicate, more natural and charming. I wouldn't at all be against choosing one here for my own.

"She needn't have money. God knows I've got enough of that. I just want a young, pretty girl with a nice figure. One who carries herself well. So that she'd be fit to be installed in my palace as my lady wife.

"If you have such a one among your stocks, you can bring her."

Well, you can probably guess this made our Khone-Leyb go half crazy with delight. Who would have dreamt it? Such a stroke of luck! The handsome fee was as good as in his pocket already!

And he already had the perfect match in mind: yes, our Mr. Leybush Suchestow's very own daughter. She had every virtue the gentleman was seeking.

He ran at once, his bit of news burning on his lips, to the home of Reb Leybush. Failing to find him there, he instead told Fraulein Regina of the great happiness that lay in wait for her.

Regina had, truth be told, never quite been able to bear this matchmaker. He was in the habit of suggesting religiously fanatical young men to her, oafish and slovenly benchwarmers at the yeshiva, the sort of boys who have their nose ever in a Talmud and in Yiddish are sneeringly labeled *khnyok*.

But today, after telling her who the match was . . . today the matchmaker was an honored guest. If she had not been too shy, she would have wrapped her arms around him and given him a kiss.

Reb Leybush soon came home and was told, too, of the pot of jam his daughter had fallen into. Khone-Leyb chewed his ear off so hungrily that he barely had a moment to ponder the matter over. All he could do was consent to the young gentleman paying them a visit that very day.

He came after dark. Fraulein Regina immediately found favor in his eyes. She had "enchanted" him—"*batsoybert*," as he put it—and that very night, accompanied by the customary breaking of plates, they signed the traditional engagement contract.

The bridegroom gifted his fiancée a golden pocket watch on a golden chain, earrings, and bracelets. He positively weighed her down in gold from head to foot. How she glimmered, how she glittered—so much so that even Reb Leybush, who himself was no pushover and not impressed so easily, attained a certain new respect for her.

"Fancy that! A millionairess!" he thought.

Naturally, it occurred to no one that it might be a worthy idea to look into who exactly this tycoon might be. They did not even ask him what city he came from or who his father was.

He gave his name as Franz Braunwald and mentioned some shtetl with a Romanian name, one that the Jews of Milanowo could not even pronounce.

The wedding was fixed for a fortnight's time, as the groom had to travel home soon, he said. Then, after several months, he would return to Milanowo, as the engineers in the region first had to ascertain whether there were indeed oil deposits to be found.

And today the wedding is upon us. Nuptials just as joyous as God commanded, with klezmorim, a wedding jester, even the requisite feast for the poor. The guests made merry until the sun came up. And as for the bride—she was in seventh heaven. What a thrill it all was!

Reb Leybush was thrilled too. He had married off his eldest daughter so well and was no longer worried about what would turn up for her sisters. Rivkele promised to take care of them, providing bountiful dowries and searching out the best that groomdom had to offer.

All the shtetl shared in Reb Leybush Suchestow's joy. Firstly, he was such a distinguished man and had been restored to his former eminence. Everyone used to be so sorry for him in the days when he, who had once been so prosperous, had to toil away for his daily bread.

And secondly, the whole populace considered it a great honor for the shtetl that a local daughter had risen so. Many were the mothers, on the day of Regina's wedding, who consoled their grown-up girls at home, themselves on the lookout for husbands, with words such as these: "You see, my child? God doesn't abandon anyone. Rivkele, Reb Leybush's daughter, waited and waited . . . until God saw to it she had to wait no longer! He'll see to it for you, too—soon you'll be a bride; I just know it's true!"

CHAPTER TWO

Like a Stone Dropped in a Lake

THE YOUNG COUPLE remained in the shtetl until after Shabbos, and every night such a feast was thrown as is fitting for a man of great wealth. These were the *sheve-brokhes*, the "seven benedictions," the nightly banquets at which the bride and groom are blessed and feted for the week after their nuptials.

And on Friday night the celebration was something tremendous. The whole shtetl was positively *bathed* in beer, and the streets were littered with the empty pods of peas and green beans.

When Shabbos ended the couple left town, before Rivkele had yet received any kind of trousseau from her new husband. Braunwald told her that he would buy her everything her heart desired once they reached Bucharest.

All she took along for her journey were the few dresses she owned and the jewelry her groom had gifted her. Her parents escorted the carriage for several miles outside of the shtetl. She vowed that as soon as she arrived in her new home, she would write them and also send along handsome sums of money.

Reb Leybush and his family bade hearty farewells to the daughter and her new husband, then returned to Milanowo and counted the days until they would receive the promised letter from their dear Rivkele—their *milyonerke*, as they called her. For several days the entire household kept a keen lookout for the post.

After five days they received a picture postcard from Bucharest. In it Rivkele wrote that she had arrived to the city safe and sound and would spend a few days there, shopping for her trousseau, before joining her husband in his hometown.

She also assured them that she would send a good long letter the next day, but that at present she was too exhausted from her journey to write any further.

Some three or four days passed, though, and there was still

no word from her. Her parents grew anxious. Impatient. They did not know what to think.

Every day they ran out to greet the letter carrier. They would even wait for him at the post office. But still—nothing. Not a sign of Rivkele. She had disappeared, like a stone dropped in a lake.

The whole shtetl knew of it. Everyone took an interest in her and was itching to learn where she had gotten to. From dusk till dawn Reb Leybush's house was thronged with neighbors, friends, and acquaintances coming to check whether or not there had been any news of the girl.

Reb Leybush, meanwhile, was nearly going out of his mind. He paced this way and that, clueless of what course to take. And every day he wrote another letter to his son-in-law, to which he never received any answer.

Finally he decided to send him a telegram.

But when he arrived at the post office to do so, he was met with another misfortune: the Romanian town that his son-in-law had named to him did not exist.

"You must have misheard him," the postmaster tried to console Reb Leybush. "Your son-in-law must have said something else, and you wrote it down incorrectly."

But Reb Leybush stated categorically that he had made sure to ask his son-in-law before his departure to make absolutely certain that the address Leybush had written down was correct, and the man confirmed that it was.

But it was no use. No telegrams can be dispatched to a place that is not on any map.

When Reb Leybush walked through the doors of his home, he looked barely alive. His daughter was nowhere to be found, his son-in-law was nowhere to be found. Disappeared like a stone into a lake.

Earlier the family had hoped that maybe, God forbid, the daughter had just fallen ill or gotten into some kind of accident—something from which she might soon recover. But now they were faced with a complete mystery. What could have possibly taken place?

No one in the shtetl could imagine the answer. No one would dare think that the rich gentleman, the millionaire, could be some kind of swindler, with intentions far less than noble.

Reb Leybush's wife, a sharp woman with a strong sense of reason, was the first to come to her senses. One day, she said to her husband, "Do what I say, Leybush. Don't lose faith. Go to my brother, the merchant in Lemberg. His business concerns stretch all over the world, and you know how much he's traveled and become acquainted with places near and far. He can advise you on what you must do."

Reb Leybush followed her wise counsel at once and, that same day, traveled off to visit his brother-in-law.

CHAPTER THREE
A Nightmarish Discovery

After Reb Leybush told his brother-in-law the whole story, down to the last detail, this intelligent, world-wise man was left with no doubt as to what had taken place.

"You've been dealt a terrible card, dear brother-in-law," he said to Reb Leybush. "Your daughter has fallen into the vilest of hands. God knows if you will ever see her again."

Reb Leybush sat there like he had just been knocked out cold. "What are you talking about? What are you saying?" he asked, in wild tones. "Speak plainly!"

"Have you ever . . ." said the brother-in-law, "have you ever heard of the sort of criminal they call a 'flesh peddler'?"

"No! No!" Reb Leybush screamed. "Such peddlers, no, I don't know what that could mean."

"And yet such peddlers do exist," the brother-in-law went on. "Their business consists of this: seducing young, beautiful girls, then selling them to brothels.

"They go about it by various means. Sometimes they travel to a small shtetl, some far-flung place, and seduce a girl, still a child, then marry her and abduct her to Turkey, Egypt, or America, where she is sold to a brothel. Other times they come pretending to be agents of factories or large companies, ones needing women to work the assembly line or to do sales, and take several girls away at once, promising them good positions with high salaries. Those ones get sold to brothels too of course."

"But my Rivkele is a good, pious, kosher Jewish daughter," Reb Leybush cried. "She wouldn't let herself be defiled. She'd run away under cover of the night, she would jump out a window . . . she would even take her own life."

"Yes, yes," his brother-in-law interrupted. "She's bound to do anything she can. But the truth is she can't do much. The girls they deceive are penned up like arrestees, like prisoners. None of them escape. She'll be watched day and night. They'll force her by the most horrific means to not be stubborn, to do as she's told.

"The strongest girl—she could be made positively of iron—eventually grows tired. She gives up. She does what they demand of her. No girl has ever come out of it clean."

Reb Leybush fell unconscious after hearing these words. It was a long while before they managed to revive him. When they did he was in a state of utter desperation. He wanted to kill himself.

His brother-in-law felt terribly sorry for him and regretted having told him the unvarnished truth. But upon reflection, he realized it would not have done any good to hide it from him.

After Reb Leybush had the chance to calm himself somewhat, and to reflect likewise, he made the following speech to his brother-in-law: "You should know that I refuse to go home until I get my daughter back again. You must do everything within your power to free her. I can hardly believe that such outrages can take place in our world and no one can do anything about it. The worst cases of crime—theft, arson, murder, fraud—are eventually cracked, and the criminals are punished. But you're telling me that against these people, these most heinous of criminals, there's nothing that can be done? Not by the police, the military, the courts? It's impossible!

"You must help me! Come, we'll run off to alert the police, the courts, the provincial governor, the minister-president! Hell—until it gets right up to the kaiser himself! I must free my daughter!"

Reb Leybush went on so; it was as if he were in the throes of a fever. But his brother-in-law listened patiently to every word. His heart overflowed with compassion for the distraught father. But what could he do?

Finally he remembered something. A certain organization had been formed some time ago to combat this trafficking of women. Societies were formed, and committees, and women came down from somewhere in Germany, along with members of the fraternal organization B'nai B'rith, and they gave long speeches and tried to combat this nefarious industry.

Until now he had not troubled himself with the matter. He was not really one for community activism, being too occupied with his own business endeavors. But now he resolved to get in touch with these societies. Maybe they would be able to help him.

He told Reb Leybush what he knew about the groups and clarified for him that getting the police or the governor or the minister-president involved would do nothing, as Leybush had no idea where his daughter actually was.

But maybe the people from the anti-trafficking organization would be able to advise the two men. These advocates have taken an interest in the whole business and may have a notion of where the captured women are eventually transported to.

Reb Leybush managed to recover a little from his agitated state. In fact, he accompanied his brother-in-law at once to the local B'nai B'rith chapter. Maybe someone there might know what to do.

CHAPTER FOUR
An Oration—and a Recommendation

AT THE B'NAI B'RITH offices, the two men met first with the secretary of the chapter, who was himself involved with combating the trafficking of women. Reb Leybush recounted the whole story to him. Once he finished listening, the secretary launched into a lengthy sermon on the proper raising of children.

"You are yourself guilty," the secretary stated. "You are bringing up your children in such a fashion that ensures you will later reap terrible trouble and grief from them.

"Let us examine what your kind does. You yourself are a learned Jew, and pious, maybe even a bit of a Hasid. You and your compatriots raise your sons according to the traditional Jewish ways. Until the age of fourteen or fifteen they are stuck in a cheder learning Torah, then they continue poring over the Talmud in a house of study or a yeshiva. And by the end they can't even sign their own names in the Latin alphabet.

"I don't mean to criticize or say whether this is good or bad. From your standpoint, according to your customs and ways, you may be doing right.

"Why is it, though, that you all raise your daughters so differently? I'm not talking about teaching them to write, or read Polish and German, or do arithmetic, and other skills of the kind. All of that is very useful, and everyone should know such things. Everyone *must* know such things. But it's not enough for your lot. Most Jewish girls, even in the small shtetlach, are now expected to be able to babble away in French or English and play the piano or the zither. They waste away their days reading novels. They dull their brains by getting involved in modern social movements, though they barely understand their true purpose or whether they might actually do a bit of good.

"Such a daughter becomes a stranger to her parents. She considers her father a religious fanatic and an uncivilized creature, and her mother an outmoded old Jewess who doesn't understand the true necessities of life. She looks upon her brother, indeed upon everyone around her, as a bunch of unusual specimens who must descend from around the time of Terach, the father of Abraham.

"And so the family comes to ruin. The father and the daughter understand each other no longer. The household's harmony evaporates, and only chaos reigns.

"But the worst of it is yet to come. Eventually the daughter who has been raised and educated in this manner reaches the age at which she must marry. Her father, the Hasid, the pious Jew, wants to secure a groom for her that matches his own ideals: a little scholar, a holy, kosher boy. But the daughter, refined as she is, her head full of love stories and cheap novels, takes one look at such young men and sees only Talmud-thumpers, pale and bleary-eyed yeshiva boys, savages untutored in the ways of modern life. She wants by no means to sacrifice her 'young life,' her precious 'cultivation,' for such a being, one who does not understand her worth, who won't drop to his knees to declare his love for her, who won't write her letters dripping with sentiment, who won't perform a gentlemanly bow to her every time he looks upon her visage, the sort of bow demanded by the latest fashion.

"Only then does the true war between father and daughter break out.

"If the father is rich, at least, and can furnish his daughter with an impressive dowry—maybe then he can still achieve his aims. If there's a bit of coin to sweeten the deal, even a cultivated Jewish maiden who can parlay-voo français can be inspired to find some store of respect deep within her for her old papa and obey his will.

"But if Papa's poor and can't give her the dowry she expects, all hell breaks loose. In one corner, there's the father weeping, lamenting over God having saddled him with such an ill-behaved daughter, one ready to claw his face off to achieve her aims. In the other, the sweet little miss, wailing over her wretched lot, having been born to such a father, one who doesn't understand her and would force her to sacrifice herself to another zealot like himself.

"Many are the Jewish daughters who, when faced with such a situation, fall ill with consumption and into an early grave. And many are the Jewish fathers who, whilst waging such a war, become old and gray before their time—and depart from this world on account of their grief.

"And it is even worse when this very cultivated daughter adds recklessness and obstinacy to the bargain. Then she does her parents dirty just to spite them by, say, falling in love with a goy and running off to a church to get baptized.

"Why, then it would be as if the sky had fallen in! The world being rent asunder! We'd raise an absolute ruckus over it! Can you imagine? A Jewish girl being converted by force?

"But who was really responsible? Why, you yourselves, the Jewish parents, with your ill-advised child-rearing! You make your sons into fanatics, people who can't even find their way in the contemporary world. And you make your daughters into lady modernists, emancipated women, bluestockings and the like. And then you dream you can pair off two such strange bedfellows? Fat chance!

"All of this is the underlying cause for these basest of criminals, the flesh peddlers, having the greatest success among the Jews of the small shtetlach. It is in such towns that they net most of their victims.

"Such a cultivated Jewish 'Fraulein,' if she doesn't want to marry a young Hasidic fellow because he's too fanatical for her tastes, also won't want to hitch herself to an upright, ordinary Jewish worker, one who earns his wages from practicing an honest profession.

"No! That doesn't suit her! A Jewish laborer as a husband? What'll she do with her French, her novels, her piano and zither?

Would he ever understand her? Would he ever know how she is to be cherished? The only choice for her is a modern, secular gentleman, the sort we call a *daytsh*, a German—not that he need be of that nationality. But a European cosmopolitan he *must* be, the only sort of person who can understand her, one who would wait on her hand and foot and whom she would be able to introduce to her girlfriends.

"And so, when some mystery man rolls into town, all dressed up in a golden chain and golden rings and a golden monocle, no one dares ask him who he is, what he is, where he's from, or how he got his hands on all that gold—whether it was from honest work or the most dastardly deceit. Not a single question. The whole shtetl merely shoves its daughters toward him from every side. For such a one as he, they forgive him his lack of piety, his going about dressed like a dandy, his distinctly non-Jewish appearance. No, he is permitted anything! He has money, after all!

"And when such a hotshot shows up and promises to give Jewish girls good positions somewhere out in the wide world, such that they'll be able to earn heaps of money and lead bright and happy lives, free of constraints, naturally no one asks what, or who, or when. They just run after him like hens do a rooster!

"Such girls are the sort that, when growing up, wouldn't lift a finger to help out at home in any way that didn't suit them or to learn a useful domestic skill—they're much too refined for that. It is precisely these girls who are most easily led astray, who fall into the deepest of mud pits. And only then, when it's already too late, does your lot come to us and beg that we come to the rescue.

"But what are we to do? How should we know who these characters are who went and seduced your children—when you haven't the slightest idea yourselves?

"It is a bitter pill, I know, but I can do nothing to help you, my good man! I can only warn you that if you have other daughters at home, make sure they are raised differently. That way you may spare yourself future heartache and your children future catastrophe."

Reb Leybush listened calmly to the whole of the lengthy oration. He had to admit to himself that everything this man said was true, much to his chagrin. He could raise not a single objection. But hearing it all, and accepting it, did not do him a bit of good. He was already miserable over not knowing what to do. Then here comes this stranger and rubs salt in his wounds.

He sighed deeply and made his answer: "You are, of course, correct, dear sir. But you too are guilty in the matter. We Jews here in the small shtetlach . . . we know nothing. We sit here, cut off from the world around us. We have no idea if what we are doing is the right thing. Each of us lives according to his custom, his inherited tradition, according to his own sense of reason, and thinks he is acting as he ought.

"But you, Jews from the great cities, know all and can name every one of our faults—so why do you keep silent? Why do you not come down to see us in our shtetlach? Why do you not take pains to enlighten us so that we may know that what we are doing is no good?

"Perhaps you hold meetings and assemblies in the big cities, and at these events you tell your horror stories about us. But to us . . . to us you never come. What do the residents of the big cities need to hear such stories for? Their conditions are completely different from ours, and perhaps better. It is to us you should come, us you should instruct, us you should help—rather than sitting and waiting, shut up in your offices, until a despondent father comes to you, one you can lecture to on right and wrong when it's already too late.

"And you put out newspapers. I've read a couple. But what

do you write in them? Empty words, ridiculous stories, what the kaiser had for breakfast, what the emperor of China has to say. Why is it you don't write about us? About our circumstances, the state of things in our shtetlach? And why do you not distribute these newspapers among our people, giving us a chance to open up our eyes and see the error of our ways?

"Maybe what you do is sufficient, all that my brother-in-law told me of. How you invite down fancy orators from Germany. Seems even ladies from there come down here to Galicia to give pretty speeches about us. But who gets to hear these speeches? Perhaps those for whom the message would be of some practical use? Of course not! I've never even heard of these speeches until now! They are given only in the metropolises, for listeners who don't need to hear them. Listeners who can only be entertained by them."

Reb Leybush spoke with fire in his voice until the secretary interrupted him: "You're right. Still, we do what we can. Consider that if we were to try to visit you in the shtetlach, at times when all is nice and quiet, you would laugh us right out of town. Now, though, when you've gotten burned badly, you confess that you do need our help, that our work is valuable to you.

"But as matters stand, your case may turn out to be just the thing that will open the eyes of our provincial Jews in the shtetlach, right along with those of the big cities, so that they all see that the status quo is not working, and we all have to do better."

"What am I to do right now, though?" Reb Leybush cried out, his voice stricken with despair. "What am I to do about my daughter, my Rivkele? So you'll go and write up the case in your newspapers. Is that supposed to satisfy me? That others will hear about it and extract a moral from it to better themselves thereby? What I want is to free my daughter!"

"And I cannot help you with that!" the secretary answered.

"Over two weeks have passed since your daughter disappeared. She could be anywhere now. No police officer could help you either, nor any court. There is but one route left for you, only one that could be of any use . . .

"In Vienna there resides one Max Spitzkopf, one of the most renowned private eyes in the entire world. He has cracked some of the most uncrackable cases and dug up some of the most dangerous criminals from their underground hiding places.

"I shall write him and relay all the details of the case. If he has the time, he is sure to take it on. And maybe . . . he'll be able to bring your daughter back to you."

"Yes, that would be . . . that would be very good indeed," Reb Leybush said, more than a little stunned. "But . . . *vehakesef meyayin yimtso*, as we say—where shall I find the money? I am, unfortunately, destitute. How could I pay this gentleman of Vienna, this . . . nobleman?"

"You need not pay him anything," the secretary answered. "Spitzkopf never asks about money first. He just gets to work."

"How could it be?" asked Reb Leybush. "He does these things for free?"

"Don't worry about it, friend," said the secretary. "Our organization will compensate him."

And so he got right to work, dashing off an exhaustive letter to the detective in which he related the whole story of Leybush's daughter and asked him to take the case on behalf of his society combating the trade in women.

Reb Leybush returned to his brother-in-law's home and waited impatiently for an answer to arrive from this Viennese nobleman. Arrive it did, and quickly too. Indeed, the very next day they received a telegram:

> I WILL ARRIVE TONIGHT IN LEMBERG
>
> COMING BY EXPRESS TRAIN
>
> SPITZKOPF.

CHAPTER FIVE

Return to Sender

AND ARRIVE he did, that very evening. He headed immediately to the offices of Lemberg's B'nai B'rith chapter, where Reb Leybush Suchestow, Leybush's brother-in-law, and the chapter secretary were all waiting for him.

Spitzkopf had Leybush repeat the whole story for him, from the beginning. He also asked Leybush to provide him with a detailed account of what the stranger looked like, how he walked, how he talked—jotting everything down in his notebook.

"It appears to me," Spitzkopf remarked, "you've fallen right into the talons of one very talented bird of prey. There is but one more thing I must know: where the man came from and whither he was bound. Can you not tell me whether the man perhaps carried foreign currency, and what kind?"

"Yes!" Reb Leybush answered. "I did once see some curious-looking banknotes on him, and when I asked him what sort of money it was, he answered, 'Turkish!'"

"Excellent," said Spitzkopf. "That's just what I needed to know. If he had Turkish money, he must have just come from Turkey, and it's likely he was going to return there too. So. We have our first clue."

Reb Leybush gazed at the calm, steely-eyed man and was astounded. Amazing the way he so simply hit upon such an important piece of information.

"Now," Spitzkopf continued, "we must make our way to Milanowo to continue following our breadcrumbs."

Reb Leybush cut in: "I swore not to come home unless I had my daughter in tow."

"*Nu*, then you can remain here," said Spitzkopf. "I'll go myself."

And so Reb Leybush stayed back in Lemberg while Spitzkopf took the next train to Milanowo.

He arrived there quite early the next day and checked in at the same little guesthouse where the mysterious "millionaire" had stayed on his visit to the shtetl. The innkeeper told Spitzkopf what had happened there recently to Reb Leybush's daughter.

The detective seized the opportunity to ask him about the mystery guest who had stayed with him. But the man's answers were so vague that Spitzkopf was unable to glean any useful information. He then asked the innkeeper to show him the room where the man had stayed. But it was difficult to find any traces of him, as a series of guests had stayed there since. Still, Spitzkopf carried out a thorough inspection of every crevice: under the bed, behind the cupboards, inside the furnace—until he found something . . .

It was in the furnace. A bit of crumpled-up paper. When he smoothed it out, he discerned that it was a piece of a torn envelope with remnants of a Turkish postage stamp and a few smudged letters left over from the official postmark. These few letters spelled out the beginning of the word CONSTANTINOPLE.

"So," Spitzkopf thought to himself, "the man received letters from Constantinople. I'd say I know now where to look for him . . ."

He then made his way to the local post office, identified himself, and asked whether the visitor may have received any registered mail or telegrams from someplace. The clerk had a look and found records stating that during his stay in the shtetl, the man had indeed received a registered letter from Constantinople, sent by someone surnamed Bärwald, and a telegram from Constantinople that read:

> AWAITING FRESH GOODS
>
> CLARA.

"Capital," said Spitzkopf to himself, nearly doing a little jump out of sheer excitement. "Now I have everything. All that remains is to travel to Constantinople and locate a brothel owned by a certain Bärwald and a certain woman working there named Clara . . .

"Naturally, I haven't quite reached my goal yet. It is possible that these people are merely the go-betweens, the contractors, when it comes to the living merchandise. Our unfortunate girl may not necessarily be with them. But this is a significant clue. If I can find these brokers, I'm sure I'll find the rest."

Later that same day Spitzkopf returned to Lemberg, where he informed Reb Leybush that he was on his way to Constantinople hoping to find a trail leading him to the man's daughter.

"But you must stay silent as the grave," the detective warned him. "No one can know that I am traveling there, nor that I have taken an interest in the case.

"We are dealing with a crafty criminal syndicate here. These people have spies posted everywhere. If they find out that someone is hot on their heels, they'll be sure to hide your daughter away so well that no one will ever be able to find her."

Reb Leybush swore to him that he would keep mum.

Spitzkopf also asked the secretary of the B'nai B'rith chapter to not write anything of the case, nor tell anyone about it, until it was resolved. The man promised. And Spitzkopf boarded the Orient Express bound for Bucharest.

"I'm going to recite psalms every day!" Reb Leybush called up to him when the detective was already seated in his train car. "May they fly up to heaven and bring you success so you may bring my daughter home to me, still a pure and virtuous Jewish girl!"

CHAPTER SIX
Constantinople

As soon as he arrived in Bucharest, Spitzkopf made inquiries at the city's various hotels asking whether or not a young couple may have checked in a couple of weeks earlier, one that matched the physical description he provided to them.

But the inquiries led him nowhere, and he came to the conclusion that the couple must have stayed in Bucharest only for a brief period, possibly not even spending the night at a hotel. And so he chose not to tarry there and bought a ticket for Constantinople.

His first order of business in Constantinople was to ask around about the various bordellos and try to ascertain whether or not any of their proprietors might be a man with the surname Bärwald or a woman named Clara.

But these inquiries led him nowhere. He struggled to elicit a clear answer to any of his questions.

"I wouldn't consider it going too far," Spitzkopf decided, "to forget my sense of honor for a while and pay a visit to these houses of ill repute myself . . . I may happen upon the characters I'm searching for at one of them.

"But it's easier said than done. In Turkey, and especially so in Constantinople, these harlot houses number in the thousands. It could be weeks before I've popped into all of them. Still—I have no other choice. The work demands that I go to any length."

He retreated to his hotel, put on clothes that a rich young playboy might wear, and went out on the prowl.

His first route was down the main streets of the city, where there was the greatest deal of . . . ahem . . . foot traffic. Along these thoroughfares hundreds of demimondaines made their nightly rounds. He reckoned they would be able to point him in the right direction.

And he reckoned well. He had barely just entered into the stream of pedestrians when, from all sides, he was thronged by dozens of young ladies, all painted and powdered and perfumed, each of them giving him a come-hither wink and many even addressing him directly: "How'd ya like to have some fun, lover man?"

He strolled around thus for quite a while before finally deciding to go off with one of the streetwalkers.

"And where shall we go, my sweet little dear?" he asked her with a smile, though her rouged-up face made him queasy and her perfume turned his stomach.

"Oh, just come on!" she said. "It ain't far from here. We're gonna have a real nice time. You'll buy us some wine . . . and after that . . . well . . ." and she exploded in a fit of giggles.

So he followed her. Seeing that she had nabbed her prey, she shoved her arm under his and dragged him off into a side street. He clenched his teeth but did not push her away. He hoped she would lead him to the place he was ultimately seeking.

"I'm an Italian girl, y' know!" she called out suddenly. "So you can bet your bottom lira that with me it's gonna be a real pleasure, a *mekhaye* . . . er, I mean, it'll be *bellissimo*."

"An Italian girl direct from the Galician shtetl of Tarnopol, eh?" he asked, and he could not hold back a chuckle.

"Ha!" She chuckled right alongside him. "Well, like recognizes like. I see you're from Milan yourself—that is to say, my land! Ha!"

He made no answer but simply followed where she was leading him.

Soon they were standing in front of a large, elegant home. She knocked three times on the door. A black woman opened it for them, and they proceeded into a handsomely appointed, brightly lit hallway.

Spitzkopf was conducted up the wide, lushly carpeted steps to the second floor, where another door was opened. He and his female escort then found themselves in a resplendent drawing room, furnished with plush, upholstered armchairs, large mirrors, and luxuriantly soft divans.

Several scantily attired young women rotated around the room, and noticing the entrance of the young, nattily attired rake swarmed him like a cluster of bees.

They buzzed around him, batting their eyelashes and humming sweet nothings, trying to attract him back to their various honey hives. But the one who had brought him there swatted them away, screeching: "This precious flower's for me! I brought him here myself! He's mine!"

"Oh, look who's the queen now!" the others cried. "But we say no! This gentleman'll taste the nectar of whichever of us is most to his liking!"

Spitzkopf sat himself down at a small table and had glasses of wine brought over for the whole swarm.

The young cocottes continued to float in a circle, skipping about, trilling bawdy songs. Some flung their arms around him and tried to give him kisses, others perched on his lap and wrapped their fingers round his neck.

The whole thing repulsed him—but he did not protest. He needed to make out whether the girl he was searching for might be among them.

He sat thus among this strange society for rather a long time. Finally he stood up and made his goodbyes.

"Leaving so soon, lover boy?" they bawled. "But why? Don'tcha wanna amuse yourself with us for a spell?"

"It so happens I haven't the time just now," he answered. "But I'll be back tomorrow."

With that he left, and he finally was able to take a nice long breath. The stagnant air inside the brothel, and the overwhelming odor of the various powders and perfumes, had all but suffocated him.

He went to a number of brothels after that, and the same scene repeated itself each time. And each time he failed to find the object of his search.

He made sure to engage some of the girls in conversation and question them as to where they came from and how they ended up there in the houses of ill repute. He hoped thereby to figure out who these two characters, Bärwald and Clara, might be. But this did not get him anywhere either.

Some of the girls had been seduced as Rivkele Suchestow

had—that is, a strange man had wed them, so to speak, and whisked them off to Constantinople. After arriving in the city, he would abandon them in a brothel, telling them it was a hotel. After that the man would leave for half an hour or so to take care of something, he would say, after which they never saw him again. Eventually the girl would be forced to start working at the very brothel at which she had been deposited.

Others were deceived by being promised that in Constantinople they would receive fine positions in dressmakers' ateliers or as salesgirls in grand department stores. And then as soon as they arrived they were dropped off at one of the brothels, and as with the other girls they never again set eyes on the charlatan who had brought them.

These girls generally came from Galicia, Russia, or Romania. Some had already become accustomed to their new situation and described themselves as happy. But most of them still dreamed of fleeing, running away as if from a terrible fire.

"As long as I still meet her standards," one of the girls told him, "the madam won't let me out of her grasp. If I ever get sick, she brings me to the hospital and the staff doesn't let me out again until she herself comes to retrieve me.

"But I am well aware how I'll end up. Several years from now, when I grow old and sickly, they'll cart me off to a hospital. Then when I am well enough they'll have me thrown out on the street, where I'll have to fend for myself, scrounging for a crust of bread.

"Yes, when I can't serve her anymore, when she can't get any more business outta me . . . only then will I be free. But what good will my freedom be at that age, in that condition?"

Another girl lamented to him: "You see me now, how I sashay around you, caress you, flirt with you. You must think I really am a lewd sort of female, that I really do want to sell myself for a couple of francs! But it ain't so! I do all that because I have to. If I don't, I'm beaten so awfully that life itself becomes a punishment to me.

"I've endured enough. At first I was steady as a rock. For over a month I could not be moved. I resisted. But then . . . I had no choice but to give in.

"Try to imagine: they take a young girl, eighteen years of age, in the absolute flower of her youth, and lock her up in a dark room in an attic somewhere, without windows, without any fresh air. They keep her bound, hand and foot, like a chained dog. They give her dry bread to eat once a day and salted water to drink. And on top of all that? She is dealt excruciating lashes with thick leather straps, with riding crops, with whips, so severe that her skin is lacerated and blood spurts out from every inch of her.

"So I ask you: How long can such a child bear it? Especially when she knows that no one is coming to rescue her because no one knows where she is. Those beatings I got then . . . I can still feel 'em. So bad that I would never dare to play the rebel again.

"I would do anything, anything, in order not to ever have to go back to that place, the 'cheder' as we call it, never to feel the straps of that cat-o'-nine-tails, like snakes made of fire attacking my body.

"We all tremble in such fear of the cheder that not a one of us dares make a peep."

As Spitzkopf listened to these testimonies, he himself trembled. He balled his fists, ground his teeth with seething rage—but he could do nothing about it.

The police in the Ottoman Empire are, so to speak, in bed with the brothel keepers. No kind of lawsuit or intervention would do a thing. Business as usual.

But Spitzkopf was resolved to discover who the scoundrels were that directed this business and at the very least to wrest away the youngest of their captives, Rivkele Suchestow, from their savage paws.

He was already getting impatient that he had not yet found any trace of her. But he was determined to visit every last one of the Constantinople brothels and not to tire of the work until he found her.

And in fact, that very first night of making his rounds of the bordellos, he had a stroke of luck.

Around midnight, he let another of the streetwalkers drag him back to her house of employment. The girls there who sold their bodies for a pair of francs did their little dances around him, flashing him their smiles so much like a bunch of grinning cats that he did not know whether he should be sorry for these poor souls or shoo them away out of sheer revulsion.

He sat there for over an hour, though, and had the girls bring wine, and entertained himself in their company, for appearances' sake. Eventually he had to get up, though, and made his way to the door.

"Why ya runnin' off so quick?" all the girls shrieked. "Why, you're the best gent we've had! And it's late. Everywhere's closed by now. Stay here with us just a bit longer."

But he wanted to take advantage of every hour that remained of the night to continue making his visits and so was determined to make his exit.

At the door he met *di mume*, as the girls called her: the auntie—the proprietress of the brothel.

"Well, had a nice time?" she asked him.

"Eh," he answered. "I like the goods when they're nice and fresh. It may cost a couple pennies more, but it's always worth it!"

"Come back tomorrow," she said to him in an undertone. "I have such a little plaything for you. No, but she's really something, ha-cha-cha. You'll have a ball."

"So why must it wait?" Spitzkopf asked. "Couldn't I have it tonight? I want to be her first." He took out his handsome leather wallet and pulled out an impressive banknote as if to say, "Let it cost a grand, and I wouldn't care."

The madam's eyes twinkled and she let out a wild cackle: "Hee hee hee! You're gonna be a mighty nice client. But come tomorrow! No one's gonna snatch away the privilege from yeh. At present the girl's still being obstinate. But I hope to have her fixed by morning."

"Fine. I'll come back tomorrow. But remember: I want to be the first."

As he descended the stairs, he thought to himself, "Finally, finally, I think I've hit upon the right track."

In the entrance corridor he stopped a moment. He heard a soft murmuring coming from up above: "She's still holding out," he heard a woman whispering. "No girl has received so many lashes before, and she endures it all. Stubborn as a mule."

"Well, then," a rougher voice rumbled. "Bring out the big whip. The cat-o'-nine-tails. That always does the trick."

"I've already thought of that," the woman answered. "But I'm afraid of scarring her body any worse than I have already. We're in bad need of truly fresh, nice-lookin' goods. None of our boys want to even catch a whiff of our old meat anymore."

"Don't think about it too much. Just run along and dredge up the cat. After a coupla blows with that, all of our sweet kosher calves have been brought to their knees. Bärwald wants his broker's fee. We've gotta start making some money off the little virgin."

Spitzkopf had heard enough. He knew everything he needed to.

He turned on his heels and left. His resolve was now ironclad. He would be freeing Rivkele the next day.

CHAPTER SEVEN
Rescued

The next morning Spitzkopf went off to Constantinople's Austrian consulate, where he presented his papers and explained the case he was dealing with.

The consul told him that he was quite familiar with such matters. More than once he had called upon the Turkish police for their help with them, but every time it proved pointless. The gendarmerie takes hefty baksheesh, by Ottoman custom, from all the local brothels and so looks the other way at their activities. Even when officers are forced to go and investigate something at one of them, they alert the bordellers beforehand so that they can be careful to not let anything suspicious be found.

Therefore, the consul was of the opinion that if Spitzkopf wished to have any success, he should make sure not to be in touch with the Turkish gendarmerie but rather should carry out his work entirely alone, lest the officers themselves give him away.

Spitzkopf did ask, however, that the consul furnish him with a few staff members from the consulate in order to help him execute the necessary arrests.

"That won't do, either," the consul answered. "The consulate does not have the right to act in these matters without the support of the local authorities. It is within my power only to ask the gendarmes here to arrest the criminals and liberate the captives. But that would only be, as I have already made clear, a detriment to your work."

And so Spitzkopf left—but quickly hatched a different plan. "I can't ambush the brothel myself. I could, maybe, free the women inside. But the perpetrators would take the opportunity to flee while I'm doing so. And they must not be allowed to do that without my neutralizing them first.

"I can't call upon the Ottoman *jandarma*, as its officers can't be trusted. But I'll play a trick on 'em myself—*opton af terkish*, as we say back home—give it to 'em Turkish-style!

"I'll locate a couple of brawny young men, dress them up as soldiers of the sultan, and bring them with me to the bordello. We'll round up the criminals together, then hand them over to the police. The authorities won't be able to back out of it by then, not when they've already got the culprits in their clutches.

"Well, all right! Now time to roll up my sleeves and get to work."

And so Spitzkopf marched off to the famous harbor of the Golden Horn, where he found a whole pack of stevedores walking around with nothing to do, having not managed to be hired on to any loading teams that day.

"Looking for work?" he asked a few of them.

"Yessir!" they answered. "Whatever work you've got for us, we'll do it. We're hungry."

"So come with me," Spitzkopf said, and walked back into the center of the city with the men in tow, where he led them into a bar and got them nice and tipsy.

Then he brought them to a secondhand dealer and rented out Turkish military uniforms for them.

"Now let me show you to a real nice little harlot house, with lovely girls," said the detective. "We'll have an absolute ball."

"Hurrah!" the men whooped, a bit wobbly on their feet. "And hurrah once more! Wine and women! Long life to this honorable gentleman!"

"Yes!" Spitzkopf chorused. "You'll have everything you desire! But to get it—you must first agree to lend your support in case anything should happen to me."

"Why, we'd leap into a fire for yeh!" all the workers bellowed, the excitement rising in their voices.

"Then follow me! And if you hear gunshots, know that someone is trying to harm me. Then you'll run like the devil to the door of the house and keep guard there. If anyone tries to escape, grab hold of them and don't let them go until I've come to you . . ."

He brought them to the door of the brothel where he had been the night before. They went in first, and the girls converged on them like a cloud of flies. Each of them grasped one of the "soldiers," then sat down with them at the drawing room tables. The men ordered wine to be poured out for the whole party. A buoyant, merry mood soon took hold.

Then, some fifteen minutes later, Spitzkopf knocked at the brothel's front door. Spitzkopf pressed a golden ducat into the hand of the black maid that opened it for him and bade her give him, in return, the key. He then used it to lock the door behind them. The woman gaped at him.

"A joke merely!" he reassured her. "And there's more where that ducat came from if you keep quiet about it."

And so she regained her composure, and Spitzkopf ascended the steps to the drawing room. When he entered, the girls hailed him with a hearty "Hurrah!"

"There's the gent what spent so much on wine for us last night!" they shouted.

But he did not bother engaging too much with them and answered in even tones: "Seems you've fine company now without me joining. Amuse yourselves in the meantime, and I'll be back before long. May I ask, where's your 'auntie'?"

"Auntie's upstairs, in the cheder," one of the girls answered, "giving it to our new friend with the cat-o'-nine-tails."

He did not hesitate to ask where the place was but merely sprinted up the stairs, all the way up to the attic.

Through a door at the top of the stairs he heard a muffled scream. He well knew what its source must be. Wasting no time, he opened the door at once with his skeleton key.

He found himself in a large empty room, devoid of any furniture. Here the screaming was even louder—a horrific yowling. But after opening a second door, he still found no one.

He did find, though, hanging on the wall, a gallery of leather straps, wooden switches, and whips. And again the screaming: now even more immediate, such that it all but tore the detective's heart in two.

The third door he busted open with sheer force, and he was met with an excruciating scene.

It was a gloomy, windowless chamber. The only furniture consisted of a bed, a night table, and a washstand with a mirror.

In the bed lay a young girl, half naked, her long hair streaming out in loose strands. Beside her stood the "auntie,"—that is, the procuress. With one hand she firmly grasped the girl's bound wrists and with the other she held aloft a large cat-o'-nine-tails, affixed with a clutch of thick, flying lashes.

But the auntie had not noticed anyone entering. Spitzkopf charged at her and seized her by the arm.

"That's enough!" he roared out, seething with rage. "You infernal beast! Release her or I'll turn you into a pile of bones."

The auntie swiveled round, her face a mask of fear. Upon seeing the unknown man, she was tempted to give him a thwack with the cat too, right over the face. Before she could do it, though, Spitzkopf gave her such a shove that she went flying to the ground and lay there, utterly defeated.

He quickly gagged her with a handkerchief, cuffed her wrists and ankles, and slid her under the bed.

Then he liberated the girl of the ropes that tied her to the bed, sprayed her with cold water, and, unscrewing his flask, poured a few drops of cognac into her mouth.

All she could do was gaze at him in abject fear. She did not know what to think.

"Steady on, dear child," he said to her in a voice of utmost tenderness. "Calm, calm. I have come to free you. You'll soon be out of here."

She still could not bring herself to accept it. Still she stared at the detective, her eyes big as two moons.

And still he spoke to her softly: "Now get dressed quickly. I'll be back before you know it and will lead you out of this place. First I have to arrest a whole band of evildoers."

He darted out of the room and fired off his revolver. Soon a rushing was heard on the steps, a mad stampede. Various characters were running down the stairs, trying to flee through the front door.

But it was locked, of course. And before they could force it open, the military impersonators had them surrounded.

Spitzkopf, meanwhile, ran down to join them in the corridor. There he found three fellows guarded closely by the "soldiers." One of them perfectly matched the description he had been given of the young man who had seduced the unfortunate Rivkele.

"If I'm not mistaken," Spitzkopf said in a voice as cool as ice, "I have the pleasure of meeting that highly distinguished gentleman, the millionaire who recently visited Milanowo."

And as he said it, he made sure to turn his revolver so that its glint caught the man's eye.

The three men were just about to dive at him when the "soldiers" rushed in to stop them.

Then the terrified working girls of the establishment came careering down the staircase. They looked on at the scene in total astonishment.

"You shall soon all be free!" Spitzkopf called up to them. "No more nightmare cheder, no more fearsome cat, no more wicked uncle, no more devil aunt!"

He then moved to cuff the three men's wrists and hauled down the auntie, kicking and screaming, from the floor above. "You're killing me!" she yelped.

Spitzkopf had two carriages summoned and packed the whole gang off to the gendarmerie.

At the police station Spitzkopf telephoned the Austrian consul and brought him fully up to date. The consul immediately dispatched one of his functionaries to the station to carry out the first interrogations of the arrestees. He did so to ensure that the gendarmes would not be able in good conscience to let the criminals go, free and easy, as they always had done before.

Rivkele and the other girls were questioned too. They all described how they had been deceived and led to this place, what horrific trials they had endured, and how much they had suffered.

Meanwhile, the band of miscreants was left with no choice but to confess to everything. Among their number was, indeed, the primary agent of the girls' abduction, the "millionaire" marauder from Milanowo we know all too well. It was his job to travel around "buying up" the new merchandise.

The second miscreant was the broker, Bärwald, who supplied the various bordellos with the newly imported stocks. The third was the "uncle" himself—that is, the proprietor of the brothel, who worked alongside the procuress, the "auntie."

Clara, it turned out, was Bärwald's sister, who herself worked as a brokeress in the trade.

All of these miscreants received the sentences that were due to them. The consul made sure of that, keeping a keen eye on the proceedings so that no amount of underhanded protection or baksheesh could save them.

That same day Spitzkopf brought Rivkele back with him to Galicia, at his own expense. Before they departed, he had a telegram sent to her father, informing him of his daughter's liberation.

The consulate, meanwhile, paid for all the other girls to be sent back to their homes right away. They had waited long enough.

It is impossible to describe the jubilation that held sway in Milanowo when Rivkele came home, still the same fine, unsullied Jewish daughter who had left it some time before. The entire shtetl rejoiced, and all of its people wished to thank the guardian angel, the wonder worker who had caused this redemption to come to pass.

But after delivering his daughter to Reb Leybush in Lemberg, Spitzkopf took the train directly back to Vienna.

After all, a very important new case was already waiting for him there.

Issue 9: The Bank Burglar

ניינטעם העפט. פרייז 20 העלער.

דער באַנק־איינברעכער.

שפּיצקאפּף ליעגט בעהאַלטען אונטער דעם שרייבטיש און וואַרט, דעם געלאָדענעם רעוואָלווער אין דער האנד. פּלוצים פאַלט אַראָב פון דער וואַנד, געראַדע נעבען אויווען, אַ ציעגעל, עס עפענט זיך אַן'אָרט פענסטערל, דורך וועלכען עס בעווייזט זיך דער קאָפּ פון אונזער פערשוין, דעם פערשטעלטען גראַף הארדעגג.

The Bank Burglar

CHAPTER ONE
Spitzkopf Gets into a Bind

THE ILLUSTRIOUS DETECTIVE Max Spitzkopf had returned home from a long journey. He was very tired and ready to kick off his shoes. He had been working on a significant case while away, which he had of course cracked with his usual panache.

But now his exertions, and the long hours of travel, had left him exhausted. There was nothing he longed for more than a bit of good rest.

When he entered his home, he did not find any of his assistants in the suite of offices. During his absence a number of intricate cases had presented themselves in Vienna, and all of his assistants had a great deal on their hands. They must have been out doing fieldwork.

The only person in the house was his old housekeeper, who apprised him of all the goings-on he had missed while he was away.

Spitzkopf took off his traveling clothes and lay down on his sofa to rest. He lay there for around fifteen minutes and managed to doze off for a spell.

Suddenly an elegant carriage drew up in front of his house. A uniformed lackey alighted and rang Spitzkopf's doorbell. The housekeeper opened and asked the man what his business was there.

"I am footman to the honorable Count Hardegg and have an important letter for the famous detective Max Spitzkopf. But I have to hand deliver it to him personally."

"Very well," the housekeeper answered. "He is at home. You'll find him in the room just over there, where you can hand him the letter."

Spitzkopf could hear that someone was approaching. He stood up and opened the door himself.

"Are you Herr Spitzkopf?" the footman asked, making a courteous bow.

"Yes," Spitzkopf answered. "What can I do for you?"

"I've brought you a letter from my master, the honorable Count Hardegg," said the man, presenting it to him. "He most adamantly requests your presence as soon as possible."

Spitzkopf opened the envelope and read the following:

> Dear Herr Spitzkopf!
>
> A terrible calamity has befallen me. A few days ago, a number of important papers were stolen from my writing desk, papers upon which my very existence depends.
>
> To wit, for some time I have been entangled in a legal dispute with my relatives over the estate of my uncle, Fürst Kinsky, and it was beginning to appear that I would win the day. All I had to do was present several significant documents that testify to the fact that I am the only possible heir to his properties and princedom. It cost me a great deal of effort and money to get my hands on the papers, and I was elated when I was finally able to do so.
>
> But the same day I obtained them and locked them away in my desk, they were stolen. The thief must be someone who is acquainted with me—perhaps even one of the officials of my comital court.
>
> I do not wish to entrust the matter to the police, for

> I do not want it to become public knowledge that the papers are missing. Therefore I turn to you, with the most serious request that you come to see me at once and take the reins of the investigation.
>
> My entire future lies within these papers, and I am certain that if you carry out the search, I shall recover them.
>
> Come soon. You shall be lavishly compensated.
>
> Paul Graf zu Hardegg

Spitzkopf scanned the letter quickly, then made his answer to the count's servant: "Shall I find your master at home?"

"You shall!" the lackey answered. "The Herr Graf made me promise to have you come with me immediately, as he is waiting for you quite impatiently. His Excellency the Count is currently residing at his villa in Weidlingau. I have brought the speediest pair of horses from his stables, and we can be there in two hours at the most."

"Good," said Spitzkopf. "Go on out, and I will join you presently." The lackey left, and Spitzkopf prepared his usual equipment: a number of skeleton keys, three loaded revolvers, an electric torch, handcuffs, padlocks, and other such articles. He tucked them all away into his pockets so that no one would be able to tell that he was traveling so heavily laden. Then he exited his home and climbed into the waiting barouche.

It was already almost dark. The lackey locked the door of this large, luxurious carriage, lit the coach lamps attached to either side of it, and told the driver to take it at a gallop. Spitzkopf took the precious opportunity of nestling deeply into the soft, plush-covered seats of the barouche. After all, it would be two hours until he arrived at Weidlingau, that village of chateaux in the Wienerwald, the Vienna Woods. He intended to make the most of the time—by getting some much-needed rest.

They had been traveling rather a long time, and Spitzkopf had dozed off. But at one point he awoke from his nap to find, upon looking through the window of the barouche, that it was making its way down a narrow street betwixt tall, mud-spattered houses. By his calculations, they must have been far outside Vienna by then. He wondered where exactly and thought to ask the coachman.

But as soon as he rose up and moved to open the door communicating with the driver's seat, he received such a blow over the head with some blunt instrument that he fell back into his seat, unconscious.

After he came to again, but before he opened his eyes, he heard two unknown voices engaged in a conversation. He pretended not to hear so that he could learn, without being found out, precisely where he was and what had happened to him. Of this much he was sure: he had really fallen into the mire this time.

He had been so exhausted when the unknown footman turned up at the door of his home, and his usual faculties so weakened, that it had simply not occurred to him that the man's whole story might have been concocted. He did not stop to think that the criminals of the city's underworld, who for so long had been wanting to do away with him once and for all, might have something to do with it. He did not consider for a second that he was being hoodwinked.

It had sufficed for him that the lackey had such a splendid uniform on and that the letter from Count Hardegg had been written on fine paper, with the count's name and his crown emblem embossed in golden ink. He took it all at face value. He did not suspect a thing.

"Oh, what a bitter, bitter pill!" he lamented to himself. "And the bitterest is that nobody knows back at home where I've gone off to.

"But just as sure as I've fallen into the mire, I'll soon be crawling my way out of it. No enemy of mine shall live to see his revenge taken on me—not nobody, not nohow!"

As all of that raced through Spitzkopf's brain, he listened quietly, hearkening close to every word the two men spoke.

"He's lying there practically a corpse," said one voice. "It was a right good wallop I dealt him. Just a shame he happened to have such a stiff hat on, otherwise I woulda been sure to smash his skull in."

And now the second voice: "It doesn't bother me a bit that the sucker's still alive. I've been itchin' to have a go at the old man for as long as I've been at the game in Vienna. First let me get my jollies out on him, then let him go free!"

Hearing these words, Spitzkopf understood where he had been taken. He opened his eyes and, blinking as if he were afraid, took in his surroundings.

He was in an elegantly appointed, brightly lit room and was sitting in a plush armchair. Beside him sat two men, each holding loaded revolvers. They broke out in uproarious laughter.

"Well, if it ain't Herr *Spitzklutz*," one of them said. "How do ya fancy the situation you've landed in?"

"Why shouldn't I fancy it?" the detective answered calmly. "I'm sitting in a nice soft chair in a lovely bright room. What's not to like?"

"And how about these two sweet pistolets, twinkling right in your eye like the brazen little things they are?" the same man asked. "Don't they make you blush a bit?"

Spitzkopf shrugged his shoulders, answering them with a chuckle: "Why should they bother me? Back home I've got a drawer full of such delightsome toys." His perfect calm took the two characters aback.

"Well, you really are quite the fella!" the second man said. "Letting yourself kid around with us when you find yourself in such dire straits! Others wouldn't be able to do nothin' but quake with fear. Very nice, very impressive indeed. But would these others have been duped so easily as the world-famous international private eye Max Spitzkopf? I wouldn't have believed it of ya!"

"What have you done to me?" Spitzkopf now asked, feigning ignorance. "I would have come with you here anyway, sooner or later, you didn't need to . . . but no matter. If you'd just tell me, please, which one of you is His Excellency Graf Hardegg?"

"That'd be me!" laughed one of the men, in hysterics now. Spitzkopf recognized him as the same man who had passed himself off as Hardegg's lackey.

Spitzkopf continued with his questioning: "Well, might you please just tell me what you intend to do with me from here on out?"

"Nothing!" the supposed "count" answered. "We ain't gonna put a single hair of that famous head out of place. But as for you . . . you've got a terrible habit. You get your kicks having free birds like us turned into jailbirds, sending us off to the clink for years at a time."

"Just so," Spitzkopf interrupted. "And I hope I can treat you to such a nice room and board soon—only the finest bread and water, in a very renowned penal institution."

"Ah, look who's got their sass back," one of the men said. "I don't consider that very nice manners. You're ours now to do with as we like. And with us your life ain't worth half a pfennig."

"Oh, you think so?" Spitzkopf laughed. "So happens I think just the opposite. You both ought to be more afraid of me than I am of you."

The two men gaped at him. They had never experienced quite this degree of chutzpah from someone they had in their clutches. "You've got a real big mouth on you!" they said. "You better be careful or we'll cut you down to size. Be a lot smaller then, eh?"

"You won't be doing that either," Spitzkopf answered, as evenly as ever. "You're not courageous enough, not by half."

"You're one nasty son of a gun!" one of them shouted. "Not even worth talking to. But we'll see to that soon. You'll be showing us respect by the end of the night.

"And you're right! We won't do anything to you. We're no murderers. Just notorious burglars—and our specialty is breaking into the biggest banks in the world.

"I've just gotten done working a nice stretch of years in America. The biggest banks in New York, Chicago, Philadelphia, Washington, Boston, Pittsburgh, San Francisco, Saint Louis, and New Orleans—I've robbed 'em all. And the world's greatest detectives have taken to pursuing me. Not one of 'em could do a thing.

"Now I've come to Europe for a change of scenery. I want to try my luck here too. And I'm going to start with Vienna . . .

"And because I've heard what they say about you—that you're a dangerous sort with a nasty habit of sticking his nose into everything and interrupting us lot right when we're getting down to business—well, I realized that first things first I had to see to you for a spell to give me the breathing room I need to get the job done.

"I'm not going to lay a finger on ya. I've arranged a lovely little room for you right here in this house, where I myself reside. I've made it up to look exactly like a prison cell, because I know how much you love to put up people like me and my friends in such places.

"So we're going to leave you in that cozy little room to enjoy a spot of rest and relaxation. Tie you up to the wall with a chain. For just a few months is all. Just long enough for us to finish our business, then you'll be free to go. You following my train of thought?"

"I'm following it," answered Spitzkopf, barely louder than a whisper. "But I'm doubtful that you're going to be able to ride that train to its destination."

"And who's gonna stop us?" the two men asked.

"Why, I myself," said Spitzkopf. "I'll wager that before you manage to rob even one bank in Vienna you'll be under my thumb."

"Delusion is worse than a disease!" said the man who had dressed as a lackey and had turned out to be an accomplished globetrotting bank burglar. "We've managed to dupe you quite easily before. It's clear you're not quite the all-knowing sage you think you are.

"So you'd better knock this madness out of your head once and for all. To make clear to you that we're not playing any games, soon we'll bring you up to your little room. You'll be singing quite a different tune then."

He then rang for an accomplice, and in lumbered a tall man of Goliath-like build, with red hair and a pockmarked visage.

"Good evening, Herr Spitzkopf!" the man called out, with a mischievous laugh. "*Sholem-aleykhem*, peace upon you! What's brought you here?"

Spitzkopf recognized him. The man was a notorious burglar, known to all Vienna as "Red Franz." He had committed all kinds of knavery in the city before Spitzkopf was able to finally catch him. The man served a six-year prison sentence.

"Why, if it isn't Franz der Royter," Spitzkopf said to him. "By my calculations, it isn't too long ago that you were freed from prison. And you're already back to your old tricks . . . well, that's not very smart of you, is it? You're digging your own grave again."

"Maybe so," said the red-haired giant. "But I'm going to drag you down with me this time. As revenge for what you did to me. I'm going to be your warden in this sweet little jail we've prepared for you. I'll pay you back for everything you did—and with a high interest rate!"

"Cut the chit-chat," said the international bank thief. "It's late already. Let's show our honored guest to his room. He must be tired. Come, Herr Spitzkopf, let's retire."

"With the greatest of pleasure," answered the detective. "You've made me quite curious to see how you've fitted out my accommodations."

Red Franz opened a door in the back of the lounge where they were sitting and, grasping Spitzkopf by the arm, led him through a number of rooms until they reached a dark corridor. The two other men followed behind, the barrels of their loaded revolvers pressing into the back of Spitzkopf's head.

In the corridor, Franz, wielding a massive key, opened a door that creaked open slowly, heavily, revealing a flight of stairs. He led Spitzkopf down twenty steps and into a cellar.

There he opened another solidly built door, this one made of iron, and Spitzkopf finally saw his absurdly cramped quarters, two meters wide and two meters long. There were no windows, but there was a button connected to an electric current. When Franz pressed it, the room was brightly illuminated. These electric lights were all affixed to the ceiling, several meters overhead.

The furniture consisted of a plank bed with a straw mattress and a small table and chair, both tightly screwed to the floor. "Here you can finally get some rest after all your hard work," said Franz as he pulled out a heavy iron chain from under the bed. He wrapped it around Spitzkopf's stomach like a belt, but so tightly that the detective felt the iron links engraving themselves into his flesh. Still, he did not let out even the slightest groan. Instead he said with a laugh: "Well, you've accoutred my room most handsomely. There's even electric lighting! It's extremely kind of you. But I don't think I shall be staying here long."

"Keep looking through those rose-colored magnifying glasses!" the international burglar laughed in return. "Soon you'll be on your knees begging for mercy, pleading for us to set you free.

"Now you, Franz, see to it that our little friend gets something to eat every day. But I would like to implore you not to open his door. Use the small opening to shove his bread and water through. We'll just see how long our little friend holds out . . .

how long he'll keep making his little jokes.

"Good night, Herr Spitzkopf! I'll come visit you tomorrow for some show-and-tell . . . You'll get to see the crisp thousand-krone notes and the glittering ducats I'll have stolen by then from the Rothschild banking house!"

And with that all three of Spitzkopf's captors left the room. As Red Franz hulked out, he turned back once more and shouted through gnashing teeth: "Just you wait, mangy bloodhound! I'll settle up with you once and for all!"

Then he locked the door and left Spitzkopf alone in his cell.

The chain with which he was bound allowed him to take only a few steps in any direction. He could barely reach the door. And as he moved, the chain pressed even more deeply into his skin. He feared it would soon open a wound.

It was certainly a dire situation he had fallen into. And on top of it all, no one at home knew where he had gone—so no one would know where to start looking for him.

His only comfort was this: one loaded revolver that still lay tucked away in his underpants, the only one that the scoundrels had not managed to find on him when they emptied his pockets.

And his only hope: that Red Franz would not be able to resist entering his room so as to goad him a little—at which point Spitzkopf would finally put an end to his mischief and set himself free.

CHAPTER TWO
Three Banks Are Robbed

THE NEXT DAY, Vienna was abuzz.

Just hours before, in the night, three large banking houses had been broken into and robbed. And certain repeating motifs could be discerned in each burglary. It was clear to everyone that one pair of hands was behind all three.

Each had been carried out in quite a mysterious fashion. All doors and windows were found to be locked, so it was a puzzle how the burglar, or burglars, had managed to get in.

At all the great banking houses a guard usually spends the night in the building. This man is tasked with walking through the bank's many rooms from time to time and making sure no break-in or theft is underway.

In all three of these banks, however, when the staff turned up at work the following morning, they found the guards lying on the floor, their wrists and ankles bound and their mouths stopped up with rags so that they could neither move nor cry out for help.

And each of the guards related the same story: "Around midnight, I was suddenly attacked from behind, and before I could even turn around to see who it was that did it—before I could even cry out that one powerful word, 'HELP!'—I had already been tied up and gagged. I don't know what else to say. I saw no one, heard no one."

This sequence of events was so unusual, so mysterious, that if it had taken place in but one bank the suspicion would surely have fallen on the guard. It would have been surmised that he was involved in the whole plot and that everything he had related was a bald-faced lie.

But because it happened in three banks, all on the same night, the accounts had to be believed, as unbelievable as they may have been.

In each of the banks only cash was missing—banknotes and gold coins. Other items of value—paper securities, assets, bonds and debentures, pensions, and the like—were left untouched. It was evident that the work had been done by a skilled practitioner, one who did not intend to load himself up with such things as would leave a paper trail and lead the authorities right to him. He took only ready money—money he would be able to easily secrete away or to change without anyone bothering him.

Naturally the police were informed at once, and the brightest investigatory minds on the force were dispatched to carry out the necessary inspections. A specialist who worked at a factory that produced safes tried to determine exactly how the thieves managed to open the heavy, meticulously secured cabinets where the money was kept. They had not used duplicate keys—keys for such high-security locks simply could not be duplicated.

Rather, it seemed they used some novel system, some entirely new mechanism that enabled them to open up the safes, then lock them back up again without damaging the locks in the slightest.

The case was so puzzling that not a single police inspector could even begin to understand it. They gabbled about this and babbled about that, exchanged bits of wisdom, suggested ideas for a plan—but could not manage to land on one to which they all agreed.

As they sat around someone came in to tell the police chief that Hermann Fuchs, senior assistant to the private detective Max Spitzkopf, wished to speak with him.

"Aha! So Spitzkopf is getting in touch!" cried the chief. "Maybe he'll have a bright idea."

Then in came Fuchs, visibly out of sorts, his face pallid.

"What's got you in such a tizzy?" the chief asked. "Have you taken an interest in the break-ins that took place last night?"

"Yes," Fuchs answered. "But that's not why I've come to see you. A more significant matter has brought me here, and I want you to listen closely to all I have to tell you."

"Do go on. What is it you wish?"

And so Fuchs sat down and gave the following account:

"My master, Spitzkopf, returned home from a long journey yesterday and found none of us at his home offices, as we were all away doing fieldwork. And so he lay himself down for a bit of rest. But then an elegant carriage drew up in front of his house. A lackey emerged and entered the house to deliver Spitzkopf a letter.

"My master immediately departed in the carriage with the lackey, neglecting even to inform his housekeeper of his destination. Later, the other assistants and I met at his home. The housekeeper told us what had happened, and we all concluded that it must be a trifling little errand that had brought him away and that he would soon return.

"But he never did return last night. We began to grow uneasy and to consider what our next steps must be. My heart told me that some sort of misfortune had befallen my master. I wanted to extract from the ancient housekeeper the necessary information—where he had traveled off to and with whom—but she hadn't a clue.

"When I heard this morning the news of the three bank burglaries I thought: 'Well, here's a moment when we need our master something awful.' The feeling prompted me to go looking in his room to see whether there might be some clue there as to where he'd gone.

"That's when I found a letter written to him by some Graf Paul Hardegg. I figured he must have traveled off to pay this count a visit. So I immediately telephoned all the counts named Hardegg who maintain homes in Vienna and its environs, but nothing of note had recently happened to any of them, and none of them had summoned Spitzkopf.

"In the book containing the names and addresses of the Austrian nobility, however, there is but a single Graf *Paul* Hardegg, who currently lives in Weidlingau. I fired off an express telegram to him and received an answer right away—he also knew absolutely nothing. It had now become clear to me, beyond the shadow of a doubt, that my master had been deceived by his enemies, the criminals of Vienna, and there was no knowing what might have happened to him since. The scoundrels have dealt so slyly this time, so skillfully, that even the ever-careful Spitzkopf did not suspect a thing but rather simply dashed out of town and left not a trace behind him."

The police chief and the officers present were in a state of shock.

They had never encountered such a case before. They had never known the legendary detective to get himself into such a bind that the police were needed to liberate him.

The chief at once ordered that every effort should be expended to meet one solitary goal: *Find. Spitzkopf.*

"Unless I'm mistaken," he said, "the trap for Spitzkopf must have been set by the very gang that perpetrated the bank break-ins. And if so, they are a flock of very crafty crows indeed—ones that we shall have to hunt using quite new, untested methods. And it seems to me that if we manage to free Spitzkopf—we will simultaneously find the tracks of the bank burglars."

The most highly trained officers were duly scattered throughout the many and sundry streets of Vienna, questioning the populace to determine if anyone had happened to see whither the elegant carriage that had stopped in front of Spitzkopf's house was bound.

Spitzkopf's other assistants, meanwhile, also dispersed themselves throughout the city. They were intent upon finding their vanished master.

CHAPTER THREE
Detective, Free Thyself

MEANWHILE SPITZKOPF remained alone in his blindingly illuminated cell.

He feared to turn down the lights lest the villains should ambush him in the dark and do him all manner of harm. He feared falling asleep for the same reason. And though he was desperately tired and enfeebled, he used the last of his strength to remain awake. He would just barely doze off, for no more than a couple of minutes, then wake up again with a fright, as though he had just had a nightmare.

He could not countenance what had happened to him. He had always been so cool under pressure, so unafraid. He had looked death straight in the eye on more than one occasion, and his courage was never found wanting. And now . . . now his nerves were somehow shot. His spirit was nearly defeated. He felt as powerless as a small child.

The iron chain cut unmercifully. He was in a great deal of pain. He ground his teeth out of pure anger, knowing that these knaves may be carrying out at that very moment the most dreadful crimes, and meanwhile he was sitting here, a prisoner. He knew what must be happening and could do nothing to stop it.

The men had left him his watch. He sat there on his plank bed, counting out the hours and the passing minutes. And that is how he passed the night: in the throes of deepest anxiety.

Around morning he heard footsteps on the stairs that led down to this dungeon. Then a small hatch built into his cell door slid open, and there appeared the visage of Count Hardegg's pretender.

"Good morning, Mr. Spitzkopf!" the man called out derisively. "Did you sleep well?"

"Awfully, thanks," Spitzkopf answered quietly. "What's the news?"

"Here's your news!" said the supposed count, showing him a package stuffed with thousand-krone notes and sacks brimming with gold pieces. "All this I received as a just compensation for the good work I did at the Depositenbank, the Hypothekenbank, and the Vorschussbank. Tomorrow I shall get even more. I plan to pay a nice visit to the Länderbank, the Creditanstalt, and the Postsparkasse. And the day after that I shall be leaving my calling card at the rest of Vienna's great banking houses.

"I can console you with the fact that after I'm done, and my little visits all come off as beautifully as it did last night, I will be leaving Vienna, and you will be set free."

There was nothing Spitzkopf could do while this taunting speech was recited other than remain silent, grinding his teeth out of seething rage.

The scoundrel's face, with its faux-friendly smile, then disappeared from the little hatch, replaced with that of Red Franz. He tossed a hunk of bread through the opening and lowered a jug of water tied to a rope. "There's yer victuals for the day!" he called out, with a mocking laugh. "Eat, drink, and be merry!"

Spitzkopf kept silent. He did not even bother looking at the giant's face.

"Angry with me, are yeh?" asked Red Franz. "Well, you're forgetting that yer at my mercy—so you better learn to get along with me and play nice."

"I'm at your mercy, eh?" said Spitzkopf, laughing right along with him. "Seems to me, actually, that you're at mine."

"Just you wait, you dog!" answered Franz, smoke all but coming out of his ears. "Just wait and see which one of us is stronger." Then he slammed the hatch shut and tramped back up the stairs. Spitzkopf was alone again.

Suddenly he was beset with sharp pangs of hunger and a burning thirst. He had not had a morsel to eat nor a drop to drink for over fifteen hours. But he refused to touch the bread and water out of fear that they may have been poisoned.

Unsettled and impatient, he sat upon his plank bed and resumed monitoring the minute hand on his watch. It seemed to beat on so slowly that he nearly sprang up out of sheer frustration.

Several times he tried unloosing the chain that bound him. But he had not a single tool, and whenever he tried wriggling to effect some movement of the chain, the iron links only cut deeper. Each time he was forced to stop his efforts as soon as he started them.

Releasing himself from the chain would not have done much good anyhow, as he knew the door of his dungeon was reinforced with iron—he would never be able to breach it with his hands alone. His only hope lay in the revolver, which he always had at the ready, and Red Franz, who would not be able to restrain himself from barging in to attack him if no one else were home. If he did, Spitzkopf would be able to figure a way out of the desolate pit into which he had been flung.

Around noon Spitzkopf again heard footsteps coming from the staircase, and again there appeared the maniacally contorted face of Red Franz in the hatch. "Hey, bloodhound!" he barked. "You ain't eaten or drunk nothin'? The bread's untouched and the water jug's full as when I left it. Afraid we'll poison yeh, eh?"

"What's it to you?" Spitzkopf responded in a fractious tone. "To the devil with you, for all I care!"

"Oh, go on, you ninny!" Franz shouted. "My friends don't want to do anything to yeh. They just wanna getcha outta their hair for as long as they've got business what needs attending to. But just you wait. Payback's coming. A payback for all times. From now on you won't get any bread and water."

"You think I give a damn?" was Spitzkopf's retort. "You can close that little door now and head straight to hell." And with that he grabbed the jug and splashed its entire contents into Red Franz's face. The giant's face was now ferocious as a tiger's.

"You're lucky I'm not alone!" the man roared. "If I was you can bet I'd squash yeh like a bug right this second. But be patient. I'll see yeh again real soon—tonight, in fact."

But Spitzkopf was not done provoking him. Now he hurled the empty jug at Franz, hitting him smack in the head.

"Just you wait, yeh filthy dog!" the man said, his eyes absolutely flaming now as he slammed the little door shut. "Just wait! I'll soon give yeh what yer askin' for."

After he left, Spitzkopf could still hear him ranting and raving on the stairs.

Then all was quiet again.

Spitzkopf was bone-tired, and though he struggled mightily against sleep, at the end he could resist no longer. He fell back onto his plank bed and instantaneously into dreamland.

He slept thus for a good number of hours. When he awoke he saw that it was already nine o'clock at night. "Oh, but how dreadful!" he thought. "I slept so soundly. If Red Franz had come upon me during this time he could have done whatever he pleased with me."

But the extended slumber strengthened him. He felt refreshed and in far finer fettle than before. "He'll be coming in soon now, I expect. I've got to tread carefully—and give him the kind of warm welcome he deserves."

He sat thus in deep thought for around an hour. Then he heard steps, and soon there appeared in the opening the face of—the bank burglar, the ersatz Count Hardegg.

"You're still here, eh?" the man said. "And here I thought they said you're such an artist at your craft! Such a famous detective as you—I would have thought you could squeeze yourself out through the keyhole itself! Why, you're nothing more than a shlimazl! The real mystery is why any of my friends are so afraid of you!

"Anyway, I've got to run. It's time for me to carry out the greatest feat of my illustrious career. I'm gonna clean out the biggest bank in Vienna! By tomorrow all of Europe will be in awe at my pièce de résistance.

"And there you are, sitting on your plank bed, unable to do a thing about it! Ha ha! You great and powerful man!"

Spitzkopf could not help but join in the laughter. "Let's not count our chickens before they hatch, shall we?" he said to the burglar. "Or count any money before it's in the bag—lest I have you yourself bagged while you're at it!"

"Oh, come off your high horse! Truly, I did not take you for *this* great a simpleton!" the burglar sneered. "I can't tell whether you're more simple than you are stubborn or vice versa! But just you wait. Soon you'll be crying like a baby for me to let you out of this here nursery."

Then he disappeared, and again Red Franz's head popped out of the opening.

"Yes, soon! Soon you and I will get to dance our little waltz together! Oh, won't it be just the absolute mostest!"

Spitzkopf said nothing in response but just held ever more tightly on to his revolver, his only salvation. Then the little door slammed shut, Spitzkopf heard feet galumphing up the stairs, and all was quiet again. He expected it would not be long now before Red Franz returned to assail him.

"He told me he'd be paying me a visit, and I should think it's in my interest to believe him," Spitzkopf reflected. "He's bound to take full advantage of the hours when the other scoundrels are off doing their work."

And so Spitzkopf undertook to do the following: He turned off the electric lights. He lay down on his plank bed. And he began snoring. Loudly.

But he was not sleeping. No, anything but. He just lay there, the revolver locked and loaded in his hand, just waiting for his foul-hearted foe to pop in.

It did not take long. Soon he heard quiet, careful footfalls on the steps above—so quiet and careful that only Spitzkopf, with his sharply attuned ears, could have heard them. Then quietly, carefully, Red Franz turned his key in the cell's heavy door. And quiet and careful as a cat, he drew up to the plank bed upon which Spitzkopf was snoring.

He had just barely groped his way to it in the pitch dark when Spitzkopf switched on the lights and bolted up to face his opponent. He pointed his revolver at Red Franz, the electric lights flashing off of it and directly into Franz's affrighted eyes.

The man sprang backward and cried, "Where'dja get a gun?

We . . . we emptied out yer pockets!"

"That's no business of yours," Spitzkopf answered. "Now put down that knife or I'll shoot you dead as a dog."

"I'm not afraid of no old popgun," said Red Franz, readying himself to tackle the detective and thrust his long, sharp blade inside him.

But Spitzkopf fired, and Franz fell at his feet. Three bullets, right into his heart. His knife fell from his hand.

"Well, there's an end to our time together, though it breaks my heart to say so . . ." Spitzkopf said, searching the man's pockets. He found a ring of keys, among them the one Franz had used to lock the chain that restrained him. Hastening to unlock it now, Spitzkopf finally breathed a deep sigh of relief. He was simply delighted, delighted to finally be free of the chain's iron embrace.

"Now you just stay down here and keep quiet while I attend to some things upstairs," he said, shoving Franz under the plank bed, the villain's life hanging by a hair.

Spitzkopf at last left his subterranean prison and locked the door behind him. He tiptoed up the stairs until he found himself in the corridor. The room at the end of it was open, and he entered. There was no one else to be found. It seemed Red Franz was indeed the only man left behind to keep watch. Spitzkopf continued to traipse through the house's rooms, and though each was brightly lit, not a soul stirred within them.

Finally, in the foyer, he found a man sitting in a chair, half asleep. Spitzkopf immediately recognized the coachman who had driven him there. He woke the man up and, pointing his gun directly in his face, asked him, "So where are your friends?"

"I know nothing!" the man yelped, staring wide-eyed at Spitzkopf as though the detective were some horrific apparition.

"You're lying," Spitzkopf shouted back. "Tell me where they are this instant—or you'll meet the same end as your crony Red Franz."

The man swore by all the saints that he truly, honestly, knew absolutely nothing.

"I see!" said Spitzkopf. "I see you're a stubborn mule, that is. And stubborn mules get taken by the reins."

He grabbed the man's collar and dragged him down into the cellar. There he opened the door and shoved him inside, into the space where Spitzkopf himself had spent so many long hours. Not once did the coachman try to struggle. All he could do was tremble like a fish from the moment he caught sight of Spitzkopf's revolver.

"Now you're going to tell me where your friends are," Spitzkopf commanded, "or I'll empty half an ounce of lead right between your ribs."

"But I know nothing," the man pleaded, in plangent tones. "I know nothing!"

"Fine, then," said Spitzkopf. "Remain here until I return, at which point I'll turn you over to the penitentiary—which is where the lot of you belong."

And with that he left, locking the door. He ascended the stairs and, in the room at the top, happened upon a ring of keys and lockpicks, quite finely made articles. Using one of them, he opened the only door he had not yet gone through. It led into a massive courtyard, surrounded by a high fence.

Not pausing to think for even a moment, he jumped the fence and, upon surveying his surroundings, saw that he was on one of the most dangerous streets in Vienna. He ran for several minutes until he found an empty cab. Jumping into the carriage, he called up to the cab-man: "To the city center, and make it quick! I'll soon tell you which street. But know that you'll be receiving a handsome tip if you get me there in a half hour at the latest."

And so, driving the horses at the most vigorous gallop they could manage, the cabman swiftly transported the detective to Vienna's center, the Innere Stadt.

Fuchs, along with all of Spitzkopf's other loyal assistants, had spent the entire day running around like people who were not quite sane. They searched the whole city: every corner, every dank bar, every hideaway, every miserable hole that they knew to be occupied by the suspected criminal gang. But not a trace did they find of their absent master.

The police too had not spared any effort in investigating the matter, researching and interrogating and tracking down any lead that might bring the officers to the missing detective—but with zero results. Neither had they managed, in all their investigations, to gain any further insight into the bank burglaries. The case remained a total riddle.

Meanwhile, the papers published lengthy reports on the break-ins, sending all of Vienna into a stew. When word got out that the illustrious detective Max Spitzkopf had vanished, this stew positively bubbled over. The telephones at various editorial offices were ringing off the hook as the Viennese populace called in to ask whether or not any clues had been found that might lead to the discovery of the culprits or of Spitzkopf. At police headquarters too people called every minute pleading for new information.

Thus an entire day passed in utter alarm and agitation, in confusion and clamor.

Around midnight Spitzkopf's assistants gathered in his office to discuss what tack to take next. Fuchs, as the senior assistant, chaired the meeting. He began by stating his opinion that Spitzkopf's vanishment and the bank break-ins were connected. That is to say, the burglars were the same men who deceived and disappeared the detective. Doing so allowed them to commit their crimes without anyone breathing down their necks. In order to track them down—and send them packing—the team of assistants would have to maintain surveillance over all of Vienna's major banking houses that night. There was no chance the culprits would be satisfied with the three they had cleared out the night prior.

And so the assistants divided up the remaining banks among themselves, each of them promising to maintain an all-night vigil at the building to which they were assigned. Perhaps one of them would happen upon something out of the ordinary.

Fuchs assumed responsibility for the Länderbank. He hid out in one of the administrative offices, through which one had to pass in order to enter the bank's strongroom.

Everything was perfectly quiet up until midnight. Fuchs had not heard even the remotest rustling. But after midnight he pricked his ears up. Now would be the time, he reckoned, that the burglars would most likely begin their heist.

He did not have to wait long. Around 12:30, he thought he heard a noise coming from the strongroom. Now that was a corner room, only accessible through the office in which Fuchs lay hidden between two large cupboards. So he could not quite believe his ears. How could the noise be coming from there? He decided to patrol through the bank's other offices to determine whether he was mistaken and the sound had in fact come from a different side of the bank.

Fuchs had seen to it that all of the offices were dark, it being imperative that the thieves not notice anyone waiting for them, if or when they did break in.

So as soon as Fuchs entered the first office adjoining the one in which he had been hiding, he stumbled . . . over a dead body. Before he had a second to take in the room or fire off his revolver, he was seized by the wrists and a wet rag was stuffed into his mouth by a pair of very dexterous hands. Then a pair of extraordinarily powerful hands wrenched his arms behind his back and bound them. He was rendered unable to move or to scream out.

He now felt himself being lifted in the air by those powerful hands and carried through a succession of spaces, by a route theretofore unknown to Fuchs, ending in the bank's strongroom. As he was deposited in a corner the chamber was illuminated by a small electric lamp, which threw a faint light onto the walls.

Now Fuchs saw, standing beside him, two characters he did not recognize—both of them big brawny men, and both guffawing right in his face.

"Well, if it ain't the little assistant of the great detective Max Spitzkopf!" one of them howled. "We've been hosting your master for two days now in a real nice, safe spot! But we're gonna make even quicker work of you . . ."

Fuchs bit his tongue and balled his fists. His conjecture had been accurate—his master was in the clutches of these criminals, and there was nothing he could do to help.

With astonishing speed the men opened a large safe and cleared it out. Then they took the trussed Fuchs and slipped him into the empty safe.

"You'll be spending the night in here, old pal!" they jeered. "And tomorrow morning, though the bank teller will find the safe empty of cash, he won't find it empty of all treasure. No, no—he'll discover a precious little weasel waiting for him inside!

"And the day after we'll see you again ourselves—at your funeral! Because you're going to suffocate in here!" And with that they slammed shut the doors of the safe, Fuchs crouched inside it like a mouse in a trap.

He could hear the men then occupying themselves in the remainder of the strongroom, opening up all the locks and doors and emptying out all of its ready cash. Yes, he heard all of it—and could do nothing but scream inwardly. He was powerless to stop them.

He sat listening to their operation for some time. Then he began to feel lightheaded. His breathing became more labored. It grew more and more difficult for him to fill his lungs. He closed his eyes, held his breath, and his consciousness slipped away.

He had already accepted that his life would soon be slipping away with it. He did not know that help was near at hand and that in but a few minutes he would be rescued. And who would be there to accomplish this extraordinary feat? None other than his master, Spitzkopf—the very man he had been so intent on rescuing himself.

CHAPTER FOUR
The Dog

DASHING ALONG at full gallop, the cab Spitzkopf had hired made its way into the heart of the city, the Innere Stadt. Spitzkopf had the driver pull up in front of his house and bade the man wait there while he was occupied inside. The detective rushed in, but none of his assistants were in the offices, only the old housekeeper.

"*Groyser got almekhtiker*, God almighty!" she exclaimed. "Master Spitzkopf! Where have you been? We all nearly breathed our last waiting for your return!"

He did not even try responding to the whirlwind of questions she blew his way. Instead he seized a ring of skeleton keys, his electric torch, and a pair of revolvers, then raced back to the front door, calling back to his housekeeper: "Stay calm—I shall be back before you know it and will explain everything!"

In the foyer lay his ever-faithful hound, a strong, sturdy hunting dog that had more than once lent a helping paw to Spitzkopf in his work. The dog, like the other denizens of the household, had been ill at ease all day as a result of not seeing his master for so long and now greeted him with a most friendly bow-wow.

"Come with me, Bob!" Spitzkopf called to him. "None of my

men are here, so you're going to be my assistant today."

The dog scampered over to his side and soon both of them were sitting in the carriage. "To the Länderbank!" Spitzkopf shouted up to the driver. "But stop a few buildings away, and Bob and I will get out and walk."

Spitzkopf sat and pondered: "That scoundrel boasted that he'd be cleaning out the Länderbank tonight. But if Lady Luck smiles on me, I'll nab him right in the middle of his wicked work."

A few minutes later the carriage stopped. Spitzkopf bounded out, his dog Bob right alongside him.

Every door of the Länderbank was locked and every window was dark. "I know we're late," Spitzkopf said to Bob. "But we've actually come at just the right time."

He then opened the heavy front door with a skeleton key.

"Looks like the burglars turned out the lights in all the offices," Spitzkopf remarked. "They wouldn't want anyone catching a glimpse of them while they're so hard at work—not when they haven't quite finished yet . . ."

Treading softly, he entered the bank. His various skeleton keys, all of the finest construction, opened all the interior doors quite easily. Brave Bob ambled along at his side, matching footfalls with his.

Spitzkopf feared using his electric torch and revealing his presence. But he held a loaded revolver at the ready. Upon entering one of the offices, he felt something soft underfoot. He carefully switched on his torch and saw lying on the floor a hog-tied bank employee, his mouth corked with a rag. Spitzkopf yanked the rag out and cut off the ropes that bound him.

The man breathed a great sigh of relief and briefly reported to Spitzkopf what had transpired.

"So . . . I *have* come too late," said Spitzkopf in response. "The scoundrel has already finished his work here. Which means that I must now go and seek him out at the Creditanstalt."

He told the employee to remain where he was—to not go

out nor breathe a word of what had happened lest the criminals learn someone was on their trail before Spitzkopf got the chance to sneak up on them at the Creditanstalt.

The detective was ready to exit the building, but Bob refused to budge from his spot. He kept snuffling at the base of the door that led to the next room over.

"Come, Bob!" Spitzkopf commanded. "We haven't any time to play!"

But the dog gave out a harrumph and tried to open the door with his front paws.

"Oh, you've sniffed something out, have you?" Spitzkopf thought, helping Bob in his task.

With that accomplished, the dog bayed raucously and zoomed over to the safe into which Fuchs had been sealed. Spitzkopf raced to get it open. It took him a few minutes, but finally he managed to twist open the heavy lock and wrest open the iron doors.

He shone his torch inside and, to his horror, found Fuchs there, nearly suffocated. Quickly pulling him out, Spitzkopf spritzed him with water and slipped him out of his confining ropes. Fuchs came to within moments and opened his eyes.

"Ah, Master! We were worried half to death over you!" he said, unable to speak any more loudly than a choked groan.

"Half to death indeed! You were worried about *me*, and here *you* are, having almost lost your life over it!" said Spitzkopf, pressing the lip of a bottle of cognac to his assistant's lips. "Now rest a little here, then go home and lay yourself down to sleep at once. I'll finish up on my own."

"No, Master," said Fuchs, recovering a little. "We won't be leaving you on your own any more. One of us must always be following close behind you."

"But someone is. I've brought faithful Bob with me today," Spitzkopf said, putting Fuchs at ease. "Look at him there. You have him to thank for saving your life."

Fuchs started to respond, but Spitzkopf could not spare another second.

"The clock is ticking. I must be off," he called out, dashing out of the building with his hound at his heels.

CHAPTER FIVE

The Burglars Are Busted

SPITZKOPF AND BOB ran to the Creditanstalt as fast as their feet could carry them. The detective did not want to take the cab again, as the thieves would surely have stationed a watchman outside any bank in which one of their heists was underway. Such a guard would spot Spitzkopf arriving, and he'd run to warn his cronies. But it was the dead of night and perfectly dark outside, which allowed the detective and his dog to remain quite unnoticed as they padded down the street.

When they turned onto the street where the Creditanstalt is located, they slowed their pace and sidled along very warily, keeping close to the buildings, making sure no one caught sight of them. They succeeded in this and arrived at the bank without incident. Inside, also, complete darkness reigned, save for in what appeared to be one small anteroom. Spitzkopf did not delay. He opened the front door with a skeleton key and crept in, faithful Bob at his side. In the entrance hall, Spitzkopf's sharp ear detected a distant noise, and his dog issued some low grunts.

"Bob, hush!" Spitzkopf commanded him, taking care that the dog not give them away, for it was clear the criminals were here, and right in the middle of their heist.

And so Bob lay down on the staircase and made not one more peep. Spitzkopf, meanwhile, opened the first door he came to and found himself in an office. He strode slowly through a number of rooms until he arrived outside the anteroom in which he had noticed the light of electric lamps.

The door to this room was crossed with iron bars and locked with heavy iron locks. Spitzkopf tried for a very long time to open it and finally managed. As he did so, from the other side of one wall, he could just make out a noise that sounded like someone very effortfully drilling into a wall.

The room in which he now stood opened directly into the bank's strongroom. Spitzkopf conjectured that the thieves had been unable to open the iron-barred door and that in order to avoid the loud noise that would be occasioned by them ramming their way through it they changed course. They must have decided instead to bore a hole into a different wall, one less solidly built, through which they would be able to infiltrate into the strongroom.

Spitzkopf stood there for a while considering what he ought to do next. But then, noticing a tall writing desk in the middle of the room, he formulated his plan.

The only other piece of furniture in the room was a small iron furnace. The drilling sound was coming from just above it.

"I'll hide under the desk," Spitzkopf thought, "and wait and see what happens." The desk was across from the site of the noise. They would not be able to sight him so quickly once they broke through.

The drilling grew louder and louder until bits of mortar started flying off the wall, landing right next to the furnace. All the while Spitzkopf lay hidden underneath the desk, a loaded revolver in his hand. Suddenly, just beside the furnace, a brick was dislodged from the wall and crashed to the floor. Through the tiny opening there appeared the visage of a character we know all too well: the pretender to the countdom of Count Hardegg. Spitzkopf did not move a muscle. He simply watched and waited.

The hole was growing larger and larger. The burglar was now deftly removing one brick after another. Soon the hole was so spacious that he could easily crawl through it. He did so slowly and let himself down into the room.

"I've made it," he said to himself. "Now to turn off these pesky lights, and we'll get right to work."

He searched along the walls for the button that controlled the lights but he did not find it so easily, as the button was in fact nailed into the desk.

When he walked toward the desk Spitzkopf sprang up to face him, pointing his revolver right at the thief's face so that it glinted in his eyes.

"Spitzkopf!" the man screamed, startled out of his wits. He snatched his own loaded revolver out of his pocket.

"Yes, it is I," the detective answered evenly. "Sorry to pop in here like this unannounced. You must have expected me to still be in that pit you sealed me up in."

"And you must be a demon, not a man, to have managed to get out of there," said the man through gritted teeth. "But now we'll settle which of us is to come out on top once and for all. Let's see who's the better shot!"

Spitzkopf laughed. "Oh, go on, bird brain!" he said. "You know very well that I shoot straighter. What good could it do you having that knowledge confirmed? You'd be far better off putting down your revolver and considering yourself as good as arrested."

"Aha!" the thief shouted back. "I can see you haven't quite got my number! Now either you put down your gun or prepare to duel. Or if you'd prefer . . . just let me go free. I'll give you my word that I'll leave Vienna for good, this very day."

"Oh, yes, I know you've a special passion for flying off like the bird brain you are," Spitzkopf answered. "But it won't serve you this time. Now drop the gun or I'll shoot.

"One . . . two . . ."

But before Spitzkopf could call out "Three!" the criminal fired off his own gun and, with catlike grace, vaulted toward the hole he had drilled in the wall.

His shot had missed. Spitzkopf followed it with a shot of his own, hitting the thief in his left foot. He caterwauled wildly but continued fleeing, clawing through the hole and disappearing. Spitzkopf gave chase, but the man cut a route through an entirely different set of rooms and reached the staircase before Spitzkopf was even in sight. He could almost taste his perfect freedom—by the time the detective made it onto the street he would be nowhere to be found.

But he was soon to taste a far more bitter pill indeed.

On the steps lay Spitzkopf's canine companion, Bob. After being splashed with a couple drops of blood from the thief's wounded foot, Bob lunged and sunk his teeth deep into the man's flesh. The thief whacked Bob on the head with the grip of his revolver, but this only served to drive the dog even wilder. He pounced on the man, knocking him straight to the floor, and stood astride him, biting him anywhere that his gnashing teeth landed.

When Spitzkopf finally arrived, it was with some effort that he managed to free the thief from Bob. The man was a shambles. His clothes were torn; blood ran in rivulets from his face, his arms, everywhere.

Spitzkopf left the man on the steps. He rushed back up the staircase to the office that contained the telephone. Picking up the receiver, he asked to be connected to the chief of police, whom he brought up to date on all that had taken place. The chief was astonished to hear Spitzkopf's voice. But he did not waste any time and left immediately for the Creditanstalt with a number of security men in tow. Spitzkopf was waiting for him there, standing on the staircase beside the seriously wounded burglar.

A doctor was called. He dressed the man's wounds, and the police chief ordered that the culprit be brought to the hospital. The man was so weakened by his injuries that the interrogation would have to be postponed.

Spitzkopf, meanwhile, made off with the chief and his officers in the direction of the street where the criminals resided. Entering the house, their first destination was the cellar, where they found the wounded Red Franz. They hauled him upstairs and immediately had him conducted, like his crony, to the prison hospital. The other criminal they found in the house was sent to police headquarters.

The hideaway was thoroughly searched, and a great deal of stolen money found. Indeed, the entire amount, down to the last heller, that had been stolen from the three banks the night prior was still untouched. The money that had been stolen just a few hours earlier, from the Länderbank, was also found, along with a tremendous sum of American dollars and British pounds. The bank burglar had been plying his trade around the world for years.

Once the police finished recovering all of the money and sealing up the house, Spitzkopf returned home, where he lay down for some rest. He was very tired after his exertions of the last two days.

As soon as the new day dawned, Spitzkopf and Fuchs, who had also had a bit of time to recuperate, traveled off to the police headquarters, and from there a squad was dispatched to the prison hospital, where the wounded criminals were questioned. Both were still so reeling from their injuries that not a great deal of information could yet be extracted. But this much was learned: that the ringleader was a career burglar from the United States who had been perpetrating his notorious crimes there for years, though no one had ever succeeded in nabbing him. He worked by the cleverest methods and used all the latest technologies. He had opened the world's strongest locks, broken through the toughest walls. It seemed as though absolutely nothing would ever hinder him in the execution of his wicked work.

The second man arrested in the house was his assistant. His beat was fixing where he and his master would stay and where the money would be kept, keeping watch, and other such tasks.

These two got to know Red Franz only after they arrived in Vienna, taking him on as the muscle, as they said, and leaving him to do the dirty work.

The infamous burglar suffered for a few days in the hospital before succumbing to a terribly painful death. Red Franz did not last long, either, and died in the hospital along with him. The third chief member of the gang was condemned to several years in the clink but did not serve most of his sentence, as it was not long before he managed to escape, and none could catch him.

As for Spitzkopf, the Viennese banking houses rewarded him for his brilliant work with an absolute *hoard* of cash, enough to fill a great big safe.

Issue 10: The Child Murderess

צעהנטעס העפט. פרייז 20 העלער.

די קינדער־מערדערין.

— גענוג שוין! דו אונמענשליך ווייב! מעהר וועסט דו דיין בלוטיגע מלאכה נישט בעטרייבען!

The Child Murderess

CHAPTER ONE

The Vanished Child

It is a perfectly, most pleasantly warm morning. Let us look in on the celebrated private eye Max Spitzkopf sitting in his office, reading a letter that had come with the first post of the day.

It was but one of the mountain of dispatches Spitzkopf had received that morning. Summonses came for the detective from every corner—people seeking his help in rescuing some persecuted person, or finding one who had disappeared, or catching a criminal.

His senior assistant Hermann Fuchs sat beside him as he leafed through the letters, and Spitzkopf would give him each one to read once he was done scanning it over.

"I would need at least ten heads, along with twenty eyes, twenty ears, twenty hands, and twenty feet, to take on all of the cases these people wish to drop into my lap," Spitzkopf said to his assistant after reaching the bottom of the pile. "They are all matters of some importance, and I simply can't decide which I must attend to first."

Hermann Fuchs smiled. "Oh, Master, more than once I've witnessed you close ten cases in a day, and I've never seen you at quite such a loss over the work as you seem to be today!"

"You're right," Spitzkopf said. "But today's different. You see, all the things they've laid at my feet today, when I say they are matters of some importance, I mean they are important—indeed very important—to the people wrapped up in them. But as far as my own work is concerned they hold no real significance. Such trivialities are things the police can take care of, and I don't know why these people would come running first to me.

"If there were but one case here that interested me especially, I would not waver for an instant to grab on to it with all my might and expend every last bit of my energy on it. But as they are all minor matters, I find myself without the requisite burning desire to take any one of them on. And so I find myself quite undecided."

"*Nu*, who's forcing you?" asked Fuchs. "You can turn them all away and take a day to rest for once!"

"I could . . ." Spitzkopf answered. "But I don't wish to. I don't need to rest. It is only in my work that I find diversion, that I find pleasure. Only in my exertive and exhilarating work! Exhaustion is all I get from going about idly." At that moment the doorbell rang, and Fuchs scampered over to open it. Spitzkopf, meanwhile, had barely finished putting the letters away in his desk drawer when in walked an elegantly attired young lady. Her face was deathly pale, her eyes wet with tears. But one could still see that she was very beautiful. Even now, in this state of deep sorrow, she could not help but be enchanting.

Spitzkopf extended a friendly greeting to her and demanded she take a seat. But she remained standing and said: "I have come to you, great master of your art, so that you might help me in my hour of greatest need!"

"I shall do what I can," Spitzkopf answered, "but first you must sit down and tell me in full detail what has happened to you. Only then will I be able to know what I can do."

The woman assumed her seat and spoke. "I don't know if it will be possible for me, in my present agitated state, to string my thoughts together well enough to fully recount to you my story of woe. But I will try . . . try to pull myself together, if it's the last thing I do, and tell it all, in as much detail as I can . . ."

She sighed deeply, used her handkerchief to wipe the tears from her eyes, and related the following. "My name is Clara Goldfeld, and I was born in a small shtetl in Galicia.

"My father was a prosperous man. For years, he led a highly successful business, and he raised me, his only daughter, in a very fine way, seeing to it that I was educated. When I was fourteen years old, the wheel of fortune started spinning in quite the other direction. My father lost all of his money and was left deeply in debt. The whole family had to leave town and relocate to Vienna. My mother could not endure this most painful period for long and died a few months after we settled in the city.

"My father worked here as a commission agent, selling goods that belonged to others and keeping part of the profit—but a very small profit he had from it indeed. So I had to find employment as a shop girl to support myself. Father did not end up living much longer either. After three years of residing in Vienna, he caught cold, and following a few weeks' illness died in hospital. And so I was left alone, a girl of only seventeen years, dependent upon myself only, with nary a relative, nary an acquaintance, nary a friend. And to add to my misfortune, I was, so they tell me, very beautiful. That which for other girls is a blessing for me was a curse.

"I needn't spell it out—as a man of experience, you can easily imagine what a single girl, an orphan, and moreover a pretty girl, with no father, no mother, and no money, is forced to endure. Whoever cast his eye on me wouldn't stop pestering me. Whoever took an interest in me courted me incessantly. I had to use every last effort to defend myself from these impudent young men. For a while I managed. But then . . . then I fell into the most horrible misfortune.

"Among my new acquaintances, my so-called 'admirers,' there was a certain salesclerk, one Adolf Schneider, who took a special interest in me. He was a capable young man, educated, with refined manners, such that he made a worthy impression on me, and it seemed his intentions were actually serious.

"I didn't reject him as adamantly as I did the others, so he used to frequently come fetch me when I was leaving work at the shop and walk me home. On days we both had off, we would sometimes go strolling together. Sometimes he would invite me to the theater. Slowly, slowly, I allowed myself to be seduced by him. We went on like this for a good few months. He had a good position, made a fine salary, and told me that he had saved up 2,000 kronen. Most important, he behaved very respectably indeed, and I believed him when he said that he well and truly loved me. And so I accepted when he proposed marriage, and we became engaged.

"Our plan was that after the wedding we would open a store of our own. As we both worked in shops and possessed the necessary skills, we wouldn't have to employ others at the start and could build up our business gradually.

"We had been planning the wedding quite in earnest. Everything was prepared. I was indeed so sure of him that I stopped being quite so careful . . . and then, in a moment of weakness, he persuaded me . . . and ruined me.

"After that his behavior changed. He began telling me stories, saying his boss wanted to open a branch in Graz and make him director of the operation. And so he wanted to give up on our plan of opening our own store. He now preferred to wait until the Graz branch opened; then we could get married. He would be receiving such a high salary that we could both live off of it. I would no longer have to work in any shop.

"I believed him. I let myself be taken in.

"In due time I perceived that I would soon be a mother. When I told him, he made out as if he were quite ecstatic about it and went on amusing little tangents over what we might call the child, what games he would play with it, and so forth. But after that he started coming to see me less frequently, and when I asked him why, he would tell me that things had just gotten so busy for him, as the new location in Graz would be opening soon and everything had to be in place for the big day.

"My condition then was such that I could no longer work in the shop and had to remain at home. He told me not to let it worry me, promising that from then on he would support me, provide me with everything I needed. I would not need to touch the bit of cash that I had saved up, a few hundred kronen. And that's exactly how it was. He occasionally gave me some money, and we decided that as soon as I happily reached the other side of my present condition he would secure a residence in Graz, and I would promptly resettle there.

"One day he came to inform me that all the preparations in Graz had finished and that he would be traveling there the next day to open the store. He left me with fifty kronen and urged me not to let it trouble me if he wrote very little in the first letters he sent from there, as he would be frightfully busy at the beginning.

"But then . . . then he disappeared like a stone thrown into the ocean. I never heard from him again.

"For a week I waited impatiently for any word from him. For hours on end I would stand at the window and watch for the letter carrier. Maybe he would be toting some message for me . . . But it was for naught. I received nothing from him. Heard nothing. The impatience was all but driving me insane. I was seized by a horrible, wild feeling of desperation. Dark thoughts began to torment my brain. A sick feeling of suspicion took hold of me.

"I tried to forgive him in my heart, to convince myself that he really was just that frightfully busy or maybe something had happened to him—maybe he had taken ill or been beset by some other calamity. Finally I resolved that I would visit his boss at the shop he'd worked at in Vienna and seek information from him. And that's when I learned the whole, horrible truth: the entire story of the branch in Graz was invented out of whole cloth. A web of lies.

"'Adolf Schneider,' his boss told me, 'gave notice two months ago, explaining that his cousin somewhere in Germany would be taking him on in his own store. I tried to retain him, as he was one of my most industrious salesmen, someone who could be depended upon. I tried raising his salary. But he could not be convinced to stay, and two weeks ago he walked away from the position.' The man's story hit me like a clap of thunder. I lost consciousness right there in the store. When I came to again, I found myself in the hospital.

"I shall not bore you with all the particulars of my life story—they won't interest you, and they only upset me. In short, a couple of weeks later, there in that hospital, I became a mother. Mother to the most darling little boy. I named him after my pious father. The child was my only consolation during this most miserable period.

"I eventually found my way back to the apartment I had been living in, paid the rent with my savings, and began thinking of a plan to support myself and my child.

"I could not recover my position at the shop, as I would have to hand the child over to strangers while I worked, and that I could not bring myself to do. And so I tried finding work elsewhere. I can embroider very nicely and do other kinds of handicrafts, and I tried finding jobs in that line, something I would be able to do at home. But I wasn't successful at obtaining such work. The last bit of savings I had left would soon be used up. I would die of hunger together with my poor, sweet little lamb, the one remaining entity that brought any joy to my life.

"I realized I had to give him up. I made inquiries as to whether there might be any honorable woman to whom I could entrust my beloved boy. About two weeks ago a certain woman came to see me. She introduced herself as someone who made it her life's work to raise young children like mine. This woman made a very solid impression indeed. She gave me her address and swore to me by all that's holy that she would take care of the child like her own flesh and blood. She lived in a village not far from Vienna. I decided to give up my baby to her.

"I paid her in advance for two months of care, and we arranged that every two months I would come pay her for two more months.

"I had intended to accompany the child on the journey to her home, but the woman persuaded me that as unsettled as I was it would only distress me further to have to wrench myself away from my child when he was already in someone else's home, and therefore it would be much better not to join them. She spoke in such a tender, warm manner, like my very own mother, that I allowed myself to be convinced.

"After that I resumed my old position at the shop and impatiently counted the days until I would be able to visit my sweet little son.

"Yesterday my boss granted me leave from work to travel to the woman's village and see my boy. But imagine my horror when no one in this tiny village could provide me with any information about the woman who had taken my child. 'No such woman has ever lived here,' they insisted. No one in the whole village was in the business of rearing other people's children . . .

"Well, seeing as I lived through that day—I must be made of iron. For several hours I careered around the village like a madwoman, searching and making inquiries. Finally I was forced to admit to myself that all my effort was in vain. I returned home despondent, arriving quite late back in Vienna.

"I did not get a wink of sleep that whole night, only wept and wept. I spilled so many tears I could have drowned in them. I woke up early the next morning, and my first errand was to report to the police what had happened. On the way there, I ran into my boss and told him of my great misfortune. 'Well, that's a puzzler, eh?' he answered. 'My advice would be to take it first to the famous detective Max Spitzkopf. The police aren't gonna do you a bit of good. It'll take 'em a good long time just to identify a few clues. So I would say bring it right to Spitzkopf, on the double. He's shed light on the most shadowy cases before, and he'll surely be able to help you now.'

"And so I followed his advice and came straight to you, Herr Spitzkopf. And I shall not be leaving until you agree to take on my case."

CHAPTER TWO
Spitzkopf's Plans

ALL THROUGHOUT the unlucky girl's recitation of her story of woe, Spitzkopf sat quietly, barely moving, as if screwed into his chair. When she finished she was seized by an uncontrollable urge to sob, and she did so, bitterly, for over fifteen minutes.

Spitzkopf waited patiently for her to cry herself out, knowing that weeping is the best remedy for a heavy heart and that this unhappiest of women would soon regain her calm, at which point he would be able to have some serious interchange with her. While he waited he had time to think over the case and hatch a plan for how to go about solving it. Reclining in his chair and blowing rounded puffs of smoke from his pipe, he retreated deeply into his own thoughts and soon had a clear picture of what had happened.

Once the girl had composed herself, Spitzkopf spoke to her: "My dear child . . . I call you that even though you are now a mama, and one who has already endured much trouble. I call you that because you are indeed still a child yourself while other girls your age are only just starting to live life. So, my dear child, be calm. I promise you I shall move heaven and earth to help you as long as there is still time.

"Now you must answer my questions. Consider them very carefully, for absolutely everything depends on it.

"First, can you tell me where exactly your erstwhile fiancé Adolf Schneider went?"

"No," the girl answered. "His boss told me he went somewhere in Germany. Where exactly I do not know, and neither does his boss."

"Have you heard anything from him since then?" Spitzkopf asked further.

"No."

"Have any of his friends or acquaintances come to visit you?"

"Yes!" said the unfortunate girl. "Right after I had the child, a few of my fellow shop girls came to visit me in the hospital, along with a young man I had often seen hanging around with Schneider."

Spitzkopf prodded her. "What is the young man's name, and where does he reside?"

"His name is Franz Schmidt. He is employed as a salesclerk in a china shop on Währinger Strasse. His exact address I do not know."

"That suffices," said Spitzkopf, jotting down the man's name in his notebook. "Do you recall anything this Schmidt said during his visit?"

The girl thought for a few moments. "Yes, I remember it quite well. First he inveighed against his friend, Adolf Schneider, for having mistreated me so notoriously. And then he questioned me as to what I would do next."

"Did he ask if you would be keeping the child with you, or instead handing it off to another woman to raise?"

"Yes, in a sort of roundabout way."

"And how did you respond?"

"I had not yet decided, so I did not give any kind of definitive response."

"Who sent the woman who took the child?"

"I don't know. She just came. She said she had heard I wanted to give my child over to someone who would raise him. I thought she must have heard it from one of my neighbors."

"Do you by chance have a photograph of your former fiancé?"

"Yes," she said, taking a small portrait out of her purse and handing it to Spitzkopf, who stored it away in his notebook.

Spitzkopf asked what Schmidt looked like, what the woman who took the child looked like, and exactly what objects the child had along with him when she sent him away. He wrote everything down, then said to the girl: "I have all the information I need now. You can return home with the peace of mind afforded by the certainty that I shall do all I can to assist you. Of course, I cannot provide you with the unshakable hope that you shall see your child again. Who knows if the boy is still living . . . But as for your seducer and his accomplices soon being within my grasp, of that I can almost assure you."

"Oh, my dear child, my last and only source of solace!" cried the woman, breaking out into a fresh deluge of tears. "I am myself guilty. Your own mama let you out of her hands! Who knows what has become of you now!"

Spitzkopf consoled her with tender words, promising her she need not yet lose heart. It is quite possible, he said, that he would be able to track down the culprits before they harmed the child. And so the miserable woman collected herself and thanked the detective for his kindness in lending her his aid. "I haven't any money to pay you with!" she said through tears. "But my eternal gratitude is all yours."

"I require no money," said Spitzkopf. "It so happens I never ask my clients whether they shall be compensating me for my labor. It is enough for me to free innocent victims and to prevent criminals from doing any further harm. That is my greatest reward!"

CHAPTER THREE
Girlish Wiles

"FUCHS!" SPITZKOPF CALLED to his senior assistant after being left alone in his office. "Oh dear little Fuchs! We've caught one—a significant case! Finally something that calls for being reeled into my net.

"But I won't be tackling the matter myself. Not just at present. I am too old for the tactic I have in mind. However, I shan't be leaving Vienna until the case is well and truly cleaned and gutted!"

He summed up the basic details to Fuchs and told him to fetch the detective's youngest assistant, Leon Fein.

Barely half an hour had passed before Fein turned up in Spitzkopf's office, standing before his master. The detective gave him a thorough once-over and said: "You see, my young fellow? Everything in this world eventually comes in handy. Take yourself, for example. All your friends used to tease you that you look like a young girl and all that was missing was you putting on a dress and lady's chapeau for every boy in town to come chasing after you trying to win your affections.

"And in truth, you really are made to play the role of a little coquette—which is precisely what I am in need of today.

"Go on over to my dressing room. You'll find all the glad rags that you require there. Change into them such that no one will be able to recognize you nor the fact that you are a male."

"Right-o, Master!" answered the assistant, a youth of barely seventeen. "I'm sure I won't let you down!"

And so the boy disappeared through the wallpapered door that opened into the detective's dressing room. No more than ten minutes later he reappeared to greet his master, transformed. He was powdered, perfumed, and wearing a lady's ensemble, complete with a modish hat. A stranger would have sworn, without a doubt, that the young person standing before him was a comely maiden, down to the last freckle.

"Well, well! You haven't let me down a bit!" said Spitzkopf. "But this most important mission is only just beginning. When you set out on it, don't forget to bring along a revolver, an electric torch, and all of the other equipment that we need whenever we hit the road to do our work.

"Your path will lead you first to Währinger Strasse number

67. There you'll find a china shop, and you'll go promenading in front of it till around noon, when the staff breaks for lunch. One of these staffers is a certain man named Schmidt."

Spitzkopf described Schmidt's appearance according to the details Fraulein Clara Goldfeld had provided. "You should allow this person to get to know you and arrange a rendezvous with him for tonight. Then report to me, and leave nothing out. After that I'll tell you what to do next.

"And one more thing—you have a new name now: Paula Mark. Do not forget it."

"You can count on me, sir!" answered the newly minted young Fraulein. She then left the office, though not before performing such an artful, elaborate curtsy that Spitzkopf burst out laughing and called after her, "Brava, my lovely child! You've got the woman's touch!"

Paula Mark sallied forth to Währinger Strasse. When she reached number 67, she stopped to contemplate the window display of the grand porcelain emporium of Meisner & Co.

It was nearly noon when she arrived, so she did not have to wait long. Just as she finished examining all the contents of the five large shop windows, the clock struck twelve. And so she began her little promenade to and fro on the sidewalk in front of the store.

Soon the personnel spilled out onto the sidewalk, all heading home to take their lunch. Paula briefly stopped in front of a window and noticed an elegantly dressed young man come to a standstill beside her. He matched the description Spitzkopf had given him of Schmidt. He bowed to her in most gentlemanly fashion and asked, "It seems you are awaiting someone here, Mademoiselle?"

She parted her lips in a coy smile and answered, "Just so! But it looks like I'll be waiting in vain today. The man I'm expecting hasn't shown his face."

"Then he must be an absolute fool—or an absolute cad!" Schmidt remarked. "I would not allow such an enchanting creature to be kept waiting, not even for a minute! Why, I'd be positively *flying* to come and greet her!"

"But not all men are so polite," Paula Mark responded with a flurry of giggles. "It seems such a happy lot as that has not been granted to me."

"Oh, but don't despair!" Schmidt cried. "You simply have to let such a man go and find yourself an even better one."

"I dare say you're right," said Paula. "But how is one to know who is the best candidate?"

"Well, you could try me on for a start, sweet child!" Schmidt said, already reaching the badgering stage. "You won't regret it."

"You young blades aren't worth a plugged nickel, the lot of you!" Paula parried, tittering again. "But I suppose anything's worth a try. Who knows? Perhaps you'll improve upon the example set by that other specimen of your sex. So. When shall we see each other next?"

"Tonight! At the Venedig, main entrance. Around eleven."

"Why so late?" asked Paula. "Are you so very busy at the shop up until then?"

"Why, no! I'll be out of here at eight! But I have to walk my friend to the train this evening, so I won't be free until eleven."

"I see . . . a friend!" Paula scoffed. "Sure you don't mean a *girlfriend*?"

"No!" Schmidt insisted. "I give you my word of honor! It is a friend who has come here for the day. On a rather important matter. And I have to accompany him to the train."

"Whatever you say . . ." said Paula. "Well, I'd like to see if you really are the peach of a man you claim to be! Fine. So tonight at eleven at the entrance of the Venedig pleasure garden, eh?"

"It's a date!" answered Schmidt, squeezing the laughing girl's hand. "We'll have an absolutely marvelous time." They walked some thirty paces together until they reached a streetcar stop. There Schmidt bade farewell to his refreshing new acquaintance, saying he would be taking only an hour's recess for lunch and so had to return home quickly to gobble it up.

"Where is it you live?" Paula asked him.

"You want to find out everything in one shot, eh?" said Schmidt. "If you're as bold as you seem to be, you'll be learning where I live before long . . ."

At that moment a streetcar came rattling to a stop. Schmidt pressed the young lady's hand once more and jumped in. She blew him a kiss and waved her handkerchief at the departing tram long enough for it to vanish from view. Then she hoofed it back to Spitzkopf's office to report on all that she had managed to do, without batting an eyelash. Well, maybe just one or two.

CHAPTER FOUR
Schneider in Vienna

As for Spitzkopf, he had not been twiddling his thumbs during the time that Leon Fein was away.

After he had dispatched his damsel, he changed into his own disguise: a young dandy, a well-heeled swell of the highest Viennese order, and sauntered off to the store where Adolf Schneider had been employed.

He introduced himself to the manager as one of Schneider's friends, from Berlin, and asked if he could have a word with his old pal.

The manager answered that Schneider had left Vienna a few weeks past and was now working with a cousin in Germany.

"Perhaps you could furnish me with his address?" Spitzkopf asked.

"No," the manager answered. "I haven't bothered myself over

him since he walked out of here, nor has he attempted to get in touch with us."

"Perhaps you will permit me to make inquiries among the other staff? I can't imagine that none of them would have any information about their former colleague!"

"By all means. But I'm not so sure you'll be successful. There was a girl here a few days ago making the same sorts of inquiries, and no one was able to tell her a thing."

"In any case, I think I'll try my luck!" said Spitzkopf. He went off to converse with the salesclerks, the shop girls, and the accountant, asking each of them the same question—whether or not they could tell him the present address of Adolf Schneider.

But none of them knew a thing.

His last resort was a certain typist, a scent-wearing, spangle-bearing young lady.

"How should I know?" she drawled. But there was something in her voice that set off his internal lie detector. "He hasn't written me a word since he up and went."

"And before that you had been close?" Spitzkopf inquired further.

"What's the big idea, interrogatin' me like this, huh?" she answered, quite stirred up now. "What's it matter to you, anyhow? Now do me a favor and buzz off with your little quizzes."

Spitzkopf begged her pardon and left the shop. But there was something about her answers he did not like.

"I asked the same questions of all the employees, and none of them were offended until I came to that testy typist," he thought. "I could swear that she knows more than all the rest of them, and it would be worth my while to keep an eye on her.

"It will be lunchtime presently, and the staff will be heading home to dine. I shall have to go change clothes in a jiffy and see where the young lady resides—and with whom she socializes. Maybe she'll lead me onto the right track."

And so he climbed aboard a fiacre and bade the coachman

drive him home. Upon returning to his rooms he disguised himself anew, this time as an old peddler. He slung a tied bundle over his shoulders and raced back to the shop.

He made good time. It was only five past twelve, and the staff was just starting to leave for lunch. Spitzkopf paced slowly on the opposite sidewalk until he caught sight of the typist. She scurried off to the second district and stood waiting at a streetcar stop. Spitzkopf scurried after her, and when she boarded a tram, he did the same.

She alighted at the Prater and struck out onto the Hauptallee. He exited from the other side of the car and made as if to go to the Nordbahnhof but did not let the woman out of his sight. She had barely gone a hundred steps when he wheeled around and followed her. He did not have to walk long. As soon as she had ventured some distance into the Prater, she came to rest at a park bench, standing beside a young man who was sitting there engrossed in a newspaper.

The man looked up in surprise, but when his eyes met hers, he extended both his arms out to her and greeted her warmly, pressing her hands in his. She then sat down beside him and communicated something to him. It must have been something quite momentous, as Spitzkopf noticed the color of the man's face change as soon as he heard it. In a couple of seconds he turned white as a sheet.

Spitzkopf inched closer to the pair. Then, standing directly behind the bench, he called out: "Buy, won't you buy from me, my very fine, distinguished people! A sweet little comb, or a dainty brush, or a graceful mirror, or a winsome brooch, or the purtiest little ring you ever did see! Buy, buy, come and buy!"

"Get outta here!" the Fraulein shouted back. "Or I'll call a guard! Why, I simply can't stand these nasty hawkers."

Spitzkopf skedaddled as if he were actually afraid of park guards. In truth, however, quite another thing had taken him by surprise: in the face of the young man he had recognized none other than the highly sought-after Adolf Schneider. Spitzkopf managed to identify him despite the man being partly disguised, having pasted on a black moustache and little black goatee, with a blue pince-nez balanced upon his nose.

"So there you are, our little flyaway pigeon!" he thought. "It seems you haven't flown far. Well, you won't be taking flight again! I figured from the start that your fingerprints must be all over this case. You! It was in your interest, yours alone! To get rid of that poor, tiny, innocent creature. So that your former fiancée would not have any claims upon you, could not force you to help bring up the wee thing! Why, you're a miscreant with a capital M!

"And now you've a mind to mosey back, meandering in a muffled manner around Vienna and moving right back to mucking around with your menagerie of mint-condition mistresses, eh?

"Meanwhile, mister's miscalculated. It won't take me but a few measly moments to make out all your malevolent mysteries. I mustn't even monitor you. I've mapped out all the monsieurs and mademoiselles you mingle with, and any minute I'll muster the manpower to manacle you."

Spitzkopf walked a good distance farther until he was deep within the Prater, then turned around and went right back along the same path. When he passed the young couple again, he observed them deeply immersed in conversation.

But he did not bother with them any further. Instead he hurried off to the next tram station and traveled back to his office.

As soon as he returned he was met by Fraulein Paula Mark, his little coquette—that is, his assistant Leon Fein in disguise. She had been waiting for him. The Fraulein reported on all that had happened on her end.

"You've done well," Spitzkopf said. "But I fear you'll be dancing on home from the Venedig pleasure garden altogether untwirled. Don't count on any fun with your admirer there, as he'll likely stand you up. We'll be scoping him out somewhere else entirely."

"Oh, don't you worry about li'l old me!" Paula piped up, quite sure of herself. "C'est la vie! As long as it gets us to our finish line, I'll be just fine forgoing my entertainment for the night."

"But your playing today is not yet finished," said Spitzkopf. "You haven't yet taken the final bow in your role as the little soubrette. I shan't skirt the issue—the show must go on, and you're our leading lady!"

CHAPTER FIVE
The Child Murderess

ON A CHARMING street in a Viennese suburb, in a small, low house, lives a woman of middle age who goes by the name Mathilde Schoppening. She is the sole owner of her little house and has little to do with her neighbors. Very rarely does anyone come visit Frau Schoppening.

The word is that she is the widow of a state official and lives off his pension, as well as a check her wealthy family somewhere in Moravia sends every month.

Whenever she does go out, Frau Schoppening always does so dressed in high style. She gives the impression of being an intelligent, well-to-do sort of lady, and the women who live nearby—generally in the habit of gabbling and gossiping about every little thing—always demonstrate a certain respect for her and never let their tongues land on her as a topic.

Naturally, none of them have even an inkling of the lady's actual vocation. They haven't the barest notion that she plies the most horrific, hideous trade that could possibly exist on this earth.

Her vocation is this: the disposal of inconvenient children.

In the teeming metropolises, there are plenty of wayward women would prefer to be rid of their children. These women often go looking for someone, anyone, to simply get the young baby burdens out of their sight.

Strange to say, this happens most often with women of some means who would simply like to live, to amuse themselves, to carouse, to be flattered and flirted with at champagne balls. Their young children become awkward to have around, nothing more than infant albatrosses about their necks.

The matter also presents itself in quite "upstanding" families—now beset with an unexpected misfortune that may lower their standing. A young daughter is seduced and finds herself in the family way before she has quite staked out a family of her own by way of getting married. In order to hide its shame the family keeps things under wraps as it tries to find a way to make the blameless child simply . . . disappear.

At other times the following situation arises: a man seduces an unwitting girl, one not surrounded by any upstanding relatives, and makes her a mama before her time, at which point the girl is forced to provide for all the child's needs. And in order to be free of this seemingly impossible burden, she thinks the best idea is to get rid of the poor creature.

In these same teeming metropolises there are accursed souls, monstrous malefactresses, who manage this bloody work in return for some takings, the kinds that clink in your pocket or fold nicely in your wallet. And all the people that undertake this work are women, of course—ones who might be able to provide care for a child. They take the children off of the mothers' hands, they say, on the grounds that they will rear them. And some of them do, keeping up appearances for a few weeks, and then . . . who knows?

There are others still more monstrous than these who murder the small children immediately—of course being handsomely compensated for it—and bury them in a cellar somewhere or fling them into some body of water so not a soul can ever find out where they vanished to.

It was to this latter category of practitioner that our widow, Mathilde Schoppening, belonged.

She had been plying this grisly trade for years. Dozens of children were rotting away in her cellar, children who had been handed to her so that certain kinds of people could go on living their comfortable lives or relieve themselves of inopportune burdens.

Mathilde Schoppening did her work quite carefully. She kept a few confidants in the "better" echelons of society who would bring her the business she craved. Hers was indeed considered the "best" brand, the "finest" of the houses that dealt in this industry, and it was to her that the élite brought their living merchandise.

And of course she consequently commanded the most "upstanding" of prices. Not just anyone could afford her.

It is almost impossible to believe that in the great cities, with their serried ranks of police officers and constables, such crimes could be carried out. But it is the unvarnished truth. More than once police have discovered such notorious criminals, ones who had been doing this abominable work right under their eyes for years, right in the middle of the hustle and bustle of the city.

It was to this Mathilde Schoppening that our Adolf Schneider, after making some sly inquiries around Vienna, had made his way, and to her, ultimately, that he had arranged for his child to be handed over—the child of his bride to be, whom he had just abandoned like the villain that he was.

Adolf Schneider, from the moment he first met his fiancée, had not a single honest intention in his heart. The lovely girl pleased him well enough, and he thought he would have a nice time with her just as he had with ten others exactly like her, then leave her just as soon as another maiden pleased him more.

Circumstances were different this time. Our Fraulein Clara did not in fact belong to that class of Frauleins who are easily taken in. He had to approach her much more earnestly in order to win her. It was not so easy.

But because she really did tickle his fancy, in time he became quite accustomed to the idea of her, such that he thought he really would resolve to marry her if she eventually forgot herself in some weak-willed moment and surrendered herself to his charms.

And as soon as she did so, as soon as he hit his target and the innocent girl sacrificed all to him, his old recklessness came rushing back. All he could think of then was how he might drop her. The thoughts grew more intense when Clara told him that she sensed she had gotten herself into a situation . . .

Now he would be bound to her, his own little ball and chain. Sold away forever and ever and off the market. The prospect left him with a funny taste in his mouth. So he started telling her the whopper about the store in Graz so as to set the stage for his eventual disappearance. In truth, though, he had no intention of going elsewhere. It would have been a pity to leave Vienna, where he had a good position and so many friends—and even more girlfriends. So he cemented a plan to stay in the city until Clara was about to give birth. He would then make himself scarce for a few weeks, staying in some small municipality not far from Vienna until the ordeal of her pregnancy was over.

Maybe she wouldn't survive the delivery. Then he would be well and truly rid of her and any responsibility to the child. Or maybe the child would not live. That would be good too.

And if not—if she made it through just fine, and the child with her—he would have to figure out some other way to free himself of the inconvenient burden.

He carried out this nefarious scheme knowing for certain that his boss would always take him back, so pleased was he with Schneider's work. The only two people to whom he divulged his plan were his new lover—the typist from the shop where he worked—and his friend Franz Schmidt. After Clara delivered her baby, Schmidt reported to Schneider that she had made it through safely and that the child also survived. Naturally, this was not good news for the young father. He resolved to exempt himself of his responsibility toward the child by any means necessary.

It was Schmidt who happened to know about Mathilde Schoppening. He got in touch with her and promised her a considerable sum if she managed to rock the baby to a nice long sleep.

The hellish scheme worked. The luckless, helpless Clara was forced to give up her child. The genteel, gracious conduct of Frau Schoppening made its intended impression on the girl's tender heart, and she entrusted the boy to her—forever. Schmidt of course told his friend right away that the situation had been taken care of. And so Schneider traveled back to Vienna in order to make sure that he was well absolved of his duty—both parts of it. He intended to pretend that he wanted to reconcile with the mother. Being confident that she would unloose hell's fury on him, with furious looks and furious words, he would not have to put on a show of begging her to take him back for long and would quickly be free of her too.

Such was his plan. On the same day Spitzkopf had learned of the case and gone off dressed as a dandy to speak with employees at Schneider's store, and the girlishly beautiful Leon Fein had gone to rendezvous with Franz Schmidt at the china shop, Schneider had gone to pass the lunchtime hour with his latest amour, the typist. In the evening he was to meet up with Schmidt and both were to make their way to Frau Schoppening's to see that everything there was quite correct. A few days later Schneider would return to Vienna and wrap matters up with his former fiancée.

But things had not gone entirely according to plan.

When the unfortunate Clara brought her case to Spitzkopf, the detective realized within a minute that Adolf Schneider must be involved in the child's disappearance. No one else in the world, after all, had a vested interest in the baby's eradication.

With his usual flair, he took matters into his own hands, and, as we have seen, in but a few hours' time he was already hot on the trail of the whole barbarous brigade.

CHAPTER SIX
The Barbarians Are Busted

"A NEW TASK awaits you!" said Spitzkopf to his youngest assistant, Leon Fein, after the boy had spent the earlier part of the day doing his star-making turn as the lovely, laughing Fraulein Paula Mark. "This evening, at seven o'clock, you will again disguise yourself as a young maiden, but of course an entirely different one than today's, so different that even your new votary, Franz Schmidt, won't recognize you.

"In this new attire, you will watch him closely when he leaves work at the end of the day—but discreetly, such that he won't notice he is being followed. But follow him you shall, wherever his way wends. You are not to let him out of your sight. In any case, I will find you soon after you begin your pursuit and apprise you of what you are to do next."

"Right-o, Master—it's as good as done!" Fein answered. "I'll have my new glad rags on by around six. Why, I'll be such a changed woman that even you won't recognize me!"

"We've a few hours yet," said Spitzkopf. "Get some rest, as we have a tricky bit of work awaiting us tonight."

And so Fein retired to his room and put himself down for a nap. Spitzkopf made himself comfortable too and sprawled out on his canapé sofa to leaf through the day's newspapers. He had already handed over to his remaining assistants all the other cases that had been left at his doorstep that day. He had reserved the case of the disappeared child for himself. His heart had told him that at the end of it, there would be a great big trout to be caught.

At around five he arose and dressed himself up as a dignified old man, sticking a long gray beard onto his face, placing a long gray wig upon his head, and balancing a golden pince-nez upon his nose. In this guise he made his way to the store where Adolf Schneider had formerly been employed.

He picked out a few items there and wandered around every department of the large establishment. He wanted a chance to observe every staff member closely. "It is possible," he reasoned, "that besides the typist there are other employees involved in this rotten business of the vanished child."

But his observation did not lead to any new discoveries. The rest of the employees, seemingly the honest, workaday sort, gave off an air of perfect ordinariness. Only the typist seemed unsettled and nervous, like someone who is expecting something quite out of the ordinary to occur and finds her heart beating faster and faster.

After bringing his purchases to the till, he asked the counterman to pack them up and prepare them for pickup the following day. "I'll be coming back early tomorrow and taking everything with me then," said Spitzkopf.

He then paid his bill and exited, but instead of returning home he went to a coffeehouse directly opposite the store. He took a window seat so he could keep an eye on what was going on there and ordered a coffee and some newspapers to be brought over. But his gaze remained fixed, never roaming, on the store's front door. Half an hour later, the employees left for the day and the door was locked.

Spitzkopf paid for his coffee and made his way out onto the sidewalk at the very moment that the typist exited the store. After walking no more than twenty spaces, she stopped beside a cab in which an older lady was sitting. Spitzkopf's eagle eye revealed the truth: that elderly lady was none other than our notorious Adolf Schneider in disguise.

The young woman then climbed in, the coachman spurred on the horses, and the carriage sped away.

Spitzkopf hailed another cab and bade the coachman drive the horses on at a gallop in order to follow the couple's cab. After around half an hour that cab came to a stop, and Spitzkopf saw yet another fiacre drawing up beside it. A young man alighted from the fiacre and climbed into the couple's carriage.

Spitzkopf immediately hypothesized as to what was going on. It had to be our Franz Schmidt who joined them. And indeed, his hypothesis quickly turned theorem when yet another fiacre arrived, following close on the tail of Schmidt's. Enthroned in this one was a preening young woman in full feather—the enchanting creature formerly known as Paula Mark, now with a sparkling new identity.

"Well done, Fein!" Spitzkopf beamed. "You shining starlet! We'll get to pick off all three leaves from this shamrock in one go—and arrest the whole nefarious gang."

The carriages were soon on their way again, and after a few minutes the first, containing the three malefactors Adolf Schneider, his lover the typist, and his friend Franz Schmidt, pulled into a narrow, handsomely kept-up lane and stopped where the lane ended. The three characters climbed out and walked some twenty paces up the lane until they stood before a small, low-roofed house. They rapped a few times at the door. It was opened for them and they entered.

Spitzkopf watched all this from afar, through the windows of his fiacre. He then bade the coachman drive a couple of blocks more, alighted, and returned to enter the lane into which the three villains had disappeared. Our Leon Fein, meanwhile, dressed as the little princess, alighted from his own fiacre and went flouncing off into the lane too.

It was now quite late. The lane was dark and there was not a soul to be seen. Just one burning gas lamp brought some light to the gloom. But the little house into which the three characters had vanished was shrouded in near-total darkness. All of its windows were likewise unlit, nothing but blackness visible behind them.

"This brutish band is carrying out its work in the shadows," Spitzkopf mused. "Indeed. It is the appropriate atmosphere for such endeavors as this. But just you wait, you princes of darkness! I shall soon shed a light on all you've done—so bright you'll be blinded!"

He waved over his disguised assistant and whispered a few words into her ear. Fein nodded in agreement, and the two of them, the gumshoe and his girlish apprentice, split up, each taking one exterior side of the house.

Half an hour after the three shady characters had disappeared into the house, our Leon Fein, resplendent in his socialite's attire, slunk up to the front door and tapped upon the door. The lady of the house, our infamous Schoppening, lumbered over and, opening the door, asked the young lady what she wanted.

"Are you Frau Mathilde Schoppening?" the young lady asked.

"That I am," answered the woman, her eyebrows rising.

"I am in dire need of your help," said the girl. "Do let me into your home, and I shall tell you all."

Mathilde Schoppening took the girl in head to foot, her sharp eyes resting upon every feature of this innocent child. Then she opened the door and admitted her. "Come in," she said, "but not so loud, you hear? I happen to have guests."

She led the girl into a small, handsomely appointed parlor, told her to sit, and asked her what sort of help she sought.

"My name is Elsa Nicker," the girl began, "the daughter of the manufacturer Nicker, who has his factory on Nussdorfer Strasse. My sister, a girl of nineteen, took a lover and has been carrying his child. It is a secret; my parents do not know. My sister is staying with a girlfriend of hers in Baden bei Wien, where she delivered the baby. Of course, my parents think my sister is merely paying the girl a friendly extended visit.

"I have come to you so that you might take custody of the child. We shall of course compensate you—whatever fee you may desire, you shall have it."

"Very well," answered Frau Schoppening. "I'll do it, and you may be sure that no one will hear a word of it. When should I come to you all?"

"This very night," the girl answered. "Other girlfriends from Vienna are coming to visit our friend tomorrow, and the child must be gone before then. If not, the whole ordeal may be exposed."

"If it must be tonight, it must be tonight. I'll do it. But just this moment I haven't the time. I have company, and I have to finish another important bit of business with them first. Stay right here until I've finished. Then I'll come get you and we'll be on our way. I believe there should be a train to Baden just around midnight, if I recall correctly?"

"Yes," the girl answered. "Let's be sure to get there on time."

"I fly," Frau Schoppening whispered in her ear. "Just remember to keep quiet while you wait. I don't want anyone knowing you're here." Then the woman lit a lamp, fanned out a few old newspapers in front of the girl, and quit the room.

Our Leon Fein, or shall we say Elsa Nicker, was left alone in the parlor. "My damsel in distress act worked!" she thought. "And my master was right about this frightful woman. Now I just have to go and give him the sign that I've done my bit—and he'll handle the rest."

She tiptoed over to the window and looked out—but the parlor she had been led to looked out on the backyard. And so, moving with great caution, she opened a door that led into another room, facing the street, and sidled over to the window there.

She opened it carefully and waved down to Spitzkopf, who

stood just below. Then she returned to the parlor and sat down to thumb through the yellowing newspapers. As she did so, she made sure to prick up her ears, listening for the slightest noise coming from elsewhere in the house.

Soon she heard a knocking, then the front door creaking open and being locked back up. "My master is inside," she thought, "and I have to be ready to lend him a hand if things get sticky."

She snuck through the house until she came to a door behind which she heard a few distinct voices—among them Spitzkopf's voice, along with Frau Schoppening's, asking him what it was he needed.

"I've come to you on an important errand," Spitzkopf answered, "but I must describe it to you privately. Could we go into another room?"

"These are my friends," Frau Schoppening answered. "I keep no secrets from them. You may say whatever you wish right here."

"That may be so. But I have things I wish to keep secret from them. And so I must speak with you alone."

"I am an honorable woman," Frau Schoppening answered sharply. "There is nothing about me that I would mind anyone on earth knowing. If you are afraid of naming the thing you desire, then this secret must be very dishonorable indeed—and I can do without it!"

"If that's so, you must forgive my coming here," said Spitzkopf. "I'll be on my way."

"No, you dirty old cheat!" the typist piped up. "Not so fast. You're a spy. I had your number as soon as you walked in here. You've been following us all day—but I'll be following your corpse out of here!"

Before Spitzkopf could make a move, he was dealt such a smasher over the back of his head with a piece of iron that he went out cold.

"Hogtie that man and stuff up his mouth!" Frau Schoppening

ordered. "And stay here to keep an eye on him. I'll go off to finish our little job. Then we'll figure out what to do with this old coot."

Left alone with Spitzkopf, the three young miscreants delighted in their captive. "Well looky here, you silly old geezer!" Schneider snickered. "You wanted to get us behind bars, but look who's gotten a dose of iron now! You'd better wake up and write your will soon, as soon we *will* be putting an end to you!"

Meanwhile Spitzkopf lay there, his consciousness only half returned, unable to move a muscle.

Leon Fein, otherwise known as Elsa Nicker, heard everything, up to the moment when Frau Schoppening left the room.

He gritted his teeth and balled his fists—he wanted nothing more than to barge in on these monsters. But he remembered what Spitzkopf's orders were—that he must find any opportunity to catch Mathilde Schoppening right in the middle of her devilish work, preventing the woman from having any grounds for denial.

So Leon turned on his heels and went back into the parlor, putting his ear to the interior door so he could listen for where the woman was headed next. From the next room over Leon heard creeping steps and Schoppening grumbling to herself. "Well, by my blessed paws! Where ever did a stinking spy spring from, just imagine! And it's already high time I should be getting on to Baden to grab up the next miserable brat. It'll have to be the last one I take on for the time being. I'll have to ease up on the business for a while, let people forget about me so I don't attract any more damn spies!"

She opened a door and Leon could discern every one of her footfalls as she descended a flight of stairs.

"Heavens, the moment's come," Leon shuddered. "She's off to finish the job. But not if I sneak up on her first!"

After fifteen minutes he opened the parlor door and slipped over to the hall outside the room where his master was being kept. Overhearing Schneider and his merry crew continuing to jeer at their captive spy, he reckoned that he could rest easy for a spell, knowing Spitzkopf was not yet in mortal danger—so he had time to steal away and set his sights on the old witch who plied her trade below.

Returning to the parlor, he continued in pursuit of Frau Schoppening, following the direction in which he had heard her footfalls tending.

Soon he found himself blocked by a heavy, locked door. He opened it with a skeleton key, then descended some twenty stairs.

A horrible stench and suffocating air rose up from below, making it difficult for him to breathe. It was also pitch dark in the staircase, and Leon did not dare use his electric torch and give himself away. So he continued making his way down, slowly, slowly, until he caught a flash of light. By that flash he was able to make out a sort of opening, just barely big enough for a person to crawl in. He stooped down to peer through it, and his eyes met a grisly scene.

A ladder led from the opening into a deep, damp cellar. Standing upon the sodden floor, in a corner of the cellar, stood another ladder with a candle resting atop it, casting a weak glow over the penetrating darkness.

In the middle of the cellar stood our Mathilde, wearing an old dress covered by a wide, torn apron and gripping with both hands a massive spade, which she was using to dig a pit in the dirt.

Beside her lay two tiny, half-decayed corpses . . . the bodies of dead children. It was too ghastly to bear. It took all of Leon Fein's strength not to cry out from sheer horror and revulsion.

Moving with great delicacy, he leaned in deeper through the opening, reaching for his loaded revolver. Then he let forth a muffled cry: "Hello down there! Frau Mathilde Schoppening! What ever are you doing?"

The woman's astonished gaze flew upward, though she did not let go of the spade.

Now Leon Fein did not hold back, and he roared: "That'll be enough, you monstrous woman! You won't be plying your bloody trade for one second longer!"

Extinguishing the candle, the murderess launched her spade up at the opening in the wall, intending to wound the little imp who had surprised her so.

It missed. Now Leon Fein switched on his electric torch and threw a blinding light over the whole of the cellar.

"Don't move or I'll shoot you down like the rabid dog you are," he barked at her. And before she had a chance to run and recover her wayward spade, Leon had descended, quick as lightning, and pointed his gun right in her eyes.

The woman realized that all resistance was in vain. Gnashing her teeth, she screamed, "Just you wait, you little viper! Such a young girl, and already a nasty little spy!"

"I'm as much a girl as you are a fine, upstanding lady!" Leon Fein chuckled. "I am assistant to the famous detective Max Spitzkopf! And he too is right here in your house of horrors!"

Hearing the name *Spitzkopf*, Mathilde threw her hands down. She knew that as soon as that detective was on the case, no salvation would ever come.

She submitted as Leon bound her ankles and wrists, stopped up her mouth with a rag, and pushed her into a corner of the cellar. She did not lift a finger to stop him. All was lost.

All she could do was gnash her teeth and let her eyes flame like those of a tigress when it is pierced through by the hunter's bullet.

His work below accomplished, Leon Fein now climbed back up through the opening in the wall and sprinted, revolver in hand, to the room where Spitzkopf lay bound and the pretty young lovers and their nefarious friend made sport over him.

"*La commedia è finita!*" Fein bellowed, kicking open the door. "You've cracked your last joke! And whoever moves, I'll be cracking his head open with a bullet."

The merry crew sat there as if frozen to the furniture. The flashing revolver had stunned them.

By this point Spitzkopf had finally come to. Leon moved immediately to slash off his ropes, right before the glazed eyes of his captors, who dared not stop the boy at his labors.

When Spitzkopf regained the free use of his hands, he also drew a loaded revolver from his pocket and called to the petrified criminals: "Now put up your hands and prepare to be tied up the way you did me—that is, if you don't want to find out what a round of speeding bullets tastes like!"

They realized they could do nothing and allowed Spitzkopf to do as he pleased with them. He tied them all up into one rather alarming-looking package, which he then hauled up onto the sofa to await pickup.

Meanwhile Leon Fein ran out of the house to alert the authorities.

The chief of police appeared half an hour later together with a number of investigators and patrol officers.

The rope-bound Frau Mathilde Schoppening was lugged up from the cellar and thoroughly interrogated. She confessed to everything. It turned out that she had plied her ignominious trade for several years, in the course of which she had strangled fifteen infants and buried them in the earthen floor of her cellar.

During the course of her questioning the bodies of these children were exhumed, and Mathilde Schoppening indicated who exactly they were and who had delivered them into her hands.

The court trial that followed joined the hall of infamy of the most expansive, most sensationalized trials that had ever taken place in Vienna.

There was an endless series of defendants, among them women who belonged to the most glittering circles of Viennese high society—women who had paid Frau Schoppening to unburden themselves of their inopportune children.

Mathilde Schoppening, THE CHILD MURDERESS, was sentenced to death.

All of the other defendants, including the three miscreants in our merry crew—Adolf Schneider, his friend Franz Schmidt, and the typist—all received lengthy prison sentences.

Clara Goldfeld, who had been dealt such a miserable lot in this life, never recovered her child. When Schoppening was apprehended, the boy had already been lying in the dark cellar for eight days, strangled to death. The girl's only consolation was living to see retribution being meted out to the man who had caused her such terrible misfortune.

Spitzkopf had to content himself with the praise showered upon him from all Vienna for his successful work. He refused to receive any compensation from Fraulein Goldfeld.

This nightmare had already cost her so much.

Issue 11: The Gravedigger

עלפֿטעם העפט. פרייז 20 העלער.

דֶער טוידְטֶען־גְרֶעבֶּער.

פלוצים עפֿענט זיך איין טרומנע און פֿוכס זעצט זיך אויף. פֿון דער זייט בעווייזט זיך שפּיצקאפּף און פֿון אונטער די טרומנעס נאך צוויי פֿון זיינע געהילפֿען. די פֿערברעכער פֿאלען פֿאר שרעק ווי דערשלאגענע אַ ניעדער.

The Gravedigger

CHAPTER ONE

Betrothed—and Betrayed?

It is a scorchingly hot summer's day. The sun's rays penetrate like burning lances. There is a clear blue sky and not even the faintest wisp of cloud. The air is calm and quiet; not a single breeze troubles its perfect stillness.

Such a heatwave has held sway for a number of days now. It has left the grass in the meadows parched, yellowed, the leaves on the trees devoid of their former luster. They droop on the branch, looking like willow leaves that have only just barely survived the custom of being beaten on the synagogue floor on the festival of Hoshana Rabbah.

The express train coming in on the Nordbahn, originating in Kraków, has now drawn up with its usual swiftness, stopping at the station in Lundenburg, Moravia.

It was around noon. And though the train would only be stopping for two minutes, out poured all of its passengers, desperate for a cold drink—whether it be a glass of water or beer or wine it did not matter, so long as it were cold. They gulped down their beverages, then climbed back aboard the train.

It was the height of the season for going to the various bathing resorts, and all the train cars were crammed full of travelers. Good luck finding an empty seat, even in first class.

Soon all were back in their spots, the conductors called out their "All aboard!" in unison, the locomotive pierced the air with its whistle, and the train chugged away from the station.

The passengers made themselves as comfortable as they could. Nearly all of them had taken off their jackets and vests and sat quietly, each in their little corner, trying to keep cool. They had closed all the curtains over their windows, trying to block out the threatening sun. The journey would not take long; just about an hour and a half more and the train would arrive in Vienna.

In a first-class car, a finely attired man paced up and down the narrow aisle that stretched between the small single-passenger compartments. Each time he passed a certain one he would steal a look inside at the quite distinguished-looking gentleman within, a man somewhat older than himself who sat pressed up against the window, lost in his thoughts. It was easy to see that this man was much distressed over something. He rubbed his hands together nervously and shook his head. It looked as if he were carrying on a conversation with himself.

And the man pacing up and down the corridor watched him. He had dashed out of the train at Lundenburg to get his hands on a cold glass of beer, and when he climbed back aboard this man had already taken his spot. No other compartment was free at that point. And the appearance of this new passenger, who had gotten on at Lundenburg, attracted his attention to such a degree that he decided to simply let the man steal his seat.

For around ten minutes the man sat there talking to himself, not paying the other travelers any mind as they passed his compartment, though they stared at him as if he were a very odd duck indeed.

Then he jumped out of his seat, burst out of his compartment, and started pacing up and down the aisle in great agitation. But the younger man who had already been doing so was an obstacle to the elder's pacing. The aisle was too narrow for two pacers doing their laps simultaneously. And so the older man turned to the other with a polite request. "You may go into my compartment and take my place now, young sir. I have been sitting long enough."

"I thank you kindly," said the younger man. "I myself was sitting there before."

"Why, that means I must have taken your spot!" said the older man. "You must forgive me. When I boarded, the compartment was empty, and so I sat down there."

"No harm done!" the younger man assured him. "I could see that you were distressed, and so I did not want to bother you."

"Distressed, you say?" the older man asked incredulously as he wrung his hands together. "Just distressed? No—I've gone half insane! For as long as I've lived, I've never undergone such a thing!"

"That thing being, if I may ask . . ."

"An awful—no, a truly dreadful—calamity! One I simply cannot bear! My heart tells me that a terrible calamity has taken place here."

"Or a crime?"

"Yes! A crime!" the older man cried out. "A crime . . . yes, that's the word. An outrageous, scandalous crime, one fit to tear the heavens apart! I'm half crazy, I tell you. I don't know what to think, what to do, where to start . . ."

"You are indeed most distressed, I can see that. You are not in a position just now to think clearly, or even to see clearly. It will not be possible for us to figure out what we must do in order to properly attend to this crime.

"If you could try to calm yourself somewhat and explain everything to me, perhaps I could help you. I am, of course, a stranger. But I believe that my name alone may be enough for you to entrust me with your story.

"That name happens to be Max Spitzkopf, chief of the private detective bureau Blitz, in Vienna."

"Max Spitzkopf!" the older man exclaimed, visibly stunned.

"God Himself has sent you to me! I know your name well, and I know every one of your miraculous deeds by heart. I am certain that just as you have helped all of those others, you shall also be able to help me."

"I shall do all I can," said Spitzkopf. "First, though, you must tell me everything that has happened. But speak softly, and don't call out my name again. These walls have ears, and no one must know that you have put your case in my hands."

"Fine, fine!" the older man agreed, sighing deeply. "I am so troubled, however, that I don't know if it shall be possible to tell you everything accurately enough to obtain a clear picture of what's taken place. Maybe it would be more sensible to wait until the train gets in to Vienna, then we'll make our way to my home, where I should be able to express myself more intelligibly."

"No," Spitzkopf answered. "I still haven't even the slightest notion of what has taken place. But if a crime has indeed been committed, every minute is crucial. If I learn all of the details on this journey, I can devise my plan even before we arrive in Vienna, and be ready to execute it too. This train makes such a racket that none of the other passengers will hear a thing you say, so you needn't worry yourself on that account."

"Then I shall compose myself as best I can," the older man decided, "and tell you all. Just listen closely.

"I am Dr. Leopold Ostermann, junior doctor at the Allgemeines Krankenhaus in Vienna. My father was a banker and left me a large fortune after his death. My wife received a likewise substantial inheritance from her late father, such that we count ourselves members of the wealthiest circles in Vienna.

"We have one daughter, nineteen years old and lovely as a painting. Well educated and finely brought up too, if I might add. This daughter is all our joy, our life's one great source of pride and pleasure. All we have ever done has been for her, all our thoughts only about her, all of our plans made entirely for her sake.

"A few months ago, at a ball, she became acquainted with a

young man who introduced himself to her as Dr. Siegfried Waldner, lawyer in training and candidate to the bar. The young man carried himself in a most refined manner and told her that he was raised in Lundenburg, where his father owned a large factory and was very well off.

"We welcomed this young man several times into our home, and he made an excellent impression. But we did not take the matter seriously; that is to say, we did not think for a moment of giving him our daughter's hand in marriage. We thought of him only as a dear acquaintance of hers, just like many other young men who were in our daughter's orbit.

"Our daughter, Clara, did not favor him with any extra attention than she gave to the other youths around her. Therefore it did not occur to us to make further inquiries about this particular young man or to find out exactly who and what he was. A few days ago he invited our daughter to join him on an outing to the Wienerwald. My wife was ailing somewhat at the time, and we had to postpone our family trip to the island of Norderney, off the North Sea coast of Germany. The weather happened to be extremely hot at the time, so I thought, 'Good, let our dear daughter go and amuse herself a little, find some cooling shade in the trees of the Wienerwald.'

"The very next day I received a letter from my daughter. This is what she wrote." He took a letter out of his briefcase and read aloud:

> Dearest parents! I know how much you love me, and for that reason, I know that you will forgive me for having taken such an important step without your foreknowledge.
>
> Of all the young men who have frequented our home, it is Dr. Siegfried Waldner whom I've liked best—and I have selected him as my future husband.
>
> I kept my feelings for him a secret from you because

> I thought that you had your eyes on another man for my groom, and I did not want to aggrieve you with my choice.
>
> Furthermore, until now Dr. Waldner had not ever declared his affection for me. I had not known before whether he loved me in the same way I loved him. But yesterday, when we set out on the excursion, he spoke the words I'd longed to hear and made me the happiest woman on earth.
>
> I am traveling with him to Lundenburg so he can introduce me to his parents. I am certain that you, my own treasured parents, will accept our couplehood with open arms and will greet us as your own dear, loving children when we return to Vienna.
>
> Your devoted daughter,
> Clara

"You can imagine how much this shocked and unsettled me," the man went on. "There was something about the whole story I did not like one bit. Not because I had anything against Dr. Waldner. On the contrary, as I've already told you, he made a fine impression on us.

"But it was precisely for that reason—because we liked him—that it seemed so unusual to me, my daughter pulling the wool over our eyes so, keeping such a secret and not telling us a thing. What displeased me most of all, though, was Dr. Waldner inviting Clara to his parents' home in Lundenburg before even introducing himself to me as my daughter's prospective groom. He ought to have received my blessing first before bringing her there.

"But my wife has forgiven our daughter. Clara is still but a child, she said, with no experience in such matters. The girl must have been so elated when Dr. Waldner declared his love that it would have been her own wish to go and introduce herself to his parents as soon as possible, and so he would have whisked her away there to please her.

"Well, I thought. The thing is as good as done, and there's no turning back time to correct matters now. We'll just have to wait until she comes home, I figured, then I'll give her a piece of my mind for her thoughtlessness, for the lapse in judgment she had made—but she is my daughter, after all. If she likes Dr. Waldner so much as all that, then it is in God's hands.

"But then a day passed, then two, three—and we did not receive another word from Clara, nor did she return to see us. I grew more and more uneasy. And so I sent a telegram to the manufacturer Waldner in Lundenburg. In return I got back from the telegraph office a message saying in no uncertain terms that unless a more detailed address could be provided, no manufacturer named Waldner in Lundenburg could be found.

"There was nothing else to do but go up to Lundenburg myself. I supposed that perhaps the man had given up his factory and it was now operating under an entirely different name. Or maybe it was in fact located not within the city boundaries of Lundenburg but in some nearby village.

"And so I took the train up yesterday, and now I am taking it back a changed man: broken, ruined, depressed, nearly out of my mind.

"No man such as I was looking for exists in Lundenburg. In fact, the city has no manufacturer, no doctor, no person of any description named Waldner. And not in any of the surrounding villages either. I visited every factory, made inquiries everywhere, asked anyone with an ear to listen, investigated, turned the whole city up and down. For nothing.

"No Waldner, and that's all! And so now I am going home with empty hands and a heart that's been ripped in twain, without an idea of what to do next. I am telling you the truth now: if I can endure this, then I must be made of iron!

"But God has not abandoned me. He has led me to you. And I am certain that you shall be able to lend me aid."

"I can make no promises to that effect," said Spitzkopf. "I am no prophet. You are mistaken in thinking that everything always goes my way. But I can promise you one thing: I shall leave no stone unturned in searching for your daughter and in bringing to justice the criminal who took her. Now, return to your compartment and take a nice deep breath. We are not far from Vienna. When we alight from the train, I shall tell you what I need you to do next."

And so the doctor plodded back to his seat. Spitzkopf, meanwhile, remained standing in the narrow aisle, lost in the recesses of his capacious mind.

CHAPTER TWO
130,000 Kronen Stolen

THE EXPRESS TRAIN arrived in Vienna at around three that afternoon. The passengers spilled out onto the platform and hurried off to the exits. It was a mad rush, people shoving each other right and left.

As our Dr. Ostermann descended the steps of the train, he felt someone shoving a note into his hand. He quickly stuffed it into his pocket and strode away in the direction of the doors, all the while glancing around for Spitzkopf but not spotting him.

When he reached the street, he drew out the note again and read: *Go directly home and wait for me there. —SPITZKOPF*

And so Dr. Ostermann hailed the best, swiftest fiacre he could find and made his way home. He found his wife waiting for him impatiently. She did not have to say a word. Her eyes asked the question for her: "So?"

He did not answer her silent query. He did not want to tell her the whole truth—but he could not lie to her either. And so he simply moved to retire to his office, saying only this to her over his shoulder as he went on his way: "Be patient just a little while longer. You'll soon hear everything."

The distraught woman could make neither heads nor tails of her husband's utterance. Her heart grew only heavier. She broke out in a flood of tears. All she wanted was a thorough account of what had taken place—the whole truth and nothing but the truth. She stalked her husband through the house, and when he closed the office door on her and locked it, she wanted desperately to open it by force.

But at that moment the doorbell rang.

The couple's manservant opened it and into the house shlepped an old, sickly woman, helped along by a young girl. "Is the Herr Doktor at home?" asked the girl. "My mother is terribly ill, and she must see a doctor at once."

The servant bade them wait in the foyer as he went to inform Dr. Ostermann that a patient had turned up. The doctor ordered that the patient be brought to his office—which also meant his wife had to leave her post at the doorway. She knew her husband well and therefore knew he did not tolerate being interrupted while treating a patient.

The old woman shlepped through the home and into the doctor's office. The girl remained back in the waiting room.

"What is your complaint, dear lady?" the doctor asked his patient, indicating a chair for her to sit down in.

"I have nothing to complain of," she responded. "You do. And I've come to help you."

The doctor looked at her, astonished. He thought perhaps her true complaint was that she suffered from insanity.

But the woman figured he must be thinking that and laughed. "It's Max Spitzkopf," she said. "I've only disguised myself so no one would know I was coming to you.

"You should know that you were being shadowed throughout your misadventure, on the journey to Lundenburg and back again to Vienna. Sitting near your compartment, in both trains, was a man who followed every step you took on your expedition.

I did not want to tell you anything of it at the train station, which is why I told you to go home at once.

"I am of the belief that your daughter has fallen into treacherous hands and is currently in grave danger. But I still hope I shall be successful in freeing her before that danger is fully realized.

"Most important right now is that you let no one learn that I paid you a visit nor that I have taken over the case. Even your wife and your servant are not to be told anything. I additionally ask that you answer a few of my questions and permit me to conduct a short inspection of your daughter's room."

"Do what you must," the doctor answered in resigned tones. "And ask away. I shall tell you everything I know."

"Did Dr. Waldner come over often?" Spitzkopf asked.

"As far as I can remember, he visited us perhaps five or six times."

"Did your daughter ever rendezvous with him somewhere without your being informed?"

"Not that I know of. It's possible, as my daughter often used to go out alone to spend time with her girlfriends."

"Are you missing any money, valuables, or anything of that sort?"

"Not that I've noticed. I never keep much cash at home. And my wealth consists mostly of the few real estate properties I own in Vienna. Besides that I own many securities, stocks, and bonds, kept in a local bank. I also keep a number of savings books here in which I record the sums I have deposited in the bank—and considerable sums they are."

"And are all these books where they should be?"

"I would need to have a look. If you would wait, I will go into my study and open up the safe."

"There will be time for that later. You can do it when I am making a search of your daughter's room. For now I just need you to answer one more question: Was your daughter still such a childish thing that she could be easily deceived and led astray, or has she in fact developed enough intellectually to be a decent judge of character?"

"As I told you earlier, Clara is our only child. We pampered her. We loved her most tenderly, spoiled her as you might a wee babe, even up to her current age of nineteen. And so, yes, she retained something of a child's spirit, and yes, she was gullible."

"Very well; I know enough for the moment. Now please lead me to your daughter's room—but take heed that no one notice us."

"Not a problem. This room has a door opening into my daughter's study, which adjoins her bedroom. You may inspect every corner as you wish."

And with that he opened the wallpaper-covered door and waved Spitzkopf through. The detective locked the door behind himself, and the doctor went off to his own study to see whether anything was missing from his safe.

Spitzkopf conducted a fastidious search of the missing girl's bedroom. He opened every drawer, every cupboard, and turned every little object over in his hand many times. In one of the drawers of a dainty escritoire he found a bundle of letters bound with a blue silk ribbon.

He opened up the bundle and found that all the letters were written by the same hand and ended with the same signature: *SIEGFRIED*.

"Just what I was looking for," he said to himself. He began reading the missives.

They were all love letters, all written in more or less the same style: such phrases as "my love," "burning love," "eternal love," "my happiness," "the heavens," and "paradise" were the common currency throughout. From these letters it was quite plain that Fraulein Clara did indeed often meet this Siegfried for secret trysts, making sure her parents did not suspect a thing. One of the last letters in the bundle read as follows:

My beloved Clara!

My resolve is firm. We must surprise your parents with the news of our engagement as a done deed.

According to the inquiries I've made, your father will not under any circumstances consent to give me your hand on account of his wishes to marry you off to a colleague of his, a young hospitalist whom you do not even know and whom you would never wish to have as a husband, not by any stretch of the imagination.

If I were to ask your father right now whether he would accept me as his son-in-law, it would only result in his dismissing my request outright—and you and I not being able to have our delicious meetings any longer.

He'd then rush to force your engagement to this stranger whom you've never even set eyes on.

And so, my darling, it will be far better to spring the news on your parents unannounced.

Tomorrow you will join me on an excursion to the Wienerwald. There you will send a letter to your parents saying that we have become engaged to each other and that we are on our way to visit my parents in Lundenburg for a spell.

Later, when you return to Vienna, your parents will surely forgive you and embrace me as their future son-in-law in order to avoid any scandal.

Your parents love you. They will do anything to oblige you when they see that you have formed a strong will of your own, one that compels you to go after whatever you desire.

I trust that you will consent to this plan of mine, and on that account, will await you tomorrow at our usual meeting place.

Your ever faithful,

Siegfried

Spitzkopf read the letter through, giving close attention to every word, and said to himself: "My first hypothesis has been confirmed. The girl was susceptible to being seduced, and her seducer must be one very bold bird indeed to have dared to fly so far to realize his rotten ambitions . . ."

At that moment Spitzkopf heard a resounding knock at the door. He opened it and there was old Dr. Ostermann standing before him, his face chalk-white, his body trembling like a fish.

"What's happened, Herr Doktor?" Spitzkopf asked.

"It's terrible!" said the old man. "My safe is missing two savings books, which together record sums held in the bank worth 130,000 kronen!"

"In which bank is this money deposited?"

"In the Creditanstalt!"

"What were these books numbered?"

"One was 5040, the other was 6761."

Leaving Ostermann standing in the doorway, Spitzkopf whizzed past him to the telephone that was in the elderly doctor's office.

He connected to the Creditanstalt and asked a clerk whether anyone had recently withdrawn the money from the accounts 5040 and 6761 under the name Dr. Leopold Ostermann.

He quickly received his answer, in black and white: yes, money was withdrawn from both accounts that very day, to the tune of 130,000 kronen.

Spitzkopf then went to the doctor, saying, "The criminal took out the money today. This is a sign he is still here in Vienna—so it will be easier to nab him.

"The question remains: Who took the deposit books from your safe—your daughter, or someone else?"

"My daughter . . . robbing me?" the old man whimpered, more broken with every passing minute. "It's impossible . . . she is not such a bad girl as all that."

"As far as we know nothing is impossible. Anyway, it's a minor point. On to more important matters. I haven't any time to lose. And you can't afford to not remain calm—allow me to get to work. And remember: not a word!"

And with that Spitzkopf left the doctor and snapped back into his shlepping act, assuming the role of the old, weak woman as he returned to the waiting room. Sitting there was the young woman who had accompanied him to the house. They shlepped together, arm in arm, down the stairs that fronted the home and, emerging onto the street, then climbed into a cab and clattered off into the distance.

The girl, it turns out, was Spitzkopf's senior assistant, Hermann Fuchs, who had dressed up as a girl specifically for the mission of accompanying his master on the doctor's visit.

"*Nu*, what did you observe, Fuchs?" asked the detective.

"Nothing!" his assistant answered. "But I will say—there is something about the doctor's manservant I don't like. The whole time I was sitting in the waiting room he was fixing me with this odd gaze and throwing glances to the door of the consulting room, then cupping his hands to his ears to eavesdrop on what you and the doctor were saying."

"That's not good news. The old bird must have gotten his beak up about us, suspecting I was no ordinary patient. We'll have to keep an eye on him."

"That's what I thought too. He might lead us onto the right track . . ."

"I dare say you're right. And as you're the one who noticed him, I'll put you in charge of watching this particular birdie."

Meanwhile, the cab had turned onto a street where Spitzkopf maintained one of his secret residences. He had deliberately told the coachman to drive them there rather than to his primary home and main office so that no one would be able to tell who these two ladies were—as he was certain they were being followed.

He was right.

When the two ladies alighted from the cab and shlepped themselves into the house, Spitzkopf slithered over to a corner of the room so that he could have a clear view of the street without any pedestrians below having a view of him.

He called to Fuchs and said: "You see, down there, that *Dienstmann* walking to and fro on the corner, seemingly ready to take on an errand for any old passerby? Well, he ain't. The man's been stalking us. He must be one of the band of criminals involved in this mess.

"These scoundrels we're always after . . . it's funny: they all think they're so mighty clever, but they give themselves away at every turn.

"This man's no exception. He's going to lead us directly onto the right path—that will lead us to the culprits."

CHAPTER THREE
Gone A-Courting—and A-Conning

In this great world of ours, there exists a sort of person called a *Hochstapler*—a confidence man, a scandaroon, a flim-flammer, a fraud.

These are the idlers and cutpurses, people who want to coast down easy street, who want to enjoy all life's pleasures without putting in the honest work, without breaking a sweat, without troubling their heads.

To that end they strive to scrabble their way up to the highest branches of society, always being careful to dress according to the latest fashions so that they look the very picture of upmarket, upper-crust gentlemandom. When they reach the heart of the ballrooms of the silk-stockinged and blue-blooded, they start to make a living by swindle and trickery, thievery and crime—until that career is put to a sudden end in a darksome prison cell.

The con artist plies his trade in a number of ways. Some are card sharps, using their cunning contrivances to win at the gambling table. Others make a dishonest living from betting on horse races. Their methods are innumerable and various. What does not vary is how much peril, how much precarity and plight, these swindlers bring to life in the big cities today.

All of the above criminals, however, are set only upon wheedling money out of people. The dupe is defrauded and de-walleted, and it ends there.

But there is another kind of conman—the *Heiratsschwindler*, the marriage swindler—who ends up taking not only financial capital but social and moral capital too. These marriage swindlers not only steal money, down to the very last groschen, from poor maidens, factory girls, and young, orphaned women and leave them with barren pockets and broken hearts. They steal their victims' happiness too, often up until the ends of the poor souls' lives. They lead them astray and into such a ditch that these women may never crawl their way out.

For these reasons the marriage swindler is the most dangerous, and the most despicable, of all the miscreant knaves of swindlerdom.

But even among the marriage swindlers there are various types. Some do not set their sights quite so high and try only to turn the head of some mere orphan or factory girl, a maid, or a young widow whom they suspect of having saved up a little nest egg. They present themselves as worshipful suitors, head-over-heels in love, and bring the girls bouquets and write them billets-doux for as long as it takes them to get their hands on their buried treasure. After that they either turn on their heels and run or find some fault in the supposed sweetheart and pick a fight with her, a lovers' quarrel that leaves them angry with the girl—forever.

Other marriage swindlers, however, hitch their wagons to a star—or more specifically to some belle of the beau monde. They infiltrate the highest of high society, present themselves as counts, barons, manufacturing tycoons, brilliant engineers, and the like, become engaged to daughters of the finest families, and end up swindling them out of their enormous fortunes. Or sometimes he will turn a girl's head, and when the parents reject the match, they pay out exorbitant sums to him in order to avoid even the faintest whiff of scandal—and also simply to get rid of him, their daughter's most insistent, needling, annoying "amour."

It was to this latter class of marriage swindlers that our Dr. Siegfried Waldner belonged.

Originally he operated quite differently. When he first managed to penetrate into high society, he worked as a common pickpocket. He attended balls and various entertainments organized by Vienna's dashingest *Damen und Herren* with the purpose of swiping the diamond brooch upon some dame's décolletage, unsnapping another's bejeweled hairpin or slipping off a dripping bracelet, or gliding up to some worthy *Herr* and waltzing off with his wallet just as the cavalier was taking a break from his dancing at the buffet table or otherwise engaged with his lady *Liebchen*.

He was pleased with this occupation for a while. He led a quiet and carefree existence as a fingersmith of the fashionable crowd.

Then, a few months prior to Fraulein Clara Ostermann's disappearance, he happened to make her acquaintance at a ball. Noticing that she was rather taken with him, he thought he would switch up his racket and try his luck as a suitor to well-bred young ladies.

He was quite good at it, one must admit. He always behaved so nobly, with such graceful and gallant manners, that no one ever would have thought of looking into his background and finding out who this dapper Dan really was.

He visited Dr. Ostermann on only a few occasions, always for but a brief time and always when there were sure to be no other guests. He was careful about not entering into the intimate acquaintance of too many people in Vienna lest he should come upon someone who was well acquainted with Lundenburg and would know he had not actually come from there.

In time he came to regret that he had not introduced himself as a foreigner from some distant land, far outside of the empire. It would have been more difficult to make inquiries there than to go poking around Lundenburg, which lay only a stone's throw from Vienna. Too late now. He had professed himself a Lundenburger at the start, so a Lundenburger he was obliged to remain.

Therefore, once he had made such a fine impression on Dr. Ostermann and his friends and family and become so stuck in among them, there was nothing else to do but twist the blade further into the young Fraulein's heart and win her for his own.

And soon he realized, with his penetrating eye, that he had landed upon a nice bit of merchandise, an easy target for his criminal designs—quite a suitable suitoress indeed. The girl had been mollycoddled. She was spoiled and naïve and full of foolish fancies, altogether like a girl no older than fifteen, though she was just shy of twenty.

Though given a fine education, she had never gotten to know the world, had little interaction with men she did not know, and seldom left the house without her mother. Such a child is easily wooed. She is susceptible to declarations of love, flowers, secret rendezvous, love letters, and all manner of trinkets. This is the kind of girl, he thought, whom you can easily have, and once you do you can have anything else you want too.

He was not wrong, this Dr. Waldner, whose real name was in fact Georg Schmidt. Schmidt had grown up a young man with no particular calling or profession. In his earlier years he had tried out every kind of employment but quit each one. He did not particularly like working. He far preferred a life of dolce far niente, and he wished to sample all the easy pleasures that came with it.

He was led onto the path of crime by a friend of his, an employee of the Währinger Allgemeiner Friedhof, on the outskirts of the city. This man, Julius Spannik, introduced the young Georg to a gang of his best pals, who all referred to Spannik simply as the "Gravedigger." The men all used to gather at Spannik's to make nefarious plans, concoct their various cons, and bring him their pilfered winnings, which he hid in a place so secret no one would ever think of looking there. The hiding spot? At the Allgemeiner Friedhof, in ancient family crypts. Hardly anyone would ever visit these dusty mausolea, and the keys to unlock them were always within Spannik's easy reach. He would hide the loot underneath the coffins until it came time to sell it and divide the profits among the members of the gang.

The men ran a tight ship. When any of them took a job his cronies were there to support him—to pack up the booty or keep an eye out for meddling do-gooders.

Now Georg Schmidt, alias Dr. Siegfried Waldner, recognized that things were right on course with the doctor's daughter—he had turned her head so resolutely that he could do with her as he wished. The time had come for his plan's final phase: wresting her away.

His initial approach was to try becoming engaged to her quite in the open. He would then let the mask fall from his face and demand hush money from her family to keep the betrothal a secret and leave the girl in peace. This approach he eventually had to give up. When he got to know old Dr. Ostermann better, he realized the man would never consent to his marrying Clara without thoroughly researching the prospective groom.

But there was another way to go about it: to drive the girl so wild, make her so incorrigibly smitten, that she would agree to becoming engaged against her parents' will.

This plan he did swing, even more successfully than he had expected.

The naïve, inexperienced girl had once heard her father say that his funds at the Creditanstalt were being set aside specifically for her and that they would be paid out to her as soon as she was engaged to marry. This had been a joke the father had allowed himself with his dear little daughter when she asked him in her artless way for whom all his thousands of kronen in the bank were intended. But she took it as the unvarnished truth and ever after considered the money hers.

When she met up with the so-called Dr. Waldner at their appointed place in the woods, they had given each other their troth, vowing to be faithful to each other for eternity. At that point she told her bridegroom that she had even brought along her dowry—her father's deposit books—and told Waldner of her intention to go to the bank and claim "her money" that was rightfully hers now that she was an engaged woman.

Dr. Waldner was quite taken aback by her account. He had not expected it all to be so easy nor the money to be quite so good—yes, as good as gold was this Clara of his.

And so he hatched a truly devilish plan.

Such a plan could not be carried out right away, however. It would have to wait a few days longer. And while it waited Waldner would bring his willing victim to stay with the leader of his gang—the Gravedigger.

On the way from the woods back to the city they stopped at a restaurant and ordered wine to toast to their "engagement." Before the young lady brought the glass to her lips, Waldner deftly slipped some powder into it, and when she drank she quickly became very sleepy. She could barely stand upright, let alone walk.

And so he hailed a fiacre and told the coachman to bring them "home." The girl fell asleep in the carriage, so he was able to deliver her to the Gravedigger without any interference. When she was in his clutches, the kingpin hid her away in the same secret location where he stored the gang's takings—a crumbling family crypt, which no person other than himself had visited for years. She would be able to rest there undisturbed for who knows how long.

The soporific that Clara had been administered, meanwhile, was guaranteed to keep her in a sleep lasting several days. It would afford the Gravedigger and his accomplices plenty of time to set their plan on solid ground and make sure it had no holes.

CHAPTER FOUR
The Gravedigger

AFTER GEORG SCHMIDT had handed over his drugged "fiancée" to the Gravedigger, and the latter made sure the girl was cozily entombed, the gang convened to discuss its next steps.

First on the agenda: they all feared that Dr. Ostermann would quickly realize that his deposit books were missing from his safe and immediately notify the bank. Then whoever went to withdraw the money would be arrested on the spot. So the gang decided to postpone that step until they got a better read on how things stood.

To that end, they made plans to follow Dr. Ostermann's every movement. Wherever he went, one of the gang stalked him like his own shadow. They wanted to determine exactly how he would go about searching for his lost daughter. When he traveled to Lundenburg one of the gangsters, disguised as another old man, was close on his heels every step of the way as he made his inquiries in the town.

This same spy also observed him chatting with Spitzkopf

aboard the train as it returned to Vienna. Spitzkopf, with his marvelously trained eye, of course noticed the spy immediately.

But Spitzkopf did not mind being watched. Not in the slightest. On the contrary, he liked it. He knew that having someone on his trail would make it easier to track down the doctor's daughter.

And he was right. Though Spitzkopf was disguised as a frail old woman, the spy recognized him. What this clever man did not realize was that Spitzkopf recognized him as a snoop just as the snoop had recognized him as a detective, and he was now keeping an eye on this snoop just as keenly as the snoop was keeping an eye on him.

Once Spitzkopf was inside his secret residence—now fully aware that the gang knew he was on the case—he said to his assistant: "Listen up to what I have to tell you, Fuchs. We must make haste—and try to arrest the culprits this very day. They managed to withdraw the money from the bank earlier. We have to recover it before they have a chance to split it up or hide it away.

"They didn't withdraw it until Dr. Ostermann left for Lundenburg. As soon as the old man began his journey, they were certain, from having followed him, that he had not yet found out about the stolen deposit books and still considered his daughter to be off with her fiancé in his hometown.

"And because the gang now knows that I am mixed in with this, they are going to be much more careful, perhaps even abscond from Vienna for a while. It would not be as easy then to nab them, especially as I am not entirely clear on how to go about the thing. Why, I am not even in possession of a photograph of the principal offender, the self-styled Dr. Waldner! But now we'll get by with a little help from our . . . foes.

"My plan is for you to sneak out of here and go on a good long walk through Vienna. That courier, that supposed *Dienstmann* who is surveilling us, will certainly move to follow you, wherever you turn. Meanwhile I'll be following *him*, wherever *he* turns. Thus will you or I eventually learn which gang it is we are dealing with and where we can find its hideaway."

Spitzkopf had barely finished unpacking his plan when out of the corner of his eye he noticed a nattily dressed young fellow approach the *Dienstmann* and exchange a few words with him. "Have a look over there, Fuchs," Spitzkopf hissed, somewhat taken aback. "I could swear that the dandy confabulating over there with the *Dienstmann* is our Dr. Waldner!"

Fuchs took a peek out of the window. "You're right, Master!" he murmured. "It must be him and none other! He's clearly burning to learn the other's news. Why, let's go and cage the street pigeon right this minute!"

"Don't count your pigeons before they hatch, Fuchs. I see you still haven't unlearned your bad habit of rushing into things. What do you think would happen if we apprehended the man now? Would you learn anything? You think he'd break down immediately and spill all his secrets, tell you who he is, who his cronies are, where the missing girl is, and where they've stashed Ostermann's money?

"No! First we must find out everything there is to be found out, and then, why then . . . the pigeon will fly right into our loft all on his own. Now, Fuchs, take off that charming frock, throw on a new disguise, and begone. I won't be far behind. And believe me, once we've gone a little way, we'll soon know what it is we must do next."

Not five minutes later our Fuchs was out on the street, now dressed as a ragged beggar, much worse for the wear, with a nose turned red from too much drink, torn boots, a disheveled mop of hair, and a wild, unkempt red beard.

It was beginning to grow dark, and the first gas lamps were already lit. The street outside Spitzkopf's secret residence was almost entirely devoid of pedestrians.

Meanwhile, the *Dienstmann* and his elegant companion were so engrossed in their conversation, and their gaze so fixed on

Spitzkopf's window, that they did not even notice Fuchs emerging from the front door and hopping over to the side of the street where they stood.

Fuchs noticed that they had *not* noticed, and it made him very glad. "Now Spitzkopf need not even come down," he thought. "I won't let these fellows out of my sight. But first I wouldn't mind getting a good look at them from up close. Maybe I'll recognize their mugs."

And so he dragged himself over to them, grunting out some obscure street song to himself in a croaking, liquor-soaked baritone and rocking back and forth like a man well in his cups.

Once he had reached them, he stared the two men right in the eyes and said to the one who was fitted out so smartly: "Heh heh heh, Herr Graf! Esteemed Count, hiccup! So you're using the *Dienstmann*, hiccup, to send a nice mushy note to some pretty baroness, eh? Heh heh hehcup!"

"Shoo, you red-nosed lush!" shouted the young swell. "Get outta here or I'll call over the night watchman!"

In lieu of a normal response, Fuchs broke forth in a hoarsely sung serenade:

Call a watchman? Call a watchman?
I'm a watchman too!
A watchman! A watchman!
Why, watching's all I do!

I watch the bar
To be sure it's stocked with schnapps!

I watch the bottle
So's I can catch the last drops!

And I watch my glass
So the pouring never stops!

Yessiree, I'm a watchman too!
Watching, watching,
Watching's all I do!

Heh heh heh!
Heh heh heh!
Heh heh hehcup!

He accompanied his song with rhythmic handclaps, all the while keeping his gaze focused on the two men.

"C'mon, Gravedigger, let's ditch this drunk," he heard the younger man saying to the other. They turned on their heels and put some distance between themselves and the noisy stranger.

They went only a short way, however, making sure to stand at the streetlamp, where the man would not dare to disturb them any longer, before continuing their discussion.

Fuchs remained where he was and carried on singing but now with a somewhat altered timbre. He was still clapping his hands—though now it was out of pure joy. No, he had not managed to recognize the criminals' faces. But the alias "Gravedigger" was familiar.

During his frequent visits to shady bars to collect information on the gangs who patronized them he had overheard the name more than once. He was beginning to guess which particular underworld clan these miscreants belonged to.

"So! It seems that in the end we are indeed dealing with a band of common criminals," he thought. "And here I thought that he was some higher breed!

"*Nu*, *nu*, we'll soon be done with him and his whole sordid gang. If only my master knew what I've just discovered!"

Wheeling around, he saw that there was no light shining in any of Spitzkopf's windows. He did not know whether his master had already left or had purposely turned out all the lights in order to better observe the two men on the street.

As he staggered about on the street, teetering this way, tottering that way, and wondering what to do, he saw the two men hail a passing fiacre and speed off.

Fuchs started to run after them. But before he knew it the criminals' fiacre was the merest speck in the distance.

"Those sly birds have flown!" he grumbled to himself, trudging back to Spitzkopf's secret residence.

But as he reached the door, something caught his eye: white spots on the sidewalk like smashed bits of chalk. It was the usual sign. Spitzkopf had indeed already left, but as he walked away he had dropped pieces of chalk at intervals and smashed them underfoot to indicate to his assistant the path he took.

Fuchs knew what he had to do. Chalk it up to experience. He strode off at once on this great white way, resolving to follow wherever it might lead him . . .

CHAPTER FIVE

Secrets, Secrets Are No Fun

It was ten at night.

In a small drinking den not far from the Allgemeiner Friedhof, four characters sat huddled around a table, holding a covert conference.

Not far from them sat an old mendicant, slumped over his own table and snoring. There was a large glass of schnapps beside his head, some of the clear liquid still left inside. The man had clearly not been able to tolerate another drop before falling into a deep sleep.

Meanwhile the foursome went on talking, quietly but incessantly, one sentence following right upon another, their hands gesturing constantly, their eyes sparkling.

There were no patrons besides these four and the sleeping beggar. The barmaid, a short, stout woman with a pockmarked face, sat beside the bar and dozed.

Soon a door opened and in came a peddler, his basket of wares slung over his shoulders. He looked around at the old barflies as if he were trying to decide whether or not he could do some business with them. Seeing how few there were, however, he shook his head as if to say: I won't earn a penny off of this pack of bums.

He decided to have a seat anyway. Parking himself at the bar, he woke up the barmaid and ordered a shot of something strong. The woman rubbed her still-not-quite-open eyes, groping around the bar to find a glass for the new guest.

The gang of four, having interrupted its conversation upon the entrance of the beggar, now resumed it, again murmuring in soft tones.

"Hey, Gravedigger, whaddya say we call it quits for the night?" the new guest overheard one of them saying. "Somethin' off about the place tonight. All these rum customers . . ."

"Bah! That drunk beggar and this ridiculous peddler got you quaking in your boots?" the Gravedigger scoffed. "They're nothing to make the likes of us tremble, no they ain't!"

"Don't be so sure," the first man answered. "You know that damned bloodhound Spitzkopf is on the case."

The new guest sitting at the bar, who was none other than our Fuchs, Spitzkopf's assistant, pricked up his ears and heard every word, even though the men were whispering. But when he caught the name "Spitzkopf" his head twitched ever so slightly—and he gave himself away.

One of the foursome—in fact, our own infamous Dr. Waldner—noticed and exchanged a signal with his cronies. Before Fuchs even had time to rise from his stool he was surrounded. The four men stood before him, each pointing a shining knife at him.

Fuchs, it so happened, had a revolver on his person, but he did not have time to take it out. It would have done him no good anyhow. The men had trapped him, one at each corner. He could not defend himself from four sides simultaneously.

"What do you want from me?" he cried out, a sob in his voice. "I am a poor old man, and have nothing!"

"You're a dirty rat is what you are," the Gravedigger hissed. "That bloodhound sent you here to spy on us. But you're not leaving this place alive."

Fuchs cast fearful glances all around him. He had really landed in the drink this time—and there was no splashing his way out of it . . .

But at that very moment the sleeping beggar suddenly awoke, and in a voice wet with schnapps croaked out: "Help! Murderers! Thieves! Save us!"

Despite its altered *spirit* . . . Fuchs made out the true identity of the voice immediately: it belonged to his master, Spitzkopf.

Redoubling his volume, the detective cried out again: "Help! Murderers! Thieves! Save us!"

"Can it, you old beggar!" the Gravedigger snapped at him. "Can it or I'll twist your head clean off!"

Dr. Waldner could not contain himself. "Why, that beggar's just another spy!" he shouted. "Let's get him too!" And he advanced on Spitzkopf with his knife aloft. But he was outmatched: Spitzkopf met it with a loaded gun, pointed right in Waldner's face.

The gang was stunned. Stupefied. Baffled and bewildered. Amid the chaos, Fuchs took the opportunity to slide off his stool and run to a corner of the bar, where he drew his own revolver. It was a perilous standoff. Spitzkopf did not want to shoot unless he was forced to. And the criminals were afraid to retreat lest they be pursued by speeding bullets.

The barmaid shouted in a rough and well-worn voice, "I don't allow folk to spill blood in this bar, house rules! Now march on outta here, the lot of yeh!"

"Ha!" said the Gravedigger. "We're regulars here! Let these new dogs on the doorstep be the ones to vamoose, the mangy bloodhounds!"

"Fine, but first put away those damn knives! And I'll let our other guests leave in peace. No one's allowed to do any mischief here. This is a respectable tavern! Blood ain't on the menu!"

So the gangsters sheathed their knives and sat back down at their table. Spitzkopf holstered his revolver, together with Fuchs. But they stood their ground.

Then the barmaid opened a back door and spoke to the two of them: "Come, I'll escort you out myself. Nothing's gonna happen to yehs. And the schnapps is on the house."

Spitzkopf reckoned she was not quite as nice as she seemed. No doubt in cahoots with the gang. But he went quietly, motioning to Fuchs to follow him as he walked through the open door. He too had heard everything as he sat there snoring. He knew all their secrets. All he had to do now was catch these criminals in flagrante, right as their hands were in the cookie jar—or, more accurately, the coffin.

If he had truly gotten into it with them there in the bar, he would not be able to carry the thing through to the end. They would have denied everything categorically, and the case against them would be ruined.

And so he left the place willingly, exiting with Fuchs through the back and into a large courtyard as the barmaid bolted the door after them.

The courtyard was lit by a small hanging lantern. From one side of the space stretched a narrow passageway, which led to an arched vestibule opening onto a little lane.

But the detective and his assistant had only advanced a few

steps when the lantern went out, leaving the men in total darkness. At the same time they felt the ground sliding out from underneath them—and then they dropped. Ten meters. As they scrambled to their feet, they found themselves up to their ankles in putrid water. Thankfully they were not injured.

After taking a moment to put themselves to rights, Spitzkopf switched on his torch and illuminated the place in which they found themselves. It was a canal through which the waste of the surrounding houses was trickling in an unending stream.

The stench was abominable, but that did not bother the two men. Spitzkopf assessed the situation and noticed a small opening on one side of the canal, covered with rusty bars. The filthy water came through them as it entered the main canal.

"We've really landed in it this time, Fuchs," said Spitzkopf. "The gang's left us well and truly in the gutter, and they've locked the opening up above. They thought they'd have us sealed down here in this foul prison forever.

"But they were mistaken. All we have to do is pry open those bars and then we can crawl our way into the main canal. Once we're there, as we wade through the dreck, we'll eventually hit upon some passageway by which we can evacuate."

The bars were well rusted over and rotted through. Spitzkopf and Fuchs grabbed them and pulled with all their strength.

It was arduous work, but after ten minutes the bars surrendered to the men's mighty effort and gave way, snapping into pieces.

Now that the hole was wide open, water came rushing through in mucky profusion. After it finished sweeping past, there was no more water underfoot, and Spitzkopf and Fuchs could see clear through to the bare stones around them. And there, on the floor of this canal, the detective saw a decomposed dead body.

"Well, ain't this a lovely crew we're dealing with!" said Spitzkopf. "We're not the first people they've sent down here. And one of them has just gone right on rotting where they left him. That's what they expected we'd do too. I'd sooner *they* rot, in . . ."

But there was no time to waste. Both men squeezed their way through the tight opening and found themselves in the wide central channel of Vienna's sewer system. Spitzkopf and Fuchs waded through the wastewater for over half an hour until finally they saw a few pinpricks of light coming from above.

"There must be an opening up there," said Spitzkopf. "Some ladder or steps to reach it should be somewhere close at hand."

And indeed they soon found a ladder and ascended. The opening up above was sealed with an iron grating with tiny holes distributed throughout.

The two men thrust their fists upward, banging at the grating, soon busting it open and poking their heads out into fresh air.

A watchman stood guard near the sewer opening. Upon seeing two rather unclean beggars slither out he charged over to them, ready to clap them in irons. But Spitzkopf identified himself immediately and asked the watchman to hail them a cab to bring them home. He did so, though the coachman refused at first to allow into his vehicle two characters who were so offensive to the eyes (not to mention the nose).

"They'll dirty up the whole carriage!" he protested.

"You'll get five florins for it," said Spitzkopf, stuffing a ten-krone note into the driver's paw. "But make haste."

The man drove his horses at a gallop and soon had Spitzkopf and Fuchs at the detective's house, where the two wasted no time in speedily cleaning themselves off and tossing on some new clothes.

While he waited, the driver gave his carriage a good wipe-down. A few minutes later, Spitzkopf and Fuchs, now joined by two other assistants, reemerged and climbed back in. "To the cemetery, the Allgemeiner Friedhof!" Spitzkopf called out from the back. And the driver cracked the whip to spur his horses on through the dark night, bearing their cargo of sleuths just starting to sniff the sweet smell of success again.

CHAPTER SIX
At the Cemetery

In a corner of Vienna's Allgemeiner Friedhof, hard by the cemetery wall, stood the family vault of the Counts of Herbersberg. The family line had gone extinct some twenty years earlier, and since then not a soul had bothered about the state of the crypt or its otherworldly inhabitants. It had been years and years since anyone had opened the heavy stone doors of the chapel-like crypt, and no pairs of Herbersberg feet had trod its cold floors for as long as anyone could remember.

It was in this crypt that the Gravedigger had sought out a suitable hiding place for his gang's stolen treasure—and likewise for the treasure stolen from Herr Doktor and Frau Ostermann: their only daughter, Clara. She was still stowed away there, lying in a trance among the coffins in the dank air of the mausoleum, as the carriage transporting Spitzkopf, Fuchs, and the junior assistants thundered toward the cemetery. And lying right beside her: the money she considered her dowry, withdrawn from the accounts kept at the Creditanstalt under her father's name.

Spitzkopf knew the Gravedigger quite well. He had not yet

managed to catch him in the midst of any of his robberies but had had his eye on him for quite a while and knew where his and his gang's regular bar was, as well as where he usually spent the night.

When he had come with the self-styled Dr. Waldner to surveil Spitzkopf at the detective's secret residence, Fuchs, with his raucous drunkard's song, had cleverly driven them to distraction so that they sought the security of a streetlamp. Spitzkopf was consequently able to get a better look at them. He recognized the Gravedigger in a trice—and knew exactly with whom he was dealing in this case.

He threw on the second drunken-beggar disguise that he kept in the apartment and headed off to the tavern where he knew the Gravedigger and company had their secret conferences. The gang showed up not long after and found him snoring in a chair. But he was not actually asleep. He had not drunk a drop of the large glass of schnapps he ordered but had rather spilled it out underneath the table. In his pretend slumber he eavesdropped on the criminals' conversation and learned that the missing girl was hidden away at the cemetery, in the mausoleum of the Grafen von Herbersberg. Spitzkopf was also quite familiar with the geography of the cemetery, aboveground and under. He knew exactly where this particular mausoleum stood, and to find it was a walk in the park.

When Spitzkopf, together with Fuchs and the other assistants, arrived at the cemetery, they gained entry by way of a side gate, opening it with a skeleton key. They did not dare wake the guard on duty so that he might open the main gate for them lest the sound of the interaction alert anyone to their presence.

They used their skeleton key to open the mausoleum too. And as soon as they entered the ancient, frigid crypt, they found what they were seeking. Lying among the coffins, which were arranged in a row down the long chamber of the mausoleum, was the sleeping Fraulein Ostermann. She was breathing gently, like a person getting some ordinary, everyday shuteye. The sleeping potion that she had been given to drink had worked so powerfully on her because of the thin, stifling air within the crypt. And so she had not yet woken up, though a number of days had already passed.

Spitzkopf let her go on sleeping peacefully while he and his men searched the crypt. They found a great variety of stolen articles hidden among the coffins.

Fuchs found, after striking a coffin with his fist, that its lid shifted ever so slightly. In attempting to lift it off, he found that its screws had been undone, and he slid it off with ease. Inside he found a heap of bones and dust, the only remains of an ancient corpse that had been lying there for who knows how long. At either end of the coffin were stashed a number of sacks filled with the money that the gang had illicitly withdrawn from the bank that very day.

Spitzkopf removed the sacks and hid them away in a nook. Then he hid himself in the shade of a massive column, while his assistants concealed themselves below the coffins. Fuchs tucked himself right inside the coffin he had opened, placing the lid just slightly off its sockets so that he could easily throw it off when the moment came.

It came soon. Spitzkopf and his assistants had barely finished their inspection when they heard someone inserting a key in the crypt door and locking it back up again after he and another man entered: it was the Gravedigger and the ersatz Dr. Waldner. The other two men who had been with them in the bar remained outside the mausoleum, standing sentry.

The Gravedigger and Waldner walked toward the row of coffins. Suddenly one of the lids flew open and crashed to the floor as Fuchs, who was inside it, bolted upright. Then Spitzkopf emerged from behind his column, and his two other assistants popped up from underneath their coffins. The criminals toppled backward, startled half to death.

Spitzkopf did not delay. Before the two men could regain their footing, he clapped them both in handcuffs and gave them a shove so that they crumpled in a heap at the base of a coffin. Fuchs, together with one of the junior assistants, tore out of the crypt to apprehend the two other bandits.

The remaining assistant took it upon himself to run off to the cemetery wall, jump it, and call two cabs to come as quickly as they could to the front gates. After no more than fifteen minutes, all four of the criminals were sitting, shackled, in one fiacre. In the other rode Spitzkopf and Fuchs, and with them—the sleeping Fraulein.

The pair of carriages rolled off to the nearest police precinct, where the detective delivered up the culprits and a doctor was summoned to medically induce Clara into waking up. It did not take long. The evil effects of the sleeping drug wore off in the cool, clean night air.

It was now two o'clock, and a new day would soon be dawning. The old doctor was telephoned and told that his daughter had been found. He came flying to her in a carriage to bring his child home again. The criminals were interrogated and found they could do nothing besides confess to *everything*. After all, Spitzkopf and Fuchs were there close at hand, repeating back to them each word they had overheard them speaking earlier that night. However, when the four malefactors were asked about the decomposed body in the sewer underneath the bar, they pled ignorance. And when the police went off to round up the barmaid, she was nowhere to be found. The gang had told her in the tavern that the two strange guests were in fact the famous detective Max Spitzkopf and his assistant, so she knew she was in for it—and made her getaway.

The Gravedigger, the marriage swindler, and their two accomplices received fittingly severely sentences, just as they deserved. The girl who had been so led astray was ill for a long period following her rescue. The ordeal she endured had taken its toll.

Her father, however shaken, was no swindler like Clara's seducer had been. He rewarded Spitzkopf handsomely for his success in saving his daughter from a very grave fate.

Issue 12: The Secrets of a Millionaire

העפט 12. פרייז 20 העלער.

דאס געהיימניס פון א מיליאנער.

חאפט נאר נישט! — רופט זיך אן שפיצקאפף, א־ויסקריכענדיג פון הונטער דעם קאמין — איהר זענד דא נישט אליין!

The Secrets of a Millionaire

CHAPTER ONE
Venice in Vienna

A WARM AND SPLENDID summer's night. It is smack in the middle of the month by the Hebrew calendar, and so the silvery moon is at its fullest, all aglimmer in its clear and cloudless heaven, its surrounding stars ashimmer. The air is pure, even fragrant. It is one of those balmy nights when even the most weary, worn-out, overworked person cannot bear to just sit at home but must go out into the street and breathe in delight from the fresh air.

In Vienna's vast, everlasting Volksgarten—the "People's Garden," with its myriad roses, beside the Hofburg Palace in the center of the city—and in the verdant, vivacious Prater Park not far away in the neighborhood of Leopoldstadt, it is as lively as high noon, people strolling, sashaying, and saluting each other underneath the light of the moon.

The famous Viennese coffeehouses are full of patrons. The Wurstelprater—the funfair inside the Prater, with its comedic entertainments, stalls selling all manner of wares, its panoramas you can watch for just a few heller, its carousels and sideshows—is teeming with the everyday folks of Vienna, out to make the most of this extraordinary evening.

But the scene is really something else at the Prater pleasure garden known as the "Venedig in Wien." A man with a sparkling imagination founded this establishment several years ago.

Though he himself had no great commercial success with it, he performed a great service for the people of his city: creating a site where they could enjoy themselves to the hilt, carousing until well after midnight.

In time, the Venedig park became a rendezvous point for lovers, groups of merrymakers, travelers from abroad hoping to seize a minute of pure pleasure, and for married men and women who wished to sample the flavor of forbidden fruits. Here at the Venedig in Wien, in its cafés and champagne gardens, in its narrow alleyways and quiet corners, such people as these can disport themselves without fear of prying eyes, as carnivalers did in times bygone at costume parties and masked balls.

But there is yet another class of people who seek out the Venedig as a perfect practice ground for their activities. I am speaking now of various species of swindlers and swizzlers, cardsharps and common pickpockets, and other such miserable marauders.

The Venedig was practically tailor-made for such as these. Amid the bustling life that convenes there, in the cacophonous clamor of the crowd, among the shoving, shouting thousands of strangers, these criminals can carry out their wicked work with hardly anyone being the wiser.

Nighttime suits them particularly well. It is only after dark when the Venedig fills up with all sorts of unsuspecting people and the program of entertainments on offer becomes truly interesting.

It was on just such a night that our story begins.

The Venedig was really hopping, its guests at the height of their revels, its hired instrumentalists and singers sending up into the air their swirling song. All the cafés were crammed full, and at the champagne bars, crystal flutes carried on in one continuous clinking while woozy bons vivants poured in the effervescent liquid and poured out drunken ditties, their voices growing hoarser with each passing glass.

Only quite late, after midnight, did the evening program end and the pleasure garden begin to empty out, belching forth its sleepy pleasure seekers in one unending stream. The tram had long stopped running. Those who still happened to have a sixer left in their pockets hailed cabs and wheeled on home. But those who had emptied out their meager wallets at the Venedig, poor souls, had some serious shlepping to do before their yawning beds could welcome them.

Among this stream of shleppers was a rather pristinely coiffed man in middle age. He had arrived in Vienna from the provinces that very day to take care of some business matters. As the long day wore on into night, he thought he would amuse himself a little and tramped over to the Venedig, where he partook in every manner of fun that was on offer. Atop the giant Ferris wheel, the Riesenrad, he took in a view of all Vienna, under the glow of beaming electric lights. And he went down a massive slide, three stories high, flying into a river and hitting the water with a magnificent splash. In one of the Venedig's gondolas, he went floating down the grand canal that snakes through the whole of the pleasure garden. Standing above the thoroughfares, he showered every lovely lady that passed by with colorful confetti.

Yes, truly fun of every flavor, and around midnight someone ushered him over to a champagne garden, where he spent a nice long time in the company of several demimondaines and was coaxed into ordering just as many bottles of bubbly.

But feeling rather tired after all of these intoxicating pleasures, he eventually found his way to the exit and trudged back toward his hotel. His head hung heavily upon his neck—it was best to go there by foot, he knew, and let the refreshing night air sober him up a little.

What he did not know, however, was that he was being followed by a certain young man, turning when the elegant merchant from out of town turned, walking onward when he walked onward. Neither did the merchant notice when the man started walking right beside him, as if he were his official escort, once the merchant had reached the grand columnar monument to Admiral Wilhelm von Tegetthoff. The old admiral is just outside the park, where a number of streets converge in the traffic juncture called the Praterstern, the Star of the Prater.

There at his monument, our man from the provinces stopped and thought for a few moments, considering what path to take next. The stranger used the brief respite as an opportunity to ask him a question: "Seems to me you're not from here. Don't know how to get home, I reckon?"

The visitor looked at the man with some surprise. But seeing how smartly this stranger was dressed, he figured he could trust him and answered: "Just sooo! I am not Viennoiserie, ewe see, and it luks like, hiccup, I've drunq just a leetle too muchchgghch. My noggin feels, it feels . . . hevvy. And I can't seems to orientuh meinself, or knows which o' the five hundred or so paths I oughtter tayk."

"Where are you staying?" asked the young man.

"At a hotels in the Innere Stadt," answered the shickered provincial.

"I also live in the city center, my good man. If you'll permit me, I'll walk with you there."

"Good, good, grood! Comes."

They walked a little way down the Praterstrasse, now nearly emptied of pedestrians. As they carried on slowly, step by careful step, the great stream of people that had flowed out of the Venedig dispersed down a hundred different streets.

"Quite a pleasant evening, no?" said the young stranger. "And what a romp they put on at the Venedig. It's been a little while since I've had such a spree."

"Me three, I spent a really loffly coupla whoures."

"Hours?"

"If you likes. But now I've got one helluva katzenjammer. Wishin' I could jest fly to bed."

"Oh, you're too good to know of such things as a hangover!

Why, you haven't the foggiest notion of how to treat it. If you go right to bed, you'll be hung over all day tomorrow too, and with a headache besides.

"No, the best thing to do in such a case is to drink down a black coffee, walk around a little, and go for a little more amusement, play a round of billiards, say, or some cards, enough to help you come to again . . ."

He carried on in this wise and at such great length that the provincial visitor could not help but be convinced, and he entered a coffeehouse together with his young companion to gulp down a steaming cup of mud.

As he drank the young gent treated him to a cigar. And as he smoked, his head started to hang even heavier than it had before. So woozy was he that he no longer quite knew what was happening to him. He barely perceived the young man taking hold of his hand, leading him out, seating him in a cab, and riding away with him.

Once inside the fiacre, our out-of-towner fell asleep. His mind did not register when it stopped nor when his guide hauled him down from the carriage and walked him into the young man's own home, where he stretched the visitor out upon his sofa.

The merchant quickly fell asleep again, into a deep and heavy slumber. Now his guide could do as he wished with him . . .

Neither did the sleeping visitor perceive when he was led out again to the street and into a park in Vienna's nineteenth *Bezirk*, the northern district located between the Vienna Woods and the Danube Canal, and was plopped down upon a park bench.

It was already well into the morning when the provincial visitor finally awoke, the sun's bright rays greeting his barely opened eyes, the heat something tremendous.

He looked around himself perplexed, rubbed his eyes, and

started to piece together all that had happened to him the night before.

When he was at last in a state to actually remember everything, and a complete picture emerged, he gave a tap to his lapel pocket and found, to his horror, that his wallet was missing. He had been keeping a princely sum of over 10,000 kronen in it, together with important documents and other valuable items.

He sat there like he had been pierced through the heart. He could barely move. All he owned had been in that wallet. With that money he had intended to open a store in his hometown. He had come to Vienna to buy up some merchandise for it. Mustering up all his strength, he lumbered over to the nearest police precinct and filed a report, recounting what had happened to him.

The superintendent of the precinct took down the visitor's statement, recorded all the details the man provided him, and assured him that the most skilled undercover officers would be dispatched to find the thief.

But a whole day passed—and the detectives came up empty. They had not succeeded in identifying even the vaguest clue as to who or where the culprit might be. Meanwhile, after his visit to the precinct, the traveler fell into the depths of despair. There remained no recourse, he thought to himself, other than to go and fling himself into the Danube.

Broken, he plodded back to his hotel and—finally—fell into bed. So exhausted was he by all he had been through that he fell asleep instantly and quickly entered dreamland.

CHAPTER TWO

The English Millionaire

THE NINETEENTH DISTRICT of Vienna, known as Döbling, is the villa district. There reside the upper echelons of society, the leisure classes who are not bound by the constraints of their business concerns to have to live in the center of the city.

No, Döbling is fairly remote, at the northern borders of the city. The air is clearer there and cleaner, the dust gathers not so thickly upon every surface as it does in the great metropole of millions to the south. Life in general is more comfortable, more perfectly pleasant, in Döbling. In several streets of this district there are nothing but villas, one after another. Each villa is surrounded by a beautiful garden and set at a congenial distance from the villas next to it.

A certain middle-aged man had been living in one of these villas for a few months now, a man with a very genteel look about him. He had no family with him, only a footman and a coachman, both of whom accompanied him when he would go for a stroll or a long hike.

His name was Henry Clerk, and he said he came from England, where he had done very well in business and amassed a fortune. But owing to disputes with his brothers, he was forced to give up his business and wished to spend the remainder of his years leading a quiet life enjoying his retirement funds and avoiding any commercial concerns—and likewise any interactions at all with his new neighbors, something he made sure of. His lackey and driver apparently spoke only English, and no one saw either of them ever chatting with anyone else in town.

Neither did the neighbors much bother with him and his staff. The English are known as proud people who do not like to have anything to do with anyone not exactly like themselves, and therefore no one wondered at this new resident keeping altogether to himself.

All they knew about him was this one fact: that he was a millionaire. He had bought his villa and its grounds for over 200,000 kronen, and what's more, had filled it with the most lavish furnishings. His whole manner, the way he held himself, his horses, his clothing—they all spoke for him without his saying a word. The man must be rich as Croesus.

One day in this Henry Clerk's villa, three men sat down for a conference: Clerk, his footman Arnold Fox, and his coachman Michael Brund. Clerk spoke first: "So we've reeled in a real whopper today, haven't we boys? That yokel Fox caught netted us over 10,000 kronen."

"I thought he might be a nice fat fish as soon as I set eyes on him positively swimming in the bubbly," Fox the footman boasted. "I watched him at the Venedig, stalked him the whole time. I saw how he flopped his money around this way and that, figured he's sure to have a nice little shoal of coin on him."

"In any case, we'd better get moving on destroying the wallet and all the other documents we found inside so they don't end up giving us away," remarked Brund the coachman. "It was a risky step, bringing the man all the way over here and then leaving him at a park just a hop and a skip away."

"I had to bring him here," Fox defended. "Even though he'd been swilling down the alc, he was still semiconscious. It wouldn't have been possible to empty his pockets without making him cozy so he could do a bit of dozing. But we needn't fear a thing. I took him into some dingy coffee bar, see, where no one knew me so there's no one to go and rat. And when I abandoned him in the park, not a person on earth was there to see it. Of course I couldn't take him any further; someone coulda spotted us."

"We needn't fear anyone telling," Clerk interrupted. "And it wouldn't dawn on anyone to search the millionaire Clerk's house. Most of all because I'm English, and wherever a rich foreigner goes you'll find people just itching to kiss his feet."

"What about our primary target, though?" asked Fox. "This new cashflow I brought in today is only bound to flow a few days. We'll need much more than that to keep things flying right."

"We won't have to bother with that old man for long," Clerk muttered under his breath. "Either he hands over the money . . . or we take it from him."

"*Take* it?" said Brund incredulously. "How? First things first we'd have to get him in our clutches, and even then, only when he's got his sack of dough on him."

"Let me worry about that," said Clerk. "The geezer's the nervous sort, and on that account it seems he carries his money on him wherever he goes. As soon as we've got him, the rest is smooth sailing."

From this conversation it will have become quite clear to you what kinds of people we are dealing with here at the Villa di Clerk. The supposed millionaire and his two apparent servants were in fact a most dangerous band of criminals who had been carrying out all manner of felonies all over the world. They did not shy away from burglary or even murder, and several unfortunate victims had met their ends at the hands of these ghastly men.

But Clerk had always been careful, always behaving in such a way as to avoid any suspicion falling upon his person. What had protected him most of all, perhaps, was the picture of exquisite deportment he presented in public. He made no secret of his wealth but was at the same time discreet and retiring. The fact that he always introduced himself as a foreigner did not hurt either.

In whatever new country he found himself in, he would always pose as a citizen of a different country. He was careful to socialize very little with others and—this was the main thing—never stay in one place for too long. There would come a day when he would disappear just as suddenly as he had appeared.

Naturally, he would change his appearance just as often as his base of operations. Sometimes he was an old, upper-crust dotard, at other times somewhat more middle-aged as he presented in Vienna, or even quite a young man or, when he felt up to it, an ancient, ailing woman—whatever guise suited him for each new scheme.

The villa he had taken in Vienna was not his own newly purchased property, as he claimed to his neighbors. He had only rented it for a set period of time. All the furniture was rented too. He asked the owner and the furniture dealer to not let on about his contracts with them. It did not quite fit the new character he was playing to be paying rent on the mansion he called home.

Meanwhile his gallant, lordly bearing impressed everyone in the district. All of affluent Döbling believed anything he told them.

And now had come the time to put into action his great Viennese scheme. He had entered into negotiations with a rich old man, offering to sell him all the factories Clerk owned back in England. He fanned out photographs of the factories, documents of patents and products he had manufactured, and financial statements and invoices, all giving testament to the apparently brilliant success of his enterprises and the high likelihood of any new owner raking in massive profits from them. In fact, he was only selling them, Clerk explained, because he no longer wished to reside in England on account of the ongoing strife between him and his brothers.

The old man fell for it hook, line, and sinker, and he and Clerk had even reached an agreement on the price for the factories. But first he wanted to travel to England to have a good look at them, which naturally did not please the scoundrel Clerk very much. His plan had been to take the generous down payment he would have extorted from the old man and then hightail it out of Austria, never to see him again. He had counted on achieving his goal quite soon.

But he had miscalculated.

The night that Fox had pinched the out-of-towner's wallet, with its nice bit of cash, there were other notable characters among the crowd of revelers at the Venedig in Wien—namely, the celebrated private detective Max Spitzkopf and his assistant Hermann Fuchs.

Spitzkopf happened to have a spot of free time that evening, and knowing that at the Venedig there constantly flitted about those funny-feathered birds that one ought to keep one's eyes on, he thought he would spend a few moonlit hours there.

He did not come across much of anything that seemed too significant, however. It seemed he had come on a fairly quiet night as far as crimes and misdemeanors go. But Spitzkopf did not mind. It was enough for him to see a couple of suspicious-looking faces and take good note of their physical appearances—that too was work.

"It's always a worthy strategy to keep a catalog in your head of as many people as you can," he advised his assistant. "You never know when it may come in handy.

"For example, see that finely dressed young gent over there, making his rounds of the champagne bars, taking everyone in? It's almost like he's searching for someone.

"I could swear that he's either a detective following some criminal or a criminal himself, taking stock of the silk-stockinged set and picking out his next victim from among it.

"And I think the latter possibility is the likelier one. Something curious about the way his eyes are flashing. It would be worth your while to keep your eye on this particular bird as he goes on circling. I entrust him to you, Fuchs, and hope to learn from you in due time exactly what species he may be."

Around midnight Spitzkopf walked home. He was obliged to take a trip down the Danube to Hungary the next day to pursue a case, and so he left his assistant behind at the Venedig to observe the suspicious reveler.

Fuchs dispatched his duty faithfully, trailing the young man—our footman Fox, of course—like a shadow, being careful, of course, to never let him notice. He followed Fox when he left the park and saw him introducing himself to the provincial visitor, then leading the man wherever the lackey pleased. Fuchs followed them into the coffeehouse and noticed how exhausted the visitor seemed to be, almost too exhausted to be quite natural. It was likelier that he had been induced into that state by aid of a sleeping drug or the cigar Fox had treated him to. And then, when Fuchs saw them leaving and Fox shoving the visitor into a cab, he did not tarry, hopping into a second cab right behind them.

But when they rode off to Döbling and entered the sumptuous villa, Fuchs began to wonder if he had been entirely mistaken, worried that all his efforts up to that point had been entirely in vain.

Why, here they were in the most luxurious district in Vienna. A distinguished personality must surely reside in this fancier-than-fancy villa there. It was near impossible that some common criminal would be welcomed inside. "Waiting here any longer would make no sense at all," Fuchs thought. "Why, it would be a downright waste of time. And I'm not likely to hit upon anything else of note in this dead old district, late as it is. I might as well head home now, rest up a bit. I'll come back out here tomorrow morning to make some inquiries into the villa, find out who lives there and the like. Then I'll know whether there's anything at all to be suspicious of, or whether in fact I—and, it must be said, my master too—were mistaken all along about that young gent."

And so Fuchs went home, in time to accompany his master on his trip down the Danube the next morning.

If he had waited just a little while longer he would have surely seen what happened next to the out-of-luck out-of-towner. But his work had not been entirely in vain. That which he had observed would indeed come in quite handy later.

CHAPTER THREE
Upon the Danube

THE STEAMBOAT *Pressburg* waltzed quaveringly, to and fro, up the ostinato waves of the blue Danube.

It was on its return journey to Vienna, and was not far now. The passengers, who had been on the boat for some two days, were waiting impatiently for it to drop anchor at the quay in the capital so they could finally feel terra firma underneath their feet.

For twelve hours the weather had been terrible. After the intense heat that had seized the region in days past, the temperature swung in the opposite direction. A cold, cutting rain had been falling in great lashes, the air was cool and damp, the sky veiled with black storm clouds.

Most of the passengers had set out in light summer suits and frocks. Now they stood on the deck and fairly turned to icicles. Others retreated to their cabins, where the wind would not whip at them quite so forcefully.

This great crowd of passengers hailing from all different regions now saw the first signs of Vienna slowly approaching. Before long they would finally be free of this journey's unexpected torments.

But there erupted a discombobulated din among them, clamor and cacophony, screaming and squalling—and stampeding. The passengers pushed and shoved their way toward the captain, who was standing on the deck explaining something. Beside him stood a Polish Jew, rending the air with a tearful lament. "I've been ruined! Everything I was carrying has been stolen from me!"

The other passengers inched forth, all eager to learn what had happened. It took some trying for the captain to calm the sobbing victim, assuring him that the thief would easily be found—no one would leave the vessel until everyone was searched.

When the victim had regained some composure, he began to describe what had happened. "I am traveling from Budapest to Vienna. I was carrying a wallet full of money, a few thousand kronen at least. I am a cattle broker, see, and the money wasn't my own. I had been given it by someone else to buy up some oxen for him.

"I had it all on my person this very morning. After standing on the deck for several hours, I became very drowsy. I thought it must be from the rotten weather, so I went down to my cabin to warm up a little. It would seem I fell into quite a deep sleep as soon as I got through the door. When I woke up I found, to my horror, that I was missing my wallet.

"It's someone else's cash, I'll remind you! This is a catastrophe! I'll lose my entire livelihood. There's a chance I'll go to jail for this too! The merchant who entrusted me with his money is a merciless fellow. Not a chance he'll believe me. On the contrary, he'd be delighted to see me locked up."

The ill-fated Jew's story made a powerful impression on his fellow passengers. They felt for him and vowed they would assist in finding the missing money. Meanwhile the captain halted the steamboat's progress and ordered all the passengers searched, every inch of the cabins inspected, every pump and paddle wheel, every saloon and smokestack, turned over and around and upside down. But not a single sign of the money could be found.

The victim was despondent and soon got back to his weeping and wailing. Observing this, one of the passengers suggested taking up a collection on his behalf, starting it out with twenty kronen of his own. Many others gave too, each according to his or her means. Soon the kitty reached nearly five hundred kronen. Kind though this gesture was, it did not equal what the victim had lost.

"What use are a few hundred kronen to me," he sobbed, "when I've been robbed of ten times that?"

At which point one passenger bolted up and blustered, seething with rage, "Just look at this Polish Jew! It's not enough that we were so good as to take up a collection for him; he has the audacity to pooh-pooh it and declare himself unsatisfied! I wouldn't put it past him to be trying to turn this whole affair into a nice little business venture for himself!"

This outburst did not at all please the other passengers. They rebuked the man for his words, telling him that the Jew did not seem to be a swindler and that there was no reason to not accept his story as the unvarnished truth. But the man refused to end his tirade, insisting that the Jew was a liar and that he had manufactured his story out of whole cloth.

Soon the captain gave his crew the order to start the ship steaming ahead once more. He promised the victim that when it dropped anchor in Vienna, he would go off personally to inform the police of the case and make sure that they immediately launched their own investigation.

Now, two of the passengers aboard the ship, it turns out, were our very own detective Max Spitzkopf and his assistant Fuchs.

They had taken the steamboat to a small Hungarian town, where they had some investigatory business to take care of. On the journey there, Fuchs gave Spitzkopf the full report on what he had observed the night before.

"There has to be something there," Spitzkopf commented when the account was finished. "We'll add it to our list when we get home."

Once they arrived at their destination in Hungary, they quickly took care of the matter that required their attention and boarded the boat back to Vienna.

Then, when the Jewish passenger announced he had been robbed, Spitzkopf immediately took the case in hand. Of course, as was his wont, he did not tell a soul that he had assumed a special interest in the matter. Not even the captain. He allowed himself to be patted down just as all the other passengers were and pretended to not take much notice of the commotion.

But when the crew's search had finished he got to work.

He ordered Fuchs to remain on deck keeping an eye on the other passengers in case anyone should stand out as a potential suspect. Spitzkopf, meanwhile, headed down to the cabins, looking for any clues.

It was clear the victim must have been drugged. The thief likely sidled his way up to him amid the jostling of the crowd on deck and placed an etherizing agent near enough to the man's nose for him to get a strong sniff of it. He might have doused his handkerchief with chloroform and held it out in front of his fellow passenger just slyly enough for him not to notice.

And so Spitzkopf went wandering down the halls of the steamboat hoping his olfactory senses might be greeted in one of the cabins by the odor of chloroform, which would in turn tell him where to look for further traces of the thief. He rotated around the rooms for a good while and encountered no particularly out-of-the-ordinary aromas.

But when he reached a certain narrow passageway between two cabins, his keenly trained nose got a whiff of it at last: chloroform, wafting out from under a doorway.

"I've found the room!" he cried out to himself in private celebration, quickly opening the locked door with his skeleton key.

As soon as he entered he noticed a stain on the carpet that he recognized as chloroform. The thief, when saturating his handkerchief in the liquid, must have let a few drops fall to the floor.

"I'm sure to find his loot here too," Spitzkopf thought, undertaking a thorough inspection of the room. He tapped along the walls, the floor, and the ceiling, trying to feel for some opening where the thief may have stashed the stolen money.

As he lay prostrate on the floor engaged in his sounding, the door of the cabin swung open, and before the detective had a moment to turn around and look he was clobbered over the head so forcefully with some hard object that he remained where he lay, unconscious.

Rivers of blood ran from his head. Soon he was lying in a veritable red sea.

Meanwhile the boat had reached the quay in Vienna. The captain went off to file a report with the police, and soon an inspector came with a number of other officers, and all of the passengers and their luggage were once again searched. But still—no wallet, and no money.

Those passengers who were carrying large sums were able to demonstrate how the money had come to them. Meanwhile, the victim lacked proof that he had ever had any cash on him at all during the voyage.

And so this Polish Jew disembarked from the ship a desperate and broken man, crying out to the heavens, "All that remains for me to do now . . . is to throw myself into the Danube!"

But the police inspector was able to settle him somewhat and brought him back to the precinct so he could take down his full statement.

As for the five hundred kronen that his fellow passengers had collected for him, the inspector set it aside in the police offices, the victim having refused to accept the donation himself.

CHAPTER FOUR
The First Discovery

FUCHS HAD NOT sat idle above deck. While Spitzkopf was conducting his search of the cabins below, Fuchs was keeping a keen eye on the passengers, seeing whether he might not read in anyone's eyes some twinkle of guilt.

The one whose look displeased him most was the man who had inveighed against the Polish Jew. Something flashed in his eyes, a sort of disquietude. It appeared to Fuchs as if he were waiting with great impatience for the boat to pull in so he could finally disembark.

And so Fuchs made sure to keep him in his sights until the onboard search was finished and the passengers had come ashore, then to follow the man and see where he repaired to.

As soon as the suspicious character descended from the boat, he hailed a cab and gave out his destination: Döbling. Fuchs did not quite hear what street and address he named, so he resolved to just follow him closely and, entering another cab, told the driver to be hot on the other's tail. He did not wait for Spitzkopf. He did not want to let his suspect get away.

From within the carriage, though, he did take this precaution: letting nubbins of chalk fall to the ground, between the wheels, so that Spitzkopf would be able to follow him by tracking the chalk marks.

The two fiacres rolled on for over an hour until the first came to a halt in front of the villa where, the night before, the cab carrying the elegant young man and his provincial charge had stopped. "Aha, back to this mysterious mansion," Fuchs reflected, alighting from his fiacre some twenty steps past the house and trespassing onto the grounds. But after he saw the man he had been following enter the villa, Fuchs turned back onto the street and asked a passing watchman who the residents of the house might be.

The watchman answered him with the reheated morsel about the secretive Englishman and his tight-lipped staff. Fuchs found it hard to swallow. "I know these larks!" he thought. "A mysterious Englishman, yes, a millionaire they say, with a footman and a coachman . . . Yes, we know such far-flying birdies quite well! I shall find it most interesting to find out what the secrets of this millionaire really are."

Fuchs walked up and down the street for around half an hour, keeping to the side farther from the villa but not letting the vast edifice out of his sight. He could not see what was happening inside, as the facade was shielded by a grove of tall trees, and he did not wish to approach any closer to the house lest he reveal himself.

But even observing the villa from afar, he was able to determine that there was a large garden stretching out behind the house. He quickly made up his mind to infiltrate it. He jumped the fence and entered.

He was not alone in this garden. He saw a man in a tattered suit with an old fedora cocked crazily to one side. This character was advancing toward the fence, taking giant strides as he walked.

Fuchs hid under a tree and watched him closely. He recognized him as the same young swell he had seen at the Venedig. He watched the man open a low gate set in the fence and exit onto the street. Fuchs waited a few moments, then followed him from afar so that the man did not notice. This fellow, in his new disguise, walked for some distance until he disappeared into a different large house of considerable vintage.

Fuchs followed him. Standing in the entrance corridor, he could clearly hear the man going up a great number of steps onto the highest floor and there opening a door and advancing into some room. Fuchs cautiously ascended the staircase. The stairs were old and fairly dilapidated, muttering and juddering with every footfall.

Fuchs tiptoed as gingerly as he could manage, hoping no one would hear. But all the gingerliness in the world would not have helped. The stairs creaked continually, and the reverberations could be heard throughout the entire house.

Fuchs finally reached the top of the stairs and stood outside the doorway into which the young man from the Venedig had disappeared. He tried to peer through the keyhole to see if he could make out what was going on within. But he had just barely bent down when the door swung open and the man he had been following loomed on the other side, now dressed quite elegantly again. He barked out, “What is it you want, and whom are you looking for?”

Fuchs was stunned and stood stock still. He pulled himself together quickly, though, and answered: “I am looking for one Friedrich Schuster. I’ve been told that he lives in this house. But I can’t seem to locate him.”

"Do come in, please," said the man with a smile. "He does indeed live here. With me."

Fuchs did not hesitate. He went right in, though not without putting his hand in his pocket to find the familiar grip of his loaded revolver. As soon as he had passed the threshold the man stepped into the hall, slammed the door shut, and locked it.

He exploded with mocking laughter from the other side of the door. "Not very lucky with us today, are yehs, you dirty bloodhounds?" he jeered. "One of yehs we battened down on the boat, and as for the other, we'll show him some real hospitality here at home!"

Fuchs could feel his jaw clenching up with rage. "So something happened to my master on the boat," he shuddered, "and who knows what. Meanwhile I, foolish and frolicsome fellow that I am, went my merry way off the deck and left him there alone!

"But now I see our hunch was correct. We're dealing with a flock of wily scoundrels here. I must think up a way to get out of here and get these birdies pent up in a cage before they take wing."

He inspected the room and found that there was a second door on the other side. It led to a dark chamber, its sole dim light source being a small window in the center of the ceiling, opening into the attic. Fuchs slid a small table over to the center of the room, directly below the window, and standing atop it, he used the handle of his revolver to shatter the windowpane. Then he hoisted himself up.

But as soon as his head breached the opening, he found himself looking straight into the barrel of a gun.

"I knew you'd try to worm your way out through that window," the young man said to him, a wicked grin spread across his face. "I've been waiting for you."

Fuchs did not bother to respond. He let his gun answer for him. He discharged it, and discharged it well. The man's revolver dropped from his hand as he crumpled to the floor. Fuchs had gotten him right in the gut. The wounded man let out a savage cry. But soon his eyes glazed over and he lay there silent, nearly dead.

Fuchs clambered into the attic. He scrutinized the injured party and thought, "The man has been rendered harmless, and he's bound to be lying here until I get back. But the injury is not life-threatening. All I've got to do now is crawl my way out of this forsaken hole.

"I don't want to bust open the door to the hall lest the other inhabitants hear. I've got to be sneaky and not put the kibosh on all the work I've done up to now. I can see I have only one choice: get out of the attic and from there let myself down to the ground."

Fuchs managed to wriggle through a small window and haul himself up to the roof. After swinging himself down so that his fingertips clutched onto the tin gutters, he released and dropped, landing in a narrow courtyard.

It all happened so quickly that no one inside the house noticed a thing.

Fuchs ran to the nearest telephone station, where he telegraphed to Spitzkopf's office, inquiring as to whether the detective was at home. He received an answer quickly, saying in no uncertain terms:

SPITZKOPF LYING IN BED. WOUNDED.

Fuchs ran on winged feet to see his master, flying as fast as they would carry him. Arriving at his home office, he found Spitzkopf under the covers, his head wrapped in bandages. The wound, it turned out, was not so very grave, but the detective had lost a great deal of blood, which had reduced him to a much weakened state.

Spitzkopf did not know how long he had lain there on the floor of the stateroom after sustaining the blow to his head. He did remember having been found there shortly after all of the other passengers had disembarked, when a lowly member of the crew was making his rounds to air out the cabins. In one of them he saw Spitzkopf lying in a spreading pool of blood.

The man sounded the alarm, and the captain followed by a number of sailors came running. The ship's doctor bound Spitzkopf's head wound. Then the captain brought the detective home in a carriage.

Naturally, the police got involved before long, and they took down Spitzkopf's statement. But Spitzkopf asked them to keep the whole thing quiet. "On no account," said the detective, "do I want word getting out that I went searching the cabins. These crime crows will gird themselves for battle if they find out it's me they're dealing with. Better they should think that they were successful in neutralizing the spy. We'll have a far easier time luring them into our trap if they do."

After Spitzkopf finished telling his story, Fuchs told him his. And when Fuchs was finished, his master commented: "Why, the yarn is even knottier than before! I'd thought that the wallet thief must have gone down to his cabin when I went to search it. But I gather from your account that he was on deck the whole time. He must have had some accomplice. But who might this accomplice, my attacker, be?

"I fear he might have been one of the ship's crew. Whoever it was, he will likely have already told his mates that the spy was none other than Spitzkopf. Which would not portend smooth sailing for us.

"All this means I must get to work at once, before the gang has time to work all this out."

"In your present condition?" Fuchs asked incredulously. "How could you possibly allow yourself to get out of bed?"

"Oh, it's water off a sailor's back," answered Spitzkopf. "I've rested plenty. Now is the time for me to stop resting and start restoring—restoring justice to Vienna, that is. And it seems to me we've made a solid start at it. It would be a downright shame to let these knaves make their getaway now."

Fuchs could see that any resistance would be in vain. So he helped Spitzkopf change and escorted him out of the house.

"Fuchs," Spitzkopf addressed his assistant as they emerged onto the street. "In half an hour, make your way to our notorious villa. Just remain in its environs, waiting for me, until I give you a sign."

Having given his order, the detective climbed into a fiacre, which whisked him away into the vastness of Vienna.

CHAPTER FIVE
The Secrets of a Millionaire

Henry Clerk sat at his desk in his magnificently appointed study, smoking a fine Havana cigar.

The contract he was to offer the old man who wished to buy up his supposed factories lay on the table before him. Clerk had been able to convince him to visit later that day in order to sign and seal the document, and he meant to fleece the geezer of his cash right there and then.

And so Clerk was a perfect bundle of nerves as he sat there in his handsomely carved chair, chomping on his cigar.

Of course, it was hardly his first rodeo. But something about it made him feel unsettled and impatient. He could not wait to have the thing over with. "Once I've milked the man," he ruminated, "and his fortune's in my pail, I'm getting out of Vienna quick as you can say *Schlagobers*. There's something about the whole thing that's starting to smell sour.

"I always have my boys carrying out little heists and swindles on my account, diving into the money pit. I'm just . . . I'm just worried we may bellyflop this time."

As he sat fretting, he heard the doorbell. "Aha, here he comes!" he thought, plucking up his courage to reel in the unwitting prey.

It was not the old man at the door, however, but rather the footman, coming to announce that some gentleman wished to speak with him.

"Who? What's his name?" Clerk asked.

"He doesn't wanna say. But he claims he's an old acquaintance o' yers."

Clerk meditated for a moment on whether to tell his lackey to let the man in. But who the devil could it be? Might even be a spy, for all they know!

But if it really were a spy, what good would it do to refuse him admittance now? He would just find his way back later . . .

Maybe it would be simpler to just let him in, and if he proves dangerous . . . well, they would cut him loose soon enough.

All of these thoughts flew through Clerk's head, each chasing the one before. Finally he decided what to do with the mystery guest.

"Let him in!" he commanded his lackey. "But stay there in the next room, and if you chance to hear us going at it, fisticuffs or the like, barge in. As for what you'd do next . . . well, you know that already."

The footman's eyes twinkled as if to say, "Do I ever!"

After a short while the door was pushed open again, revealing an elderly man dressed in extremely fine and expertly tailored clothing. "Good morning, Herr Baron Hammerstein!" the visitor greeted the supposed millionaire. "You must not have expected to see me here!"

Clerk looked him up and down as his face first turned white as a sheet, then bright red. He did not know how to answer.

"Cat got your tongue, old friend?" the old gentleman asked. "Don't you recognize me? Seems you've already forgotten about the business we did together in Belgium, before you skipped town and forgot to settle up with me before you did."

All Clerk could do was sit there, perched on his desk chair like he had been fired into a hardened mass of clay. Not a word could he utter in response.

"Yes, indeed!" said the old gentleman. "You were calling yourself Baron Hammerstein then and passing yourself off as an Austrian. Now it seems you've transformed into Henry Clerk and are suddenly English. Why, I suppose soon you'll be called Something-or-Othernandez, a Spaniard, *¡jajaja!*"

Finally Clerk hit upon a course of action and said with resolve in his voice: "I don't know what it is you want. And you have no proof of anything. Any claims you may have upon my property have not been duly authorized. Why, the only thing I'll be paying out to you is a scream of laughter in your face!

"And I'll tell you another thing. It's no concern of yours if I've taken on a new name. That's my affair.

"But I don't want you leaving here complaining you were ill-treated. So I'll give you a parting gift. What is it you desire?"

"What do I desire?" said the guest. "None of your gifts, that's for certain, and no pity either. All I want is what you owe me."

"And how much would that be?" Clerk asked, growing ever more impatient.

"Oh, don't play dumb! You know quite well what I'm owed. But to jog your memory, here's the invoice," said the man, pulling a long scroll of paper out of his briefcase and presenting it to his host.

Clerk took a glance at the bottom line and spluttered out, "What? Ninety thousand francs? You must be off your rocker, old man."

"Me? You haven't even read through the calculations and already you're apoplectic! First have a good look and then tell me if my accounting isn't right."

"Right or not right," Clerk went on, "I wouldn't dream of giving you even half of that total! Listen here, if you want five thousand francs, it's yours, if it means washing my hands of you for good."

"My dear Baron Hammerstein! Is this really the sort of hospitality you show to your guests? You haven't even invited me to sit down. But I don't stand on ceremony—and so I'll sit, whether you ask me to or not." At which the man relaxed into a chair that faced Clerk's, on the other side of the desk, crossed his legs, and lit up a cigar for himself from Clerk's collection.

Clerk merely glared at him with flaming eyes, his teeth gnashing in purest indignation. "I am asking you once more, and politely this time: leave me!" Now Clerk was well and truly bellowing, projecting his voice out to the door. "Or things won't look so pretty for you."

And in stormed the footman, along with the coachman. Clerk gave them a nod, and before the visitor had a chance to turn around and see who had entered he found himself being wrested out of his chair and held fast, his arms pinioned to his back.

"You're deluding yourself," the visitor said in clear and even tones. "Don't think I'm the only one who is on to your schtick. If you hurt me, others will follow in my wake. The little part you've been acting will soon be ended, then it's curtains for you and your whole troupe."

Clerk was about to issue his retort when the doorbell went off again. "Here comes the old man I *was* waiting for," Clerk cried out, evidently shaken. "Gang, go and show this chattering magpie to someplace comfy where he can have a nice long rest. I haven't the time to play any more games with him."

And so his two henchmen hauled the man off to an anteroom. In the middle of it stood a large trunk, sealed with heavy ironwork. They quickly moved to tie the man's wrists together and gag his mouth with a rag, then shoved him into the trunk, closed the cover, and locked it.

The doorbell rang again. The coachman retreated into another room. Clerk wiped off the cold sweat that was beading up all over his head and hands, fixed his hair, and sat back down in his lordly desk chair, awaiting his new guest.

The footman opened the door and let in yet another venerable looking old gentleman. This one, however, Clerk greeted with a controlled and affable smile.

CHAPTER SIX
Entrances and Exits

When Spitzkopf left his home office with Fuchs, he set off for Döbling on the double.

Bidding the fiacre to stop a few houses before the villa in which the alleged English millionaire resided, he alighted and walked the rest of the way. When he arrived near the mansion, he kept his distance while scrutinizing the edifice from all sides.

It so happened he knew it quite well. An aged physician had lived there until he was attacked one night by a pack of burglars and murdered. On that occasion Spitzkopf had conducted a thorough inspection of the home and its surrounding gardens, so he knew every corner like the back of his handcuffs.

Now, considering how best to enter the home without anyone noticing, he remembered something he had noted on his prior inspection: that one could let themself down to the main floor from the attic by sliding down a large chimney that opened out into a grand English fireplace situated in one of the stately front rooms.

As soon as the bright, shining idea was ignited, he did not wait for the smoke to settle. He walked around to the fence gate, opened it with a skeleton key, and strode through the sprawling garden until he reached the walls of the house. Not a soul was about, and the windows were covered with heavy curtains such that those within could hardly see outside. Spitzkopf opened the back door carefully and slipped inside, then, tiptoeing all the way, ascended the stairs to the attic, where he found the opening into the broad flue. Moving soundlessly, he snaked his way down the chimney until he found himself down below, in the living room of the purported English millionaire Henry Clerk.

With his loaded revolver in his hand, he withdrew deep into the recesses of the fireplace and eavesdropped on the conversation that was underway in the room. He observed two bottles of wine on the table. Evidently Clerk wanted to loosen his victim up a bit so that his designs could be realized as smoothly as possible.

"Well, Herr Glicksberg," Spitzkopf heard Clerk saying. "You've read over the contract. Are we all agreed?"

"Yes, I've read it," answered the elderly gentleman sitting across from him. "But as to whether we're agreed, that I won't know until later. Not until I've had the opportunity to inspect your factories, enough to convince myself that everything is as you've portrayed it to me."

"What do you mean, you need to inspect the factories first?" Clerk asked in a tone of astonishment. "You've got everything here you need: photographs, the official appraisals from authorized experts, inventories, all the financial statements from the past five years, certificates of manufacture and export—in short, all that you could ever want to be sure of the success of my operations. What do you need to see the place for?"

"What ever could you mean, 'What do I need to see it for?' You think I'm going to buy a pig in a poke? The money we're talking about is nothing to sneeze at! Imagine sneezing at a sum like the one inscribed on that contract! Such business is not entered into blind!"

"I am not demanding you get the entire payment to me up

front," said Clerk with practiced composure, though his eyes might have given him away, burning bright like a tiger's in the forests of the night. "All we've stipulated in the contract is that you're to give me a quarter of a million kronen as a down payment, and the rest you'll pay out once you've actually acquired the properties and they're in your name. There's nothing to fear!"

"*Nu*, and to you a quarter million kronen is a couple of pennies?" the old man retorted. "That is not the sort of sum I'm accustomed to paying in exchange for a bit of sweet talk!"

"Then how do you mean for us to get this done? I want to get the deal squared away."

"Quite simply! We make our way across the water. I get a good look at the factories, and once I'm satisfied I get you the down payment. You'll receive the rest once you transfer ownership of the factories over to me."

"But I'm not in a position to travel now. Neither do I want to. What good does it do me to drag myself off to England? And what if it turns out you're just playing me once we get there and you haven't a cent to your name?"

"If I didn't have any money I wouldn't have come here to take up your time," the elderly gentleman protested. "I'm also dragging myself to England, and I wouldn't do such a thing to no purpose. Why, I have the money on me right now!"

"And you're going to hand it over immediately, and we'll get this thing signed and sealed!" Clerk barked at the man. "I'm not going to let you take up a moment more of my time. You either do as we've agreed, or . . ."

"This kind of talk doesn't please me a whit, Mr. Clerk," the old man answered evenly, rising from his chair. "There must be something underneath your wanting to get the money from me before I have the chance to see the factories with my own two eyes. If these are the conditions you're presenting, I'd rather call the whole thing off right now."

"Call it off?" Clerk thundered, gesturing wildly. "*Call it off?*

And where does that leave me? You think you can make a fool out of me? That would be your biggest mistake yet."

The hand-waving was the sign Clerk's men were waiting for. The footman and the coachman tumbled into the room and bore down on the terrified old man. Meanwhile Clerk sprang out of his chair, grabbed the leather briefcase the man was holding, and tried to pry it from his hands.

But the old man was defiant and did not loosen his grip, clutching the case with all his might.

And so Clerk's accomplices joined in the struggle, seizing the man by the arms as all three bandits now attempted to free the case from his iron grasp. They were so concentrated on their pulling and prying that they did not hear Spitzkopf emerge from his hiding place. He knew his moment had come.

"Hand over the bag, you ancient buffoon," Clerk snarled, "or I'll split that buffoonish pate o' yours in two!"

"Not so fast," Spitzkopf roared as he crawled out of the fireplace, "or I'll shoot you down like the vicious curs that you are!"

Then the detective gave out a loud, shrill whistle, a signal to Fuchs to come running. Barely a second passed before a window was flung open and Fuchs leaped into the room, a loaded revolver in his hand.

Seeing two armed men standing directly opposite them, all the criminals' courage evaporated, and their hands fell to their sides. Not hesitating for a moment, Spitzkopf went to cuff Clerk's wrists, and Fuchs took care of the other two scoundrels.

Amid all the excitement the old man could not get a decent breath in. Spitzkopf laid him out on a sofa and telephoned for a doctor. Then he phoned the police to inform them of these developments. An inspector soon came, along with a dispatch of officers, who hauled the criminals off to the clink.

Fuchs went off with one of the officers to the old house where he had shot the criminals' associate and left him lying in the attic. The man was barely breathing and was promptly transported to the hospital.

After all the criminals were taken care of and led away, Spitzkopf undertook a thorough inspection of the entire villa, hoping to find clues that would indicate who these men were and where they came from.

He found a massive cache of papers that revealed to him they were dealing with a dangerous international crime syndicate.

Walking into an anteroom within the mansion, he thought he heard a sort of groaning coming from the locked trunk that stood in the center of the space. He opened it and found inside the nearly suffocated old man the crooks had confined earlier.

Spitzkopf pulled him out of the trunk and found that he recognized the man. It was someone he had come across before, another dangerous criminal, in fact, one who had been sent to prison before through Spitzkopf's efforts and had spent several years there.

"How do you do, my friend?" Spitzkopf laughed. "Here you are *boxed in* by me once again, ha! I heard tell that you busted out of the big house a couple of years ago, and the authorities haven't been able to find you since. So why would you commit such a grievous blunder now and return to show your face in Vienna? Perhaps you thought I was not still living?"

"You're no better than a dog!" answered the sworn criminal. "Someday I'll give you what's been coming to you all these years. But for now I'm pleased with you. Pleased as punch—that you've punched that nasty gang off to the pokey. You'll be my proxy in taking my revenge on them!"

"That will take care of itself," said Spitzkopf. "But first you will assist me by informing me of everything you know about all the crimes this gang has committed. And then we'll see about *you*."

Spitzkopf called over an officer and ordered that this fellow be sent off to jail too, where he and the members of the terrible troika were duly interrogated.

CHAPTER SEVEN

Curtain Call

Rather an interesting discovery emerged from the gang's interrogation. Photographs of all of them could be found in the police's rogues gallery. And it turned out Henry Clerk was indeed a native Englishman. He came from a very wealthy family, and his brothers were in fact major manufacturers in Britain—and millionaires to boot.

Henry Gordon (for that was his actual name) was reckless as a youth, a complete wastrel, really. Some twelve years before his sojourn in Vienna, he had gotten to know the daughter of his brothers' factory manager and did her dirty. Fearing he would do time for it, he made himself scarce and hopped across the ocean to America, where he assumed a new name.

He did not flee with much money, and he had spent what little he did have within a few weeks in America. As he did not want to work, he soon fell in with a crowd of common criminals. It did not take him long to rack up a number of crimes of his own. He eventually was arrested, convicted, and sentenced to ten years in the most feared and unforgiving of American penitentiaries, Sing Sing.

Soon after he was locked up, a revolt broke out. Our Henry was the leader of the insurrectionaries. A number of wardens were slain, and several prisoners, including Henry, escaped.

The runaway Englishman sailed for South America. While on board, he robbed the ship's purser, and when one of the sailors found him out, Henry stuck a knife in him and killed him instantly. Another sailor was identified as the chief suspect in the murder, though, and Henry arrived safe and sound in South America.

He did not remain there long either. After carrying out a string of various peccadilloes, he had to vamoose.

His next destination was Europe. For a number of years, few

of the continent's great capitals were safe from him and his devilry. Police departments all over issued warrants for his arrest; his photograph featured prominently in every rogues gallery. Knowing this, he made sure to always assume a new identity in every new place he turned up in, disguising himself so skillfully that detection proved impossible. Not for the detective known as Spitzkopf, however. It took his involvement to finally cage this plume-shifting peacock.

Henry's cronies operated more or less as he did. They all had dozens of serious crimes on their conscience. And in every city where they touched down, they found new accomplices. One of them was the fellow who had shown up at Henry's door the day of the gang's arrest, demanding his share of the loot from Belgium only to be left for dead in a sealed trunk.

This was the man, the criminal flyabout turned clay pigeon, who sang like a canary, providing the police with a full account of the criminals' activities and forcing Henry's hand. He and the others ultimately confessed to everything.

During the thorough inspection of the villa that followed the arrests, the wallet and papers that had been stolen from the provincial visitor by the footman, Arnold Fox, were finally located. So was the money stolen from the Jewish cattle broker.

That latter thievery had been the handiwork of the "millionaire's" coachman, Michael Brund. Another career criminal, he was constantly traveling, by rail and by sea, and to pass the time en route, he seized any opportunity to ruin some poor soul's life. On the ship he happened to have an accomplice: one of the crew, an old friend of his. It was into this salty seaman's room that Spitzkopf had penetrated, searching for the wallet, and it was he who attacked the detective.

In the end all of these men were brought to justice, and everything they had stolen was recovered.

Clerk, who had also added a number of murders to the bargain, was sentenced to hang, as was Fox, his footman. The others were given a good many years behind bars.

Spitzkopf, meanwhile, received all of the monetary prizes that the police departments in several European capitals had offered to whomever it was that might finally succeed in sending away these shapeshifting criminals and giving each of them one final role to play: convicted felon.

Issue 13: The Bride on Holiday

די דערטרונקענע כלה.

דערזעהענדיג דאס בילד, שפרינגט דער פֿערברעכער אָ דערשראָקענער אויף. דער הינטער איהם שטעהענדע שפּיצקאָפּף לעגט די האנד אויף זיין פּלייצע און זאגט: אַי האסט דו שוואכע נערווען!

The Bride on Holiday

CHAPTER ONE

The Bride on Holiday

A FEW HOURS from Salzburg is the paradisiacal Austrian health resort Zell am See.[13] It is nestled among the towering, imposing Kitzbühel Alps and hugs the shores of the sprawling Lake Zell, which stretches out for several kilometers. A number of hotels kiss the water's edge. There, guests enjoy windows directly overlooking the crystalline expanse. Further hotels and villas, dozens of them, are scattered nearby.

The views from Zell am See are nothing less than enchanting. In the summer months, thousands of guests converge there to take the cure, chiefly the highest-ranking aristocrats and the idlest and richest of the idle rich. The pleasures of Zell am See do not come cheap.

One of the shorelines is graced by a vast veranda, crowned by a gleaming glass roof. Twice a day calm and healing music is played there, and in the evenings, concerts are given, along with dances, parties, and other such revels.

In the earliest hours of the morning, the spa guests bathe in the lake, but in the afternoons they float above it, going out in little boats, laughing and frolicking and making mischief. Or sometimes they form little hiking parties and enjoy a jaunt into the surrounding mountains.

Sometimes on such fine afternoons, when the train from Salzburg to Innsbruck is passing through Zell am See, passengers will not see a single holidaymaker cavorting near the hotels, in the glass-roofed pavilion, or upon the surface of the water. It is as if all life there has come to a standstill. The truth is all the guests have either gone into the mountains or sailed off to the other side of the lake.

Our story begins on one of these fine days, a perfectly splendid, clear-skied, soul-refreshing day you could only experience in a place like Zell am See. Not even the remotest whitish plumes that might at some point gather to become a cloud mar the azure expanse of sky. The air is clean and cool. From the nearby gardens, from the nearby mountains, there drifts a heavenly fragrance of blossoming trees and wildflowers. You would not be much to blame if you mistook this corner of the world on such a day for the very Garden of Eden.

Often on days like this, Zell am See appears perfectly unpeopled and quiet, nearly lifeless. But today nearly all of the guests have congregated noisily around the great veranda, impatiently awaiting the arrival of the express train and discussing, at fever pitch, the shocking event that took place the day before.

Several days earlier, a couple of new spa guests had turned up at Zell am See: the businessman Heinrich Taussig and his daughter, a maiden of twenty summers. Taussig had booked a suite at one of the hotels facing the lake, and before long his distinguished comportment, amiable demeanor, and obvious intelligence had attracted the attention of all the other cure-seekers.

His daughter, a highly educated, impeccably brought up girl who was moreover lovely to look upon and always wore simple but exquisitely tasteful clothing, was nothing to sniff at either in that respect. She immediately turned the heads of the young men, many of whom soon counted themselves her most devoted admirers.

Within days she had become the dazzling, golden sun around which all of the hotels' younger denizens orbited—for this Fraulein Taussig was not merely beautiful and clever but also very, very rich. Her father was a merchant and landowner of considerable prominence in Prague and had promised this only daughter of his a dowry of half a million kronen.

But all the young male hotel guests' efforts to ingratiate themselves with her were in vain. Fraulein Hedwig Taussig was already betrothed.

She was still quite young, and her father had no intention of giving away his only daughter so very soon. But the prior winter she had made the acquaintance of a young man, the manager of a factory in Aussee,[14] where the girl had traveled to pay an extended visit to an aunt. The young man pleased her so well that she stubbornly insisted her father allow her to become engaged to him.

Herr Taussig hemmed and hawed, but after the girl's aunt gave the suitor a glowing review, telling her kinsman that this was a very upstanding young man, dedicated to his work and with a promising future ahead of him, old man Taussig agreed to the match.

This suitor, Rudolf Kolb, made off for Prague at once to introduce himself to his future father-in-law. He showed himself off to fine effect, displaying his fine manners and impressing Herr Taussig with his educational credentials and his professional expertise. By the end Taussig was just as convinced as the aunt had been: this was a worthy match. The couple's intention to wed was soon announced publicly.

All of this had happened a number of weeks before the Taussigs, father and daughter, ventured off to the sunny climes of Zell am See. The girl's fiancé had spent only a few days in Prague, expressing his regrets that he could not leave the factory for so long. But he promised the girl that in a few weeks he would be receiving a month's worth of vacation, and he planned to spend every waking moment of it with his sweet fiancée.

It was also decided that as soon as his vacation began he would take the train to join the Taussigs in Zell am See. Herr

Taussig had even reserved a number of rooms for him in the hotel he was staying at with his daughter.

On the fourth day of the pair's holiday in the town, a beautiful afternoon, Taussig went off with a few acquaintances for a foray into the mountains. He left his daughter back at the hotel, as she preferred to take a boat out with some of her girlfriends.

Taussig returned to the hotel late that night. To his surprise, he found that his daughter was not in their suite. He went down to speak with the hotelier and the staff, asking after her, but no one could supply him with any information.

All of the other guests at the establishment, meanwhile, had already gone to sleep. It was not possible to make further inquiries. And so Taussig spent that dark and lonely night in a vigil of anxiety and fear. As soon as the first rays of the creeping dawn entered his room, he got to his feet and went to walk the perimeter of the lake, hopeful of finding some sign of his daughter. His heart told him something terrible had befallen her.

When the rest of the guests woke up and the lakeshore began to bustle with activity, he made his rounds among all of his acquaintances both old and new, asking them whether or not they had seen his daughter the day before.

But no one could put him at ease. None of them had joined her on any excursion; indeed, no one had even laid eyes on her.

No one, that is, except one old, ailing woman, who did have something interesting to share. She was staying in the same hotel as Taussig and had spent every hour of the prior day inside, as she was not feeling her best. Sitting beside the window in her room, she had thought she saw Fraulein Taussig rowing off in a boat with an unidentified man, leaving the waterfront a considerable distance behind them.

Herr Taussig ran around town all day, driven almost to madness. Feeling beyond desperate, he rented out the resort's entire fleet of boats and hired local country folk to cast out onto the lake and search far and wide, through every marsh and meadow, leaving no stone unturned and no ripple unchecked in pursuit of his daughter.

It was all for naught. There was not a trace of the missing girl.

Finally, the evening before all the guests convened to watch for the arrival of the express train, the girl's lifeless body washed ashore.

Old Taussig fainted upon hearing this most dreaded of news, and it took several hours for him to be resuscitated. The body was laid aside in one of the rooms of Taussig's hotel, and the authorities in the nearest city were notified.

Now the express train from Salzburg was arriving bearing the commission that the court had dispatched to investigate the case. All of the resort town's guests were deeply invested. The fate of this unfortunate child had devastated them, and they truly felt for the unhappy father who had still not managed to be restored to his former self. He lay there in his room, nearly dead himself, deranged with grief, haunted by an unending, fitful dream of his departed daughter.

CHAPTER TWO
Mystery Guests

The train in which the court-appointed investigative tribunal arrived also happened to be carrying Rudolf Kolb, the fiancé of the drowned maiden. He wanted, he said, to surprise his betrothed and so had not told her and her father of his imminent arrival.

One can easily imagine his surprise—and his agony—at the kind of reunion that awaited him. Wild with despair, he flung himself at the body of his bride, covering her with tears and impassioned kisses, as if he wanted to blow new life into her with his gasping breath.

It took a number of people, pulling hard, to draw him away from the body. The judicial commission had to begin its work.

Once the investigators had fully inspected the body and confirmed that which was already clear to everyone—that Hedwig Taussig had suffered a death by drowning—they began a criminal inquiry.

But aside from the testimony of the old woman, no one had any information worth hearing. No guest of any of the surrounding hotels was unaccounted for, nor was any boat. Meanwhile, none of the boats' owners claimed to have seen Fraulein Taussig out on the lake on that most sunshiny and yet infinitely dark afternoon.

It was a mystery—a complete and utter mystery. The judicial commission could not see a path forward.

But Rudolf Kolb declared he would move heaven and earth, turn the world upside down, do anything and everything to find the person who drowned his love. It had become apparent to everyone that a terrible crime had indeed been committed, for if merely an accident had occurred, the man who had been sighted with her in the boat would have drowned too, and his corpse would also have been found.

But Rudolf Kolb was at a loss. He must find his wife's killer, and yet he had not the faintest notion of how. One thing he did know, however: he could not expect much help from the court-appointed commission.

The case was so opaque that he needed highly skilled criminalists investigating it, not just functionaries of some backwoods provincial city who had never faced a case of any real gravity in all their lives.

And so he sent off a telegram to an acquaintance in Prague, asking him whether he might know of any talented private detectives, experts in forensic science, who might be persuaded to take on the case.

Herr Taussig, meanwhile, gradually broke free from the spell of fevered anguish he had been under and was finally able to drag himself out of bed. In the course of but a few days he had aged twenty years.

A steady stream of guests passed through the room where the dead body lay. Locals, too. All just to sneak a peek at the remains of the ill-fated girl.

It was decided that the next day a train would transport the body to Prague. Today it was to be sealed up in an iron casket. Around evening, after nearly all of the cure-seekers had come to see the body, the hotel's staff set about moving it into the casket.

Rudolf Kolb was standing nearby. In spite of his troubled state, he had barely left the side of his drowned fiancée since the moment he arrived in town.

Just as the body was about to be lifted two men entered, hoping to catch a glance at it. It irked Kolb tremendously, and he thought to himself: "How strange these people are. Here they are coming to see the body, just as if they've bought tickets to see some comedy or other at the theater. How dare they!"

But he kept silent and merely stood to one side of the room, watching the two men. One of them appeared to be of middle age, perhaps some thirty years older than himself. The other was much younger, likely around twenty-two.

Both scrutinized the body from every angle, not letting themselves be bothered by the entreaties of the staff, who tried over and over to shoo them off, telling the two men that it was getting late and that they would soon have to lock the room up for the night.

Suddenly Kolb witnessed the older man picking up a hair that appeared to be enclosed within the girl's fingers and secreting it away in his notebook. Then he shot his young companion a glance, allowing a twinkle of satisfaction to flicker across his eyes. It was too much for Kolb's patience.

"The audacity of you!" he cried. "You are desecrating a dead body! Either you scarper off at once, or I'll have the police come and arrest you."

One of the hotel staff helped him as he tried to shove them out of the room, all the while inveighing against these "bats out of hell." But the two mystery guests stood their ground, and the older one said to Kolb: "Pardon me, but what's it to you what we do here?"

"What's it to *me*?" Kolb shouted, incredulous. "This is the body of my bride to be you're disturbing! If I was not able to protect her from her murderer, at least I mean to protect her body from insolent, importunate . . ."

But before he could finish, the two men broke free from Kolb and the bellhop and quit the room.

The staff duly took the body in their hands, deposited it into its eternal bed, and sealed the casket. It was only with great effort that they were able to convince Kolb to retire to his room. He could find no peace there, though. He paced to and fro like a madman before realizing he had a new obligation now: to search out Herr Taussig and try to comfort him in the midst of his mourning.

And so he left the room, locked it, and went off to visit with the man who was once to have been his father-in-law.

CHAPTER THREE
The First Clues

THE NIGHT HAD advanced, and it had grown quite dark outside. The weather had recently turned. The sky was now shrouded in blackish clouds, rent by streaks of lightning followed by blasts of thunder. Tubfuls of rain soaked the lawns and walkways of Zell am See.

In the lakeside hotels and upon the veranda, a dark and dreary mood took hold. No music had been heard in the days since the girl had gone missing, and no guest sought out any entertainment. Zell am See was a ghost town.

On this night most of the guests had gone to sleep. Their windows were veiled with heavy curtains. Only in a few of them could some stray flickers of light be seen.

One of these was old man Taussig's. His electric lamp was just barely turned on, casting a faint glow over two men, kinsmen in sorrow, sitting inside: Taussig and Kolb. Both of them were slumped forward, heads hanging, lost in their mournful ruminations.

Then there was a knock at the door, and before they could even turn around a stranger stood before them. Looking up to regard his features, Kolb recognized at once the man with whom, only a short time earlier, he had the most upsetting interaction beside his bride's body.

"What do you want from us?" Kolb asked him, clearly unsettled by his renewed presence. "Why do you insist on disturbing our peace?"

"I cannot restore your peace to you," the man answered calmly. "But as for helping you to solve this darkest of cases, and perhaps uncovering the identity of the culprit . . . in these tasks you may find me a most eager partner."

"Who are you?" asked Kolb.

"My name is Max Spitzkopf," the stranger answered. "I am a private detective based in Vienna."

"It is a name with which I am well acquainted," Herr Taussig piped up. "What brings you here, and who sent you to me?"

"I was in Salzburg with my assistant on an excursion. It was there that we heard of the terrible things that transpired here. I never wait to be summoned. If it's possible, I do all that I can to rescue unfortunate victims and to see that guilty persons are punished.

"Hearing of this tragedy and happening to have at present a bit of free time, we traveled here at once. Thankfully, we arrived only moments before the body was due to be sealed up in the casket. The discovery we made in that room was so significant that I came here immediately to inform you that I am taking the case in hand. And that I hope to have the culprit clapped in irons before long."

Taussig and Kolb stared at him with eyes widened and mouths agape. "How did you make such an apparently significant discovery in such a short time?" Kolb queried. "You were only beside the body for a couple of minutes. And the judicial commission had inspected it for hours on end and found nothing of import."

"I do not know what the commission was looking for and what it found. I only know what it is that I saw, and that is enough for me.

"I must demand two things of you both, however. The first is that you do not breathe a word of my involvement in the case. And second that you provide me with clear and forthright answers to the questions I will be asking you. The rest you can leave to me."

Kolb took the detective's hand warmly in his own and said to him: "I thank you sincerely for your readiness to find this person. Ask what you will, and I shall answer you. And you may be confident that none shall know that you have taken an interest in the matter.

"But before we go any further, I beg of you, please tell me what this discovery is you have already happened upon. It is not mere curiosity that inspires my question. I believe that if I know everything there is to know, I may prove useful to you."

"I must say," Spitzkopf said, "I am not in the habit of revealing to others the nature of my initial clues. But I shall make an exception on this occasion, as I happen to agree—you may indeed be able to help me.

"I have determined that your fiancée engaged in a physical struggle with the man who eventually drowned her—that she defended herself against him. Upon her neck and one of her hands, I perceived the marks of intense pressure. And in that hand she was holding a single long, black hair. From that piece of evidence I concluded that the culprit must have black hair and sport a black beard.

"Finally, I have reasoned that we are not dealing here with a single culprit but rather two, as the traces of pressure on the body appear to have been left by two very different hands, one of them small and delicate, the other large and coarsely hewn."

"You saw all of that in one minute?" asked Kolb in a tone of utter astonishment.

"You may postpone that question to a later date," said Spitzkopf. "We have more pressing questions to answer at present.

"Now, one thing is abundantly clear to me: that the solitary motive behind this murder was vengeance. No robbery seems to have been involved, as all of the victim's valuable rings and earrings were found on her person. Even her wallet was intact and still lodged within her pocket. Nor was this a sexual homicide; the judicial commission found no sign of the victim having been raped. And so, by process of elimination, we find it must have been an act of vengeance. For that reason, it would behoove us to know whether or not the victim may have had some enemy who sought to take revenge on her."

"My daughter, as far as I know, did not have a single enemy on earth," Herr Taussig answered.

"Did no man ever propose marriage to your daughter only to be ultimately rejected by her?"

"No, I know of no such case," said Taussig.

"Do you, Herr Kolb?" Spitzkopf continued.

"No!"

"And yet, the fact that neither of you was aware of such a thing happening does not suffice. It is possible that she simply did not tell you. But we shall look into that in due time. I will let the matter rest for now. As for you, Herr Kolb, might you perhaps have a sworn foe who might have targeted your fiancée as a way to harm you?"

Kolb reflected for a moment, then answered: "I could only possibly suspect one such man—a colleague of mine at the factory, as it happens. He is a rabid antisemite and takes any opportunity to spew his hatred of Jews. He simply cannot tolerate that I, a Jew, have risen to become manager of a factory owned by Christians. I have had little direct communication with him. I mainly concern myself with the technical operations at the factory, while his work is in the city office, so our paths rarely cross.

"But last winter I ran into him at a ball I was attending with my blessed fiancée. I was enjoying myself when suddenly he charges up to me, clapping me upon the shoulders—rather impudently, I should say—and roars, 'Our Herr Direktor has nabbed such a pretty young thing for a bride! She's just the belle of the ball, ain't she! Go and introduce me to her, why don'tcha, and let her dance a waltz with me, just one!'

"I answered him quite coldly, 'But you're always ranting about how much you despise all Jews. So why now, all of a sudden, would you want to go and dance with a Jewish girl?'

"Somehow this set him off, and then, through gritted teeth, he growled, 'Just you wait, you goddamn Jew—I'll make sure your soup's so peppered you retch at the very sight of it!'

"I could see that he'd had a few too many, so I didn't fancy brewing him up any further by arguing. We just slipped away and gave him a wide berth."

"Does this man have black hair?" asked Spitzkopf.

"Yes," answered Kolb. "But it's my belief that if you mean to go sniffing around in that direction, you'd be mistaken. First of all, he hasn't got it in him to commit murder; he's not half so volatile as all that. Second, he's not such a specimen when it comes to physical prowess as to be able to drown a robust, healthy individual. The righteous personage who was to be my bride was a good, strong girl. And third, how could he have even gotten here? As far as I know, he's been off in Bad Reichenhall[15] the past ten days."

"I'm not saying for certain that he is the culprit," said Spitzkopf, "but your reasons to the contrary do not add up to much. As I've said already, the crime appears to have been committed by two people working in tandem. And this of him being in Reichenhall is also not of great significance. He could have very easily hopped over here; the journey from Reichenhall to Zell am See takes but a few hours. The real question is whether he could have known that your fiancée was vacationing here."

"I'm not sure. It's possible he knew it. My colleagues at the factory were aware that I would be spending my holiday in Zell am See, where my fiancée was."

"That's all that I shall need to know for today," Spitzkopf concluded, rising to his feet. "I'll set about uncovering the remaining details. It seems to me we're on the right track. But the main thing for you to remember is this: mum's the word."

"You can be sure of that," said Herr Taussig and the young Kolb. "Mum as a Japanese flower."

"Fine," said Spitzkopf. "Oh, and one more thing: see to it that the body of the deceased remains where it is for now."

"Consider it done," said Kolb.

And so Spitzkopf took his leave.

CHAPTER FOUR
An Express Letter to Reichenhall

As surreptitiously as he had come up the stairs, so Spitzkopf now padded down them, opening the gate outside the hotel with a skeleton key and emerging onto the street. He was careful that no one notice him leaving.

A walk of only twenty paces brought him to the midst of a

sprawling public garden. There, in the shadow of a beech tree, his assistant Hermann Fuchs awaited him.

"*Nu*, Fuchs, *vos iz nayes?*" Spitzkopf asked.

"No news," said Fuchs, "other than that just now I happened to see our birdie sending off an express letter. I could tell it was an express delivery from the couple of special stamps I noticed on the envelope. I didn't manage to catch the address, however."

"I'll find that out in due time," said Spitzkopf. "He was too late in sending it for it to go out today anyhow—the last train has already left town, and no more mail will be delivered until the first train tomorrow morning. And you can stamp it as certified that I'll be at the post office before then, and neither snow nor rain nor heat nor gloom of night shall stop me.

"Neither shall they stop me from getting myself into my yawning bed now. I'll be seeing you at the train station, Fuchs—be there in time for the arrival of the first train in the morning. Stand by until then for your next assignment."

Spitzkopf then made off for his hotel while Fuchs headed in the opposite direction to his. Erring on the side of caution, they had decided to stay in two different establishments so as to prevent people from suspecting that they were working together.

Spitzkopf did not end up staying in his yawning bed for long. The following day, at the break of dawn, he was back on his feet again—and once they had stepped into shoes, they carried him directly to the post office.

Now, within a minute of Spitzkopf entering the room where the body lay the day before, a suspicion had already formed in his mind about the bellboy, the one who had flamed up so when he and Fuchs had approached the body to take a good look. He had tried to steer the detective and his assistant out of the room as soon as he saw Spitzkopf storing away the stray hair in his notebook.

Spitzkopf conjectured that this hotel employee must be the accomplice of whomever it was that slew Hedwig Taussig. He was confident that the man's next step would be to immediately send word to his partner that the heat had gotten turned up a few degrees.

And so the detective ordered Fuchs to keep an eye on this hotel lark, to see where the bellboy went and what he got up to. Fuchs discharged his duty wonderfully, observing that the man had dropped off an express letter at the post office, addressed to some unknown destination.

Arriving at the post office, Spitzkopf presented his credentials, verifying that he was a private detective, and asked the postmaster to show him the express letter that had been deposited at the office the night before.

"It has already been sent off!" said the postmaster. "You've come a hair too late. But I myself marked it for delivery, and as it was the only express letter in our first batch of mail today, I still remember the address: Fritz Berger, Bad Reichenhall, Villa Immergrün."[16]

"Please accept my profoundest thanks for this information," said Spitzkopf. "I am authorized to order that the letter be recalled—but I won't do it. Who knows if it will ultimately contain much evidence demonstrating the guilt of these nasties. Such people can be quite careful in their methods.

"The more expedient thing would be to send my assistant Fuchs off to make this Fritz Berger's acquaintance. Then he'll be able to tell me what tune these popinjays hop to."

After carrying on in this way, Spitzkopf asked the postmaster to keep everything that the detective communicated to him a secret. Leaving the office, he headed directly to the train station, where he found Fuchs waiting for him.

"In half an hour a train will be leaving here bound for Salzburg," he told his assistant. "You will be on it. Once you arrive in Salzburg, take the connecting train to Bad Reichenhall. You will arrive in Reichenhall at around nine this morning. Try to book a room at the Villa Immergrün, and establish a rapport with the Fritz Berger who is staying there. As you gain information and get a hunch in one direction or another, I trust you'll be able to figure out what to do next. In any case, send word as soon as you can confirm that we've hit upon the right track."

And indeed, Fuchs was on that train to Salzburg, and the connecting train to Bad Reichenhall, where he arrived right on time.

CHAPTER FIVE
Reichenhall → Salzburg

SURROUNDED BY colossal, skyscraping mountains, in a magnificently beautiful valley, lies the health resort of Bad Reichenhall, barely an hour's journey from Salzburg.

Fuchs arrived in the town at nine o'clock and practically jumped out of the train, eagerly asking to be pointed toward the Villa Immergrün. Upon making his way to this establishment, which, it turned out, was no more than fifty paces from the train station, he successfully snapped up a free room for himself.

After changing out of his traveling clothes, he walked, hungry for breakfast, to the so-called Viennese Coffeehouse across from the hostelry. On his way there he saw a letter carrier, with an express letter in hand, entering into the garden that surrounded the villa. Fuchs suspected immediately that this must be the letter due to be delivered to Fritz Berger. And so, by following the letter carrier with his eyes as the man went to deliver the item to Berger's door, which opened onto the garden, Fuchs soon learned what room this wayward waterfowl was nesting in.

The conviction building in Fuchs's mind grew only stronger as he witnessed what happened next. As soon as the letter carrier had left the villa, Fritz Berger appeared at his door, the express letter in his hands and a clearly distraught look on his face.

"That must be our mucky duck," Fuchs thought to himself, turning on his heels to continue on to the coffeehouse and his breakfast.

Soon Berger turned up there too. Fuchs observed that his right hand was lightly bruised, and two of his fingers were bound together in a bandage. The man sat down at a café table not far from where Fuchs was and ordered a coffee. As Fuchs sipped his, he did not let his eyes stray for a moment from this fellow customer.

He saw the lout taking the letter out of his pocket again, reading it through, then putting it back, saying to himself in a barely audible murmur, "Well, how do you like this jolly bit of news? Those demon detectives stick their long noses in everywhere."

Not a doubt remained. Fuchs was certain that he was indeed on the right path. Now he only waited for the right moment to strike up a conversation with the man.

It soon came.

He heard Berger asking the waiter to bring him the train timetable that showed the departures from Reichenhall. Waiting until he was through glancing it over and had set it on the table, Fuchs walked up to the man and made this polite request: "If you would please allow me to borrow that timetable, I'd like to see when the next train from Salzburg to Zell am See departs."

"Ah, you're headed to Zell am See?" the man asked. "It so happens I am too. The next train leaves Salzburg at one this afternoon."

"Very good," said Fuchs. "I've got to be there today, and that should get me there on time."

"We can travel together if you like," said the man.

"It would be my pleasure," said Fuchs. "I'm Julius Braunstein, from Vienna."

"And I'm Fritz Berger, from Aussee," said the man, confirming everything Fuchs had assumed.

After they paid their checks, Berger returned to his room to prepare for the journey. Fuchs, meanwhile, went off to the post office to telegraph Spitzkopf. He informed the detective that he would be returning to Zell am See by the afternoon train, accompanied by none other than their person of interest, Fritz Berger.

Soon after Fuchs and Berger met each other again on the platform at Bad Reichenhall, the train pulled into the station. And almost as soon as it left, it arrived in Salzburg.

The two men shared a compartment but spoke little. Berger was too lost in his thoughts for casual conversation. It was not hard to tell that he was quite agitated. Uncharacteristically, Fuchs was not putting on any kind of character this time nor wearing a disguise. He did not think it necessary, as he was traveling between small towns, out in the provinces, where he was confident no one would know him.

But he was mistaken. And that mistake landed him in deep trouble.

When they arrived in Salzburg he saw someone waiting on the platform. It was the bellboy from the hotel at Zell am See, the very one whom Spitzkopf had suspected of also being involved in this affair. Fuchs wanted to make his escape, but he could not. He was right beside a window, directly beside Berger, and the bellboy had seen him.

When they alighted from the train, Berger and the bellboy withdrew at once into the depot's waiting room while Fuchs remained behind on the platform, carefully considering his next steps.

He burned with curiosity to find out what this terrible twosome might be getting up to next. The bellboy would obviously be warning Berger that Fuchs was one of the interlopers who had taken such a keen interest in the case of the drowned girl. It was possible that the duo would not even be continuing on to Zell am See but rather would simply make a break for it, never to be seen again. He would probably be well advised to keep a close eye on them so he could detain them as soon as they tried to fly the coop.

But then he thought, "What if all of my worries are for naught? This bellboy saw me just yesterday in Zell am See. How could he explain my having suddenly turned up in Reichenhall, and now returning? Surely he'll think that he must be mistaken in thinking that I was one of the fellows examining the body yesterday."

And so Fuchs decided to let the matter slide and continue on to Zell am See as planned, just as if he were not bothered by a thing.

He would not speak further to Fritz Berger, though. The man had been joined by another acquaintance after all, and, anyhow, he and Fuchs had not exchanged more than a few words on their prior journey, from Reichenhall→Salzburg.

CHAPTER SIX
Fuchs Outfoxed

THE TRAIN REMAINED at the station in Salzburg for three quarters of an hour to allow for a customs inspection to take place, having just crossed the German-Austrian border. When the conductor rang his bell and announced "All aboard!" for those traveling to Zell am See, Innsbruck, Bregenz, and other destinations in the Austrian Alps, Fuchs eyed Berger and the bellboy getting into a car near the front of the train.

He wasted no time and climbed right into the same car, settling himself into another compartment, though quite close to them. He knew he had to maintain his watch.

As the train started rumbling out of the station, though, Fuchs got to thinking that his initial suspicions may have indeed been unfounded. The bellboy had surely not recognized him, for if he had, these two would not have continued on with such apparent peace of mind toward Zell am See, where a welcoming party may have been eagerly awaiting them—a welcoming party with handcuffs at the ready.

At the midpoint of the journey from Salzburg to Zell am See, the train had to pass through a tunnel around a hundred meters in length. Fuchs was sitting quietly in his chair, altogether minding his own business, when the train entered the tunnel. Suddenly everything went dark. At that moment a bar of iron connected with his skull with such force that he immediately lost consciousness.

His head had been cracked open, and soon the small compartment he had been occupying was filled with his own blood.

When the train left the tunnel and the eyes of his compartment mates were met with this horrific sight, they raised a hue and cry and pulled for so long on the emergency stop cord that the train was forced to screech to a halt.

There was clamor and commotion and cacophony everywhere you turned. But it seemed no one could do a thing. The few others who had been sitting in the compartment with Fuchs swore on their lives and their mothers' lives that they absolutely and positively had nothing to do with this hideous attack—indeed that they had not even seen nor heard a thing and were without a clue as to what had happened.

Nothing could be done in the open field where the train had stopped anyway. And so the train proceeded onward, pulling into a station where the fading Fuchs was carried out and left in the care of a local doctor who bound his head wound and took pains to resuscitate him.

It took a good long while, and when he finally did succeed, Fuchs was so weak, and spoke so faintly and indistinctly, that it was impossible to hear him and learn who he was and what his business had been on the train.

He was conducted to a hospital, where the doctor warned the staff that it might be several days before anything about him could be learned—other than the fact that he had been gravely injured.

Once Fuchs had been borne out of the train, the train got moving again. All any of the passengers could talk about was the shocking incident that had just occurred en route. At around four that afternoon, Spitzkopf turned up at the depot in Zell am See, awaiting the train from Salzburg and expecting for both his assistant, Fuchs, and the suspect, Berger, to be on it. But not a soul would have guessed it was he. No one would have taken a glance at this old man—with his silvered hair and the long gray beard, the golden pince-nez balanced upon his nose, hunched over as he leaned upon a sturdy cane—and guessed it was that Viennese super-detective, so famously agile of body and mind.

Spitzkopf had been informed that the suspicious bellboy had suddenly disappeared from his work at the hotel. The detective assumed he had taken the first train he could out of Zell am See to go and meet his chum. And so Spitzkopf made sure to be at the station when Fuchs was set to arrive, eager to hear his assistant's information on either of these men.

But the train arrived and there was no sign of him. Instead of being greeted by the face of his assistant, he was met with the fine and dandy bit of news of what had happened to some unknown passenger on the train. Naturally, Spitzkopf assumed it must have been Fuchs.

But the other two men he had expected did not alight from

the train either. True, he had never seen Fritz Berger's face, but he would have of course recognized the bellboy, and he was nowhere to be seen.

Spitzkopf was faced with a mystery. But this much was clear: these two scoundrels must have recognized Fuchs, figured out who he was, and decided to get him out of the way for a while as they themselves took flight.

But where to look for them? What was to be done next? He had never before been confronted with a set of circumstances quite like it.

For some time he remained standing there at the train station, turning the matter over in his head and trying to hit upon a plan of action. Finally he decided: "The first thing I must do is go and see my Fuchs. Before anything else, I must find out how he's doing. And maybe I'll glean some helpful details from him. These birdies won't be flying long—they've dug their talons into the wrong detective's assistant . . ."

CHAPTER SEVEN
At the Tunnel

SPITZKOPF WAS on the next train out of Zell am See and made his way to the small hamlet where Fuchs was convalescing.

He could not engage him in serious conversation, as Fuchs was not quite lucid yet, but he did take the opportunity of thoroughly examining his wounded head. The doctor told him that the injury was not life-threatening but the patient would have to be on strict bed rest for at least two weeks. He had been severely debilitated by the loss of blood.

It was clear to Spitzkopf that there was not much he could do by remaining there. When he learned that the tunnel where the assault took place was barely half an hour's journey by foot from the local train station, he decided he would use the remaining daylight hours to walk there. Maybe he would find some trace of the vanished murder of crows.

His instincts told him that these crows had taken wing as soon as the train stopped in the open field just beyond the tunnel. They would not have dared to travel on to the station with the other passengers.

His instincts were clever things. As he walked up to the tunnel, his hawk's eye narrowed in on something at once: the impression of fresh footprints in the grass. There were two pairs of them moving in a line. Spitzkopf knew it must mean two people on the move, and moving quite briskly, as each pair of footprints was a considerable distance from the next.

"It's all clear to me now," the detective thought to himself. "Berger's chum, the bellboy, must have joined him partway through the journey from Reichenhall, at the connection point in Salzburg. Fuchs would have acted indiscreetly, forgoing a disguise, so the bellboy surely recognized him. And in order to rid themselves of this nuisance, the pair decided to attack him en route, when the train passed through the dark tunnel.

"There is no path forward for me other than the one presented to me by these footprints. By following them, maybe, just maybe, I'll close in on the scoundrels, like they did my Fuchs."

And so he went along, carefully treading the exact same path that the two men had before him. Their tracks extended quite a distance in the grass until they brought him to a broad river, at the banks of which the prints faded away.

"My once-solid idea of where to go has now turned rather watery, it seems," Spitzkopf said to himself. "Even here where the riverbed is dry it's hard to pick out any specific footprints—one can see the ground's been well-trod. There must be a lot of foot traffic around these parts. And these two might not have even walked along it; they could have taken a carriage from here for all I know."

For the moment all Spitzkopf could think to do was walk

along the riverbank. The sky began to darken. He walked for nearly half an hour when he heard a horse-drawn conveyance clattering toward him. He remained where he stood as this farmer's wagon drew up, then he called to it: "Reckon I could hitch a ride to the nearest train station?"

"Well, sure," said the man. "Hop on in."

Spitzkopf hopped in. Then he thought he might try to chew the cud a bit with the farmer. "Is it a good ways away to the station, or nothin' but a stone's throw?" he asked him. "You get a lotta folks makin' their way over yonder, in gen'rul?"

"Ain't far, no," said the farmer. "No more'n an hour's drive from here. Funny thing, this is the second time I'm carryin' passengers 'round here today. Right after the clock struck noon, I happened to bring two young gents to where they were headed, folks I met along the way jist as I did yerself.

"But unlike you, my word were they in a rush! Offered to tip me extry jist for drivin' my ponies along fast as they could muster. So I whupped 'em on, you can bet I did, fast as my whuppin' arm could swing that lash. And it still weren't enough for these two!"

Spitzkopf listened keenly, then thought he would try milking the farmer for some further details: "And to what station d'ya reckon you brought 'em to, if you don't mind a body askin'?"

"Not to any kinda station!" said the farmer. "Naw, it was to the next village over I took 'em. They skittered out at the first inn they done lay their eyes 'pon."

"Well, gosh darn it, if that's so, take me to that village too!"

The farmer turned to look at him with a pair of eyes big and round as milk pails: "But you said you were makin' for the train station!"

"I was, see, but I think those were my old pals what you were ferryin'! And I'd sure like to see 'em, I would."

"Doesn't make a lick o' difference to me," said the farmer, pulling his reins in a different direction.

Within half an hour the wagon pulled up at an inn situated in a piddling little village. Spitzkopf scurried out of the carriage and moseyed on up to the inn, as the farmer giddied up his horses off into the middle distance.

CHAPTER EIGHT
The Cinematograph

UPON ENTERING the inn, Spitzkopf did not see the two men whom he had been seeking, nor did he wish to go and inquire after them right away. He thought a more indirect approach to learning their whereabouts would be more expedient.

By now, night had settled thickly over the landscape. After the intense heat of the day, it was now relatively cool outside, and the inn soon filled up with rural folk looking to enjoy a few hours of company and comfort.

Spitzkopf spent half an hour sitting at a private table set against the wall, nursing a glass of beer and silently watching and listening to the jawing and joking of the gathered rustics. Then a peasant with a whip in his hand barreled into the inn and demanded a beer.

"Heya, Michel," another asked him. "Where ya been?"

"Jist been on a little journey, that's all," said Michel. "To Grünbüttel.[17] Real lively crowd they've got there today. They've brought down a magic cinematograph, conjurin' a whole slew o' comic scenes enough to make a body bust a gut."

"All right, but what in tarnation brought *you* there?" the other peasant continued his questioning.

"Well, that coupla slickers what were here earlier, they asked me to give 'em a lift over to them parts," Michel answered. "Real fine gents, upstandin' kinda fellers. Gave me a real upstandin' tip, too."

This was like music to Spitzkopf's ears. "Again the mention of two strangers who arrived at this inn today," he thought. "Again a mention of a healthy tip. I should think these are my fellers."

As far as he knew, the small climatic spa town of Grünbüttel was not far from the locality in which he now found himself. If he put a little spring in his step, he figured, he could be there within three quarters of an hour.

He did not tarry, and after placing the few coins for the beer he ordered onto the bar, made his way out of the inn. He thought better of hiring one of the farmers inside to conduct him to Grünbüttel in a wagon. By the time he would have been able to settle on a price and they to bring around their horses, he could already have been halfway there. No, it would be walking this time, though not mere walking—the detective took giant strides, rocketing forward on his own two feet, blazing across the darksome night.

On the way he passed by a small forest. Screened by its deep shadows, he disrobed and donned a short jacket and lightweight pants. He was keen on being able to move even more comfortably and briskly, and in these changed habiliments the bellboy would be less likely to recognize him, seeing as he had been wearing more formal clothing back at the hotel in Zell am See. That prior ensemble he tied together into a neat parcel and left under a tree.

At around nine o'clock Spitzkopf was able to just make out, twinkling from a distance, the first lit-up buildings of the town.

Grünbüttel is a tiny health resort not far from Salzburg. It is tucked away in a pocket of the tall surrounding mountains and frequented by cure-seekers in the summer for its clean, vivifying air. These guests do not come in hordes, however. There is simply not the space, as Grünbüttel has only a handful of suitable lodgings. The place has much more the feeling of a small, sleepy rural hideaway than do competing resorts like Zell am See.

From Salzburg, however, on occasion, choral societies do come down to pay a visit to Grünbüttel, along with theatrical groups and those exhibitors who charge a couple of heller to peek at a rotating panorama of some charming artistic scene. These show people would put on a performance or two and make good money out of the cure-seekers desperate for an evening's diversion in the quiet town.

On this day it so happened that a man with a cinematograph machine had made the journey down from Salzburg. His stock in trade was projecting a succession of glowing images onto a screen, what they call these days a "motion picture." All of the visitors to Grünbüttel, along with a sizable clutch of farmers from the town and its environs, came to witness this entrancingly novel exhibition.

Spitzkopf reasoned that his two stray birdies would also be there, attracted by the shiny object. Probably they had planned to spend a few days roaming around the mountains so that they would be spotted at a number of different locations, giving them a workable alibi if called to account for what they had done to Fuchs.

As always, Spitzkopf had reasoned accurately. He had managed to follow their every step. And now they were practically in his grasp. When he took his first steps into the hamlet of Grünbüttel, he heard music being played some distance away. Following the lilting sounds, he soon found himself in front of a large barn that served the residents and cure-seekers of the place as a sort of theater, a venue where they could enjoy a variety of little entertainments.

This particular night, though, was a very big night at the barn. The cinematographic demonstration was truly something, and the most fascinating, extraordinary pictures promised to be on view. Spitzkopf bought a front-row ticket and entered the so-called auditorium. None of the other patrons noticed him. Their eyes were too busy chasing the succession of marvelous images that passed across their vision, projected onto the swath of white linen that covered the front wall.

Spitzkopf's eyes focused elsewhere. Though it was dark inside, the sharp-eyed detective did not fail to pick out the two men he was looking for. They were also seated in the first row, watching the flashing images. And these images were most diverting and diverse indeed. There was an express train whizzing by the patrons' eyes. Why, it seemed as though it could come hurtling right into the auditorium, flattening all of those present under its tremendous wheels.

As the train departed, it was followed by a comic scene: a policeman chasing a thief across the rooftops of a city. The thief darted ably from roof to roof, and the officer had little hope of catching him. Then the thief jumped down from one rooftop to the ground below as the officer remained above, twiddling his thumbs. The thief flipped the obscene gesture of the fig up at the officer, then scurried off into a nearby garden.

As soon as he disappeared from the screen, a couple of young newlyweds appeared thereon, in their bridal chamber on the night of their nuptials. The bed was still made up. The newlyweds began to slip their clothing off. The viewers' curiosity was now thoroughly aroused, thinking they would soon be treated to the most piquant scenelet yet. But just as things were about to get extremely interesting, the image suddenly cut out, and the audience was left there sitting like a bunch of fools, mouths hanging open . . .

The show had left all of them quite excited. They applauded heartily after each of the moving pictures came to a close, waiting impatiently for the screen to brighten again and the next one to begin. Naturally, the projected images were far less interesting to Spitzkopf. He was only thinking about how he might turn this unusual context to his advantage.

Soon it flashed across his mind with all the brilliance of the cinematograph. Just as quietly as he had come in, he now crept out of the room, exiting through a back door and exchanging a few words with the owner of the cinematograph machine, who was also the "director" of this show. He then silently reentered the auditorium and, while the viewers were still lost in rapturous contemplation of what they had just witnessed, slowly and furtively approached the two men he had been watching.

After the last images had disappeared from the screen, the house lights had gone up. The program was over. But now the director stepped onto the stage and announced that, "In honor of you very dear guests," he would be projecting yet one more playlet, a most captivating picture, one that would present a truly gripping dramatic scene to the eyes of the assembled.

This news was met with a raucous chorus of bravos as the viewers hung on the edges of their seats, eagerly awaiting this extra picture. The room went dark again, even darker than it had been during the earlier projections. And on the linen sheet, a lovely mise-en-scène now came into view: a glowing moon in an inky midnight sky. In the background there was a sea, its waves set a-rippling and a-roiling by a stormy wind. Then came a little boat, tossed about violently on the waves. And in the boat: a young woman beside a stylishly attired young man sporting a black beard.

Suddenly the man lunged at the woman and tried to force her overboard into the churning sea. But the girl grappled with him, doing all she could do to defend herself against this watery fate. The man took her by the throat, closing his fingers tighter and tighter around it. She tugged at his beard, clawed at him, bit down hard on his hands. But the man was stronger than she was. Now holding her in a viselike grip, and assisted by a brutal shove with his foot, he succeeded, and she went tumbling backward into the deep.

The viewers were deeply affected by these images. They contorted their faces as though the girl's painful struggle were their own and averted their eyes, unable to look any more at the sickening scene.

But affected even more than the rest was one of them in particular—one of the very men we have been following. Spitzkopf's steadfast gaze was fixed upon him, just as if this man were actually the night's featured entertainment. He saw how as soon as the present scene flashed forth on the screen the man started to fidget uncontrollably, clearly disturbed, looking for all the world like someone who wished to escape from a blazing fire.

His unease was heightened at the moment when the horrible tussle between the man and the woman broke out, and by the time the man viciously pushed her into the water, he had lost all control, and a jolt of terror sent him leaping out of his chair.

Spitzkopf, who was standing just behind him, put a hand on his shoulder and said with studied calm: "Startle easy, eh, pal?"

"I can't take a second more of this horrible picture!" the man cried. "I have to get out of here."

But as soon as he said it, the cinematograph stopped whirring and the lights went up. The viewers all turned around to see a deeply agitated man shaking like a leaf and batting at the air in front of his face as if trying to drive away some unseen phantom. "I don't feel well!" he shouted. "Somebody bring me water!"

"Yes, water!" Spitzkopf chorused. "The waters of Lake Zell!" That only intensified the man's convulsions. His legs threatened to buckle beneath him, and he fell back onto his seat.

The other patrons could not understand what was happening. They looked on with astonishment as they witnessed the new guest standing over the trembling man, laying hold of him with both hands and fixing him with a steely, unwavering gaze.

Then the doors of the barn opened and in stormed two gendarmes, the only two employed in the village. They stationed themselves at the entrance and watched for what would inevitably transpire, though they did not intervene. The audience members, meanwhile, were so enormously intrigued by the goings-on that they did not notice the officers' entrance.

Finally the man Spitzkopf was pinning down regained some

composure, rose to his feet, and said to his companion: "Come on, Georg. I'm nauseous from the heat. Some fresh air would do me a world of good."

"Do you know where you might have mislaid a bit of your beard?" Spitzkopf deadpanned.

"What are you on about? What's any of this to you?" the man asked gruffly.

"Why, it's so much to me," answered Spitzkopf, "that I just so happen to have kept a hair from your beard for safekeeping right here in my notebook. If you've been missing it, I'll gladly return it to you!"

At which the second scoundrel—the bellboy we know all too well from the hotel at Zell am See—readied himself to charge at Spitzkopf, a heavy iron bar appearing in his hand.

"Lay off my friend," he screamed, "or I'll crack your idiotic head in two!"

But before he could move an inch, a loaded revolver was pointed directly at his face, and Spitzkopf said to him in even tones: "That iron bar's seen a lotta action lately, no? It did you a good turn earlier in the rail tunnel not far from here, I believe. Why yes, I can still see the bloodstains on it. You won't get far with it on me, though. Put down the bar or I'll treat you to some metal myself—lodged right between your ribs."

The detective then cuffed the first man's wrists, and as he did so noticed how battered and bruised his hands were. "You didn't have such a sweet time of it with that girl, I see," he said, a sardonic smile playing on his lips. "Seems she bit you but good!"

Only now did the other patrons begin to understand what might have taken place. They silently watched as the gendarmes arrested the two men, shackling them and leading them out of the barn. Spitzkopf followed them to the village lockup, and a couple of the most curious audience members joined him. For them, the show was only just beginning.

CHAPTER NINE

Waves of Grief

THE WHOLE business of the incriminating motion picture was Spitzkopf's idea. When he went to speak to the cinematograph's operator, he identified himself as a detective and described the case he was investigating at present. He asked the operator whether or not he may have a draughtsman on hand who could quickly sketch up a few pictures that could be projected to the audience.

It turned out that the operator was himself a dab hand at illustration, and in but a few minutes he had some pictures at the ready, done up almost exactly in accordance with Spitzkopf's specifications. However, instead of the two people grappling with the girl on the boat, he had just drawn one, owing to the constraints of time. After all, he still had to make the necessary preparations for projecting the images onto the screen.

The missing detail did not matter in the end. The plan went off like a charm—the picture was the thing wherein they caught the conscience of the culprits.

The chief perpetrator, upon seeing the images, gave himself away by his violently distressed reaction to them. His companion gave himself away too, threatening Spitzkopf with the same iron bar with which the man had attacked Fuchs.

The two scoundrels were left with no choice. They confessed to everything, and the complete story was now made clear.

Fritz Berger had identified Fraulein Hedwig Taussig as a potential conduit for taking his revenge on the factory manager Rudolf Kolb, whom he despised so deeply. Hearing that Fraulein Taussig, Kolb's bride, was on holiday in Zell am See, he hatched a plot to journey there, make her rather too-intimate acquaintance, and carry out his will using her as a target. Upon arriving in the town, he realized that the bellboy at the girl's hotel was an old school chum of his who had been expelled from the academy and forced to give up his studies permanently on account of some rather troubling stories that had been told about him.

Berger had the bellboy let the Taussig girl know that a friend of her fiancé's had turned up in Zell am See and wished to speak with her. Now, Hedwig's plan that day had been to go boating on the lake with a friend of hers, but hearing that a treasured colleague of her groom was in the vicinity, she hurried off in his direction.

Berger cut a dashing figure and presented himself as charmingly and elegantly as he could. The girl was easily persuaded to join him aboard a little boat for a short cruise around the lake. The bellboy duly arranged for them to take out one of the hotel's vessels, and the company of three launched off, though from a distant corner of the lake so that no one would spot them.

When they reached the middle, Berger started to pester the young woman for her affections. But Hedwig rejected his advances vigorously. She reproached him for taking advantage of her being on this boat with him, so alone and so defenseless. But each defiant word of hers provoked his rage, which soon turned murderous. By nature he was a wild, manic young man, and the bellboy, whose own character was made up of rather less than noble parts, incited him further. He teased Berger for allowing a Jewish girl to insult him so shamelessly. And so, seeing that no one was about, the two men seized the young woman and dashed her into her watery grave.

When they reached the shore, Fritz Berger made his getaway, leaving Zell am See, while the bellboy returned the boat to its usual spot at the hotel's docks. Berger had promised him a generous gift for his cooperation, and it was in the bellboy's own interests to keep his mouth shut about the matter anyway, seeing as he was an accomplice to the crime.

The two of them had thought they would emerge from the whole thing with barely more than a scrape. But when the bellboy saw how deeply interested Spitzkopf and Fuchs seemed to be in the corpse, he figured they must be undercover policemen. He immediately sent word to his friend that things had gone south, telling him to return at once to Zell am See so that the two of them could form a plan for evading the authorities.

But after dispatching the express letter, he realized that it might be more expedient for him to go and meet his crony in Salzburg so that they could begin to discuss everything sooner. As to how matters progressed after that, the reader has already been treated to a full picture of it—and one glimpsed upon a linen sheet in a flash of terrific light, too.

Fritz Berger and the bellboy soon received their sentence. They were both condemned to death by hanging.

The body of the drowned Fraulein Hedwig Taussig was transported to Prague, where it was laid to its eternal rest.

Old Herr Heinrich Taussig never recovered from the shocking tragedy that had befallen him. He had taken ill as soon as his daughter was found and remained so for some time, dying a few months later. He willed a substantial portion of his wealth to Spitzkopf for his heroic efforts. Rudolf Kolb also richly compensated the detective for all he had done to identify and capture the men who had murdered his bride.

Fuchs was confined to a hospital bed for two weeks following his attack, but once he left was in fine fettle once more. His robust constitution had helped him to get over the potentially lethal injury, and before long he was back to work alongside Spitzkopf, greeting new cases with a will that you might justifiably describe as *iron*.

Issue 14: The Missionary

העפֿט 14. פרייז 20 העלער.

מאַקס שפּיצקאָפּף
דער קעניג פֿון די דעטעקטיווס.
דער וויענער
שערלאָק האָלמעס.

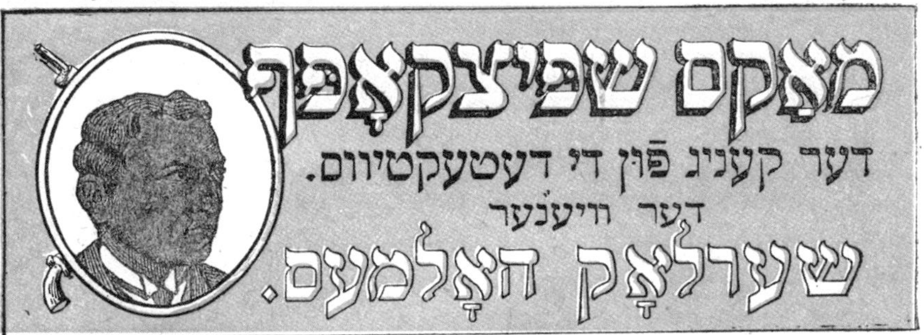

דֶער מִיסִיאָנֶער.

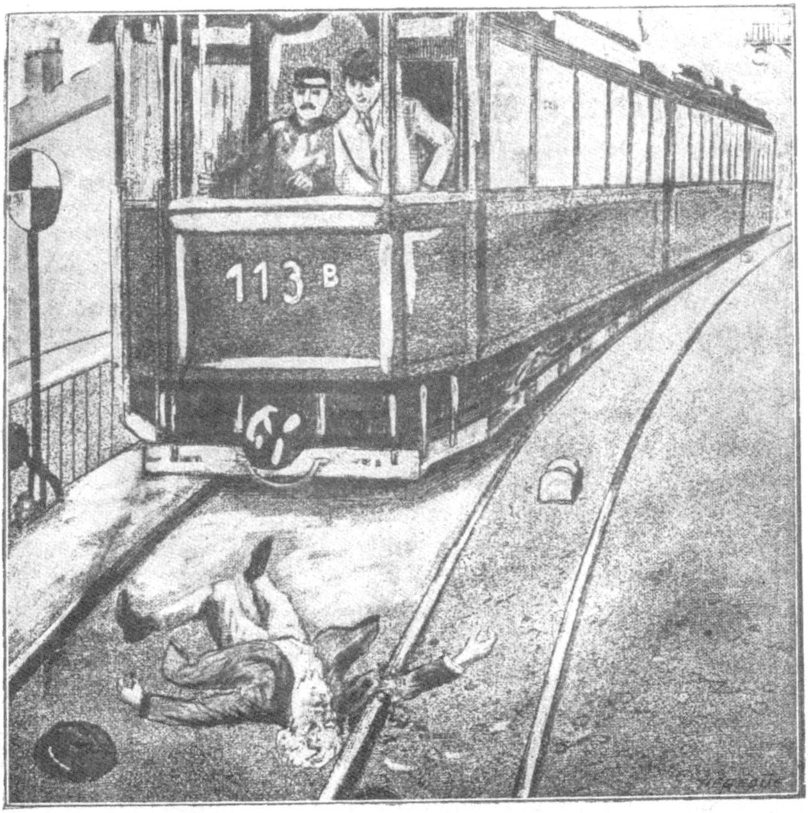

פלוצים בלייבט דער טראמוואַי=וואַגען שטעהן. אויף די שיענעס ליעגט אַ טויטער מענש, שפיצקאָפף דערקענט תיכף אין דעם טויטען דעם אָבערדירעקטאר פֿין די מיסיאָנס-אַנשטאַלט.

The Missionary

CHAPTER ONE
A Perilous Mission

EVERYTHING IS AT sixes and sevens today in Nurazvo, a small shtetl in Galicia.[18] The whole place is abuzz and abrew, boiling like a teakettle. People are scurrying this way and that, in the marketplace and through all the streets of town. Beside the little prayer houses clutches of townspeople are gathered, and they stand around chattering, bickering, battling.

For something terrible has occurred.

The rabbi's son, a man only eighteen years of age, a worthy Torah scholar with a fine head on his shoulders, has fled town, see—and joined the missionaries.

The rebbetzin, his mother, cannot stop fainting. Her husband is practically catatonic, unable to speak a word to anyone. Their relatives' hands have gone red from too much wringing. Though the calendar does not give the date as the ninth of Av, the Jews' national day of mourning, it might as well be, for all the shtetl of Nurazvo's lamentations over this recent tragedy.

Rabbi Yosele Feuermann was a very learned man, a distinguished Talmudist, a deeply pious and passionately devoted Hasid—simply put, a Jew with all the fixin's. He raised his only child, Osherl, in the only way such a man could have. He made sure this son had the best teachers, and once he had grown up a little, the rabbi assumed the task of educating the boy himself. His intent was to make a true prodigy of him so that Osherl would one day—may it be in a hundred and twenty years' time—be worthy of inheriting his father's position as rabbi of the shtetl.

The child's brilliance made it clear that Rabbi Feuermann's efforts were not in vain. When he turned thirteen, on the day of his bar mitzvah, Osherl delivered a long and complicated homily on the weekly Torah portion, which he had written without help. All present were simply flabbergasted by his sharply tuned mind and keen insight.

From that day on the rabbi no longer taught his son. He merely left him to sit in the study house and pore over the holy books on his own. But from time to time, on Shabbos or a holiday, he would engage the boy in an intellectual colloquy on holy topics, at the end of which he was always convinced of Osherl's astounding progress and readiness to enter the rabbinate.

What the rabbi did not know, poor soul, was that in addition to sitting for hours on end in the study house unspooling intricate passages in the Gemara, occasionally Osherl undertook learning of rather a different variety. When no one was watching, he would steal away to visit the new teacher who had recently moved to the shtetl and take lessons from him in Polish and German.

This teacher was something of an old-school maskil, an adherent of the Jewish Enlightenment, the sort for whom the very word *Enlightenment* had a sacred resonance. When you went to him to learn German and Polish, you did not just learn to read, write, and understand them, no siree. You were immersed in philosophy, in novels, in poetry, and in such other higher pursuits as fire the fantasy of a pupil and veritably make his head spin.

It was this sort of education that Osherl was treated to by the teacher; he was treated to so much he had fairly stuffed himself with it, and the meat of his earlier life seemed pale food in comparison. His native shtetl began to feel too narrow and crowded; he lost his appetite for Talmudic argument and Biblical verses. His broadened imagination had ushered him into another world, where every human being is free and lives freely, allowed to enjoy an existence unbounded from all constraints.

For a good while the boy led a sort of double life. Among his father and friends and people in the town, he was still the same Osherl they knew—the dedicated Torah scholar and upstanding youth who sits all the day and half the night in the study house preparing himself for becoming a rabbi like his father before him. But to himself, in the innermost chambers of his heart, he was quite a new Osherl, a "cultivated young gentleman" with brand-new ideas and brand-new ambitions—and a brain doing dizzying somersaults trying to contain it all.

This carried on for several years without anyone being the wiser. That is, until a certain occasion when the growing blister popped wide open . . .

A missionary from London descended upon the shtetl and began distributing free books among the Jewish boys. Our Osherl, upon hearing that literature was being given away, dropped in on this strange visitor. He was eager to get his hands on a couple of volumes, imagining they might be some truly precious and important objects.

When he entered the missionary's lodgings, he also entered into a conversation with the man on various global issues. This experienced man, who had traveled the world over and knew so many splendid things, made a profound impression on Osherl. It was not his religious teachings that particularly intrigued him—Osherl was too clever for those—but rather his discourse in general that further whetted his appetite for seeking his freedom and traversing the earth to do whatever pleased him. And so he found himself susceptible to the missionary's offer to take him along on an imminent journey to Hamburg, and the boy accepted.

Osherl carried out his preparations for the trip under such a veil of secrecy that no one was aware of his plans. Then one fine day he vanished, and not a soul knew whither.

The day he disappeared, the rabbi and rebbetzin were beset

with the most sickening fear that their only child, God forbid, might have been in an accident or been harmed or wounded one way or another. But soon folks around the shtetl began to whisper that this or that person had seen him entering the stranger's rooms on various occasions. Soon it became the principal rumor: Osherl had gone off to join the missionaries.

Meanwhile there was not a trace of the boy. He had fallen like a stone into the deepest waters. He did not write, and no one reported the boy having come to say his goodbyes or breathing a word about what his intentions might have been.

Finally, a few days later, the rabbi received a letter. In it the missionary related the news that his son was with him and that all would be "right as rain."

Now the thing they had most dreaded was corroborated. There was nothing they could do. Osherl had been bewitched. And no one could rescue him from such dark magic.

The rabbi sat shiva for his lost son, mourning over him for seven days and seven nights. To him the boy was dead. The rebbetzin regained her composure more easily and managed to find a modicum of calm amid the frightful storm.

As for the shtetl, however, the case was still on the lips of all its idlers and layabouts for a good many weeks following. It was all they could talk about: that fine young scholar Osherl, who had gone off to join the missionaries. Such a good and bright and talented boy, *nebekh*, poor creature . . .

CHAPTER TWO
The Big Business of Saving Souls

THE MISSIONARY who had come to visit the shtetl was one of a group of emissaries dispatched by societies in England, America, and parts of Germany. These societies consider it their goal to propagate the Christian faith among the nonbelievers of the earth. They concentrate their efforts primarily on those peoples of Africa and Asia whom they consider wild and uncivilized.

Millions are spent yearly on such holy "missions." In New York, London, Hamburg, and other great cities, there are schools and institutions where missionaries are carefully trained, and then, once they know all that is necessary, they are deployed to various countries so that these foreign lands might be conquered for Christendom.

These missionaries' work consists primarily of distributing dogmatic pamphlets and giving speeches on the glories of the Christian way of life. Most of these people are deeply committed Christians themselves and consider it their sacred duty to bring the heathen unto the light. As for whether such work is worth their trouble, whether these missionaries actually succeed in winning very many souls for their savior, is not precisely known. But considering the enormous expense these societies take on in pursuing the work, this much is clear: that the price of a soul rings up to quite a few kreuzer indeed.

Some of these societies' leaders eventually got it into their heads that it would be a good idea to try and "save" Jewish souls too, and they soon began to set up "missions to the Hebrews." This work turned out to be even more expensive than that carried out in more remote climes to the south and east—and more thankless. The Jew who could be persuaded by one of these missionaries to convert to Christianity is rare as hen's teeth. And the singular case that does is always some sorry creature who agrees to be baptized only for money or for some excellent position that has been promised to him.

Those operating these missions to the Jews are themselves some of the most dissolute characters on earth: people devoid of moral character, people who prefer to be supported by some outside flow of easy cash rather than actually work for their supper. As soon as they can string a few words together, they are anointed as missionaries, travel off to those cities and towns where Jews are to be found, and start disseminating the propaganda of their societies.

In the big cities like New York, London, Constantinople, Jerusalem, and so forth, these societies run a number of schools, hospitals, and other so-called beneficent institutions. But their true aim is not beneficence, not charity, not mankind—but rather mission-kind. These schools deceive poor families into sending them their children, promising to give them a fine and free education and provide them with fine jobs once they complete their studies. The mission hospitals accept Jewish patients and treat them at no cost. But once they are in, the missionaries seize upon the opportunity of hammering the heads of these children and patients with stories and sermons, trying to seduce them onto the path of conversion.

There is even a whole body of literature prepared especially for these missions and written in Yiddish—some even in Hebrew. Books, magazines, pamphlets, all printed expressly for Jewish audiences and handed out to them for free.

A standing position for a representative of the missionary societies is set up in each of the major cities, and this person "works" on behalf of his organization. But there are also dozens of traveling missionaries, who venture out into the tiny shtetlach and spend a few days in each, peddling free literature and thinking up ways of enticing Jewish youth to join their religion.

All in all, the whole enterprise is run like a big business, with central offices and branch offices, directors, inspectors, principal agents, and traveling salesmen. And all of these directors, agents, and salesmen make a pretty penny from their work. That money goes straight into their own coffers, although the spiritual returns are very low, netting a conversion as seldom as they do.

When they do manage to save a Hebraic soul, they are naturally unable to do so by methods that are strictly above board. It is impossible to win over a Jew to the belief that the Christian religion, especially this mishmash of hokum that the missionaries preach, is superior to the Jewish religion. Such fools simply do not exist among the Jewish people.

And so whenever they do accomplish a bit of "business," it is with one of these: a youth who has gotten it into his head that he would fancy a bit of travel, a bit of seeing the wide world; a young man who does not enjoy matrimonial harmony with his wife and cannot see a way out of being with her other than joining this group of strangers; or simply some nincompoop with dollar signs in his eyes who dreams of the easy commercial potential in assuming a new religion. As for these Jews who become missionaries—well, the less said about them the better. They lack even the basic courage to identify publicly as Christians. Rather, they claim that they alone are the "true Jews"—ones who have accepted the true Jewish redeemer, that is. They raise their eyes up to the heavens with such perfect sanctimoniousness that any Jew who comes into contact with them cannot help but retch out of sheer disgust.

At times these missionaries succeed in luring some Jewish youth onto their path. This person is confined in their institutions as a sort of captive and not allowed to leave until he surrenders himself entirely. If this unfortunate prisoner does not possess enough good sense to try and disguise his intentions a little—to play it cool and sweet-talk about his "true faith" just enough for his warders to believe him and so not keep such a strict watch over him—then he is doomed to endure the most wretched of torments during his confinement.

It was into just such a pit of doom that our own Osherl had recently fallen.

CHAPTER THREE
In Hamburg

Osherl had not been persuaded to accompany the missionary because he believed with a sincere faith in the muddled mishmash of dogma the man mixed up for him—he was much too smart for all that, as we know. No, he did it because within the first few seconds of his meeting the missionary, Osherl saw a way out of the double life he had been leading for years. It was only on the path this missionary trod, it seemed, that he would be able to strike out and be liberated from the suffocating society in which he was raised.

He did not stop to ponder long; goodness, he hardly even thought for a moment. He made a quick decision and the next day, poof—he was gone.

The missionary, overjoyed at having caught such a fine kosher fish, brought him to the Prussian border, where they awaited the director of the man's organization. When the director arrived, he conducted the boy to Hamburg, where this society's headquarters were located.

On the first few days of his sojourn there, Osherl walked around in a dreamlike trance. The society's building with its many chambers, its grand reading room and dining room, its sprawling garden—it all pleased him marvelously. He was in ecstasy.

What he did not notice was that the sprawling garden was bordered by a high stone wall and that the finely hewn arched doorway of the building was kept locked and that a guard stood beside it at all hours, not letting anyone leave without explicit permission from the general director. Nor did Osherl notice that all of the faces of the young men who stalked the society's halls were downcast and streaked with tears, not reflecting even a sliver of the jubilant light that emanated from his own face. Not until a number of days had passed did Osherl finally open his eyes. But by then it was too late.

Osherl's room was on the third floor of the institute. His windows looked out onto the garden. One afternoon, seeing how lovely the garden looked from that vantage point, he decided to leave his room and go down for a stroll. As he descended, lost in his own thoughts, he did not realize that he had passed right by the landing that would have taken him into the garden.

He just kept walking down, down, down until he found himself at the entrance to the cellar.

As he stood there he thought he heard a kind of muffled moan. He put his ear to the door and could make it out more distinctly. It was a horrible wailing, a heartrending scream, like the sort emitted by a person who is being mercilessly beaten. It was muffled only by the thick cellar walls. Osherl remained fixed to the spot, a violent tremor running through his body. He was petrified with fear. He felt he could not move an inch in any direction.

Then the door opened—and out came one of the directors, accompanied by one of the institute's domestic staff. When they saw Osherl standing at the door, the director greeted him with a couple of resounding smacks to the face, spluttering with rage and barking at him: "What is it you want?" Osherl was too terrified to speak a word in response.

"Aha! So we've got a sniveling little snoop on our hands, eh?" the director roared. "We'll whip that temptation out of your system soon enough!"

Before Osherl could make any kind of answer he found himself being lifted into the air as the servant's hand closed tightly around his collar. Then the cellar door was opened again and he was flung inside, followed by the tormenting twosome.

Osherl was bewildered and paralyzed with fear. He could not comprehend what was happening to him. He started to feel lightheaded. Losing all ability to act, he could only submit to being acted upon however his captors wished.

"Now spit it out. Who are you, and what is it you wanted to see down here?" the director asked.

Osherl said nothing.

"So it's gonna be the quiet game, eh?" said the director, stamping his feet. "Well, I can play that too. And my winning strategy? If you can't open your mouth, I'll have it forced open. Rudolf, you know what to do."

Osherl heard everything the man said but as if filtered through a dream. He did not see the servant removing a short whip from the wall. He did not feel the man hauling him over to the wall, or shoving him down onto a sofa, or tearing off his clothes. It was only when he received the first vicious lash to his half-naked body that he came to, and a howl of anguish tore from his throat as he cried out to his absent mother in Yiddish: "*Oy gevalt, gevalt! Mame, mame!*"

He could not count how many lashes he received. But this much the boy did know: when the flogging was completed, he found that his every limb and muscle throbbed in horrible agony; that his arms, his legs, his entire body were crisscrossed with black-and-blue excoriations; and that whenever he dared to move, a jolt of pain seared through him from head to foot.

In a sort of daze he looked around and saw that he was back in his room, lying upon his bed. He could not understand what had been done to him or why. Thoughts raced in his despairing, delirious mind.

And in his heart, he felt the first pangs of regret for the step he had taken.

CHAPTER FOUR
Looking for Osherl

"A DEAD PERSON is eventually forgotten. But the living can never be."

So they say, but our Rabbi Yosele Feuermann, Osherl's father, actually did take pains to forget his wicked son, this youth who had brought so much shame upon him.

But it was not possible. He had forced himself to sit shiva for the boy, but his heart he could not compel to quietly mourn. He tried to never speak Osherl's name, but in this too he failed. Try as he might, his only child's face always came floating back to his mind's eye, all day and all night. Osherl appeared in his dreams with a face bathed in tears, his arms outstretched to his father as if the boy were begging for mercy, begging to be liberated from evil hands.

For a few days the rabbi was able to restrain himself from telling anyone of the sad thoughts that plagued his mind or recounting the dreams that came to him at night. But eventually he could not hold back any longer, and he unburdened his heart to his wife, the rebbetzin. She instantly broke forth into piteous sobs.

"It is the same for me," she wailed. "I too see my Osherl every night in my dreams . . . his sad face . . . his pleading eyes . . . They break my heart. I can't take it anymore."

"We've made a mistake," said the rabbi, "in not bothering to try and find out what happened to our son. Perhaps the whole scandalous story is a lie. Perhaps he never went off with the missionaries at all. Perhaps some terrible misfortune has befallen him."

Upon listening to these words, the rebbetzin's cries became only louder and more uncontrollable.

"But all's lost now," the rabbi went on. "Where could we possibly seek him? Whom could we ask about him? Who knows what on earth might have happened to him?"

At that moment the rabbi's personal attendant came in to tell him that his cousin Reb Motele Schwartz was at the door. Motele Schwartz lived in the same shtetl as the Feuermann family. He was a successful merchant and was in the habit of making the journey to Vienna several times a year to buy up new stock. Although he was a fairly ordinary, pious Jew, due to his dealings with strangers from other parts of the Austrian Empire and his frequent travels, he was more well-versed in worldly matters. And so the rabbi, upon hearing his cousin's name, was seized at once with the notion to consult with him about his son's case and to ask him what the best course of action might be.

Reb Motele had come on quite a different, private matter. And he was in a hurry, as he meant to leave for Vienna on the next train. But upon seeing the rabbi and rebbetzin in tears, he asked what had them in such a state, and the rabbi told him everything. "To tell you the truth," said Motele, "it disturbs me that you didn't bother looking for your precious son. Even if it were true that he went off to join the missionaries, it was surely just some momentary insanity that took hold of him or some absurd brain wave. Osherl is too clever to be talked into something like that. And he's too decent a boy to sell his soul for a bit of money."

"What are you on about?" asked the rebbetzin. "He's been bewitched, and that's the end of it. It's well known that the missionaries practice this kind of sorcery. As soon as they get one of their nasty books into a boy's hands, he's compelled to join their ranks, and then it's nothing doing—not a soul can free him after that."

"Cut the poppycock," said Reb Motele. "Their magic is just money, nothing more, nothing less. With a mountain of mazuma, you can mesmerize any man. But precisely because of that, I don't believe that Osherl was indeed seduced by them. I know the boy very well. He wouldn't have done such a thing for a few shiny coins."

"You don't believe in the tricks these missionaries have up their sleeves," the rebbetzin interrupted. "So let me tell you a story I heard from my grandmother, may she rest in peace. You won't doubt me then.

"Some fifty years ago, a young Jewish man from the city of Lemberg went off to join the missionaries too. They took him with them to Constantinople, gave him his own little house for him to seclude himself away in and study their teachings. But before he got to work on that, they had him gulp down a glass of water in which they'd placed a bit of paper—and told him to swallow the paper right along with the water.

"He drank the water—but left the paper in his mouth. And as

he was alone in the house he locked the door, took the paper out of his mouth, and unfolded it on the table. And then, right before his eyes, it was transfigured into a little snake that grew and grew by the minute and was soon not so little but rather a towering, venom-spitting serpent.

"Then this serpent slithered down from the table and installed itself as a sentry at the door, preventing the boy's escape. When he tried going to the window, the serpent did too and got there in a second. And for a while they chased around the house like that—until the serpent sank its venomous fangs into the boy.

"At that moment, the boy realized that he hadn't put on his tzitzis. He bolted over to grab a set out of his luggage, flung it over his head, and cried out our eternal prayer *Shema yisroel*—Hear, o Israel! As soon as the words flew from his mouth, the serpent hurled itself out of the window and crashed to the ground, dead.

"'You're lucky,' the boy's rabbi later told him, 'that you didn't swallow the paper. If you had, the snake would have emerged right there in your throat, and you'd have had to become anything the missionaries wanted you to—if you didn't, the snake would have choked you to death.'

"So you see, Reb Motele," the rebbetzin concluded, "it cannot be denied that these missionaries are infamous warlocks."

Reb Motele could not help but laugh. "I don't see anything of the sort," he said. "I've merely been listening to an outlandish story. And I'd rather not listen to its like any longer. A waste of time."

"Then what are we to do?" the rabbi asked. He also did not quite believe in the supernatural explanation. "You're a worldly fellow, cousin. Give us some advice. There's no one else I can confide in. You're the only one."

"What kind of advice can I give?" said Reb Motele. "The only thing to do is make every effort to find out where Osherl is now. When we know that, we can think about how we shall go about rescuing him."

"*Nu*, that goes without saying," said the rabbi. "So give me some advice on how I might find him. Maybe we ought to inform the police?"

"The police won't do a thing," Reb Motele answered. "But wait a minute. I've just had an idea. A few months ago I read in the newspaper about this Jew from Vienna, Max Spitzkopf, who pulled off quite an extraordinary trick in the shtetl of Dorokhov—and not the sort your wife has described—this year before Pesach. There was a blood libel case there; the Jews were suspected of slaughtering a little Christian girl to use her blood in their matzos. Spitzkopf found out who actually did it—and saved the entire community.[19] I think this Spitzkopf could help us here too."

"How do we get hold of him?" asked the rebbetzin.

"I'm on my way to Vienna now," said Reb Motele. "I'll ask around to learn where he lives and tell him everything. If he takes on the case, I am certain he'll be able to discover where they've hidden Osherl. This man is the investigatory profession's greatest artist."

"I cannot begin to fathom what sort of person this may be or how he can find out such things," said the rabbi. "But if you think that he can help us, you may petition him. As long as he doesn't ask for a fortune. As you know, we are not wealthy."

"I'll talk to him; then we'll see," Reb Motele answered. Then he bade the rabbi and rebbetzin farewell, shouting out as his wagon sped off, "*Zayt gezunt*—be well!"

"May you have a safe journey!" they called back to him. Then they added: "And, please God, success . . ."

CHAPTER FIVE

The Sorrows of Young Osherl

FOR A NUMBER of days Osherl lay sick in his bed, recovering from the punishment he had been dealt. He had not seen any of the missionaries since then, just a doctor who paid him a visit twice daily and the servant who brought him his food.

His mind was still addled. He did not understand what was being done to him. "Why did they whip me?" he asked himself. "And what do they want from me now, keeping me pent up here like a prisoner?" But as hard as he thought, considering this possibility and that one, he could not arrive at any answer.

It was only on the fifth day after the doctor's having judged him to be perfectly well that the servant came in to tell him to get dressed, then led him down to the director's offices. The director looked at him with a pair of furious green serpentine eyes, just as if he wanted to bore a hole through him with his glare. Osherl stood there for a few moments, stock still, until he took courage and asked: "Why was I whipped?"

"Because we don't need spies here," said the director in a steely tone. "And those won't be the last lashes you'll receive either."

Osherl could not stop himself from trembling out of utter fear, even as he made his retort: "What do you mean, spies? I wasn't spying."

"So what were you doing at the cellar door?"

"I was lost in my own thoughts and had accidentally gone all the way down to the basement instead of out into the garden. Then I heard somebody crying out. And so I stayed to listen for where the noise was coming from."

"So you see now. You spied. Oh, don't worry, we know all about little spy pigeons like you. You fly over here to stick your beaks into what we're doing, try to find out everything you can about it so you can tell all the Jewish newspapers and try to wreak havoc with our reputation.

"But we make quick work of such pigeons and will soon have you roasted. Yes, you heard some screams from the cellar. It so happens that was a spy just like you. He's been down there for weeks. And every afternoon gets his daily portion of lashes. But it doesn't have to be that way. This birdie's stubborn and refuses to change the tune he's chirping. You'll end up just like that if you keep on with your little quips."

"I'm not making any quips. I didn't come here to spy. And you still haven't asked anything of me, so I'm not being stubborn in refusing it."

"We'll see about all that. Do you wish to convert?"

"Convert?" Osherl stammered, shaking even more than he had been. "But the missionary told me I didn't have to. I could remain a Jew and still . . ."

"That's true enough. You don't have to convert right away to do missionary work. We don't force people. We wait until they come to the true faith on their own. But with you it's different. Since we suspect you of being a spy, we're going to put you to the test. See whether you're sincere about wanting to join us. And so you will have to convert. Immediately. Only then can we be sure you're not a spy."

Osherl was so sorely confused he could barely move. It was only just beginning to dawn on him on what a truly miserable, inescapable situation he had landed himself in. A hundred thoughts flew through his brain with every passing second. He wanted to yield to these people out of a desperate compulsion to shield himself from the lashes. But he soon realized he could not and decided on a different course: not to yield but rather to find a means of letting his father know what had happened to him and then beg to be rescued.

But the director soon shattered this reverie when he broke in: "You can plainly see how obstinate you're being. How you don't want to bend to our will. An incontrovertible sign that you're a dirty spy, one we'll soon be dealing with exactly as we ought."

"I'm not being obstinate!" Osherl cried in a voice of anguish. "I don't know what you want from me. The missionary in my town promised that golden expanses would open up before me . . ."

"Indeed. You'll receive all you've ever dreamt of if you convert," the director dictated coldly. "And if not, you'll be kissed by the lash for as many days as it takes for you to kiss your old religion goodbye. But I'll be merciful. I'll give you three free days. At the end of them I'll demand your answer: yes or no.

"You won't get to spend these three days in your room. No. You'll be locked up in a dark chamber of the cellar. We've got to keep surveillance pigeons like you in a tight cage. Wouldn't want you flying away, would we?"

Osherl had barely a moment to answer before the servant approached, seized him by the collar, prodded him down the steps, and bundled him into a dark cellar chamber, locking the door behind him. Osherl could hear the man turning the key, then trudging back up the stairs. As the sound faded away, Osherl, overcome with the torments of the day, crumpled to the floor, unconscious.

He had not the slightest notion that the mission to free him was already well underway . . .

CHAPTER SIX
Spitzkopf to the Rescue

Reb Motele Schwartz took care of his business errands in Vienna, then started making inquiries about Max Spitzkopf. When he arrived at the detective's office, he related to him the whole story of what had happened to Osherl. The detective listened in silence. Only once Reb Motele had finished did he ask, "And what is it that you wish from me?"

"For you to find the runaway and bring him home. You'll have done a tremendous mitzvah."

"Could you not tell me what country this missionary came from, the one who put these ideas into the young man's head?"

"No. The man was barely thought about during the time he was in the shtetl. No one knows what evil wind carried him there."

"A very bitter pill indeed. How am I to search for the boy if I don't even know what country he may be in?"

"Are you truly saying that not even you can do anything to help us?" Reb Motele asked, his voice breaking.

"You need not lose all hope just yet. It will be difficult, that's all. But not impossible. Come back to see me early tomorrow. In the meantime I'll try to find out where this missionary came from before he began making his rounds in Galicia."

Reb Motele left and Spitzkopf called for his assistant Hermann Fuchs to apprise him of the case.

"That's as easy as apple strudel," said Fuchs after hearing all the details. "There's a Viennese missionary who frequents the coffeehouse I like going to. I think I can find out everything from him."

"In that case, don't delay for a second," said Spitzkopf. "Get me an answer by tonight. You know I'm set to leave tomorrow for Berlin on another urgent case, and I'd like to have this matter taken care of before I go."

Within half an hour Fuchs was sitting in the famous Café Zweig.[20] But this was not the same Fuchs who could be seen sipping a coffee there once a day. He was now a provincial, pious young Jewish fellow from some far-flung Galician shtetl with tightly wound *peyes*, a long black frock coat, and a yarmulke resting underneath his big black hat.

Russian and Polish Jews are commonly seen congregating at the Café Zweig, so the appearance of this new yeshiva bocher surprised no one. Fuchs looked all about him, trying to catch sight of the missionary who came there daily, always occupying the same spot in a corner beside the window.

And indeed there he was. Wasting no time, Fuchs went to sit down one table over, ordered a coffee, and buried his face in a newspaper. It did not take long for the missionary to strike up a cordial conversation with this young man who had attracted his notice. He asked the disguised Fuchs what his name was, where he came from, and what he happened to be doing in Vienna.

"*Nu*, *nu*, I'm called Yerukhem Grünzweig," said Fuchs, "and I am commink from Boyberik.[21] I spent de best years of mayn life in the study house, but now I'm tirink of det world, and I'd like to go off to study at de goyishe uniwersities. But I don't got even a kopeck for all det, so I'm commink here to Vienna, vere I am vishink dey'll give a poor bocher a bisele gelt for me to achieve mayn sveet dream."

"And has fortune been smiling on you here?" asked the missionary.

"No! Verever I'm turnink, dey gib mir de kalte shoulder and I am ending up mit gurnisht, nuttink! All of dem say dere're already enuff yong yidishe boyess here who've decided to go in for school studies. Det dey vant I should be learnink a trade instead. But I refuse to do dis, no metter vot happens tsu mir!"

The missionary's eyes positively glittered with unabashed glee. "Well, isn't this a nice little fish that's wriggled its way into my net!" he thought to himself. "The more desperate the young herring, the more quickly he'll be kippered!"

Soon he directed the conversation onto the topic of religion and eventually made it known what his own line of work was.

Fuchs listened to him with apparent interest so that the missionary believed he was right there with him. His apparently keen interest led the man put the question to him directly, asking Fuchs whether or not he might wish to become a missionary himself.

"Such young men as you could spread the Holy Word very far and wide indeed," the man said. "You're bright and learned and could soon rise to the rank of director. You'd receive a handsome salary and lead a quiet, most agreeable life."

Fuchs pretended to give his hearty consent to the plan, devouring all the details and drinking up the missionary's visions of what the young man's path might look like and what his life could become. His first step would be to travel off to the society's institute in Hamburg, where he would be trained in everything he needed to know.

"Hamburg?" Fuchs gasped. "Un here I tought all missionaries are commink from London!"

"A network of German missions to the Jews is currently operating around Galicia," said the man. "And all of the missionaries serving in it were dispatched by our institute in Hamburg. They're doing top-notch business out in the Jewish towns in Galicia. Why, just a few days ago a friend of mine succeeded in sending the son of a Galician rabbi off to Hamburg."

That was all Fuchs needed to know. He declared himself ready to enter the institute.

The missionary did not let him out of his sight. When they left the café, he took Fuchs home with him to spend the night. As soon as they awoke, he personally conducted Fuchs to the German border, where a representative of the institute in Hamburg awaited them.

And although the missionary from the coffeehouse watched Fuchs like a hawk, fearful lest the young man should begin to regret the steps he was taking, Fuchs managed to eke out an opportunity to keep Spitzkopf up to date. While still at the Café Zweig, he excused himself so he could ring the detective and tell him what he had learned and inform him that he planned to set off for Hamburg the next day. Spitzkopf was pleased with the nice little job his assistant had pulled off and informed him that as soon as he finished his business in Berlin, he would skip over to Hamburg to free the rabbi's son.

The following morning Reb Motele paid Spitzkopf the visit the detective had requested. Spitzkopf told him, not wasting many words, that he hoped soon to have the boy liberated. The game was afoot. "But this must all remain a secret," Spitzkopf warned him. "No one is to know I've taken the case on. All my work could be for naught if you blab."

"God forbid!" Reb Motele vowed. "I shall be as silent as the night."

CHAPTER SEVEN

Telling Tales out of School

Leopold Kunstmann, the general director of the Hamburg missionary institute, was sitting at his desk in his impeccably furnished office, gazing at the pile of letters, books, and newspapers that towered precariously in front of him. Sitting across the desk from him was his secretary, Julius Krumbein.

Kunstmann was an older man, a robust sixty-something. His hair had gone gray and his face was haggard, but from his eyes there still flashed an untempered fire.

Krumbein, the secretary, was somewhere in his forties and powerfully built, with a ruddy neck and broad shoulders. You could tell from looking at him that he lived well and seldom deprived himself.

These two characters were at the moment deep in conversation. And both appeared to be highly agitated.

"I promise you, Kunstmann, I'm not going to wait any longer!" Krumbein bellowed, punctuating his words with a wild flurry of hand gestures. "You're making a fool of me!"

"It won't be but a short while now," Kunstmann responded, gritting his teeth so as to respond as calmly as he could. "You've gotten so much from me up until now. You can be sure you'll get the rest."

"What do you mean by a short while, huh?" Krumbein roared. "I cannot, will not, wait a minute more! You know very well that I'm not here for my own pleasure!"

"But wait you must. There's no need to rush things. What've you got to lose, eh? Seems to me you've managed to save up a nice little nest egg for yourself in the years you've spent here."

"That's none of your affair. I've squirreled away no more than you have! You think I don't know that you've got your own wheelings and dealings around here? Just like before, back in your hometown, when you were a flesh peddler? There you sold off innocent girls to the whorehouses, and here you sell Jewish souls. But whether it's this or that, you're always raking it in!"

"Don't you dare remind me of my past sins," Kunstmann thundered, unable to contain himself any longer as he sprang up out of his chair. "You know how much you have to thank me for. If not for me, you'd have dropped dead from hunger long ago!"

"Well, well, well, look who's playing Moses the Liberator now!" Krumbein laughed. "You forget that if I hadn't kept mum you'd have been rotting away in prison now for years. You've got such a rank pile of crimes on your conscience that just turning holy roller wouldn't have been enough to save you from the pokey!"

"And what do you want now?" Kunstmann asked, regaining some of his calm. "You want to have me thrown in jail after all these years?"

"If you don't give me what I'm due, I'll do whatever I damn well please! And I won't wait!"

"You forget your own mountain of debt you've yet to climb! All the phony IOUs you wrote out to folks over the years . . . when were you planning to make good on those, eh? You haven't got a leg to stand on—how dare you threaten me! It would be better for us both to give up our gripes and try to live in harmony.

"But it's a bit of dough you want, eh? Fine, then. It's just about in the oven. As soon as I've managed to knead this Galician kid into converting, I'll be nicely frosted with a prize from the society, and I can get you anything you need, hot and fresh. So just wait a few days longer. That tough bun's been proving in the cellar for three days now. I'm certain he's become more . . . pliable."

"Very well. You've given the boy three days' time to rise to the occasion, so that's what I'll give you too. But I'm not going to just loaf around here for any longer than that."

That was the sort of holy conversation that played out among the two overseers of the missionary institute in Hamburg. They both spoke their peace looking each other dead in the eye, listing off the sins each one had committed in his time before joining the ranks of the missionaries.

Naturally, they did not know that every word they spoke was being overheard by a person they did not know, someone keenly intent on learning the secrets of the missionaries.

That person was none other than our own Hermann Fuchs.

Two hours earlier he had arrived in Hamburg, where he was led immediately to the general director, who meant to welcome him into the institute. But the director was busy with his secretary, having the argument that we have just been listening in on. Fuchs had to wait in the adjacent vestibule until the conversation was finished.

And so, waiting there all alone, to pass the time he pressed his ear to the door. His sharp sense of hearing allowed him to catch every single syllable the two men uttered. Now he knew exactly what sort of people he was dealing with. He also realized that this Galician boy who was undergoing a forced conversion and being kept in the locked cellar must be the same young man he and Spitzkopf had been tasked with finding and freeing.

"These louts are making my work easy," he thought. "I've learned all their secrets without a lick of effort."

Soon the two men's conversation had come to an end. They made up, and the secretary bade the director a friendly goodbye. Now Fuchs heard the director calling for the new guest to be brought in.

Fuchs played his role beautifully. He laid on the same sob story for the director that he had told the missionary in Vienna the day before. The director was highly pleased with him. "This is just the kind of boy I like," he mused. "I'm not going to have any trouble with him, no indeed."

"Let me have you shown to a room where you'll be able to get some rest," he said to Fuchs in a voice dripping with hospitality. "In two days I'll be sending a highly capable teacher over to you. He shall instruct you in everything you must know. I shall hope to soon be making a very fine man out of you."

After being led to his room, Fuchs took some time to rest as he thought up what his next steps ought to be. The general director, meanwhile, remained behind in his office, delighted by the new boy he had been brought—and equally delighted at the thought of the pretty penny he would be awarded by his society as a prize for the fresh new soul that had come flopping right into his net.

CHAPTER EIGHT
Bound for Glory

THE THREE DAYS the director had given Osherl to change his mind had passed. Osherl had not been allowed to leave the cellar. He was kept in a dark chamber and brought food twice a day. During this time he had ample opportunity to reflect on what he had done and for deep remorse to wash over him for the choice he had made to leave home. And he had come to a firm resolution: continue disobeying the director's commands.

"He can kill me if he likes," Osherl said to himself. "But I won't give in. I'll stay a Jew for as long as I live. Even if I'm dealt ten times as many lashes as they've given me already. Even if they mete out the most horrific tortures, throw all the torments of the Inquisition at me . . . still I won't surrender. I'll take it all as a worthy punishment for my sins, for being so foolish as to let myself be deceived and led astray."

On the third day the general director had the boy brought up to see him. "Well, my son, have you reconsidered?" he asked Osherl.

"Yes, I have," Osherl answered in a clear and untrembling voice.

"So you agree to be baptized?"

"No."

"And that's what you call reconsidering?" said the director

with a smirk. "Seems to me the three days in the cellar didn't do the trick. Have you forgotten the whipping you were administered just the other day? Would you like a second helping?"

"I must tell you the truth," said Osherl, his resolve steady. "What I've reconsidered is the step I took in coming here. I shall never become a missionary."

"Well, well! You think it's as easy as saying 'I don't want to'?" the director fumed. "No! You'll return to that cellar to rot for as long as it takes for you to change your mind! Your willfulness shows me that you really are a dirty spy. I'll make sure you're given a whipping today that leaves you with such an acrid taste in your mouth that you'll lose all appetite for life itself."

"Do as you wish," Osherl answered. "You won't prevail."

The director pressed his electric bell and in came two musclebound servants. The director gave them the sign, and before Osherl had a moment to look around they were holding him by the arms and legs.

"Take that rat underground where he belongs!" the director ordered, shaking with rage. "Down to the very deepest pits of the cellar!"

"Think you can carry this off so quietly?" Osherl said. "Don't kid yourself. The whole institute will know what atrocities you're committing!"

And with that Osherl began to scream at the top of his lungs: "Help, help! Murderers! Thieves! Save me!"

His outcry was so piercing, so anguished, that it set all the residents aquiver. The students of the institute raced, terrified, from their little rooms and out into the corridor, trying to figure out where the screams had come from. The director gnashed his teeth. He had not imagined the boy would dare to do this.

"Just you wait, you dog!" he vociferated. "I'll teach you how to show respect!" And he seized the boy and stopped up his mouth so that his screams could not be heard.

The servants moved quickly too, throwing a sack over him

and tying it fast at his neck so that Osherl could barely breathe. His cries were muted. All he could do was gasp and wheeze like someone who was being drowned.

The monstrous director reissued his order for the boy to be brought down to the cellar. A number of the young students of the institute were now standing in the corridor and witnessed a large sack being carried out of the director's office and hauled away. They had no idea as to what it might contain.

The director, who was following behind the servants, fulminated against these onlookers: "What are you standing around here for, you idlers, you good-for-nothings? Go back to your rooms and study!"

Quite startled at his outburst, the boys followed his command and retreated to their chambers.

But one of them stayed in the corridor. He knew exactly what was going on.

This, of course, was our own dear Fuchs.

Fearing what evil might be wrought upon the boy he had come to free, fearing even that Osherl might be killed down in the cellar, he decided that there was only one thing for him to do: free him now, without delay. But amid the confusion of the scene, he forgot to act with the necessary discretion and, rushing at the director, he shouted: "Release that boy or I'll shoot you dead as a worthless hound!" He pointed his loaded revolver directly at the man's face.

For a moment the director just stood there as if turned to stone. He could not believe what he was seeing and hearing. But he quickly came to and, making another sign to the servants, took to his heels, running off between them.

Fuchs gave chase, his gun still aloft, but when he got near the servants they grabbed hold of his arms and shoved him so forcefully against the wall that the revolver fell from his grasp. Then all three of the men, the director together with the servants, tackled him like a pack of wild animals. Fuchs defended himself as best as he could, demonstrating the fighting will of a man a thousand times larger than he, but he could hold out only so long. They overpowered him, tying up his wrists and ankles with rope.

Then they brought him down to the cellar right along with Osherl, flinging him into another pitch-dark chamber and making sure to confiscate his second revolver, his electric torch, and the other sundry equipment he had on his person.

Bound and unable to move, Fuchs lay upon the stone floor. Any hope of being saved seemed choked by the damp, suffocating air of the cellar.

Meanwhile the director, panting from his exertions, dragged himself back up to his office.

"My word!" he said to himself. "I've certainly not seen the likes of this before. Seems we're dealing with a crack band of spies. They've decided to have quite a go at us. All I'd like to know is whom they're looking for and what it is they want. Is it me they're after? Some detective's recognized me at last, perhaps, and wants to send me off to prison?

"It's no good, no good at all! I've got to get away. I've saved up enough money to live on. The rest I'll leave here for the others."

And after managing to calm himself down somewhat from all the hullaballoo, he started to formulate a plan for gathering all his earthly possessions, the whole kit and caboodle, and making his getaway.

CHAPTER NINE
The Old Missionary

The general director of the Hamburg missionary institute was sitting in his office, lost in his thoughts. He had not been able to find a moment's peace in the two days that had passed since the smash-up with the pair of young men who had joined the mission.

Frightful notions haunted him . . . his conscience tortured him . . . he was afraid of his own reflection. Evil dreams ruined his sleep and evaporated any doubt that remained within him: he must leave this place. He had already made all of the necessary preparations for his absconsion. He had gone to the bank to withdraw the money he had hoarded during his years at the institute in Hamburg and stashed it inside a leather pouch, stitched fast and concealed underneath his shirt. He had burned all of the documents that could implicate him in his crimes. His plan was now to disappear without warning so no one would have the vaguest notion as to what had become of him.

Only one loose end needed tying up before he could make his escape: settling his account with Fuchs, that new recruit who had turned out to be such an infamous spy and had gone so far as to threaten the director's life.

He did not have to wait long. That very night the institute's executive committee—the general director himself, the two assistant directors, and the secretary—would be meeting to decide on the spy's sentence.

And that sentence was sure to be something tremendous, something terrifying, something truly Inquisitorial.

Now, in the institute there was a small chapel in which the new recruits would eventually be baptized. But this chapel also served a different function. In one corner, beside a table covered with a black cloth, there stood a large flat stone. When a button on the table was pressed, the stone, commanded by a hidden mechanism, would open in two, and anyone standing upon it would plummet into a gloomy dungeon fifty meters below. The floor of that dungeon was fitted with razor-sharp spikes, and whoever fell upon them would be impaled and killed instantly.

This chapel had been built in the good old days, when the Inquisitors held Germany in their bloody grip. In that period, in the Middle Ages, the dungeon served as a brutal execution chamber. The missionaries later took over ownership of its enclosing chapel, which became part of their institute. They carried on the proud tradition of the former stewards of the chapel by making use of the same execution method their forebears had initiated. Who was subjected to it? Those poor souls whom the missionaries feared would betray them and tell the outside world of all the abuses that took place within the institute's walls.

And this same grisly death was now in store for Fuchs.

Tonight was to be his inevitable sentencing. And as soon as the hungry spikes had pierced through this traitorous scoundrel's flesh, the director would be off, leaving Hamburg with nary an auf Wiedersehen. This was what the general director was now daydreaming about—until a knock at the door woke him from his reverie.

"Come in!" he called out.

The door opened and in came one of the servants, escorting an old, stooped man hunched over a cane. His hair and beard were white as snow and his body bent almost in the shape of a question mark, but his eyes sparkled with a brightly burning flame.

"Who are you and what do you want here?" asked the director.

"I am a missionary from the London Society for Promoting Christianity Amongst the Jews,"[22] the stranger answered. "I have been working for the last twenty years in the Caucasus, preaching the Gospel to that region's so-called Mountain Jews.

"But I am now on my way back to London, as I have grown old and begun to feel the weight of my years. And as my ship is to leave tomorrow evening, I wish to ask your leave for me to spend the night in your institute."

"It would be the greatest honor," the director said, flashing a flattering grin. "I am greatly pleased to have such a worthy guest in our midst."

He then asked the old man to have a seat and ordered for a

good bottle of wine to be brought in. They both drank and toasted to each other's health.

The old missionary regaled the director with one interesting tidbit after another about the Caucasus, about its exotic inhabitants who lived in the highlands of Azerbaijan astride the Caspian Sea, what their lives were like, and how he managed to carry out his holy mission among them.

"And God be thanked, all my toil was not in vain!" said the old man. "In fact I had great success. I led over a thousand Jews to accept the hallowed sacrament of baptism and was richly rewarded for it by my society back home. And because of this, I shall be able to spend the last few years I have left on earth living comfortably, free of worry."

The old man's account made a strong impression on the director. A certain thought dawned on him. Perhaps he should make moves forthwith to assume the old man's post in the Caucasus—where no one knew him. He would have not a soul to fear, not a single suspicious face. And he would be able to rake in a nice new fortune there, even more than he had to his name now.

And so he lavished the old man with obsequious smiles, and seeing that the man responded in kind, he thought he would be so bold as to put the question to him right there and then: whether or not it might be possible for him to take over the pensioner's position.

"Certainly it would be possible," said the old man. "The London Society has not yet named my successor, and if you'd like I could introduce them to you and recommend that they choose to send you to the Caucasus. To that end, if you're ready, I'd suggest you join me on my trip to England, and we can get right to it."

Naturally, the director agreed to the plan. He was already set upon leaving this place, after all, and this was as good a way as any. Perhaps even the best way. And before he left, he would ask one of the assistant directors to pay out a nice bundle to the old dotard as a show of gratitude for leaving the position in the Caucasus to him.

The director and the old man went on chatting about all manner of things, among them the sentencing of the spy that was to take place later that night.

Meanwhile the sun had gone down, and the director showed the old missionary to a room to get some surely much-needed rest. At the door the director promised that after the spy's sentencing, he would return and invite the missionary to join him for supper.

CHAPTER TEN

A Sentence Written in Blood

THE CHAPEL was half submerged in darkness. But in one niche, standing upon a large table covered with a black cloth, two black candlesticks filled the room with a dimly flickering, spectral light.

Four men sat around the table, dressed in long black cassocks with black masks obscuring their faces. It was a most chilling tableau they presented to the eye. In front of the table stood our own Fuchs. His wrists and ankles were still bound, and he wore a long white robe.

"Wilt thou confess who thou art and what thou didst desire from us?" asked one of the masked figures. His voice he could not mask, however—it was clear that this was the director of the institute.

"No," answered Fuchs, in an unwavering voice.

"Then none other than death itself awaits thy person," said the director. "There is but one recourse remaining to thee: immediate baptism and a solemn vow to remain within the walls of our institute for a period of ten years, where thou shalt be kept under close surveillance at all times."

"I won't be doing either. I'm not afraid of dying, not a bit. You lot are all much older than me; you've much more reason to fear death than I do."

"You haven't lost what you Jews call chutzpah, that's for certain!" the director snarled. "But you'll be eating your kosher words before long, I can assure you."

And with that he smashed down the button installed at the end of the table.

Fuchs could feel the floor underneath his feet wobbling and the stone he was standing on starting to give way. He was beginning to slip down through the crack that had suddenly appeared within it.

At that moment an unknown man sprang out from behind a column, seized Fuchs by the collar, and with a powerful effort wrenched him away from the widening void.

The stone at this point had opened up completely, revealing a large hole a meter wide. The four judges of the tribunal were in utter shock, as if welded to their seats. The stranger now pointed two loaded revolvers in their faces and his voice boomed out: "You damn dirty scoundrels! So this is the kind of sacred work you get up to, eh?"

The director snuffed out the candles, throwing the chapel into total darkness. But the stranger drew out his electric torch and illuminated the room once more. Now he saw only three judges before him. The director had vanished through a back door.

The stranger leaped to the remaining masked figures, tied a thick rope around them, and kicked the tripartite parcel under the table. Then he took hold of the stunned Fuchs, carefully untied him, and said: "I'm glad I got here before it was too late. Now take this revolver and make certain that this gang doesn't budge. I've got to go and catch that old mangy dog who just hightailed it out of here."

And with that he dashed out into the street. Just as he did a tramcar came rattling toward him and he jumped on, intending to make his way as quickly as possible to the nearest precinct, where he could enlist the help of the local police in sniffing out the runaway.

But the tram rattled on for only a few minutes until it came to a dead stop. A corpse lay on the tracks. The mysterious man bent down beside the conductor and easily identified the body—it was the man he was looking for. He no longer had to pursue him.

Sprinting back to the institute, he found Fuchs standing where he had left him, keeping watch over the three bound culprits. "Ah! Master Spitzkopf!" Fuchs cried out with surprised glee. "What brings you here?"

"I always arrive at the right moment," Spitzkopf answered—for the unknown man had been none other than the detective all along. "I received no word from you when I was in Berlin and surmised that you must have gotten yourself into a bad scrape again. So I disguised myself as an old missionary from the Caucasus and wheedled out everything I needed to know from the director.

"I'm so relieved that I didn't arrive even a second later. My only regret is that the old rogue is dead. A dyed-in-the wool criminal he was."

"Well, now we've got to free the Galician boy," said Fuchs. "God knows how he's faring at this point."

"Right you are. Do whatever needs doing while I take care of these characters here." And with that Spitzkopf hauled the bundle of missionaries out from under the table and demanded that they tell him everything.

They gave up their entire tale, along with the key to the cellar where Osherl was being kept. Fuchs soon had the boy redeemed from his captivity, along with two other young Galician fellows who were confined. These two other students, well aware now of what kind of hell this was that they had fallen into, made their way back east and to their family homes that same day.

Spitzkopf turned over the assistant directors and the secretary to the custody of the Hamburg police. The director, of course, could not be tried—his trial had ended with the ferocious onset of a speeding tram. Running madly from the avenging angel that had appeared in the chapel, he had been run over by a streetcar and was killed on the spot.

Osherl made the journey home the following day. He quickly reconciled with his mother and father, the rabbi and rebbetzin of Nurazvo, and solemnly swore he would remain an upstanding and faithful Jew for as long as he lived.

Issue 15: Lady Luckless

העפט 15. פרייז 20 העלער.

די נאכטוואנדלערין.

האלט דיך איין! רופט שפיצקאָפף — די פרוי איז אונשולדיג.. זי איז היפנאטיזירט !...

Lady Luckless

CHAPTER ONE

The Diamond Ring

THE LEGENDARY Viennese detective Max Spitzkopf is sitting in his home office, deep in concentration as he makes his way through the giant heap of letters in front of him. He has only just returned, but a few hours ago, from a couple of cases that had taken him to Germany. There, in Berlin and Hamburg, he had again pulled off a couple of those extraordinary feats that have made him the legend he is.

Though exhausted from his travels, he had not gone immediately to bed. No, his first destination was his mountain of mail to see whether or not there might be some important bit of news and whether, indeed, he had to get right back to work.

A satisfied smile crossing his face, he can now be glimpsed pushing aside the opened envelopes and letters and saying to himself in a cheerful tone: "Thank God! Nothing too disastrous seems to have taken place in my absence. Why, I've barely missed a thing. Just imagine—perhaps I'll even be able to catch a bit of shut-eye after all of my exertions over the last few days."

Then, having disrobed down to his winter woolies, he stretches himself out on his canapé sofa and tries to sleep. It is a cold, overcast day in the middle of the snowy season, and outside all is damp and drear. But in his rooms, it is most agreeable and warm, and Spitzkopf soon dozes off.

This sweet slumber was to be short-lived. It had not been more than half an hour when the detective was awoken by the doorbell. With eyes only halfway opened, he sprang up out of the canapé and stepped into his slippers and robe, guessing that he was being paid some important visit.

He had guessed accurately. As soon as he turned on the electric light in his room, his housekeeper opened the door and in came a man dressed with great distinction, a most impressive-looking gentleman. Spitzkopf invited his guest to take a seat and asked him what he desired.

"My name is Baron von Schellenburg," said the stranger. "I have come to you, honored sir, on a very pressing, but also very discreet, case. I ask you therefore that what we say today be kept strictly confidential."

"That goes without saying," Spitzkopf answered. "I keep everything under lock and key. I can assure you that on my end you need have no fear of any unwanted divulgements. Now, do tell me what your business is."

"I am a very wealthy man," said the baron. "A few months ago I married the Baroness von Wellerstein, herself a very wealthy orphan. My wife is not only ravishingly beautiful; she is also highly cultivated and was given the finest possible education. I fell in love with her head over heels.

"She is worthy of such love. And I should know. I am a very cosmopolitan fellow and have enjoyed the opportunity of mingling in the finest society. I have never been lacking for female companionship, and I don't have enough fingers to count the number of well-born ladies who would have positively leaped at the chance to become my wife. But of all of these acquaintances, it was my beloved Helene who struck my fancy the most, and at our wedding I do believe I was the happiest man on the face of the earth.

"After our nuptials we embarked on a honeymoon trip to Paris, as well as Rome and other Italian cities. We saw one lovely panorama after another, *bellissimi*, the loveliest anyone ever set their eyes on, and returned home to Vienna last month.

"Then, two weeks ago, my wife announced, rather insistently, that she wanted to go to Monte Carlo. I had rather important business to attend to here in Vienna, and as I had been away from home for several weeks I found it very hard to leave town.

"But what won't a fellow do for his lady love? I gave in, and off we went.

"Truth be told, life in Monte Carlo didn't please me too much. I was well acquainted with the casino there, and so I knew it to be nothing but a bunch of smoke and mirrors for plain thievery.[23] So I didn't take part in the gambling and instead spent my afternoons and evenings in the company of a couple acquaintances of mine from Vienna who had come to Monaco for a bit of rest and relaxation.

"My wife visited the casino far more often but didn't actually play all that much, and when she did it was only for small change. Just to pass the time, you know. What little money she did lose bothered me not a whit, so I didn't try to get in the way of her enjoyment.

"Then, just a few days ago around midnight, I was walking back from the theater with one of my acquaintances. I found my wife headed back to the hotel too, on the way back from the casino—in the company of a horrid-looking, short little man. From the moment I first set my eyes on him I knew I didn't like him.

"When we were back in our room, I asked my wife who this man was. She told me it was a Parisian physician, a certain Dr. Farré, a very learned and well-educated man who would soon be named a professor at the university there in Paris. Though there was something about the man that irked me, I said nothing to my wife, as I could tell she liked him very much and found it very pleasant to spend time with him.

"Two days later I ran into the man at a coffeehouse and was astonished to notice upon his finger a highly valuable diamond ring that belongs to me. This ring happens to be an old heirloom in my family, and a very fine piece of work it is. The setting is something really rare, and it would be very hard to believe that there is another ring just like it in the whole world. So I went to our hotel at once, scrabbled about in my jewelry box, and what do you know? No sign of it.

"Now, my wife and I are the only two who hold the key to that jewelry box. It would be impossible for some unknown person to remove the diamond ring from it. So in those first moments I felt creeping up within me a horribly suspicious feeling about my wife. If she had been in the room then, who knows what frightful thing would have happened next. But she returned hours later, and so I had some time to sit with my findings and think the matter over. And the more I thought, the more it seemed to me that my suspicions were entirely unjustified: it was out of the question that my wife could have somehow been unfaithful to me with this Parisian character.

"His loathsomeness, his positively repugnant appearance, were already enough to render it unthinkable for a gentlewoman of such refinement, with such a highly developed feeling for the aesthetic as my wife has, to fall in love with such a one as he. Her sense of morals is no less keen, and so I simply cannot conceive of her being prepared to betray her husband barely two months after the wedding.

"And anyhow, even if it were possible, if this man had somehow managed to put the hex on her and she managed to forget herself entirely, it would be quite another level of insanity for her to have immediately gifted him my ring, this ring I hold so dear and would recognize from a mile away.

"In this way I arrived at the assumption that there must be a very knotty mystery at play here, one I would not be able to disentangle alone. When my wife finally did return, lively and laughing as ever, and I looked deep into her eyes, I saw in them such intense love and devotion, such tenderness and attachment to me, that any lingering trace of doubt left me. My wife is an angel, and I was ridiculous ever to think otherwise. I became convinced that there was some dark secret behind all this, and none but the most ingenious detective could find it out.

"As for how I got away, I decided I had to be dishonest to my wife for the first time since I met her and told her that there was to be an important meeting at my club today that I absolutely had to attend and she must therefore excuse me for three days and permit me to travel to Vienna.

"I figured she would by no means allow me to leave her behind in Monte Carlo and would likely demand I take her along with me. To my surprise, however, she did not resist the idea all too forcefully. All she did was cry a little and get a little peeved that I'd be leaving her alone in a foreign city. But when I suggested that she accompany me home, she explained that if it came to hauling all the way there and back again, she'd just as soon be on her own in Monte Carlo for the few days I was gone. So that's what she decided to do.

"This alone drove me nearly up the wall again. I already began to regret the plan I'd made to leave. But knowing that the longer the case remained unresolved the heavier it would weigh on me and the less I'd be able to endure this agitation to my soul, I firmed up my resolve to leave at once and, that same day, set off on the journey here.

"My first stop was to you, Herr Spitzkopf, confident in my belief that you will be able to solve this mystery that torments me so unbearably."

Spitzkopf listened to Baron von Schellenburg with the utmost calm and patience, not interrupting him even once in the course of his long narration. As soon as the baron had finished, the detective responded in an even tone: "I am quite ready to help you unpack this case, Herr Baron. But it will not be possible for me to do so from the comfort of my home. I must go to Monte Carlo and see everything with my own two eyes.

"Tomorrow morning we shall make our way there by the luxury train. We'll discuss the rest of the details once we've arrived. For now, though, there is but one thing you must know. I shall be traveling under the assumed name of Ludwig Goldthal. No one can know who I am nor even that I am traveling with you. Now head on home. I'll meet you tomorrow morning at the train station."

The baron took his leave of the detective with some cordial words. Spitzkopf, meanwhile, remained in his office, making preparations for the task ahead. No rest for the quick-witted.

CHAPTER TWO
Taking a Gamble

IT WAS FULL steam ahead on the luxury train to Monte Carlo.

Lulled to a delicious drowsiness by the long journey, the passengers lay back in the plushy seats of their first-class cabins and dozed. They had already become fast friends with their fellow travelers, already told everything about themselves there was to tell and asked everything there was to ask. Now they were silent, each wandering in his own solitary dreamland.

All morning they had been in raptures over the passing panoramas, the splendid landscapes that whizzed by outside their large windows. They had warmed themselves in the powerful rays of the burnished Italian sun. They had forgotten all about the reality that back home in Russia, or in Austria, it was bitter cold outside. And now, after night had fallen, there was nothing to do but sink into the soft embrace of the seat cushions and sleep. The imminent approach of glittering Monte Carlo had filled them all with a certain nervous anticipation, and they could no longer quite find it within themselves to carry on the expected confabulations.

In one of these first-class cabins, however, three gentlemen could still be observed deep in conversation . . .

"So, Herr Baron von Schellenburg," said one of their number, an older man with a long gray beard, "are you still not prepared to believe that there is a system by which one can become a millionaire through gaming the Casino de Monte-Carlo?"

"No indeed, Herr Hinnrichs!" the baron answered. "As far as I've heard, not a soul has ever left the place with a single sou in his pocket. It ain't for nothin' that they call the casino doors the gateway to hell! Just as you don't find anyone coming out of hell happy, so you don't see folks leaving the gaming tables of Monte Carlo with a smile on their faces!"

"Oh, you're nothing but a born pessimist!" Herr Hinnrichs countered. "You believe all the tall tales that the scandal sheets report about Monte Carlo and don't take a moment to consider for yourself whether it all might not be exactly as it's printed."

"And why don't these papers ever print anything good about the casino, I ask you?"

"What do you mean, anything good? Have you not read the story of the Hungarian magnate Dezidori, who walked away with a jackpot of millions of francs from the Monte-Carlo?"

"No, I am quite sure I haven't."

"In that case, allow me to regale you. You must first be aware that I, as a player with my own signature system, am highly interested in any others who have their own systems, and therefore you must consider all my findings right on the money, if you'll pardon the pun. Now listen up good."

Herr Hinnrichs went on: "The Hungarian magnate Dezidori, after many long years of devoted study, landed upon his own system for winning big against the house at Monte Carlo. Exactly what this system constituted I am not able to tell you. He refused to reveal it to a soul. But it's a plain and simple fact that he used it to win millions.

"The first year he made his pilgrimage to the gaming rooms at Monte Carlo, he won over a quarter million francs. He rarely took a loss. The year after he raked in over half a million. And the year after that even more. The higher he bet, somehow, the more often he would win."

"Maybe he was just lucky!" the third gentleman cut in, who had been sitting in the corner quietly listening the whole time. "Could be Lady Luck was simply on his side."

"Think so?" asked Hinnrichs, his pulse quickening. "Then listen to this: A certain Spanish nobleman who thought just like you—convinced that all Dezidori's success must be pure chance—was sure the Hungarian's good fortune would dry up at some point, and then it would be his own time to shine. So he waited for a day when the roulette wheel wasn't spinning altogether Dezidori's way and started placing big wagers, always on whatever the Hungarian didn't. When Dezidori bet on red, it would have to be black for the Spaniard; when Dezidori bet on black, the Spaniard only saw red.

"They battled it out like that throughout the day, and when it got to be evening and the game was up, the Hungarian headed back to his rooms with his pockets bulging to the tune of 150,000 fresh francs while the Spaniard had lost over a quarter million!

"I needn't talk your ears off. Suffice it to say that Dezidori, before he started visiting the casino, had been very much down and out, all his most precious property pawned, all his capital tied up in more promissory notes than he had hairs upon his head. But after his years of plenty at Monte Carlo, he was able to pay off all his debts, bought up brand-new real estate, and became one of the wealthiest men in all the Kingdom of Hungary."

"And?" prompted the third gentleman. "How does the story end?"

"How should it end?" Hinnrichs snapped, rather put off by the man's questions. "A person doesn't live forever. As for Dezidori, he lived long enough that there came a day when he eventually died."

"Just so," said the third gentleman. "He died. But not as a millionaire, no sir. As a beggar. And what's more, as a common criminal, penned up in a prison cell. How do I know, you may ask? Because I took an interest in the case myself. Dezidori was awash with luck only until it completely dried up. And when it did he lost everything he owned, down to the last centime. That season, bent upon saving himself from ruin, he began to cheat. They caught him. And he received his due punishment."

"If you're so damn interested in these things," said Hinnrichs, "you must be a regular player at Monte Carlo yourself."

"Who I am is irrelevant. The point is that I don't go telling cockamamie stories, and if I do I don't stop right before the end."

"You're clearly upset," said Hinnrichs, "so there's no use discussing the matter with you any further. Perhaps you take me for someone who has an interest in others losing their money?"

"I don't know who you are or what you are," the unknown gentleman rejoined, "nor am I interested in finding out. I just like to tell the truth is all."

Hinnrichs could see there was no kidding around with this fellow. "Well, I'd like to smoke a cigar," he said, "and we happen to be sitting in a nonsmoking compartment. If you'll permit me to take my leave for a moment . . ."

"Of course," said Baron von Schellenburg.

As soon as Hinnrichs exited the compartment, the baron closed the door hard behind him.

"So you see," said the unknown gentleman to Schellenburg, "that man happens to be an agent of the casino, one of those officials I was telling you about earlier. The Casino de Monte-Carlo sends its agents out all over the continent trying to lure more willing gamesters to come and sacrifice themselves at the roulette table, the unholy altar of the dice demon. All their stories about some kind of brilliant system for winning are made up out of whole cloth. The only system in place is that the bank is bound to win—it's designed to. Even when some player rakes in a hefty sum, it's never long before he has to give it all back.

"For years I've been fascinated by what this casino gets up to. I'm rather pleased that now I'll finally have the opportunity to see all its nasty little tricks up close."

"But are you sure . . . Herr Spitzkopf . . . that this Hinnrichs is an agent of the casino? Maybe he's just another one of these miserable gambling dupes."

"Oh, no," said Spitzkopf, for the mystery gentleman in the compartment was indeed none other than the great detective. "I have a good eye and can't be had quite so easily. That Hinnrichs is a practiced hustler, and I've riled him up quite on purpose—so that he'll warn his colleagues back in Monte Carlo all about me."

"Won't that be dangerous for you?" asked Schellenburg, a note of fear edging into his voice.

"No indeed," said Spitzkopf. "It will be better for them to take an interest in me. That way I'll have a better chance of securing a tête-à-tête with the top brass there and uncovering the full extent of their chicanery. And my instincts are telling me that your wife happens to have been caught up too in the net of just such a swindler as he who gave us the displeasure of his company here." At that moment the door opened, Hinnrichs reentered the compartment, and Schellenburg and Spitzkopf's conference came to an abrupt end.

The baron now took a moment to closely examine this man and saw that Hinnrichs's eyes were flashing bright as a tiger's—a tiger ready to pounce upon its prey.

"Herr Spitzkopf is right," he thought. "Such a fiercely blazing pair of eyes as Hinnrichs's aren't two a penny. I can only hope that startling gleam helps the detective shed some light on my case."

CHAPTER THREE
High Rollers

IT WAS PAST midnight, and Spitzkopf had spent all day gambling at the casino.

This was the day after his arrival in Monaco. Just like every other newcomer to the Casino de Monte-Carlo he first had to be thoroughly questioned as to who he was, where he came from, and what his occupation was, then provide documents to confirm his identity. After he had met all of these demands and paid his entrance fee, he was handed his ticket to that infernal money pit.

As soon as he entered he started to feel dizzy on account of the utter splendor, the dazzling luster that greeted his eyes. The walls were gilded in glittering gold, vast mirrors stretched out wherever you turned, and the electric illumination cast a glow that outshone the sun. Columns of marble achieving near-mythic proportions supported the ceiling, which was itself bursting to vivid life with the most fantastical tracery, done up in paint and carved wood.

It was in a state of pure wonder that Spitzkopf began to take in this most grandiose of gambling halls, more radiantly beautiful even than a king's palace.

The playing tables were crowded to capacity, thronged at every corner with gentlemen and gentleladies, all of them eager to nose their way up to the front to try their luck. And Spitzkopf nosed up right alongside them, pushing and shoving so that he could gain a vacant spot at the table as quickly as possible.

But when he got there he did not remain long. The bit of money he had on him soon slipped through his fingers and right into the bank. With empty pockets he jostled his way out of the throng just as soon as he had jostled his way in.

He began to notice the staff leading a succession of men from table to table, asking each croupier to confirm that each man did indeed lose as much money as he claimed to have lost. These gamblers would appear to be one of that class of poor chumps who lose their last centimes at the tables, then beg the casino management to be so good as to at least give them enough to cover their expenses to get home.

When the croupiers confirmed that the chumps had indeed lost as much as they claimed, they would duly receive money to cover their expenses on the condition that they would reimburse the casino the next time they visited. Whoever failed to pay back the bank would never again be welcomed back.

If someone else had been watching Spitzkopf as closely as he watched all of those milling about, playing, dealing, and supervising in the *salle de jeu*, they would have seen the detective's lips curling upward into a cynical smile.

"The management isn't giving these people cash for the journey home out of a sense of compassion," Spitzkopf thought. "They just don't want to have these poor creatures' blood staining their precious carpets in case the players kill themselves after going broke. They just want to get rid of them. They just want to quiet the din of any potential scandal." As Spitzkopf stood there formulating his judgment of the scene, a sudden collective movement in the hall caught his attention. From all sides he heard the excitable chorus: "She's coming, she's coming!"

"Who's coming?" he asked the gentleman who happened to be standing beside him.

"The American millionairess!" the man answered. "She's been coming here to play every day for several days now. She always places the biggest bets, and even though she always loses, she doesn't seem to care a whit and just goes and doubles her wager right after."

"How interesting that must be," said Spitzkopf, elbowing his way up to the roulette table at which the American lady had seated herself.

It turned out there were two ladies. One was young and comely, and the way she had fashioned her hair, made up her face, and adorned herself was the very paragon of elegance and taste. The diamonds and pearls that dripped from her neck and ears and wrists bore testimony: here was a woman with a queenly fortune.

Beside her stood an older lady, likewise decked out with the utmost elegance, seemingly the mother of her younger companion. Behind them both stood a uniformed lackey, holding two heavy purses in his hand, weighed down with cash.

The younger woman drew out a handful of gold ducats from one of the purses and staked them on number nine. The roulette spun round and round, but the ball, that true coquette, landed on number eleven, and the lady lost. Not losing her calm for an instant, again the young woman placed a fresh pile of coins on nine. Off went the wheel, ça *roule*, ça *roule*, on the ball rolls, and again—eleven.

This same routine went on for a good long while. The lady stubbornly chased her luck at the nine, and the ball stubbornly evaded her, popping in every time at eleven.

When the lady finally relented and moved her bet to the ball's preferred number, the little minx skittered just past it and landed on fifteen.

At this point both coin purses were empty, but this did not seem to bother the young American in the slightest. She simply made a sign to her lackey, bidding him bring her new bags of money. And in a trice he reappeared, two fresh bags in his arms, and the lady went on playing.

"*Holà! holà! holà!*" cried the croupier. "Come on, come on, *mais faites vos jeux*, place your bets!" And the lady placed hers. Her piles of staked coinage grew even more towering than before, but not once did she win. Finally she grew tired of the game and, still as cool and collected as ever, a pleasant grin on her face, she left on the arm of her older companion. In the course of this couple of hours, she had lost close to a quarter of a million francs.

These were the sorts of scenes Spitzkopf saw playing out again and again on the casino floor, but he did not return to a table to play again himself.

Finally he began to feel rather drowsy. All his senses had been overstimulated; the unceasing flashing and clanging of gold coins set his head reeling and his ears ringing. And so, his limbs dragging, he stumbled out of the hall and walked up a side path that ascended from the Place du Casino—when suddenly he felt himself being pulled backward by his right sleeve.

He whipped around and saw a diminutive man with a rather unpleasant visage standing before him and shouting up to him: "Where is it you'd like to go, good sir? The only people that tread this path are those who have lost all hope, but I didn't see you losing a sou!"

"I don't catch your meaning," said Spitzkopf evenly. "Who are you, and what do you want?"

"I am a good person," said the stranger. "And I consider it my noble duty to save other people teetering on the brink of total despair—while there's still time.

"This path generally carries these miserable souls to their end, people who have lost all they possess at the gaming tables and are too proud to ask the management to cover their expenses home. Don't you see, up there, those cliffs overlooking the sea? Suicides are committed there daily, my friend, by these wretched fools. It's for that reason the path we're walking is called the Lane of the Lonely.

"Every evening I wend my way over here, and seeing these lonely wayfarers I make every effort to hold them back as they move to take that dreadful step . . ."

"But what are they to do?" Spitzkopf asked. "It would seem there's truly no path left to them other than this one."

"Why's that? The management would cover their expenses if they only asked, then once they're home they could stock up on cash and return to win back what they've lost."

"And so this is what you call your good deed?" Spitzkopf quipped in a tone of biting irony. "You want to lead these unfortunate souls to bring back even more foreign money and throw it away right into the casino's coffers? Thanks kindly, but I'm afraid I'd have to decline a good deed like that."

"I'd rather not argue the point with you. But surely you'll concede that, as you haven't even played tonight, you truly needn't go up this path where so many much more miserable than you have gone before."

"And how would you know whether or not I've gambled tonight?"

"Because I've been observing you the entire time you've spent in the gaming room."

"Observed me, eh?" Spitzkopf laughed. "Seems to me you're not some champion of the down on their luck but rather a champion of the ones what brought 'em down so, a benefactor of the bank! Or rather—the bank is *your* benefactor. Monte Carlo's got you in its pockets, has it?"

"Well, aren't you a case!" the stranger fumed. "Absolutely cuckoo!" And off he went with nary a goodbye.

Spitzkopf stared at him with a grin on his face as the man's already diminutive form grew smaller and smaller in his descent, and he said to himself: "So I'm the cuckoo, eh? But it's you I've got in my cage. I knew it. You're an agent of the casino. I had your number right from the start, figuring that your relationship to the baroness, Schellenburg's wife, was founded on nothing but the bank's own interests. It's got its eyes on Schellenburg's fortune. But this time I dare to say it's placed its bet on the wrong color. Red, black, bother it all—you must be green if you think you can outwit Spitzkopf . . ."

CHAPTER FOUR
Up and at 'Em

AN HOUR LATER Spitzkopf could be found cozied up in the sitting room of Baron von Schellenburg's hotel suite. Even though it was terribly late, Spitzkopf knew he had to go and pay the baron a visit.

The detective had not seen the man for hours, intent as he was on spending his first day in Monte Carlo getting to know the way of life in the casino. But now, confident that he was on the right track, he had hurried off to Schellenburg, eager to hear whether the baron had any news for him and in turn to report on his own findings.

After knocking on the door of his suite, a barely audible "Come in!" drifted back. Entering the opulent sitting room, Spitzkopf saw the baron sunk down in a plush armchair, holding his head with both hands. It was clear that he was quite upset.

"How glad I am that you've come," said the baron. "I'm going half mad here from pure agitation, pure hopelessness . . ."

"What's happened now?" Spitzkopf asked, unable to conceal his surprise.

"It was around midnight," the baron answered. "I'd been asleep for a while. Then I woke with a start, thinking I heard footsteps inside my suite.

"I thought I must just have dreamt it, and being exhausted I closed my eyes again and tried to fall back asleep. But then . . . then I heard the door softly opening and closing again. I jumped out of bed and turned on the lights. Imagine my surprise: my wife's bed beside me was empty, and her clothes that she'd hung over the chair beside the bed were gone too. To think that my wife has let her infidelity go so far that she dares to steal out of our bedroom in the middle of the night . . . It's dreadful, dreadful. I can't take it anymore."

"Calm yourself, Herr Baron," urged Spitzkopf, now rather calm himself. "My hope is that you soon shall be convinced of your wife's innocence and of the possibility that all these strange deeds of hers were carried out under the influence of external forces. I am not able to give you a full explanation just yet, but I hope soon to discover—"

"You're speaking in mysteries," said the baron. "I beg you to speak more plainly."

"I can't. I am not in the habit of offering up any definitive answers before I am quite definite. At present I am only entertaining a conjecture. I am still waiting on two more pieces of evidence. First I must speak with your Frau Baronin, but altogether anonymously. She cannot know who I am or why I've chosen to speak with her. Second, I have to arrange another tête-à-tête with that rather short-statured, unfortunate-looking man whom you believe to be her seducer. This shall all take place tomorrow. Until then you will just have to be patient.

"For now, do try go to back to sleep, Herr Baron. And if you happen to hear your wife returning, pretend you haven't noticed a thing. Please take heed of what I'm telling you."

"Your word is my command, detective—though it's asking a lot."

"I'm afraid I'm not done asking. I have a few questions for you before I go."

"*Bitte sehr*, certainly; ask away."

"Did you not come upon that slight, decidedly unattractive Frenchman sometime before, on your honeymoon trip to Paris and Rome?"

"No! I saw him for the first time here in Monte Carlo."

"Is it not possible that he acquainted himself with your wife at some point on the journey over here?"

"I don't see how it could have happened myself. But I suppose it's not outside the realm of possibility. And it's true that when we were in Paris I did go off hunting with some men I know while my wife remained in the city with her own friends. It is possible that she came across this man then. Here in Monte Carlo she seemed to have already formed a rather lofty opinion of him."

"Does your wife have a nervous disposition?"

"I'm not the best judge of such things. That is to say, from my vantage point she has always seemed perfectly even-keeled. I've also never given her any cause for becoming upset. Whatever she's ever wanted I've done for her. But it does seem to me, now that you mention, that she may have nervous proclivities.

Sometimes when she's in ill humor she gets this odd look, stares straight ahead with a sort of unnatural fire in her eye."

"That's all I shall need to know for now, Herr Baron," said Spitzkopf. "And now I am able to let you in on some of my own hypotheses. That stunted, miserable-featured man is an agent of the Casino de Monte-Carlo. The bank sends out its emissaries all over the world to reel in fresh victims. By some means this man managed to introduce himself to your wife. He's the one that led her here, and since she's come he has only continued leading her about. He intends to lead her right to your ruin at the gaming tables, having her play until she's relinquished to the bank everything you own.

"And I think I know by what means he's been influencing her. But I shan't breathe a word of that to you until I've convinced myself beyond a shadow of a doubt that my hunch is correct. In the meantime all I can tell you is this: your suspicion of your wife's infidelity is unfounded. You need no longer worry on that score."

And with that the detective took his leave of the baron and quit his hotel room. The baron returned to his bed, crawled back under his covers, and was soon fast asleep.

CHAPTER FIVE

Miss Fortune

Baron von Schellenburg kept his word. As soon as Spitzkopf left his suite he went right back to bed and fell almost immediately into a sound slumber. He did not hear his wife's return, and when he awoke the sun was already streaming through his windows. His wife was there snoring in the bed beside him. The baron emerged from under his blankets, dressed himself, and waited eagerly for Spitzkopf's return and whatever news he might bring.

But by the time the clock struck twelve, there was still no

sign of the detective. The baroness had now also gotten out of bed and dressed for the day. Schellenburg did not exchange a cross word with her. She seemed so at peace, was so entirely free in her movements, that she seemed to have a perfectly clear conscience.

"A woman behaving like that can't be feeling guilty about some terrible wrong she's done," Schellenburg thought to himself. The only unpleasant sight that did meet his eye this morning was something on the chambermaid's face, something that made it quite clear she knew his wife had slipped out of the hotel in the middle of the night.

"Maids the likes of her," he thought, "have got big mouths. Please, just let it stay closed this one time—or she could set a thousand tongues wagging. But there's nothing I can do. I dare not tell her to keep mum. That'll only make matters worse."

As the baron was lounging in his preferred armchair in the suite's sitting room, lost in these thoughts, the bedroom door opened and in flounced his wife, nicely turned out, as always, in the very finest attire.

"Where are you off to now?" the baron asked.

"To the gaming rooms, of course!" she answered. "I'm going to really try my luck. Today I'm going to place my biggest bets yet."

"You know, my dear Helene," the baron cooed, "that money's not so very important to me. It doesn't bother me if you go and lose a certain amount at the casino. As long as it makes you happy I've nothing against it. But why must you place such big bets? Is it that you want to strike it rich? You've plenty of money as it is, and it would be a crying shame to risk losing all we've got. It's simply not worth the stress."

"To tell you the truth, I myself couldn't quite put my finger on what my goal may be," the baroness answered him. "I haven't taken a moment to consider whether it actually brings me all that much pleasure. I'm just . . . I'm just drawn to the casino, as if by a magnetic pull. I simply must go there. Nothing in the world could stop me."

And before the baron could get another word in she was gone. He remained sitting there, stunned, as if he had become one with the armchair. His wife had left him with the impression that she was not altogether in command of her mental faculties.

"Ah. Now I am beginning to understand what Spitzkopf was trying to tell me," he said to himself. "Some secret power seems to be controlling Helene. Her will is not her own. She is in the grasp of some external power. But what am I to do?

"If only Spitzkopf would come. But not a word! Not the slightest clue that he'll ever be back!"

With restless strides the baron paced back and forth around the sitting room. He cracked his knuckles out of pure anxiety, drummed upon the windowpanes, smoked one cigarette after another. He could not find peace. Then, while standing at the window, he caught sight of a sumptuously fitted out barouche rattling past on the street below. A man and a woman were seated within the carriage. Peering into their faces the baron recognized his wife and the grotesque-visaged monsieur. Schellenburg was now at his breaking point. He let out an anguished cry: "It's enough to drive a person stark raving mad! I shut my mouth and don't say a word, wanting to avoid even a whisper of scandal. But here's the scandal coming out all on its own, sallying forth in a sumptuous barouche!

"If my wife is riding around in broad daylight with that monstrous-looking specter, half the world will be discussing her by the evening. This cannot go on a moment longer. I have to put an end to it."

With a quick, rash movement, he seized a loaded revolver out of the desk and hurtled himself down the grand staircase of the hotel. Flinging open the front doors, he whistled down the first fiacre that passed and bade the coachman bring him to the casino.

"But do make haste, driver! Whip those steeds to their limit!"

And whip them the man did as the fiacre tore through the streets of Monte Carlo with incredible speed. A few minutes later the Baron von Schellenburg was in the Place du Casino. He bounded out of the carriage, paid the driver, and started racing toward the entrance. Then, hearing a sudden clamor break out behind him, he wheeled round and saw a great passel of people bellowing and bickering. Changing course, he approached this group and saw someone laid out upon a stretcher, bleeding profusely from a number of open head wounds.

"This man was just found at the Lane of the Lonely!" the baron heard someone crying out beside him. "It must be one of those ill-fated gamblers!"

"No, it mustn't!" a second voice rung out. "This man has been attacked, and viciously, too! He's the victim of some rotten criminal!" At this point the baron had managed to push his way to the front. Looking down at the face of the wounded man, he was horrified to find it was none other than Detective Spitzkopf.

It was too much for the baron, whose blood was already at full boil. He fell helplessly to the ground, unconscious. Now the gathered crowd had to start concerning itself with yet another of the day's casualties.

All this time the baroness was standing at a roulette table in the *salle de jeu*, engrossed in her game, without the faintest idea of how cruelly the wheel of fortune was spinning just outside.

CHAPTER SIX
The Assault

THAT MORNING Spitzkopf's first order of business was to arrange a little unplanned meeting with the unhandsome little man.

From the very beginning he had guessed that this man must be a hypnotist. He would have been employed by the casino and assigned to prey upon persons susceptible to hypnosis, such as the baroness. And his ultimate task? By means of his hypnotic power, to induce them to empty out their coffers and thereby enrich the almighty bank.

In order to test his hypothesis, Spitzkopf sought to engineer another meeting with this tiny but dangerous bird of prey. And it took place just as he had hoped, the morning after the full day Spitzkopf had spent carrying out his observations in the casino.

Upon entering a café in search of breakfast, he found the birdie he was looking for pecking away at his. Spitzkopf took a seat at the same table and engaged him in conversation. Naturally, Spitzkopf had disguised himself so that the old scoundrel would not recognize him as the same man from the day before in the gaming hall and later on the Lane of the Lonely.

The casino agent first launched into an enthusiastic discourse on Monte Carlo in general: its best attractions, its fine weather, and so forth. Then he moved on to the casino and claimed—as do all such agents—that the service that institution provides is a true boon unto the entire world and that every year thousands make pilgrimage to it and emerge fabulously wealthy.

"This I don't believe," said Spitzkopf in response. "In fact, it seems to me that it's rather the opposite. It's the casino itself that hits the jackpot every day, and it's these thousands of visitors who lose their entire fortunes—and their lives too—in the bargain. And the best evidence for it is the Lane of the Lonely."

They went on chatting in this manner for a while. The vertically and aesthetically challenged man, being the practiced con that he was, knew he was dealing with someone whose intent was to spy out all the bank's secrets in order to publicly disgrace it. And so, as the man sat there, he formulated a plan to make sure not a word of what his interlocutor had observed would ever pass this busybody's lips. If he swung it, management would be sure to reward him handsomely.

After Spitzkopf arose and made to leave the café, the little man rose to follow him, picking up their conversation right where they had left off. And in the course of the stroll they ended up on the Lane of the Lonely. There the hypnotist began to ply his trade, trying to work his mental tricks on Spitzkopf and render him putty in his hands so that he would do whatever the little man bade him.

But Spitzkopf's mind was resistant to hypnotic suggestion. This art is only effective upon people of rather more feeble, more nervous dispositions.

In order to deceive the scoundrel that his tricks were successful, however, Spitzkopf produced his best impression of a trance. He closed his eyes, let his hands fall to his sides, and altogether pretended to be fully under the man's spell. But the scoundrel was rather too clever for such a ruse as this. He was so cunning a practitioner of his art that he immediately saw through Spitzkopf's performance. Taking advantage of his subject's eyes being closed, the little man grabbed a heavy stick from the side of the path and swung it into Spitzkopf's pate with such remarkable force that the detective immediately fell to the ground unconscious.

Seeing his victim lying at his feet, apparently near death, the scoundrel then seized a heavy stone from the wayside and bludgeoned him over the head with that too, opening such grievous wounds as would have killed any human being made up of more ordinary parts than was our Spitzkopf. Then the man fled the scene, off to continue his demonic work.

But Spitzkopf's robust constitution saved him. After some time lying there, he eventually came to and managed to drag himself down to the Place du Casino, where he was immediately found by the passing holidaymakers.

The minute mesmerist had not an inkling of his victim's recovery. He sat in the gaming room with a smirk upon his ugly mug, well satisfied that his latest trick had been a stone-cold success.

CHAPTER SEVEN

The Hypnotist's Gambit

SPITZKOPF HAD not erred in his hypothesis.

The Baronin von Schellenburg had indeed been hypnotized by the Lilliputian, loathsome-featured man who had introduced himself to her as Dr. Farré. And she had indeed met him in Paris, when her husband had set off to the countryside to hunt with his companions and she remained in the city. Among the girlfriends she disported herself with there was one with whom the hypnotist himself kept company. When this woman introduced the young and comely baroness to him, all his senses perked up. He saw in her every possible sign of being susceptible to hypnosis, and upon learning that she was very rich besides he knew she would make a perfect target. He at once devised a plan for putting her in a trance and popping in the suggestion that she come visit Monte Carlo.

Setting aside his remarkably hideous, even repellent physical appearance, he was really quite good company. He knew the world, was well traveled, and used his sundry experiences to tell a great variety of piquant and interesting anecdotes for the pleasure of his listeners. In this way he ingratiated himself with the young, inexperienced baroness, flattering and fascinating her, this promising prospective entrant into the gaming hell of Monaco.

The man was indeed trained as a physician. He had graduated from his medical studies with great success and could have won a fine reputation in the field had he chosen to pursue it nobly. But it so happened that he was not only frightful in appearance and short of stature; he was also short on virtue, being of a wicked and deceitful nature. Once he commenced his medical career, he in short order committed a very serious crime against one of his patients and was duly stripped of his license to practice the trade any longer.

It was then that he decided to market himself to the Casino de Monte-Carlo as a worthy agent, and he soon began applying his expertise in methods of hypnosis to the luring of innumerable victims to its gaming tables. From that point forward he was on a winning streak, raking in a constant stream of gold for the unquenchable bank. He had now placed his bets on the baroness.

Exploiting a moment when they happened to be alone, Farré hypnotized her and issued a suggestion that she come to Monte Carlo on such and such a day. The insensate baroness did just as he asked, soon arriving in that glittering city by the sea. And when she did, working again by hypnotic suggestion, he guided her into the teeming epicenter of the casino.

Thrilled by his success with the baroness, and observing that her husband, the young baron, did not try to hinder her in anything she wanted to do, he made ready to make good on his chief objective: influencing her to play so recklessly, betting such large sums, that she would surrender the entirety of her and her husband's fortunes for the immediate financial gain of the casino bank.

In order to assure himself of the baron's reluctance to interfere with her activities, he eventually planted the suggestion in the baroness that she remove the most valuable article from her and her husband's jewelry box and bring it back to him.

This she also did.

Then he commanded her to openly roam about with him around Monte Carlo—a task she readily performed.

And to all of this provocation the baron issued nary a peep of protest. The hypnotist could not fathom why. He did not know that the baron was only being restrained from acting by distinct order of the most accomplished, most assiduous detective in all the world, a virtuoso who promised to have the scoundrel playing to his own merry tune before long. Nor did he realize that Spitzkopf, by virtue of his hawk's eye and wealth of worldly experience, had already found out everything and was hot on his trail.

In short, the scoundrel was perfectly confident that he would soon be bringing his wicked designs to their ultimate fruition.

That evening the baroness would be supping with the director of the casino in the restaurant the scoundrel had dictated to her. After that she would be headed to the gaming hall to promptly lose everything she owned. The hypnotist was sure to be richly compensated if it all went according to plan.

He had banked on it.

CHAPTER EIGHT
Spitzkopf Calls Their Bluff

In a small room furnished in grand style, in a side wing of the palatial Casino de Monte-Carlo, Spitzkopf was laid out on a cot to recover. His head had been washed clean of blood and his wounds dressed. He took labored breaths in slow succession. His extensive loss of blood had weakened him considerably.

But for all that he was still sound of mind and knew what had happened to him. When he was lugged up to the doors of the casino, management was informed as to what had happened. He was immediately admitted and allotted a private room in which to recover. A man was brought to clean him and a doctor to carefully wrap his head in bandages.

The casino directors were of course deeply wary of any scandals breaking out in Monte Carlo. They knew that if one did the casino would also attract attention and be cruelly besieged by the global population. They did not want to give their enemies any occasion for laying into them. And so they moved quickly to give the wounded man refuge and keep him well away from prying eyes.

Spitzkopf understood this. And knew that he would not be let out of the place quite so easily as he was let in, especially if he was fully healed and had identified himself and informed management in what line of work he operated and why he happened to be in Monte Carlo. He decided therefore to feign complete frailty and an inability to speak. "That way this pack of thieves will leave me alone," he thought, "and in the meantime I'll take the opportunity of sidling on out of here and nabbing that runtish man."

Presently two of the institution's directors came to check up on his condition. Spitzkopf was lying in bed, pretending to be fast asleep. And while he put on this bravura evening show, he heard every word that was spoken by these two.

"He's sleeping," said one of the directors. "Let him. We'll have time to question him later."

"Have you heard?" said the other. "Dr. Farré is worried that this man is a spy, and he's the one what gave him such a nice and thorough dousing. He's already asking for a handsome payout of blood money for a job well done."

"If that turns out to be true," said the first man, "he's not wrong to ask for it. He deserves such a prize."

"He deserves it for something else," said the second. "Namely, for that young, lovely baroness."

"Ah, you must mean the Baronin von Schellenburg. You're right: he caught quite the golden goose when he got her into his coop. I lunched with her today. A wonder of a woman."

"And I'm going to have dinner with her tonight, at the Restaurant Bellevue. The shame is that we're only getting to meet her in her hypnotized state. If she were fully awake I daresay it would be much more pleasant, much sweeter . . ."

"Such a decaying dotard and still slavering after pleasures like that?" laughed the first man. "Go on, you old coot! The thing to focus on here is her cash. After you dine with her tonight, she'll be depositing with us every last centime in her possession—on an eternal loan, let's say. Let us not get in the way of that. We'll leave her pure and holy, as far as her husband's concerned."

"But look, it's already eight o'clock," said the old coot. "She'll be here soon. Let's mosey."

Spitzkopf had heard everything, and throughout the conversation he lay there as if on a bed of pins, only able to keep still by an enormous concerted effort. If only he had not still felt quite so debilitated he would have leaped out of bed instantly and torn apart that pair of brutes with his teeth. But he knew the best thing was to keep still lest he nullify all the careful work he had done.

When the men quit the room, he began to breathe more freely and tried to sit up. His steadfastness, his hidden stores of energy, and his iron will to bring an end to this whole ignominious game being played in the casino—all these lent him the strength he needed to raise himself up and climb out of bed. Once he did he quickly pulled on his clothes and walked to the window.

He did not want to leave through the door, determined that no one catch sight of him and detain him. The window, meanwhile, opened out into a garden, which was now shrouded in darkness, not a soul to be seen. Spitzkopf opened it, climbed down onto the grass, and found himself at a little gate that provided access onto the street.

The gate was barred, but as no one could be seen on the street either, Spitzkopf decided to jump it, clearing the low palisade with ease. A fiacre happened to be passing just as he did so. Spitzkopf stepped into it and asked the coachman to take him to his hotel.

He had a pounding headache, but he did not let it bother him. When he arrived at the hotel, he slithered up the stairs and slipped into his room as surreptitiously as he could, still eager that no one notice him. Once inside he dashed off his clothes and rubbed his wounds with a salve he had brought from his home apothecary, one he kept handy wherever he went.

He now felt refreshed and with a new lease on life, just as if nothing very inconvenient had happened to him merely hours before.

Standing at the open window he heard someone calling out

on the street below: "Driver! Hello there! Have you any room? I'd like to go to the Restaurant Bellevue." Spitzkopf recognized the voice. It was none other than the Baron von Schellenburg.

"Disaster will be on the menu," thought the detective. "I've got to hurry off there myself and prevent it at all costs." And so he flung his clothes back on, stuck a loaded revolver into his bag, and after a paltry few seconds he was back out on the street. There he jumped into the first fiacre that came rattling by and bade the driver conduct him to the Bellevue with all possible haste.

CHAPTER NINE
The Game Is Up

THE BARON VON SCHELLENBURG had fainted when he saw Spitzkopf lying nearly dead at the Place du Casino. His last modicum of hope had been obliterated. He would never be able to free himself from his terrible quandary all on his own.

Thankfully, among the clutch of people that had gathered in the square around the two compromised individuals was one of the baron's acquaintances. He immediately recognized his friend and arranged that he be transported back to their hotel.

There a doctor was summoned who took steps to revive the unconscious baron. As his fainting spell had been due merely to a moment's distress, he soon came to and rebounded with ease.

But the distress did not disappear. On the contrary, it increased from minute to minute. He could not think clearly. His addled brain alighted on one confused notion after another. His one fixed idea was revenge and how best to enact it upon his wedlock-breaking wife.

He was too weak to make his way back to the casino. Better to wait in their suite until she returned.

But she did not.

Not until evening, when she suddenly appeared at the threshold, and in such fine form, so full of life and love, overbrimming with kindness and caresses as though she boasted a conscience cleaner and purer than the snowiest Alpine peak.

As might be expected of a person whose nerves were so miserably on edge, the baron's mood was quickly, mercifully soothed by the woman's tenderness. He could not even find it within himself to dare to ask her how she had spent her day.

But later, when she got on her glad rags again and told him that she was off to the Restaurant Bellevue for supper, his burning jealousy was newly enflamed. In a searing speech, he condemned the course she had taken and strictly forbade any further steps in that dangerous direction. But she resisted the ban, though in oddly mechanical fashion, and left the suite against her husband's will.

This was more than Schellenburg could take. By a monstrous effort he managed to wrench himself from the bed where he had been convalescing, seized a loaded revolver, and went after her, taking a cab in the direction of the Bellevue.

Upon arriving at the restaurant, he espied his spouse sitting at a little table in a corner beside some unknown gentleman. The place was bustling, so no one noticed the enraged baron shoving his way up to their table. Nor did anyone notice him drawing his revolver and pointing it at the baroness.

As soon as he did Spitzkopf lunged at him from behind and yanked both his arms back. "Stop right there!" the detective roared. "Your wife is innocent! She's been hypnotized!"

The baron dropped the revolver out of pure shock and erupted into an uncontrollable, hysterical bout of sobbing. Spitzkopf took him by the arm and led him at once into a small side room, where he took pains to calm him.

Meanwhile the incident provided quite the dinner show for the restaurant patrons, all of whom looked upon the scene with utter astonishment. They began to crowd around the table where the baroness was sitting, and those who could not get close craned their necks for a better view.

The baroness herself, however, had not noticed a thing. She continued eating her dinner quite as placidly as ever, not at all as though she were the focus of the entire establishment's attention—or of the barrel of her husband's gun.

The hypnotist was among the diners at the Bellevue that night, and Spitzkopf recognized him as soon as the half-pint of a man walked into the restaurant.

Later this villain positioned himself at the door to the room into which Spitzkopf and the baron had retreated in order to eavesdrop on what was being said within.

Spitzkopf had managed to put the baron at ease again before long, and when he did the detective made to leave the room and check up on the man's wife. But when he threw open the door and saw the hypnotist standing just beside it, his fury was rekindled, and he fulminated: "You contemptible varlet! Not only have you ruined his wife's existence, now you think you'll eliminate his own?"

It was clear to the hypnotist that Spitzkopf knew everything. He pulled out his own gun and prepared to fire it at the detective . . .

But before he could do so Spitzkopf fired off a bullet of his own, which promptly lodged itself directly in the hypnotist's heart.

At that moment the baroness awoke from her hypnotic state. When a hypnotist dies, his hypnosis loses all its power. Spitzkopf knew this and, not tarrying too long to bother himself over the slain culprit, he rushed toward the baroness and with a mighty effort dragged her into the room where her husband was waiting.

"Herr Baron!" said the detective. "Your lady wife is free from her psychic fetters! And he who fettered her lies there dead. His hypnotic spell has broken."

Breaking out in fresh tears, the baron embraced his shaking, shell-shocked spouse, who had not the dimmest conception of all that had befallen her.

As soon as Spitzkopf saw a carriage approaching out the window, he led the embattled man and wife out of the restaurant, and all three traveled back to their hotel, where the detective finally related to the woman all the details of her nightmarish ordeal. Deeply moved, the baron offered his profoundest thanks to the detective for his masterly work, as his wife wept like a small child.

The bloody traces of the dead hypnotist were soon wiped clean from the restaurant—and from Monte Carlo. The management of the casino did not want any scandal, after all.

Spitzkopf made his way to the police headquarters, where he delivered his full and honest report of all that had occurred and was immediately set free. The casino's directors were in fact quite pleased to see him go.

The Baron and Baronin von Schellenburg joined him on the train back to Vienna. They compensated him with a truly baronial sum for all he had done to save them and pledged to him their eternal gratitude. In the great game of life, their one incontrovertible stroke of luck had been landing upon him, the peerlessly sharp head of Vienna's private sleuthing agency Blitz—

MAX SPITZKOPF, KING OF DETECTIVES.

Endnotes

1. The Galician town of Oświęcim was at this time home to a sizable population of Jews and served as an important rail junction. From 1940, when the town was under Nazi control, until 1945 it hosted the infamous complex of concentration and extermination camps known as Auschwitz, after the German name of the town.

2. Today known as Darakhiv, a small town in western Ukraine, about a hundred miles from Lviv.

3. Warsaw was at the time in the area of Poland ruled by the Russian Empire. The border referred to is that between Russian-ruled and Austrian-ruled Poland, the latter being part of the region then known as Galicia. Kraków, near to which the children plan to make their crossing, was close to this border, on the Galician side.

4. At the time in Galicia, the town was home to a sizable population of Jews and served as an important rail junction. From 1940, when the town was under Nazi control, until 1945, the infamous complex of concentration and extermination camps was located on the outskirts of the town.

5. Mayor of Vienna from 1897 until his death in 1910; known for his Christian Social Party's antisemitic platform.

6. "Franzensfeste" more or less translates to "Franz's fort." Construction on the fortification was initiated by its eponymous emperor, Franz I of Austria (the last of the Holy Roman emperors, from 1792 to 1806, as well as the first emper-

or of Austria, from 1804 to 1835). The fort, along with the surrounding village (later also named Franzensfeste), are today in the northeastern Italian province of South Tyrol. Innsbruck, the Austrian city in the Alps from which the news telegram was sent, is about fifty-five kilometers away.

7. In the period during which this Polish city formed a part of the Austro-Hungarian Empire, its Jewish community constituted nearly 30 percent of the population. Much of the Przemyśl Jews' economic activity consisted of manufacturing and supplying goods to the local military base, where Silbermann's regiment was stationed.

8. An allusion to Alfred Dreyfus, a Jewish army officer wrongly convicted in 1895 of treason against the French Third Republic and exiled to the French penal colony of Devil's Island, off the coast of French Guiana. The Dreyfus Affair divided French opinion and riled up anti-Jewish feeling in the country, its flames fueled, as here, by an antisemitic press.

9. Today in South Tyrol, Italy, known in Italian as Mezzaselva (with the same meaning as Mittewald, i.e., Mid-Wood).

10. Today in South Tyrol, Italy. Known in Italian as Bressanone, it is the oldest city in the international region of Tyrol.

11. A form of currency in use in the Austrian Empire in the nineteenth century.

12. Today a small village in eastern Poland. Its closest large city is the regional capital of Lublin.

13. "Zell by the lake." At the time these stories were written, the resort town was a playground for European aristocracy and

royals, including Kaiser Franz Joseph I and his iconic empress, Kaiserin Elisabeth of Austria (popularly known as "Sissi," for whom a hotel in the town was named). The von Trapp family, famous to American audiences as the subject of *The Sound of Music*, maintained a residence there. It remains a fashionable resort town today.

14. There are a few localities that go by this name. The resort towns Bad Aussee and nearby Altaussee are both in the Salzkammergut region, which is a beloved summer destination for vacationing Viennese, Jewish and Gentile alike. They are both only about 80 kilometers east of Zell am See and 60 kilometers from Salzburg. The Czech town of Usov, known in German as Mährisch Aussee ("Moravian Aussee"), is much farther north, some 190 kilometers east of Prague, but at the time of this story's writing was also part of the Austro-Hungarian Empire. Its Jewish community, centered on a hill in the town, was decimated in the Holocaust.

15. Another picturesque Alpine spa town ("*Bad*" means "bath" in German), it is located close to Salzburg, in the German region of Upper Bavaria.

16. German, "evergreen."

17. "Green bailiff" in German. According to the *Historisches Lexikon deutscher Farbbezeichnungen* (*Historical Lexicon of German Color Terms*), by William Jervis Jones (Berlin: Akademie-Verlag, 2013), it means a "*grüngekleideter Gerichtsdiener*"—a court bailiff dressed in green. Here it refers to a small locality, likely invented by Kreppel, perhaps nodding to the law's encroaching power over this story's errant criminals.

18. No shtetl by such a name appears on maps of the region nor

in annals of Jewish habitation in Europe. It would seem the name was invented by Kreppel, perhaps to avoid the suggestion that denizens of any one shtetl were particularly susceptible to such a fate as that suffered by the son of the rabbi of "Nurazvo."

19. This narrative forms the subject of Spitzkopf story three, "The Blood Libel."

20. This appears to be an invented name. In lists of the notable coffeehouses operating in Vienna in the early decades of the twentieth century, no Café Zweig is to be found.

21. Invented geographic name in the works of the classic Yiddish writer Sholem Aleichem, where it is a summer colony just outside of Yehupets (Sholem Aleichem's fictionalized name for Kiev), populated by wealthy holidaymakers to whom Tevye the dairyman delivers his products. Sholem Aleichem based the name on the Ukrainian town of Boyarka. That this is an imaginary name, from a series enormously popular among Yiddish readers, may indicate that Fuchs is having a bit of fun at the missionary's expense, as the man would not have realized it was not an actual place. Still, it is possible that Fuchs is referring to the similarly named Boyberke, the Yiddish name for the Galician town of Bibrka (also within the borders of contemporary Ukraine).

22. An actual organization known today as the Church's Ministry Among Jewish People. Founded by evangelical Anglicans in 1809, its missionary work extended to other parts of Europe, as well as Africa and Palestine, where it helped to establish Christ Church in Jerusalem, the oldest Protestant church in the Middle East.

23. Charles III, Prince of Monaco, built the lavish belle epoque-style casino in Monte Carlo between 1858 and 1881, expanding and remodeling it several times. Monaco's famous gambling institution still occupies the building today, as does an opera house. The fabulous financial success of the casino enabled the prince to abolish taxation in Monaco, and Monte Carlo remains a popular gaming destination—and tax haven—for foreigners.

DEDICATION

For my father, Dr. Gary Yashinsky, who used to read the books of kid sleuth Encyclopedia Brown to me and my brother Sam as bedtime stories.

When we correctly solved each whodunit to match the book's provided answer, always printed upside down, we were rewarded with the prize of Dad reading us another.

—MY

Acknowledgments

The following kindly and clever individuals would make up my own sleuthing agency, if I had one. In their helpfulness and wisdom and clarity of purpose they could rival Spitzkopf and his merry men.

All the staff members of the Yiddish Book Center are dear to me, including those who saw with excitement the potential of these stories, chiefly the edifying David Mazower and the enterprising Lisa Newman, she who spearheaded this book project, supported by the keen editorial eye and organizational powers of Ezra Glinter, Jeff Hayes, and Greg Lauzon. Aaron Lansky and Susan Bronson have led the vital work of the Center that has made my work on Spitzkopf possible (at the most basic level by collecting these bound fiction pamphlets from 1908, if not for which I might never have clapped eyes on them!). My friends Elissa Sperling and Jordan Brown ("Mendl" to me) were among the first to put their hands on that volume when we were research fellows at the Center, bringing it to my attention—and to the attention of Jesse Finkelstein and Francine Hermelin, who were delighted by the existence of such a figure as Spitzkopf and first commissioned me to translate a few of the stories, in 2017. Konstanze Kunst, Judaica librarian at Yale, was so good as to send me scans of the remaining Spitzkopf capers beyond those five held by the Center. Historians Klaus Kreppel, Evelyn Adunka, and Thomas Soxberger wrote the indispensable German-language biography of Jonas Kreppel. Kreppel's descendants have enriched us all by upholding the legacy of their famous relative. My grandmother Elizabeth Elkin Weiss and the Vilna partisan Fania Brantsovsky, both of blessed memory, were among my earliest guides in the world of Yiddish literature and lore, and I still feel their holy influence when I put pen to paper. My teachers at Harvard, Maria Tatar, Lisa

Parkes, and Juliet Wagner, helped turn my mind toward scholarly contemplation of the German language and Vienna. My former colleagues at the Theater an der Wien, Sebastian Schwarz and Claudia Stobrawa, gave me the opportunity to travel to the city when I worked as an intern at their beautiful opera house as a college junior, an experience that proved most useful while traducting these stories as I hotfooted through Viennese alleyways on Spitzkopf's trail, retracing the steps I had taken all those summers ago. The ingenious Danielle Bendjy will never be too ashamed to join me in using a word like "traducting." Courageous Jeremy Walsh's industriousness and sense of noble endeavor inspire my own. Joshua and Zachary Bayer were my next-door neighbors as a boy, and as we grew together, so did our imaginations. My mother Debra, father Gary, and elder brothers Gabriel, Joseph, and Samuel gave me a childhood full of brightness and colorful incident. Such a childhood has caused my eyes ever since to gleam with delight when reading properly adventuresome tales, tales like the ones that appear within these pages.

Last but far from least: Jonas Kreppel was a man of serious intellect and endeavor who was also, quite clearly, unafraid of having a bit of zany fun. I have had a great deal of zany fun at his side this past number of years. *A sheynem dank dir, lieber Herr Autor.*

Biographies

Jonas (Yoyne) Kreppel was born into a Hasidic family in Drohobych, Galicia, in 1874, the fourth of seven children. After apprenticing as a printer, he found his calling as a journalist, civil servant, and author. Kreppel attended the Czernowitz conference in 1908 that adjudicated on the future of Yiddish, was active in the Orthodox political movement Agudas Yisroel, and edited several Jewish periodicals in Galicia. After marrying the daughter of prominent Kraków printer Josef Fischer, he began anonymously writing for his father-in-law's press the fifteen stories of fictional supersleuth Max Spitzkopf, whose exploits would thrill vast swaths of Yiddish readers, including the young Isaac Bashevis Singer. Settling in Vienna in 1914, Kreppel's chief activity for the next three decades consisted of editing a German-Jewish weekly, penning historical and political tomes in German as well as another series of popular fiction pamphlets in Yiddish, and serving as a press officer for the Austrian diplomatic service. As a prominent Austrian-Jewish intellectual and outspoken critic of Nazism, Kreppel became a target shortly after Austria united with Hitler's Germany in 1938. He was sent first to Dachau and then to Buchenwald, where he was murdered on July 21, 1940.

Mikhl Yashinsky was born in Detroit and graduated with a degree in European history and literature from Harvard. Now living in New York, he works as a teacher and translator; performs in Yiddish theater (singing and acting in *Fiddler on the Roof* directed by Joel Grey and in the title role of the operetta *The Sorceress*, both *New York Times* "Critic's Pick" productions); and is one of the few people in the world writing original Yiddish plays and musicals. He co-authored the award-winning new Yiddish textbook *In eynem* (White Goat Press) and is the translator of *The Mother of Yiddish Theatre: Memoirs of Ester-Rokhl Kaminska* (Bloomsbury).

About White Goat Press

WHITE GOAT PRESS, the Yiddish Book Center's imprint, is committed to bringing newly translated work to the widest readership possible in English. We publish work in all genres—novels, short stories, drama, poetry, memoirs, essays, reportage, children's literature, plays, and popular fiction, including romance and detective stories.

WHITEGOATPRESS.ORG
The Yiddish Book Center's Imprint